KEEP IT FUN

By

Lindsay Wesker

This book is dedicated to the people that make my life so good (and, for the most part, make me look good!):

My wife, Claudette
My mum, Dusty
My father-in-law, Darkon
My children: Natasha, Werner, Clarissa, Katie, Jerome Jr. (JJ), Shadae, Elijah, Josiah & Orrett Jr. (OJ)
My siblings: Daniel & Elsa
My nieces/nephew: Phoebe, Miriam & Jonatan a.k.a. Yung Lean
My goddaughters: Alicia & Nicole
My family (Mum's side, Dad's side & Claudette's side)

My friends (some I've known for more than 40 years!)
The Beautiful People (my gang)

The staff & DJs at www.mi-soul.com

Andy Dennis at Speedy Disco (www.speedydisco.co.uk)

Everyone that listens to my weekly radio show and/or attends my gigs.
Everyone that interacts with me via Facebook, Twitter, Instagram, WhatsApp & text messages!

Many thanks to Marie Harvey-Harris for your encouragement a.k.a. whip-cracking and many thanks to Joy Balfe for your impatience and eagle eyes; your proofreading skills are scary!

This book is also dedicated to all the songwriters, musicians, singers and producers that make the music. Without music, what would our lives be like?

And, of course, everything I write is dedicated to those we have loved and lost.

Thursday

"What are your expectations?" I asked.

Roz looked up from her phone and wrinkled her nose like a perplexed mathematician.

"Good question!" she replied.

It was a truly beautiful London day: clear blue skies, a light breeze, relative calm and, as we sat on a park bench overlooking the city, the world seemed our seafood platter.

I normally took two seven-day holidays a year. One with the boys and, in the past, I'd taken one with Trish, but I never took a random day off. Roz had a work-free day and had convinced me to join her. I didn't take much persuading! Max was more than capable of manning the fort and, for longer periods of time, I could always count on The Amiable Alvin. I could always count on him.

"So, what do you want to do on your day off?" she asked, expertly changing the subject. "There are museums and galleries to visit. Always something nice at The V&A!"

I would have to return to my question at a later date. For the time being, I would just enjoy Primrose Hill. In the distance, I could see it all. Our beautiful city. I would have to get an answer to my question later in the day, or maybe later in the week? Or maybe later in the year? It's the question that no woman wants to answer. That might sound like a generalisation but expectations are crucial yet vague; absolute deal breakers but also blurry and almost invisible, like distant vessels on a foggy sea!

Women have expectations but they don't like being put on the spot. They don't want to be specific. Born diplomats, women don't actually want to commit to a list of rules, plus it's so much easier to say, "After all this time, you still don't know me?"

I remember listening to Trish talk about men and thinking to myself, "What do you expect?"

"Why is it so hard for a man to be gentle?" she would say. "You're all such bloody oafs! You think you're being funny but you're not! You can't make jokes about a woman's hair, or her body, or the way she walks! Why don't men get that? Women are not men; we're different! We like laughing but don't laugh at us!"

Intuitively, we all know what we expect and, when those expectations fall beyond a certain mark, loud alarm bells go off! Before you know it, your expectations have not been met and you're finding fault with everything. My Dad used to say me, "Those little habits and quirks you found so amusing at the start will eventually come to aggravate and anger you."

And women will try and simplify it by saying, "I just want you to be kind, considerate, generous, perceptive, attentive, loving, passionate, charming, witty ..." In short, 50% of the abstract nouns of the dictionary!

Why did I need an answer to my question? I was curious. I genuinely wanted to know what this shrewd operator expected from me and, in a perverse kind of way, I also wanted to make her sweat; make her accountable for herself and, anyway, being assertive was a good look for me! This woman did not want a compliant wimp! No matter how they try to bend you to their way, women do not want a 'yes man' falling over himself to please her. It was vital I let Roz know I was scrutinising her words and actions.

Love need not be a battlefield; should you choose, it can be a civilised game of backgammon?

For the next few minutes, we did nothing! I looked into the distance, while Roz tampered with her phone. I absolutely loved that gentle breeze blowing past my ears. Shades on, bright, breezy and not too hot; perfect walking weather.

"The right angle for the selfie," she said, turning round and facing uphill, "is with our backs to the view." We paused and posed and, in an instant, we had captured the moment. Selfies aren't indulgent or narcissistic, they're moments in time. 20 years later, you look at a photo and it can fill you with any number of emotions. "That was a good day!" or "I was so slim!" or "At that point, I was still optimistic!"

We stood and looked at our selfie. "Perfect," she said. "Now let's make everyone jealous!" She quickly posted it on a variety of sites with the caption, "You're stuck at work and we've got the day-off!" She looked suitably pleased with her sadistic act. "I'm always working!" she added. "I deserve a day-off!" Who was I to argue? It was my day with Dora The Explorer. Who knew where we would end-up?

We wandered down the hill and into Regent's Park. We walked and smiled and breathed and observed the runners, joggers and walkers, the mothers, the children and the dogs; one of those 'feels good to be alive' moments.

"I don't have any expectations," she said. "I'll be grateful if you don't sleep with other women!"

"Very funny!" I quickly said.

"Not very funny!" she replied. "And a real danger! If you're up for it, they'll imagine we're not serious. If you give them any scrap of encouragement, they won't think twice about making themselves available! Other women don't care about me!"

"Yes, but I do! I care about you. I care about this. You don't do the whole daredevil, Indiana Jones routine, find the precious artefact and just throw it in the recycling bin! That would be foolish!"

"Glad you see it that way," she said.

At that moment, a cyclist attired in tight, luminous, lime green clothing whizzed past us, as if he was literally the only person on God's green earth and there was 0% chance of him crashing into another human being.

"I think," Roz continued, "expectations are not as important as fun. As long as we're laughing and having a good time, everything will be okay. When it stops being fun ... we're done!"

Thus, her expectation of me was: keep it 'fun'. In other words, she needed me to be witty, conversational, charming, insightful, perceptive, empathetic, imaginative, spontaneous, generous, chivalrous, creative and, of course, great in the sack! A tall order but one that I felt I had the measure of. If I failed, I failed, but I would die trying. I'm a trier.

But what did 'keep it fun' mean? A million relationships had struggled and floundered trying to 'keep it fun'. I'd seen articles entitled, 'How To Keep It Sexy In The Bedroom'. Who the hell wrote these things? Clearly people who hadn't dated Trish! It's not that Trish was cold and unapproachable, but you can't keep it 'sexy' in the bedroom when there is no 'bedroom'!

Within the confines of a real life, long-term relationship, there is work, there is food, there is television, there is bad breath and there is sleep. There is no 'bedroom' and there is no 'sexy'. You can keep it as 'fresh' and 'adventurous' as you like; if you're both fast asleep on the sofa, Sexy can have the night off!

Thankfully, Roz and I hadn't even known each other six months. We were not on a go-slow or at sexual stalemate. We were still at the fuck-anywhere phase. A magical phase! I struggled to keep my hands off Roz and she the same. A great part of a relationship! How long would it last? A year? 18 months?

No, 'keeping it fun' would have to be more than bedroom toys and games. 'Keeping it fun' would mean keeping it light and airy; studiously avoiding difficult questions and contentious matters. 'Keeping it fun' would mean doing what a million couples fail to do: compromise. It would mean not arguing about the same old shit; rifling through the same old rubbish bin, tossing over the debris to see if the bin will smell any different. No, the bin won't smell any different, no matter how many times you re-visit the contents; it will still smell rotten!

As we walked, I suddenly heard, "Roz?"

A ferociously-fit blonde bounded towards us, attired in designer gym gear and looking the picture of good health. Her straight, white teeth glistened in the sunlight and her lustrous locks were held back with an industrial knot. She looked very neat and tidy; the organised type who has five nights of dinner in her fridge, stacked carefully in Tupperware containers!

The two women hugged and kissed for what seemed like an eternity.

"I used to work with Joanna. We were in and out of each other's pockets for about ..."

"Four years?" added her friend.

"Close to five years, I suspect?"

Joanna held out her hand and I shook it. "This must be the elusive Wilson, right?"

"God, no!" said Roz, looking embarrassed. "He proved far too elusive! It got very boring waiting for him to have time for me! I'm not a bit-part player in somebody else's movie!"

"Of course not!" said Joanna, back-tracking furiously. "You are?"

"I'm Wes. Quite a new addition to Roz's life."

"Pleased to meet you!" said Joanna, ensuring the knot was tight and not a hair out of place. "I never actually met him! I began to think he was a figment of Roz's imagination!"

"This one," began Roz, gesturing towards me, "this one actually likes me, actually wants to be with me, remembers the stuff I tell him, always picks up his phone, always returns his messages promptly. This one likes being my boyfriend!"

"That is very handy!" said Joanna, beaming. "A definite plus! In my circles, it's a bonus!" Sidling up to me, she continued, "Take it from me, Wes, Roz is a bona fide keeper. Not perfect but an absolute catch!"

Roz pinched her playfully.

I nodded and smiled. What the hell did "not perfect" mean? Nothing was going to spoil my day off, so I left it alone.

The two women exchanged pleasantries and made a plan and a promise to meet up soon. Our mental diaries are full of broken promises.

We continued walking.

"God, I'm so sorry!"

"It's okay," I quickly replied and, to be honest, it really was okay. Roz's past was Roz's past. Beautiful women are always in demand.

"It must have been quite serious?" I added.

"On and off for about two years. When a relationship lasts that long and ends, you really appreciate the amount of time we waste! I gave him a lot of my time that I will never get back."

I thought back to Trish and I. We had both invested a lot of time in each other. Maybe it was time wasted but I chose to look at it as a crucial learning curve. With hindsight, I could genuinely say I'd learnt a lot about me and my own self-worth. I ain't worth much but I'm not worthless. Some men are. I'm not.

And, if I hadn't dated Trish, I wouldn't know how remarkable Roz was! Not wasted time at all.

"Did you like him?" I asked.

"Yeah, I liked him!" she said, sadly. "He's a camera man. A photographer in his spare time. He spends his life looking at beautiful women through a lens. We did a lot of shoots together. Travelled the world; interviews, award ceremonies, recording studios. He absolutely loves being a single man! He must be early-forties? Takes care of himself. He genuinely thinks he can be single forever! Fool! He will die a lonely man."

I thought about my glorious collection of single mates. Would they all die lonely? Well, Tony T the jeweller was showing definite signs of wanting to jack it in! He wasn't the most effective *Don Juan,* so there was no pretending he was! He kept developing feelings for his sexual conquests. Rookie mistake!

In truth, Tony T was much more rooted in reality than all of us. Sensible job, conventional hours; he did what he loved all day and, as a happy man, he actually wanted to share that happiness with another person. Tony T got invites to glamorous fashion-world parties but never had a companion! He was about to make some woman very happy!

Tony F the wine merchant had been married and definitely had the capacity to be a husband but his current view on women was not for public consumption. These days, if you got Tony talking about the fairer sex, you'd be forgiven for thinking he was describing devil worship and ritual sacrifice!

Having been cheated-on and left by his first wife, his rejection by Jill had left him very focused: life was about work and work alone. Female customers: he could tolerate, the rest could not be trusted! Women were, at best, a waste of time, at worst, sub-human swamp-dwellers!

Melvin was very single and very happy to be single but I somehow sensed his loving and caring nature would catch up with him! You can't be that loving and caring and not fall in love at some stage? Melvin loved organising for us and derived real pleasure from making us happy.

I remember when we hit one holiday destination in Croatia; me and the boys couldn't even talk! The taxi dropped us at this old hotel and, as we stood out on the terrace to watch the sunset, none of us could speak. It was too beautiful for words! We all turned to shake Melvin's hand.

"How the fuck did you find this?" I asked.

Melvin shrugged his shoulders and soaked-up the adulation. Being a PA/concierge was what he excelled at. A fine art. He knew how to book a hotel and he kept a file of the best restaurants. Good restaurants that always deliver are hard to find! Tony F was notoriously fussy about his food. Not just his wine and champers! Mids was on a lifelong journey to find the perfect steak, and had almost found it on a few occasions but the search continued; Baggers was hell-bent on finding Mids the ultimate piece of meat!

Out of all of us, Tony G the *maitre d'* would – yes – probably die a single man. He would never be lonely. He was quite happy with his own company. He liked his own space and his own routines. He would never be able to cope with compromise. When you're in a relationship, you wake when they wake, eat when they eat; that would never be Tony G! He liked 24/7 freedom! He liked whims! He liked doing whatever he wanted when he wanted! That, for him, was life! Anything else was torture!

At that moment, Roz farted! "Excuse me! Last night's Lentil Curry!"

"Significant moment!" I observed.

"Indeed, it is!" she said. "The real definition of intimacy!"

I felt very close to her. It felt good to be in her world.

"We're a few minutes from the zoo?" she said.

"Nah, don't really fancy the zoo!"

I was quite happy walking. I felt healthy, the sun was on my face and I could hear the excitable squawking of toddlers. Besides, I was still digesting 'The Elusive Wilson'. Did she still think about him? Did she still have feelings for him? And, if he was a photographer, he must have taken a million photos of her, many of them in states of undress!

God, why does a woman's past mess with your head? No wonder they're so secretive!

Roz's phone began ringing. "I'm turning this thing off!"

She put the phone to her ear and began talking. "I'm out with Wes. We've got a day off!" She listened to the other person for a while. "I'll be home for dinner and, yes, I'll be alone. See you later."

She shook her head and scratched her scalp quite aggressively. "Silly bugger!" she said.

"Who?"

"Benjamin! The Elusive Wilson didn't need me. Benjamin does! I'm like his security blanket. I keep him calm."

I had no reason to worry about The Elusive Wilson; my No. 1 irritant would always be Benjamin, hanging around like a bad smell; a constant, whining voice in Roz's ear, trying to prick her conscience, trying to get her to aspire to higher things and higher beings. She liked The Elusive Wilson but he didn't give a damn about her! And, while Benjamin adored her, she viewed him as a sickly nephew, constantly coughing and blowing his nose. She would never view him as boyfriend. He was firmly in The Friend Zone and he hated it!

Benjamin was one of her housemates. One of her five housemates. They'd all known each other since university and, 20 years later, they were all still living together in a place I called The Haunted House. Not because ghosts resided there but because some of her housemates had actively tried to dissuade her from dating me! Scarily antiquated behaviour in my book!

They should have trusted their worldly-wise friend. Roz was the kind of woman that attracted men; a friendly, inviting personality that welcomed you in, and a warm, engaging nature that made your soul sing. She was an exceptionally beautiful woman who had known a lot of men. She knew what she was doing and knew what she needed. Her housemates should have trusted her judgement but they didn't! Jill thought she was slumming it, the lovelorn Benjamin couldn't bear to see her with another man, while the rest were worried Roz wanted to leave home and break up the party.

It was a curious arrangement but I'd got used to it, and they'd have to get used to me and my friends!

"Well, if you've got to be home for dinner," I suggested, "let's just grab a movie?"

We walked round to the Swiss Cottage Odeon and looked at the programme of films. There was nothing that really excited us, so we agreed on something that looked vaguely interesting and got involved with the snacks.

There was a tray of nachos with three different dips. Roz became very animated when she saw this. "My God, nachos and hot, cheesy sauce? This is too much! And look at those bloody hot dogs!"

Once we'd finished virtually buying the entire concession and spending a king's ransom on God knows what, we staggered into the small screening room. The first showing is usually empty. We had space to stretch out and, having purchased a five-course meal, Roz was in hog heaven! She slurped loudly on a huge vat of Coke and belched!

"We're getting your full repertoire today!" I said.

"Sorry! This is breakfast!"

The film was surprisingly good. We had no expectations, so we were pleasantly surprised. It was the traditional, Hollywood love story. I'd seen it a million times; lots of pretty people struggling to communicate. As the credits rolled, Roz rushed to the toilet! I met her outside.

"That was fun!" she said. "Haven't seen a film in ages!"

We began walking in the general direction of The Haunted House, not really knowing where we were going but merely enjoy our day-off.

"How's Trish?" she asked.

I didn't really know. I hadn't seen her in weeks. Our last contact had been a phone call; a casual, friend zone phone call. Polite chit-chat about nothing! Of course she'd asked me about Roz. I'd been non-committal. I didn't owe her any details. I didn't want to get into it. The Roz thing was big fun but still relatively new. I wasn't totally sure where I stood.

"She seems fine!" I began. "She's going to focus on her business."

"To get over the disappointment of you?"

That seemed unnecessarily cruel but it made me smirk. I hadn't really thought about it. This was a first for me! I was popping my heartbreak cherry! It was fair to say, Trish was heartbroken. Not a good thing but it was her own fault! Fancy walking out on me! Like I was a nobody, not worthy of a goodbye or an explanation! Six months! Not a text, not a phone call. I ain't worth much but I'm not worthless.

"Yes," I admitted, triumphantly, "to get over the disappointment of me!"

"Silly girl!" Roz said. "Never take your lover for granted!"

Trish had definitely taken me for granted! I was there for her; at all times: when she was low, when she had flu, when she was doubled-over with cramps, when she was too tired to drive, when she was nervous about a job interview, when her mum discovered a lump in her breast. I was there for her. At all times. Like a good boyfriend. But, because she didn't view me as 'father material', she had gone walkabout!

Trish had taken me for granted and consciously placed me in a file marked, 'Not Father Material'. In my book, fathers are meant to provide unconditional love and support. I can do that. And I'm fun! Damn it, I'm fun! I'd be a great father!

"You should meet my parents!" said Roz.

I paused to absorb and fully appreciate these words.

"Farting, belching and now parents? This is a big day!"

"You'll like them! They are the most easy-going people in the world! So hospitable, so generous! And so tolerant! How they tolerated me when I was growing-up! I was a bit of a know-all, a bit of a brat, but they always smiled and let me do my thing!"

"You turned out just fine!"

Roz beamed. "Yes, I did!"

Parents? Wow, this was turning into a really big day for me! After being rejected by Trish, it was difficult not to feel smug.

"I'll get the siblings in too! Sophie's fine but her husband's a bit of a bore! My brother Marco is arrogant beyond words but his wife is a delight! God knows how she puts up with his incessant babble!"

Oh, this was turning into a big day! I was going to meet the family. And, to be honest, having been though the horrors of The Haunted House, by comparison, these people would be like church mice! Having gone 12 rounds with Benjamin, Roz's family would be a stroll in the park!

"It'll be a Sunday. As soon as I can organise it. Might take a few weeks?"

I really didn't mind how long it took. I was meeting her family: this was big!

Having walked Roz home, I was knackered! My day-off had been a five-course junk food feast, a film and a ten-mile hike. I could feel my calves throbbing! I got on a bus and headed home. I wondered who I'd see sitting on the wall outside my little house but, on this occasion, there was no one waiting for me, just an IKEA catalogue sitting on the mat inside my front door. Where had that come from? My nearest IKEA was miles away.

I put the catalogue on the kitchen table and looked in the fridge. My fridge still looked pitiful; nothing very exciting to eat or drink. No ingredients. No goodies. This had to stop! My mum's fridge never looked like that! She'd have been mortified!

Somewhere in my schedule, I had to find time to visit a supermarket. This was turning into a huge, life-changing day! I needed a supermarket and a full fridge. That's what grown folks do: they open their fridge and say, "What would you like to drink?" I tried it on for size and said it out loud. "What would you like to drink?" Maybe I could invite the boys over to my house?

None of them had spent a prolonged period in my house. They'd picked me up, dropped me off, used my toilet, and Low had even crashed on my sofa one night, but I'd never had a dinner party! Not once! Trish had never suggested it. I guess she felt she saw the boys often enough?

I looked at the IKEA catalogue and then looked around me. Most people had too much stuff, I had virtually nothing! Most people go to the recycling plant every week to get rid of stuff they thought they needed! I had nothing. My house wasn't minimalist, it was threadbare and severely lacking in personality. It was decor-less! Half an idea but abandoned soon after! Stop-And-Start Deco!

My peace was disturbed by a banging on the door. I went to open it. Marie stormed through the door, her cheeks red with frustration, her eyes watery and bloodshot, her dress – as ever – covered in flour and icing sugar. She threw her coat on my sofa and sat down with her arms folded, staring straight ahead of her, not saying a word.

Something told me that, at any moment, the gangly fool would also be arriving at my house. I didn't bother asking Marie anything because I could feel the rumbling thunder of melodrama approaching. Sure enough, another knock at my door.

And there he stood, looking apologetic. "Sorry, mate. Is your sister here?"

I opened the door wide, so Percy could come in. He wandered into my front room and stood looking down at her. "I'm sorry," he said. Marie said nothing. I left them to it and went back into my kitchen. I wanted to look at my IKEA catalogue.

With my primitive knowledge of marital disagreements, I knew there was nothing I could say. We already had two people being illogical and talking shit, we didn't need a third!

If they needed me to mediate, I would but, in truth, what could I say? There was only one thing to say: "Stop fannying about and get on with it!" The chances of my sister finding someone as besotted as Percy were slim to none. This long streak of piss was so captivated and so enamoured with my sister, he had taken to wearing very expensive after shave. At all times, he now smelt like a high-class escort, ready to jump at her ladyship's every command.

Even with the door closed, I could hear them mumbling and muttering in the front room. I really didn't want to mediate. I'd had a difficult day eating nachos and hot, cheesy sauce. I was almost weak with exhaustion. Besides, this IKEA catalogue was full of fascinating things! For a few quid, I'd be able to provide Roz with her own bedside table, with a drawer for her eye-catching underwear and her lady-business stuff!

In fact, my fridge was so depressing, I decided that supermarket visit time was now! I looked at my phone to find opening times and my local Sainsbury's was open! This was a big day!

I left the two lovebirds to it and clambered into my car. Within moments, I was at my local supermarket and, even though it was after 8.00pm, it was full of customers! Who were these people?

So, my objective was to fill my fridge with things that would NOT go off in two days' time! I wandered up the beers and spirits aisle and gawped at all the different brands of beer! Some I'd never seen before!

"Fancy seeing you here?"

I span round to see Trish with a trolley full of groceries and a look of both shock and delight on her face. "You're in a supermarket! On your own!"

"My fridge is an embarrassment."

"It is." Trish looked into my totally empty trolley. "You've just arrived?"

I looked-up at all the different beers. "I could buy what I know ... but there's so much choice! Maybe I should try something new?"

"My God!" she said. "You wait until you get to the biscuit aisle!"

I randomly began pulling bottles off shelves. Different coloured bottles. Different shaped bottles. Names I would never pronounce.

"Wow, look at you! You're in a supermarket, alone, and you're hosting your own beer festival!"

"I'm going to invite friends over and I'm going to say, 'What would you like to drink?' It's about time."

Trish nodded and smiled to herself. "Look at you! You are different! It's like a switch has been flicked! You are switched on!"

"It's about time."

I continued shopping and Trish tagged along, ensuring not to do the girlfriend, backseat-driving thing, which she knew I hated!

I was on unchartered territory, so I walked slowly, gazing wide-eyed like a tourist. When we got to the crisps and snacks, I had no option but to stop and marvel. So many flavours! Sweet Chilli With Dorset Sour Cream? Chargrilled Steak & Chimichurri? Had it been created by Dick Van Dyke?

I picked up a bag of this and a bag of that. So many bags of hopelessly artificial, tasteless yet crunchy things so lacking in nutrients, it wasn't even worth considering nutritional value. It was basically cheesy air or pungent, savoury lint, but they would go down a treat with my flash, Belgian lager.

Trish watched with amusement. I was literally like Tom Hanks in 'Big', touching female flesh for the first time. Every time I picked up a different box of cookies, I was liked a stoned junkie fingering his rucksack, uncovering the mysteries of another zip and another pocket.

"What's the party to celebrate?" she asked.

"I haven't organised a party. It's all about the off-chance. Just in case someone comes by. I want to be prepared. My mum always was. Whenever anybody turned-up; she could always feed them. I want to be able to say, 'What would you like to drink?'"

"I get it," she said.

Trish was very quiet, almost nervous to speak. She had bridges to build with me and she knew it. After years and years of being treated like her boyfriend, her fella, her companion, her hubby, her after-thought, I had finally stepped out on my own. I was an individual and someone who could not be taken from granted!

"Wes, I want you to know I'm sorry! I should have contacted you. Should have let you know where I was."

"It's okay," I said, and I almost said, "It's turned out for the best," but I didn't. There was no need for that but it was – oh – so true! I was more than happy with the crazy girl with the wild hair. She was a revelation and power-packed with energy, information and opinion. Trish was a pretty fountain, while Roz was a raging waterfall. Trish was your uncle's front lawn, while Roz was The Palm House at Kew Gardens.

Roz's constant commentary on everything was always amusing. You could even tune in and tune out and she'd still be talking! She made Trish look like a tasteless 'classic triple' from the sandwich section.

Was I angry with Trish? Not really. Not anymore. In the first few months, I'd been irate but that soon passed as I sank into a depression. Did I feel sorry for her? Not really. She was a lovely girl and sure to find someone new; someone suitable. A better fit.

I didn't feel the need to make conversation with her, though. I wasn't yet at the stage where we could have fun. I didn't feel relaxed around her. It would be a while before we could descend into laughter and silliness.

"What are you doing this evening?" she asked.

"I'm going to unpack my shopping!"

"Another first!" she said.

"I'm quite excited!"

Trish almost looked sorry that she wouldn't be sharing this first with me. Not much of a first but a first nevertheless. I didn't want to tell her about Marie and Percy. Trish was one of Marie's oldest friends but I had to learn to deal with The Volatile Twins on my own.

Strange. Marie had never been one for such drama. That passionate kind of love is such a scoundrel! Plays havoc with your emotions. Shouting, crying, irrational theories, illogical conclusions. Roll on the latter stages of a relationship! After a while of being with someone, give it 10 or 20 years, the shouting is over! No one cares! True, the sex has stopped, but so have the arguments!

I drove home and brought my grocery shopping through my front door. I listened to see if the argument had subsided. Silence. They were both still in my living room but it was silent. A terrifying thought crossed my mind. I shut my front door and went to hide in my kitchen. If Marie and Percy were now having make-up sex, I didn't want to hear it! I would leave them to it and, hopefully, they'd let themselves out?

By the time I'd unpacked my shopping bags, my fridge was full and my cupboard was full too! Not for anybody, not for any reason but at least I was ready. Just on the off-chance. I looked up at the clock. 10.30 already! I looked down at my phone. A message from Roz. "Kill me now! Would rather be there with you! Benji has bored me to tears and caused me to finish a bottle of wine. I'm pished! (smiley face)"

Tonight, I would sleep in my bed alone. I wandered into the bedroom. Where would Roz's chest of drawers go? Yep, there was definitely space for it on her side of the bed. I would surprise her. I would go to IKEA and purchase this item. She would either be touched or terrified, but then she had suggested that I met the parents! I wasn't jumping the gun.

Downstairs, I could hear Marie and Percy coming out of my living room and going out of my front door. Whatever they'd done to make-up, I hoped they'd cleaned-up after them!

Friday

The morning after, I opened the shop and the phone immediately began ringing. I didn't even get the chance to turn on the lights as I lunged for the receiver.

"Wheels Of Steel, how can I help?"

"It's my 50th birthday!" said a woman with a big grin on her face. She could barely contain her giggling. "I'm going to be 50!"

"That's wonderful!" I said.

There was a pause on the end of the line. "I'm turning 50!" she repeated, this time more solemnly.

"We cater for 50th birthday parties all the time!"

"Do ya?"

"Often joyous and often very raucous affairs!"

She laughed again. "Really?"

"It's almost as if ... the shackles have come off!"

I could hear her gasp. "Yes, that's how I feel! I'm 50. I'm an old woman and I no longer care what people think of me. I'm free!"

I could hear her processing her thoughts. Max came in and could see that I was on the phone and in the dark. He switched all the lights on and pulled up the shutters!

"Right," she began. "I want a big party. I've got quite a big garden and I want your gear and DJ outside, under a marquee!"

"Not a problem!" I replied. "Do you have a date?"

"It will be a Sunday in late May. Hopefully the April showers will have passed?"

"Hopefully?" I scrambled for the diary and made a note in the two last Sundays in May.

"I want you to play all my favourite songs!" she trilled, getting excited. "What if you don't have all my favourite songs?"

"Madam, we have everything!"

"Do you have 'Light My Fire' by Jose Feliciano?"

"Yes, madam."

"Do you have 'Oh Lori by The Alessi Brothers?"

"Of course, madam!"

"That's my name! My name's Lori!"

"Whatever you want to hear, we will play."

When people are happy, they'll dance to anything. The opposite when they're pissed-off!

I gave her some estimates and we finalised the details. It sounded like the perfect assignment for Amiable Alvin! Alvin was an absolute diamond in these kinds of situations. The patience of a saint! I'd never seen Alvin angry. He was always smiling, always upbeat, no matter how demanding the client. Alvin had been part of my crew for about 11 years. He knew about gear too, so I could rely on him to set-up and dismantle.

Lori wanted a ton of disco lights. I was getting vivid images of this day; a large collection of 50-something women, swigging from tall glasses of bubbly and singing at the tops of their voices. If they're dancing, you've done well and, if they're singing too, you've hit the jackpot!

I turned to look at Max, who was grinning and looking very pleased with himself.

"What?" I asked.

"It's going so well!" he replied. "The radio station: they want to do a big all-night event. Big venue! I'll be playing to maybe 1000 people?"

"You are on your way up, Maxi! This is what you wanted."

"1000 people!"

The phone rang again. I picked it up. "Wheels Of Steel: how can I help?"

"Do you hire out disco equipment?"

"We do."

"Actual vinyl turntables?"

"Yes!"

"That is brilliant!" said the voice on the phone. "We want to play vinyl all night!"

"No problem!" I replied. I liked saying that. And I was looking forward to saying, 'Would you like something to drink?' I thought about my full fridge and bulging snack cupboard. A strange thing to think about, I know.

He sounded very young, about 18-19, and someone who'd never seen a record player before. I could hear him stuttering, as if he had something else to ask me.

"We don't have many vinyl records," he continued. "We don't even know the best ones to buy!"

I invited him to the next Wesday Wednesday and promised to point him the direction of the best record shops. He sound elated. "Thank you, thank you," he kept repeating.

Ping went my mobile phone. I looked down. A text from Roz. "Rescue me! Can't stand another night of introspection!"

"Come to mine," I texted back. "My fridge is full!"

"Full?" she replied. "I am intrigued!"

The phone rang again.

"Wheels Of Steel: how can I help?"

"Good morning!" said quite a stern mother. "My son is turning 16 and he wants a birthday party. And I'm not invited!"

I stifled a laugh. "Dates and location, Madam?"

"We're down in Chislehurst. We've booked a function room in a hotel. And me and my husband will eat dinner outside while we wait for them to finish. God, I hope they don't break anything!"

"No problem, Madam, I have just the man for the job." I turned and smiled at Max.

We finalised more details and I made sure I jotted everything in the diary. I turned to look at Max, who was communicating on two mobiles and listening to something on one of them. His head was rocking back and forth at quite an alarming speed. I calculated 140bpm. It was probably some new and horrendous genre? Spot The Melody time!

"It has been a busy morning!" I said.

Max wasn't even listening. If he continued headbanging like that, his skull would surely come loose? He didn't seem to mind. He was happy and I was happy. My fridge was full and a pretty girl was coming to visit. Nothing could harsh my buzz.

Until Midders came barrelling through my door. He sat down on one of the counter stools and didn't even say anything. We looked at each other and said nothing. He had a carrier bag in his hand. He reached into it, pulled out two bottles of bubbly and plonked them on the counter.

"Is it lunchtime yet?" he asked.

I didn't even need to look at the clock. "No," I replied. "Can we at least wait until the sandwich girl arrives?"

"I don't even feel like working today," he said. "I'm depressed."

"Really?" I asked. "Over Jill?"

Mids didn't say anything but I could see he was still seething. Still seething over something that had happened months ago!

Jill was one of Roz's housemates. The Mother Hen of the house. The sensible one. The person that made the house run smoothly.

She and Mids had enjoyed a little afternoon delight and, for the first time in ages, I'd seen a glint in his eye. Jill was just his type: brassy, bossy and buxom. After the disappointment of his marriage, he really thought he'd found someone!

For a few days, he was back to his best but, when she started ignoring his calls and text messages, Mids quickly understood he was being fobbed-off!

The Mids & Jill Stand-Off. What an intense night that had been! A wretched and torrid four-hour analysis of two hours of passion. Jill frantically trying to make it a one-night-stand and Mids desperately trying to understand why no woman wanted a relationship with him!

Mids held one of the bottles in his hand and looked at it. He rubbed his finger over the label. "I think this is going to taste nice."

Thankfully, Sandwich Girl arrived and we were able to buy lunch.

"Great sandwiches!" I said to her.

Sandwich Girl blushed. "Thank you."

Mids picked something up, ripped it open and bit into it. "This does taste good! What do you use?"

Sandwich Girl smiled. "Family recipe!"

Mids was chomping into his sandwich like he hadn't eaten in days. He began talking again but, his mouth was so full of food, we couldn't understand him! Sandwich Girl and I shared a smile.

Mids picked up two more sandwiches and I settled the bill. Eventually, he finished his mouthful and looked rejuvenated. "What's your name?"

"Belinda."

"You are Belinda The Rescinder! You have revoked my bad mood and sent it back to where it belongs. These sandwiches are bloody marvellous!"

Belinda looked very confused but figured a simple 'Thank you' would suffice. We brought the sandwiches back into the shop and let Belinda complete her route. Mids popped open one of the bottles and we found some plastic cups to pour into. Max declined.

"Sandwiches!" said Mids. He ripped open another one and began gorging on that. "They're only bloody sandwiches!"

"Where there's good, there's always better!" I said to him.

Mids looked struck by this. "It's true! I've had good champagne and I've had better. I've had good steak and I've had better. Still haven't found the one! That one sublime piece of steak!"

The bubbly was going straight to my head. It tasted good but I was dizzy. I frantically finished my sandwich to soak up the alcohol. What the hell was I doing? Drinking on the job. Nevertheless, Mids looked much happier, so I was relieved.

"I can do better than Jill," Mids finally blurted out. "What is she like? A total contradiction! She is organised down to the last paper clip but, when it comes to this 'attached' man, she loses it. Absolutely loses all sense of reason!"

"She's in love?" I offered.

"Christ, who needs that kind of love? That kind of love detaches you from your brain! Jill married him in the hope it would break-up his long-term relationship. Where's the logic? Where's the sense? When it comes to this man, she becomes a different person."

"You can do better," I said, trying to comfort him more than anything else.

Mids really didn't feel like working! He spent the whole of the afternoon with us, taking urgent phone calls on his mobile and doing business from my shop. We talked about our customary subjects, finished one bottle of bubbly and then Mids decided to open the second one! I begged him not to. I was drunk by 4.00.

We were providing gear for four different functions that night, so there was a steady flow of my set-up and delivery boys in and out of the shop. I didn't have to DJ that night. I don't think I could have! A night-off! I needed it.

Thankfully, Max's favourite tipple was Red Bull, so he was sober. Max took all the phone calls, answered all the e-mails, and looked on as these two old fools reminisced about the eighties and slurred their words. I couldn't even see straight and, when Roz arrived at 5.00, she was amused to find us laughing at some joke, the punch line of which neither of us could remember!

Mids virtually fell on top of Roz in his attempt to give her an affectionate hug. "This man," he began, as if embarking on a best man speech, "is one of the finest men I know."

Roz nodded politely.

"A man amongst men!" Not that any of us really understood what that meant.

"This man," he continued, "is someone that can be trusted, someone you can rely on, someone who will always come through for you."

"A glowing reference!" Roz said, taking my plastic cup and swigging back the contents. "Mmm ... very nice!"

"We'll finish the bottle!" said Mids, topping-up her cup.

"This is a bit better than toast the birthday boy! This is one to savour!"

"Indeed, it is!" said Mids, impressed. "Your taste buds work!"

"I can taste almonds. I love almonds!"

"My goodness!" said Mids, mopping a little film of perspiration from his forehead, "This girl is good! You two ... together ... it's powerful!"

I looked at the crazy girl with the wild hair and felt a huge rush of affection. She looked so beautiful riffing with Mids about bubbly. She was talking his language.

She took another sip. "Almond and ... apple?"

Mids was mightily impressed and nodded with approval. No more words were necessary. He didn't even have the strength to speak. He sat back down on a stool, exhausted, and collected his thoughts.

Roz looked at me. "We should go," I said. I turned to Max. "Will you shut up shop?"

"Will do."

"Come on, old son," I said to Mids, putting my arm around him. I managed to drag him to his feet. He felt tired, inebriated and a bit pre-occupied.

"I'm alright, mate," he said but I could see he was unsteady on his feet.

"You'll have to drive!" I said to Roz.

Even though Mids didn't need me taking care of him and even though we'd entertained him all afternoon, I still felt responsible for him. Roz and I picked up some Chinese from the local take-away, and we managed to get Mids into my house and on the sofa.

"Back in a sec, mate!" I said to him.

We left him there, watching the news.

I held Roz's hand and escorted her into the kitchen.

"What would you like to drink?" I said, proudly, opening my fridge.

Roz stood back and gave me a polite, mock round of applause. "That's as full as our fridge and I've got six in my house!"

I had really gone overboard but it would last. Roz rifled through the contents and pulled out a bottle of Prosecco. "We should celebrate!" she said.

"Celebrate what?"

"Your fridge! And the fact that it's Friday!"

It was Friday! Mids had totally thrown me! I barely knew what day it was! We made him a plate of food and I carried it into the front room. Mids was already sprawled out on my sofa, fast asleep.

I carried the plate back into the kitchen and wrapped it under some foil.

"Poor bugger! That Jill thing has really knocked him for six!"

Roz poured us two glasses of bubbly and I dug into my dinner. I needed it, if I was going to stay awake!

"The Jill thing has really upset the house!" she began. "Jill set the tone, she made the rules, everybody abided by the rules. Now she's broken her own rules, Wendy wants the option to break them too! Wendy's got this hot, married doctor she wants to bring home!"

"Anarchy!"

"Virtually! Jill set the tone. Not only that, she now looks embarrassed and actually looks distracted. You can't command your troops if you look embarrassed! She's not focused. Not concentrating. We ran out of sugar yesterday! Do you know how major that is? We never run out of anything! Jill makes sure of that ... well ... Jill used to ..."

Roz and I enjoyed our dinner and talked about this and that. I wanted to ask her about The Elusive Wilson but she kept talking about Benjamin. I was happy to listen to her talk, though. I could barely string a sentence together. The afternoon drinking session had me slurring my words but I could hear a mobile phone ringing.

"Not mine!" said Roz, holding her phone in the air.

I went outside to the coat rack and found my phone ringing in my jacket pocket. It was Max, talking fast and sounding quite stressed. One of our DJ crew had gone down sick, gastric flu or something, and Max was suggesting, as it was an eighties party, maybe it was best if I went to cover it?

I was drunk, disorientated and now a bit sleepy after my dinner but, thinking about it, I was the only man for the job. "I'll do it," I said. "Text me the postcode."

I went back into the kitchen looking sheepish.

"Problem?" asked Roz.

"One of my DJs is ill, I have to cover his gig and I need to ask a big favour ..."

"I'll drive you! Why not?"

I fell to my knees and kissed her hands.

"While you're down there ..." she said, winking at me.

"Later!" I foolishly promised, knowing full well I'd be dead meat by midnight.

"It's Friday night!" she said, excitedly, finishing the last of her glass. "What kind of function is it?"

"It's a 40th birthday party with an eighties fancy dress theme!"

Roz laughed. "Of course it is! Your life is like a Carry On film!"

It was true. My life was ridiculous. And the evening ahead looked particularly bizarre. I gathered up two bags of CDs and, with Max's text, we headed down to the venue, which turned out to be a boating club in Kingston-Upon-Thames.

A lovely, traditional function room with framed photos of the boating club committee members on the wall. Perfect for weddings! I pictured balmy weekends by the river, enjoying the water, the weather and high spirits, and the committee members and their guests enjoying huge pitchers of Pimm's.

On this occasion, the venue was full of forty-somethings dressed as eighties pop icons and, as this was the decade of outlandish fashion trends, the birthday guests were a coat of many colours! Some had Boy George's dreadlocks, some had Freddie Mercury's huge black moustache, others were wearing Madonna's 'Desperately Seeking Susan' outfit, while a few had Steve Strange-style white make-up with extravagant splashes of blue eye shadow.

Roz and I entered the room and, even though I was fatigued, we both smiled. We both knew, intuitively, this was going to be one silly evening. The outfits, the make-up and the props were superb. This was a group of people who were ready to have fun. True, they were forty-somethings and they would ache for days but, as it was a special occasion, they were going for it!

A woman rushed up to us and hugged us both enthusiastically. "You must be the DJ! I think we're all ready!" Turning to Roz, she added, "That is a great Kate Bush outfit!"

"Thank you," said Roz, graciously. The woman twirled into the distance and Roz looked at me. "Your life!" she said, laughing. "Your life! Your people! Pure comedy!"

The guests had already consumed their buffet dinner and a few drinks, and I could see a few of them hovering at the edges of the dance floor, tapping their feet and seeing if their hips could still work.

'Billie Jean' never fails! That beat and that bass line immediately lured the nervous out to the middle. It wasn't going to be a great display of dance moves but it didn't matter; these people were amongst old friends; it was all about smiling and laughing and memories.

The obvious eighties favourites like Human League's 'Don't You Want Me' had the floor full and everybody singing but it was actually the dramatic, non-dance records that provoked the biggest response. When I played Queen's 'Don't Stop Me Now', all of the Freddie look-alikes took centre stage on the dance floor, and a few even had cut-down microphone stands to sing into.

Probably the highlight for me was three girls dressed like Robert Palmer's backing band in the 'Addicted For Love' video. Tight black skirts, black high heels, tight white shirts, big red lips and fiercesome faces. Plus, they all had plastic guitars hanging from their necks. Brilliant! When people are happy, they will dance to anything!

Not really Roz's decade but she knew most of the songs and worked her Kate Bush look to the max, thrilling the men with souciant flicks of her magnificent mane. I watched her dancing and smiling with other men, many of whom were probably there with their wives. I was still struggling to understand why this breathtaking beauty would want anything to do with me. Every so often, she would blow me kisses from the dance floor, and I was happy for her to stay there; I didn't need anything more to drink. The effects of an afternoon's drinking were starting to wear off.

Mercifully, we were done by midnight! The forty-somethings looked out on their feet and ready for some Horlicks. In fairness, they'd done themselves proud; the costumes, the performances, the dance moves and the high-volume karaoke had given the birthday boy a night to remember.

Roz was smiling from ear-to-ear. "Wish my mates could have been here!"

"Me too," I replied. "Trust me: there will be many other occasions! I took bookings for a few this afternoon."

I was sober now, so Roz could sleep in the car on the way home. When we got home, Mids was still in my front room, watching telly and eating Chinese food.

"Fuck me, Wezza! Your fridge, mate!"

On the floor of my living room there were three empty bottles of exotic lager.

"I like this bar," he said. "Have you given it a name?" Mids suddenly noticed that I was carrying my CD bags. "Have you just done a gig?"

"It was brilliant!" chimed Roz. "Classic eighties all night long."

"Aww, shame!" he replied. "I would've enjoyed that!"

Roz sat down in my armchair and kicked off her shoes, while I went to make some hot chocolate for she and I. When I got back to the living room, Mids was talking about his ex-wife. I'd heard this story before but Roz wanted all the gory details.

"When I discovered that my wife was cheating on me with one of our employees, it helped me see how I actually felt about her. We set up the business together, worked hard to establish it, we got married, we bought a place together, we had a sex life but I didn't really care about her. How does that happen?"

"It probably happens to a lot of people," said Roz. "They just drift from a friendship into a relationship."

That had been Trish and I. One thing followed another. Before we knew it, we were a couple.

"When I discovered what was going on," said Mids, "I didn't feel betrayed. God! Betrayal! What a word! I was just worried about the business and the disruption to my life. I didn't really care. Didn't care about her, didn't care about them, didn't care about me."

"And now business is good!" said Roz.

"Yes!" said Mids, shovelling Singapore Vermicelli into his mouth. "Yes, business is good! And you liked that bubbly you tasted earlier on?"

"Delicious!" she replied. "You serve that with posh nosh!"

Mids looked at me and almost looked emotional. I could tell something vaguely profound was about to emerge from his groggy brain. "Wezza! You're a lucky bastard! This is a very classy woman. I think we all know you are punching above your weight."

"Cheers, son!"

"Nothing to be ashamed of," he continued.

Out of the corner of my eye, I could see Roz grinning and winking at me. Mids wasn't finished yet. "It might not happen for me, mate. I might never find anyone that I truly connect with; someone special for me."

"Give it a rest!" I said.

All the bubbly and the three bottles of beer had made him very tired and emotional. "It might not happen for me but it has truly happened for you! This is an exceptional woman. Do not fuck it up!"

"That's right, Wes," chirped Roz, "do not fuck it up!"

I had come such a long way and people were still taking the piss out of me. I thought the days of 'Wes ridicule' were over?

"Thank you, Tony, I will try not to fuck it up!"

Mids continued eating his food, while Roz and I sipped our hot chocolate. I could feel myself relaxing and slowing down. I would definitely be asleep soon.

"So, Wes," Mids continued, as if in the middle of thought, "that sandwich girl? Belinda The Rescinder. Know much about her?"

I shook my head. "Nope. I'll get her card for you."

"I could do with some of those very tasty sandwiches at some of my events!"

Mids had finally finished his plate of food. He looked full and sat back on the sofa with a glow of satisfaction.

Roz got up. "Sleep well, Tony. See you soon."

"Night, my lovely one! You'll need some of that nice bubbly for your house?"

"I will!" Roz picked up her cup and shoes and headed upstairs.

Mids and I looked at each other. "You alright?" I asked him.

He was prone to depression, so I knew any answer he gave would be some kind of flannel.

"I'm fine, Wezza. Thanks for everything today."

"My pleasure. You can kip on the sofa, if you want?"

"Nah, mate, the fresh air will do me good!"

He put his shoes back on and gingerly pulled himself up from the sofa, rubbing his belly. "Need to work off some of this grub!"

We hugged and he pulled his jacket off my coat rack. "What are we doing tomorrow?" he asked.

"I'll call Baggers and see if he's got any bright ideas."

By the time I got upstairs, Roz was fast asleep. I was off the hook. If I'd attempted any kind of oral sex, it might have definitely gone south!

Saturday

By the time I woke up on Saturday, Roz was up and in the shower. I could hear her singing 'Girls Just Want To Have Fun'.

I looked at the clock. 8.10 a.m. I would need to open the shop at 10.00. It would be a busy day but Roz and I had time for breakfast.

The bedroom door opened and Roz came through it wearing one towel around her body and another towel around her hair. She began walking towards to me and within seconds she was standing above me. She undid the bottom towel and threw it on the bed. She then crouched over me and sat on my face. A promise is a promise. Breathing optional.

I knew that Roz was a coffee and toast girl so, while on my mammoth supermarket expedition, I made sure I bought her some nutritious bread, some spreadable butter and a selection of artisan jams.

When we eventually got downstairs, we moved around the kitchen as if choreographed, not saying a word. She made the coffee, because she was good at that, and I sorted all the toast. At one point, she squeezed my bum. No comment, just a quick and cheeky squeeze. This is a very clear sign that a woman likes you. If the squeezing or touching or groping or rubbing disappears from your relationship, you've got problems. A squeeze of the bum speaks scholarly volumes!

I think Trish squeezed me once. I thought about it. Yes, once. And I made it easy for her because I was bending over. Did she really love me? Or was I an obedient lap dog? I think I was just 'him indoors'. I think it was easier to have me as a boyfriend than have a load of interfering relatives ask her, "So, have you found a man yet?"

Yes, we had drifted; drifted from a friendship into a relationship. No, there was no dynamic, cataclysmic passion. No jealousy, no possessiveness, no madness. Our relationship was as mild-mannered and sedate as a quaint county fayre. So, what was she so upset about? I guess it was inconvenient to be single again?

I got to the shop just before 10.00 and my first customer was waiting for me on my doorstep.

"Johnson," said the man, shaking my hand enthusiastically.

"Yes, Mr. Johnson, it won't take long to load up your gear. Where's your car?"

"Just here," he said, pointing proudly at a khaki green, four-door Jeep Wrangler sitting right outside the shop. "I'm so excited!"

He had this wonderful Brian Blessed thing going on! Tall, stout, big beard, booming voice. He was beside himself. It was 10.00 a.m. but he couldn't wait to start playing tunes! We quickly loaded-up two vinyl turntables, two CD players, mixer/amp and speakers.

"It is so easy to assemble," I said to him.

"It won't be a problem," said Mr. Johnson. "It's my wife's 60th birthday. We met at a local pub more than 40 years ago and, on that night, I was the DJ! I haven't DJ'd since! We're going to be playing all her favourite rock & roll, R&B, Motown and a few nice reggae tunes! Haven't touched my vinyl in almost 40 years!"

"Sounds brilliant!" I said. "That's an enduring love affair!"

"Heavens!" he boomed. "We've had our ups and downs! She decided to cheat with the bloody postman, so I had a fling with our local vet. You know what couples are like! Bloody mad!"

"But you still love her?"

"You young people are so soppy!" he laughed. "Haven't you heard that Tina Turner song? What's love got to do with it?"

He paid his deposit, signed all the paperwork and promised faithfully to return the gear on Monday morning. "Have you still got your vinyl?" he asked, halfway out the door.

"Two boxes of guaranteed floorfillers!"

"Good lad!" he said, bounding out the door and clambering into his Jeep.

Max staggered in. "What was that about?"

"Customer No. 1: sorted."

The morning was a flurry of activity and then, bless him, Baggers arrived with three drinks from Costa. He'd remembered that Max didn't do coffee or tea, so he'd bought him a healthy smoothie. They greeted each other with some convoluted handshake and hug, almost Wakandan?

Melvin looked very pleased with himself and actually pulled a clipboard out of Bag No.1. "So, here are your Saturday night plans: I have procured tickets for an art exhibition ..."

He paused. I looked at him quizzically. He continued, "... an erotic art exhibition."

The penny dropped. "Ah, nice!"

"Unclothed women AND men!"

I shook my head and gave him my disapproving look. "Am I bovvered?"

"And then," Melvin continued, "I have V.I.P. tickets to a very exclusive party at a swanky house down in Dulwich Village, hosted by a professional footballer, who I just happen to know is bi-sexual!"

"Will we be the only straights there?"

"No, it will be full of bloody footballers and their wanky WAG wives!"

"Outstanding!"

Melvin's ever-expanding afro was now in very neat corn rows across his head. "Nice barnet!" I said.

"I met this handsome Ghanaian boy, went back to his house, and his sister lost her mind! Told me my hair was unruly, unkempt, not businesslike. Told me I had no future with hair like that! I had to sit on the floor for four hours while she did this!"

"Looks good!"

Melvin reached into Bag No. 2 and pulled out a bottle of lemon-scented bleach. "Tonight, last one out, empty all of this around your shop toilet bowl and leave it over night. Been meaning to do this for ages! First impressions and all that!"

How could you not love him? Maybe there were a number of people who were already in love with him and would treasure being his partner but, for right now, Melvin was having the time of his life. We were going cool places, meeting cool people, laughing our tits off, Melvin was having night time fun a-plenty and he had a forever circle of mates who adored him. He knew he was loved.

"I love you!" I said.

"I know you do," he replied and he waltzed out the door.

"He's a cool dude!" said Max, and that was the highest of high praise from someone who didn't say very much.

I immediately called Roz to tell her of our Saturday night plans. I think I actually heard her wet herself. She was laughing and crying with excitement. "Fabulous! Can I bring Wendy?"

"Of course!" I said. Beautiful Nurse Wendy was seriously low maintenance. Compared to the other tortured souls in The Haunted House, Nurse Wendy was Tinkerbell and Mary Poppins combined! A bit of sweetness and light would not go amiss.

We were meant to shut at 6.00 but one customer was delayed. We forgave him, though, because he brought us a packet of chunky chocolate biscuits for the shop.

Not only did our last customer take music-playing gear but he took every last piece of lighting.

"What are you boys up to?" I asked him.

"An epic, house party; a psychedelic, seventies happening!"

I looked at him; he was only late twenties! "You weren't even born in the seventies!"

"I know but what a decade! Free festivals, free love, free spirits. There were people all round the world protesting for their freedom; their basic human rights! You had Richie Havens passionately singing about freedom at 'Woodstock', and all this despite a group of politicians that actually wanted to restrict our freedom! I want everyone that comes to this party to feel free! You know, dance like no one's watching!"

It sounded like a great concept; I hoped it didn't result in vomit on the bathroom floor.

We shut-up shop and went our separate ways. Max had a bollocks-out Saturday night ahead of him! At some point on Sunday morning/afternoon, he would crash into a bed. Max was booked to play at one club and two private parties. He wasn't making big money anywhere but he was in-demand. Being in-demand: is there any sweeter feeling? Max was flavour of the month but he wouldn't hold that status forever. It was now my job to help turn hobby into career; help him monetise it.

The logical step was making music. Many DJs make music. Some of it is half-decent? If I could get Max collaborating with an in-demand producer and an in-demand singer, they could create something now and relevant. Creating something timeless would involve a musician. I wracked my brains: did I know any musicians? Roz's world was full of arty-farty types; she was bound to know a musician!

I also needed to keep Max's feet on terra firma. He was modest, polite and kind and I really needed to keep him that way. You can't be a jerk on the way up 'cause you'll sure-as-hell meet those same people on the way down! If Max only learnt one thing from me, I wanted him to be nice. Be nice. Two of the shortest and blandest words in your vocabulary but – by Christ! – put 'em together and you're made!

Wesday Wednesday – Max's creation – was going really well. It was always a mad day: lots of people popping in and out, enquiries, questions, activity. Max had actually stimulated the business and, come Wednesday, his crew always came down for a mid-week mosh inside the shop. It was definitely a good look to have a shop full of cool youngsters. As ever, I would play them a selection from my trusty record boxes. It always amused me to watch them hear seventies and eighties music for the first time. The horns and strings and percussion never failed to blow them away, as if I were revealing the mysteries of the universe.

We were seven, so we needed a largish vehicle. Mids had the biggest car, so we all headed over to his flat and got into his spaceship. Three rows of seats. Very comfortable. As ever, Melvin had created his own travelling playlist for the journey. Tonight's theme was girls names. 'Valerie' by Stevie Winwood, 'Gloria' by Laura Branigan, 'My Name Is Not Susan' by Whitney Houston. You get the idea.

"A night out with the boys!" said Wendy. "Different boys!"

"Very different!" said Roz.

We were all different. Low and I had a lot in common but we were poles apart. I wanted to see Roz at breakfast in the morning; Low didn't want to see anyone!

"It's Saturday night!" Topper began. "I'm going to enjoy it! I get cabin fever down in my workshop!"

"So how did you get into jewellery?" Wendy asked.

"It was the punk era, really. All of a sudden, both men and women were piercing everything! I used to make mad earrings for people. And then I developed this shamballa obsession; I was making bracelets for everyone!"

"I wore mine day and night!" said Mids. "Wore it out! And then it broke!"

"It led on from there," Topper continued. "Created a primitive workshop at home and now I have a workshop in town; surrounded by other craftsmen and women, making all sorts of pretty things. You should pop down?"

"That would be hazardous to my bank account!"

"Do a contra deal, Nurse Wendy!" suggested Low. "You can check-out that strange lump in his scrotum?"

"What lump?" said Wendy, sounding alarmed.

"Don't listen to him!" said Topper. "He's the only strange lump in this car!"

The banter was flying. Typical Saturday night banter. Ridicule, sarcasm, near-the-knuckle jokes, thankfully not all aimed at me; everybody was getting it in the neck! The boys were boisterous and, if I'm honest, the *double entrendres* were a bit blue. Wendy was a nurse, so she was used to anatomical references and bizarre blockages but I was still concerned; the two groups of friends were not yet one happy family!

The art exhibition was being staged in an old, untouched building in Holborn and, as soon as we entered the majestic room, we all knew we'd have to rein it in, keep the volume levels down and be on our best behaviour. We were greeted at the door by the gallery owners who took our invites and then by waitresses who gave us champagne. Mids gave the thumbs-up; it was good stuff.

This was a breathtaking collection of erotic paintings and drawings. Jaw-dropping images! Huge, expansive, expressive pieces of love, lust and – to be honest - pornography! Images you could never hang in a family home, although I could see them working well in The Haunted House!

Resplendent in some high-fashion finery, the assembled guests were doing their level best to be cold and analytical but – for crying out loud – these images must have been stirring a few loins! Or maybe not? These were professionals. This was art. This was their life. This is what consumed them.

It was almost as much fun watching the guests looking at huge paintings of enormous naked bodies, watching them absorb, analyse and discuss. There were naked human bodies to suit everyone's taste! Some being bitten, some being fisted, some being spanked. My senses were literally tingling! Many of these images brought back memories and even brought back long-lost sexual fantasies. I was back in my bedroom at my parent's house.

I stood next to this elderly gentleman who, as far as I could see, had been gazing at this drawing of a young woman for about three or four minutes. He could feel me standing beside him.

"Exquisite," he said. "I love his work. Simple but so sensual."

"It is," I replied. "I'm not familiar with this artist."

"I must confess," the man began, "this is the work of my nephew! I'm speechless! Where did he get this talent from?"

"My grandfather could paint!" I said. "Sadly, it missed a few generations."

"What do you do?" he asked.

I hesitated. "Music critic," I replied.

"Wonderful!" he said. "What brings you here?"

"I'd heard it was worth the journey and it is! I'm glad I came."

"Me too," said the man, not moving.

In the distance, I could see Roz and Wendy transfixed by a huge painting of a naked middle-aged man. Must have been in his forties! Fit, flat stomach with a spectacularly huge penis! Flaccid, of course, but something that was definitely going places! I stood beside them and looked up at him.

"He's gay, right?" said Roz.

"Probably," said Wendy.

The waitresses began to pass out these elaborate *entrees!* I wasn't totally sure what I was eating but they were delicious. Definitely sushi-like! My eyes, my heart, my soul, my taste buds were being enriched at this wonderful exhibition. We should do this more often, I thought to myself. Why not? My group of friends can be anything they want.

Suddenly, Low was behind us. "Mine's bigger than that!"

Typical Low! Born troublemaker!

Wendy turned round. "Is it now?"

"Definitely!" said Low, smiling.

Wendy turned back, disinterested.

"And what about the painting?" asked Roz.

Low looked and thought for a second. "Leaves me cold."

"Okay," she replied.

And it was okay. We were a group but we were all different. We loved each other but we wouldn't all love everything. I pulled Low away from the painting.

"Amazing place, right?"

"Oh, yes!"

"If the images don't rock your world, then make conversation, make new friends! I'm sure there are some dynamic women in here!"

I didn't want the girls thinking Low was some kind of sleaze. He was only joking but his jokes were sometimes clumsy. I wanted Roz and Wendy to love my friends.

"I hear ya!" said Low, feeling chastised.

I watched Low walk towards a group of women who were wrapped around a sculpture. I saw him strike-up a conversation with one of them and I saw her smile.

Melvin needed no help at all. He was very comfortable. As he always looked so smart and stylish, everyone assumed he was a model and part of their world. Melvin wasn't even looking at the images on the wall, he was deep in conversation with some chiselled, elegant man. This exhibition was a social gathering for him. I watched him for a while. Always a smile on his face. I made a mental note to smile more often.

I looked around me; the event, the people, the minds, the brilliance on display. My dad would have been thrilled to see me here.

"You're getting a window into their soul; from their brain straight out on to a piece of canvas," my dad would say. "An astonishing transfer direct from their heart!"

As a kid, Mum and Dad would drag me round The Tate Gallery and, back then, the shapes made no sense. I was your normal, spotty kid. The modern stuff looked like the paintings I'd done at nursery school and I definitely wasn't interested in portraits of 16th Century kings and queens!

Trish was a creative person but not a gallery person, so we'd never spent any time looking at art. We did films and plays and concerts but never art galleries. "Damn!" I thought to myself. "There's a lot I haven't done. No wonder I'm so dull!"

I thought about music. I thought about my favourite acts using their lyrics to tell me their stories and giving me a window into their soul.

With a simple question, "What's going on?" Marvin captured our bewilderment.

With her words, "You don't know what you've got 'til it's gone," Joni predicted the gradual breakdown of society inside a three-minute hit record. Such genius!

I could hear Stevie crying, "You haven't done nuthin'!" 30 years later, nothing's changed.

This was the same. That transfer from brain to canvas. Standing in that gallery, I knew I was in the right place. I guess it takes you a while to work out where you should be?

As a jewellery-maker, Tony T was also very comfortable; chatting easily with everybody, getting into conversations about body art and body jewellery, and handing out his card to all sorts of people. This was definitely Topper's world.

He sidled up next to me. "Now, I want a big fuck-off house!" he said. "I want high ceilings and huge walls, so I can hang some of these enormous paintings! My every day is tiny things, tiny gems, tiny stones, small and delicate parts. I need some big in my life. Big house. Big walls."

"Maybe we should all live in a big house like Roz and her mates?"

Topper's eyes begin to sparkle and I could see his cluttered noggin calculating figures like a big old hard drive. "Now, that is a great idea! Could we really do that?"

"My friends can do whatever they want!"

"Back in a sec."

Topper looked energized and went off to find the powder room.

Roz and Wendy came to join me in the middle of the room. They had been sharing private jokes and their cheeks were red with laughter.

"I just want to strip-off and let these artists paint me!" said Wendy. "Can they make me look that good!"

"Of course!" said Roz.

"I assume The Elusive Wilson has some lovely shots of you?"

"Hundreds!" replied Roz.

"Will I see you in an exhibition like this one day?"

"Probably."

She shrugged her shoulders. I knew the answer anyway.

This had been the perfect start to our Saturday evening but where was Mids? I looked around the room but couldn't see him anywhere. "Need to go and find Mids." I said to the girls, who were now sampling a new tray of delicacies that had just arrived.

I wandered around the gallery. Topper was talking to some people, Melvin was still talking to that man, Low was still talking to that woman, but Mids was nowhere to be found. The pretty waitresses were still handing-out champagne to incoming guests and then I thought, "Ah, the kitchen!" Wherever there was catering, Mids was sure to be and, sure enough, there he was, chatting and laughing with the catering manager. Doubtless, they were talking about champagne; hopefully they were talking about dining and dating? I needed someone to put a smile on Tony's face.

As everyone was happily occupied, I could just stroll and enjoy. I could take my time. I paused at a simple line drawing of the back of man's head in the upper thigh region of a woman. He was kissing a thigh and one could only assume where he was headed! That was me. I was a simple line drawing. A man of simple needs. Not a simpleton but someone that loved the simple things: music, art, a full fridge, a woman's thighs. If you had those things, what more could you need?

Suddenly, that squeeze again; Roz's hand pinching my bum! "Are you enjoying that image?" she asked.

"I am!"

"We'd better pull you away!" said Wendy. "Don't want you getting too aroused! Saturday night is just beginning! Are we ready for some vacuous footballers and their even dimmer wives?"

"As long as the music is good, I'll be happy!" I said. "There's nothing I hate more than crap music!"

Roz laughed. "Your life! What must it be like?"

When it came to music, my life could be bloody painful! Music was my thing. My skill. My talent. My subject. Listening to amateurs and wannabes made my skin crawl. And there were certain songs I couldn't listen to anymore; great songs but songs I was over! For me, played-out!

The beautiful building we were in must have been a school or university. I found myself looking at the ceilings and windows more than the drawings and paintings. Maybe a big old house was the way to go? We'd all been living in pokey single men's abodes for too long. Maybe we could all get on and live together like Roz and her friends? Though it would probably look like a brothel most nights of the week!

Eventually, people gravitated towards the centre of the room, and it looked like we had done the exhibition.

"Thanks to Melvin for the invites!"

"Baggers done good!" said Low. "I have made friends with a talented young painter called Jemima."

"Please don't tell me she'll be painting you naked!" wailed Wendy.

"The world deserves to see my body!" said Low, confidently.

"How lucky we are!" said Wendy

We clambered back into Mids' over-size car and started weaving our way down to Dulwich Village. Now, as you know, Dulwich used to be a punch line for sixties comedians like Tony Hancock and Kenneth Williams. They would joke about Dulwich or Penge or East Cheam but now, unless you're an oil baron with a fleet of camels, you can't afford to live in such places; these ordinary suburban houses are commanding million plus price tags. Because property prices keep going up, some people are calling it 'gentrification'. As in, the locals are being forced out because the gentry are moving in. It happens everywhere. It's as natural as night following day. There are few guarantees in life but one is: house prices will go up.

Melvin's travel playlist was keeping us buzzing: 'Lucy In The Sky With Diamonds' by The Beatles, 'Stacey's Mom' by Fountains Of Wayne, 'Maria Maria' by Santana etc.

We were headed for a gated community and a security guard met us at the gate. Baggers flashed our gaudy, gold-flecked invitations and we were let inside. As we approached the house, it was clear we should dump the car ASAP and walk the rest of the way. Right up to the front door, broad, highly-varnished, souped-up, customised cars were double and triple-parked. Sod the consequences: let's party! Parking etiquette was the least of their concerns. Getting out was the other guy's problem. And this attitude really characterised the evening. Not so much 'I'm Alright, Jack' more 'I'm Alright, Talk To My Agent'.

At the front door, two burly security men and one stern security woman took our invitations and frisked us, looking for knives and guns! According to Low, all he was carrying was his giant appendage. Oh, how we laughed!

The first thing that hit me was the music. I could instantly feel my skin crawling. House versions of soul and disco tunes! The original songs had been created by some of the best black music makers on the planet: bass players, guitarists, keyboard players, saxophonists and violinists coming together to create a living, breathing, shifting groove, and here was a new guy with a machine imposing a simplistic beat on top, reducing it to a tedious, metronomic drone, virtually sucking all the soul out of it!

I took a deep breath and kept walking. This was my problem and my problem alone to deal with. No one else would be affected. Everyone else in my group looked absolutely thrilled to be in this huge, opulent, gadget-laden house. In front of a huge cinema-screen TV sat four professional footballers playing ... football! No one was dancing. Everyone was too busy doing business.

Next to every footballer was a small man with a moustache and two mobile phones, and draped over every chair and sofa were glamorous women wearing sprayed-on dresses. There was so much thigh and cleavage on display, there was actually nothing to look at! People are blasé about naked flesh in a nudist colony.

The boys recognised assorted celebrities and I could see them whispering and trying not to point. Wendy and Roz didn't know who the women were, but they knew how much their clothes cost! Many of them were wearing the absolute latest and hottest!

We decided to saunter, to find the bar and, naturally, to view the house. Suddenly I heard Roz scream, as she fell into the arms of this slight, effeminate man, a TV presenter, someone she'd worked with many years ago. We left the two girls to that conversation and kept walking.

Wall-mounted and floor level TVs everywhere, autographed and framed photos of David Beckham and Cristiano Ronaldo on the wall, unusual installations or pieces of metallic sculpture strategically placed, plush furniture, classic furniture, futuristic furniture, and a disturbing, walking, talking mini-robot butler, who kept getting under everyone's feet! And, naturally, patio doors leading to a huge garden and heated, outdoor swimming pool.

Finally, we reached the bar, complete with bow-tied barmen serving us whatever we required. There were huge jugs of cocktails and I opted for a Long Island Ice Tea. It was delicious! These guys were experts; top of their game! I finished it very quickly and got a refill.

Roz and Wendy came towards us, dragging this TV presenter.

She turned him towards me. "Wes meet Aaron!" I shook his hand.

And then she turned him towards the boys. "And, Aaron, if you can believe it, this is Tony, Tony and Tony."

Aaron shook three more hands. "What happens when you call out Tony's name?" he asked.

"We have the T.I.T.," said Roz, expertly pointing at my friends. She'd heard this story before! "The Tony Identification Tree. This one is Topper, this one is Mids, and this one is Low, based on their previous history, personal traits and dubious hygiene standards!"

"Oi!" said Topper. "I smell as fragrant as a field of flowers!"

"Yeah, like an old tin of air freshener!" said Low.

Topper gave him a not-very-discreet middle finger.

Wendy continued with the introductions. "You've met Tony, Tony and Tony, well, this is the weirdo of the bunch: Melvin."

Aaron shook Melvin's hand. "I know you, don't I?"

"I've been to Paul's before," said Melvin.

"Thought so."

"Aaron and I worked on this short-lived pop music show," Roz began, "travelling around the country, interviewing hot, new talent in 'exotic' locations. Unfortunately, not very exotic locations and, as it happens, decidedly lukewarm talent! The acts are long gone and so is the TV show!"

"That's television!" said Aaron. "An endless stream of mediocre ideas. One or two work, most don't." He looked around him. "So, what do you think? Nice pad!"

"Very nice!" said Mids.

"Once he'd got his new contract, Paul was able to buy this."

"How do you know him?" asked Low.

"I went to school with the little shit! He was always captain of every football team. We all knew he'd become a footballer!"

Aaron put his finger to his lips, as if he were about to share a secret, and beckoned us to follow him. We all obediently followed, past the bar, past the buffet, past an empty dance floor, down some stairs, down to Paul's private screening room. You literally felt like you were in a small cinema, complete with the smell of popcorn. The cinema was showing one of the recent Star Trek movies. One wall was completely taken over by a screen, with built-in speakers projecting the rumble of huge spaceships.

"We could have one of these rooms in our house?" said Topper.

"What house?" asked Mids.

"The one we're all going to live in!"

Mids turned to me. "What's he talking about?"

"Tell ya later."

Aaron beckoned us again, so we kept following him. This time through a closed door to a smaller room, a much more private room: endless shelves of VHSs, DVDs and CDs, a desk, a comfy armchair, a laptop, some filing trays, and a widescreen TV on the wall displaying a silent, slow-moving slide show, photos of Paul as a kid, photos of his family, photos of him on holiday with his friends; a live, personal photo album, constantly whirring round and round, always there, not hidden in books or drawers, a reminder of his beginnings and his loved ones. We all stood and watch the slide show for a while. There were even a few shots of Aaron with Paul. Yes, they definitely had known each other a long time!

I made a mental note to do exactly the same. What a perfect way to chill and relax; wallowing in great memories. Me and the boys had certainly shared some memorable moments and, now that I'd hooked-up with the crazy girl with the wild hair, life was about to get even more eventful. I think we were all touched this intimate insight into Paul's life. No one spoke. As if we'd been allowed into a sacred tomb.

Aaron beckoned us out of the rooms and we returned to the party. Melvin and he disappeared somewhere and we all headed back to the bar. I needed some more of that Long Island Iced Tea! Low was itching to get on the dance floor. He could see some pretty girls hovering around the edge, just waiting for that one big tune, but the DJ was playing obscure nonsense, playing for no one and literally playing with himself.

Roz and Wendy didn't need to dance. Not while there were celebrities to talk to. They took their drinks and circulated, while me and the T's sampled the glamorous life. It was certainly a long way from the back room of a pub in Turnpike Lane. These weren't necessarily wealthy people but they were wealthy right now. Old money is wealthy forever but these people had a good gig this month and they were going to spend their fee on designer clothes!

Finally, Low could wait no longer and asked one of the pretty girls to dance. Mids and Topper took their cue and invited the others to join them on the dance floor. Suddenly, my rent-a-party crew had got the party started, and there were curious onlookers observing proceedings, as if they'd never seen people dance!

Low was throwing his best shapes and I could see the girls smiling. Something told me to stay off the dance floor. I got the feeling I should be look-out, just in case The Three Ts were indulging in illicit behaviour! Who knew if these girls were single or taken?

Sure enough, moments later, a burly footballer and his mates came towards the dance floor and wanted to know why his girl was dancing with another man. This geezer was at least 6'4" and some of his mates were taller. I was praying I wouldn't have to mediate. Thankfully, his girlfriend, a slip of a thing, came off the dance floor and began to give him a piece of her mind. I watched him visibly cower and retreat. She must have been saying something like, "You're off doing business and you've left me alone!" Within minutes, the footballer and his mates had done a U-turn, and the girls could continue having their fun, but Low now knew what the boundaries were: look but don't touch.

But that wasn't really in Low's nature. Some men just can't help themselves. All men flirt and, for most of them, it's just a harmless way to pass the time. The woman knows this too! She knows it means nothing. In fact, the flirting can get quite graphic and intimate, with references to bouncing boobs and shapely rear bumpers, but both parties know it's just male/female interaction. It's what men do around women. They literally can't stop themselves from showing-off!

But, with Low, if you left the door ajar, he would stick his wanger into that gap and prize the door open. If you thought you were playing innocent card games with Low, you were wrong. Low didn't play gin rummy! He was competitive in everything and snaring a willing filly was his favourite sport. He had a gift and it was too much fun not to use it.

He had a variety of approaches. Approach No. 1 was to be conversational, funny and charming. Quite a legitimate move but – oh – so deadly! As they smiled and laughed, Low would edge in closer and, before the woman knew it, lips were locked. Approach No. 2 was the connection to famous people route. If the victim seemed aroused by casual mention of celebrity names, Low had hundreds of bona fide stories about actors, singers and footballers. The possibility of moving into the high life has an irresistible lure and Low made it work for him. Approach No. 3 was reserved for cynical women; smart women that recognised Low. For such women, Low had the balls-out honesty approach; total, unforgiving, unrelenting 'truth'. After an hour of Low spilling his guts, some of these women actually felt as if he were opening his heart and soul, though it was just an act!

Thus, with these WAGs, Low observed the look-but-don't-touch rule but, when he got the chance to share a drink and engage in conversation, Low's faultless technique moved through the gears. Just like the Joe song, 'All The Things Your Man Won't Do', whatever she complained about, Low had a sympathetic ear and a halo. "Blimey, darling, that's not on, is it? You wouldn't catch me behaving like that!"

Even though Topper wasn't trying, he seemed to be getting on famously with one young woman. Tops had this way of dancing that was almost comical. As if he were ridiculing his own moves. It was part-Travolta in 'Saturday Night Fever' and part-Travolta in 'Pulp Fiction'. Whatever it was, it made women smile. In fact, this girl was dancing and laughing so hard, she had to come off the dance floor to get a drink and Topper followed her.

I didn't know if the girl was attached or married but she really seemed to like Topper! In fact, I should have known she wasn't attached or married! She didn't have that ultra-groomed WAG look. She must have been the friend or sister of one of them? Not knocking Tops but the super-pretty ones would never have danced with him. This young woman was forgettable to look at; shop assistant more than customer. Almost 'Don't fancy your mate much!'

Once she'd finished her drink, they didn't even go back out on the dance floor! I saw them slink-off to some plush sofa. At this point, Tops was going to talk about rings, bracelets and necklaces, and she would be enthralled!

This left Low and Mids out on the dance floor, and I could see Mids was getting tired! These girls were much younger than him. At that moment, Melvin and Aaron arrived and the pressure was off Mids. The two younger men had some devastating moves and it took all the girls' skills to keep up.

Oh, I liked it on the edge of the dance floor! You know most DJs can't dance. A Dad Shuffle, if you're lucky. I liked my observational post. Supervisors have super vision. I needed to have eyes everywhere and where was Roz? Now, that was a good question! Where was she? But did it matter? If I scurried around looking for her, what would that look like? The nervous, jittery, insecure boyfriend; not a good look!

Suddenly, there was another man at my shoulder. He eyed me up and down. "You're not a footballer!" he said.

"No, I'm not! I'm here with friends of friends!"

"Aren't we all?" he replied. "I seem to have mislaid my girlfriend!"

"Me too!" I said and extended my hand. "Wes."

"Robbie," he replied and shook my hand. "I'm editor of the official website. I know more about these people than anyone here. Probably too much!"

We both stood and observed. That's what we both were: observers; odd sorts that derive pleasure from being on the outside: looking and listening. I became aware of volume increasing, louder laughing, people moving more rapidly, rushing from room to room to see where the excitement was. The clueless DJ was still pumping out lifeless re-mixes of familiar songs, and Robbie and I drank it all in; just another C List celebrity party in another overpriced house.

Suddenly there was screaming and splashing and, through the patio doors, we could see people jumping into the heated, outdoor pool. I was not surprised to see Roz and Wendy in their undies jumping in! There were speakers outside, so everyone in the pool was bouncing, waving their arms and singing.

"That's my girlfriend over there," I said, pointing at Roz, "the one in the black lingerie." Robbie nodded.

"That's mine!" he said, pointing at another girl. "She's the one in the blue!"

We were both dating nutters. We shrugged our shoulders.

"Mine will do anything for a laugh!" said Robbie.

"Mine likes doing new and different things," I began. "A try-anything-once girl!"

Robbie understood. Robbie knew. He nodded. We virtually now had two dance floors; Baggers, Mids and Low were on one, and Roz and Wendy were floating in another.

"Is it normally like this?" I asked.

Robbie nodded again. He'd seen it all. Out of nowhere, some waiters arrived carrying towels which they piled on to a wooden table. Eventually, these drunk people would realise they were cold and rush for a towel. It didn't take Roz and Wendy long. They were soaked through, cold and shivering but still laughing, so it had been worth doing. They'd be travelling home without their undies! No big deal in the grand scheme of things.

Out of the corner of my eye, I could see Topper and his plain jane getting very close. A few more minutes and it would be on! In fact, all round the room, there seemed to be couples very close to intimacy. Was this about to turn into an orgy? Roz and her friends had attended a few but this would be a first for me.

"F-f-f-reezing!" said Roz, getting close to me to get some warmth.

"We'll just go and change," said Wendy.

"Good idea!" I said.

I turned round to see what kind of progress Topper was making and he and his plain jane were not there!

"How many bedrooms in here?" I asked Robbie.

"Six," he replied.

I wasn't worried about Tops. He was definitely old enough to take care of himself. We wouldn't need to worry about him getting home. He and his plain jane had clearly graduated from sofa to a bed somewhere!

Robbie's girlfriend whizzed by him, wrapped in a towel, shivering. "They always do that!" he said. "It's a heated pool but they forget how cold it is outside. This is England, after all! Paul's bathrooms are always full of damp underwear!"

"Does he hold a lot of parties?"

"Lots!" said Robbie. "He was an only child from quite a poor family so, now he's got money, his house is always full."

An elderly black man with a trolley full of seven-inch record boxes passed by us. He walked round the dance floor and positioned himself to the right of the DJ. I saw him whisper something in the DJ's ear and the young guy nodded in acknowledgement. Attired in a three-piece tonic suit, the old man must have been pushing 70. His long, grey locks were pretty wayward but his hardcore, NHS specs kept him moving in the right direction.

The young DJ played his last song and the old man opened his record box and plucked out a seven-inch single with a huge juke-box hole in the middle. It sounded like

Alton Ellis or John Holt. The entire mood of the party changed! Paul, the host, joined everyone on the dance floor and it was clear that this was his music. He was in Heaven! The music his Mum and Dad had played was the music he loved. He knew all the words.

Joining him on the dance floor, Paul's friends knew all the moves and it was clear this was a big part of the evening. The small foreign agents had served their purpose. The wheeling and dealing was over. Now Paul was going to have his fun. The old DJ knew just what to play. He'd been playing the same set for decades.

Even the pretty young things that Mids and Melvin had been dancing with, who can't have been born when these tunes first came out, instantly caught the mood of the music and followed Paul's lead. There were some wonderful hybrid steps being executed on the dance floor; old school reggae moves performed by perma-tanned WAGs in Manolo Blahnik pumps!

Robbie had seen it all but my jaw was open with astonishment. "What is going on?" I asked.

"Same at every party. Eventually, Paul wants to hear his music, so Lester comes along and plays him his favourite tunes. I think he's an uncle? Paul seems to have a lot of uncles!"

It was a delight to see. Within a few bars, we'd all been transported to a dancehall in Kingston, Jamaica, circa 1975. A different era. A different vibe. Paul was in his element! On a Saturday afternoon, he was hero to the fans on the terraces but, come Saturday night, he was a young man from Selsdon, brought-up on the music of Ken Boothe and Delroy Wilson. As a DJ and music lover, it was a delight to see; people dancing, singing, smiling and interacting with one another. Fore-foreplay. Next stop: slow dances, touching, kissing and who knew what?

Roz and Wendy emerged from the bathroom, wearing their clothes (commando style) and they were as bemused as I. The party had changed. Roz had that mischievous look in her eye. I just knew she was going to drag me on to the dance floor! This was not good. She hadn't seen me dance yet and I didn't want to lose my new girlfriend!

Nevertheless, I'd read in a book that real men face their fears, so I found myself on a dance floor at a private party in a gated piece of property in Dulwich Village. It was another Saturday night adventure with the boys but, this time, the crazy girl with the wild hair was with us and, for some strange reason, she wanted to dance with me. Naturally, I had a sense of rhythm but, interpreting the music, I may as well have been a member of the walking dead; my lifeless limbs did little to complement these wonderful old rhythms.

Curiously, Roz seemed happy enough. Maybe The Elusive Wilson hadn't even humoured her? At least, I was present. I was right there, doing my laboured, twisted bump and hustle. This lovely old reggae music sounded good, I was smiling and enjoying myself, and I suddenly realised it was a brand new experience: dancing with a woman, together as one, cheek to cheek and in-synch. Keep it fun, she had said. I must have been scoring brownie points!

3.00 became 4.00 and it was fast approaching 5.00am. We were all flagging. Mids was sweating profusely. I could see him wishing he were fitter! I signalled to Baggers that we were going; he waved his hand at me in a special way. It was Melvin-Code that he would make his own way home.

We'd already lost one, and now we'd lost another! It meant Wendy could lay down on the back seat. I was home before daybreak and the birds were already tweeting (but not social networking.)

Sunday

When I woke up on Sunday morning, almost Sunday afternoon, I was alone. Roz had wanted to finish her evening with Wendy, so we'd dropped them off at The Haunted House, both carrying their damp underwear in small plastic bags, and laughing at all the things they'd seen and heard.

My first thought was Topper. Where was he? I dropped him an innocent text. "Hope you're well? Text me when you wake up."

For me, the night had been a triumph! Roz was the queen of wild adventures but I had demonstrated (courtesy of Melvin) that I was more than capable of showing her a good time.

From out of nowhere, I had slow danced with a woman! Where had that come from? Untapped dance moves! What an experience! Though I was basically following Roz's lead. Where had she learnt to dance like that? It was virtually dry humping!

My phone went 'ping'. It was a reply from Tops. "She is the one!" it read. "I've finally found her!"

Not what I was expecting. Not what I was expecting at all! 'The One'? Only girls say that! Our texts were usually about a woman's blow job technique or her amusing, kinky requests. This was very different. Intuitive feelings hadn't always been my forte but The Roz Effect had affected every part of me. My intuitive feelings were kicking in! I was inside Topper's head!

Naturally, I was happy for him. Good friend. Old friend. I knew he'd been lonely for a while but had he really found someone special? Or was he just anxious to find someone special? The Roz Effect had made me a wise old man. Well, it felt like that. I felt I had something to contribute. Having been through what I'd been through with Trish, Roz and the residents of The Haunted House, I felt I could help Topper and it was all about expectations.

Whatever he thought he'd found and whoever she said she was, Topper would have to be patient. This woman would not be showing her true colours for quite a while. It was vital he kept his expectations realistic; bargain basement low!

My wisdom told me not to say one solitary word. I lay there thinking, "Crikey, this wisdom's good, innit?" I definitely wasn't going to say to Topper, "Ooh, be careful, mate, I know you're anxious to find your own Roz but don't jump in!" He was a grown man. A sensitive, gifted man. He knew about expectations. All men do. Don't they?

For my own piece of mind, I needed to spend some time with Tops and his plain jane. Get a sense of what kind of person she was, listen to her words and observe their dynamic. Of course, given time with Tops and his girl, Roz would quickly surge into some kind of voyeuristic frenzy. She seemed to love people-watching, particularly dysfunctional couples. Her Jill stories were becoming epic! I couldn't wait to tell her about Topper!

I sent Tops a quick text. "Great to hear you've had such a special Saturday night. Can't wait to meet her!"

Then I sent a text to Roz. "Good morning/afternoon! Hope you had fun last night? What are you doing today? Topper says he's found 'The One'."

I jumped into my shower and stood there for a while. The hot water felt good. I was in no hurry. I could scrub and rinse thoroughly. Melvin had bought me a Bluetooth speaker, which sat on my shower wall, looking pathetic, waiting for me to bring my iPhone into the bathroom. How hard was it? Play music, flick Bluetooth switch on iPhone, listen to music in shower. Not complicated!

Melvin had also procured me an expensive exfoliating sponge which, if I could be bothered, actually cleaned my body. I squeezed some Christmas present shower gel on to my sponge and began scrubbing everything. My skin literally tingled!

I thought some more about the idea of us all living together in one big house. Everyone else was renting! I was the only person with a mortgage. Pooling all our resources, in order to buy a big house, we'd have to move slightly north, maybe Finchley or Southgate? That was okay.

What would the house be like? Empty most of the time, I imagined, like our current abodes? It would only really come alive at the weekend and, most weekends, we were out and about? It would, however, be the perfect party venue. The idea of ridiculous theme parties appealed to me enormously. I pictured Roz and her friends in authentic costumes, though it was still hard to picture any of them smiling!

Having enjoyed the best shower of my life, I returned to the bedroom. Two missed calls from Roz and another text from Topper.

"Lunch today? Double date? 2.00pm?" said the text.

Roz had been too excited to text. She wanted to know what was going on. "The One?" she squealed. "The One? What happened? I must have missed that!"

"You were otherwise occupied!" I said.

"Who is she?"

"Don't know," I replied. "Tops has invited us to lunch to meet her. Are you free?"

"How exciting?"

"She might not be The One?"

"I know," said Roz. "Who cares? Let's go and grill her anyway!" And she cackled with pleasure.

Tops gave me the details of the restaurant, and Roz and I made our way down there. Fortunately, not deepest South London! A nice French bistro close to the Southbank.

Roz and I settled in with two drinks and waited for the new couple.

"She was with that group of WAGs that the boys were dancing with. They left the dance floor for a drink, they talked for a while on a sofa, and then she and Tops sloped off somewhere!"

"Where?"

"I don't know! There are six bedrooms in that house! I asked the editor of the club website, who knows everything about everybody!"

"One man and six bedrooms?" she exclaimed. "What do those footballers earn?"

"Silly money!"

"Good day to you!" said a loud, animated voice on the other side of the restaurant. Topper walked towards us, holding the hand of his plain jane. They both looked deliriously happy with huge cartoon smiles on the faces!

"Wes, Roz, I'd like you to meet Francine!"

We both shook her hand and she smiled at us; a toothy, genuine smile of almost admiration. "A real pleasure!" she said. "Tony has talked about you non-stop. I feel like I'm meeting Marvel super heroes!"

Topper embraced Roz; a lingering, grateful embrace; as if to thank her for bringing sanity to our reckless, single lives. She seemed to understand.

"You okay, Tony?" Roz asked.

Topper could barely speak. He was twisting his head like Stevie Wonder and trying to formulate a sentence but nothing would come out. Finally, he grabbed Francine's hand, to calm his nerves. "I'm okay," he said. "A bit confused but okay."

Francine was a plain jane. No getting away from it. She was not an attractive woman. Even if you didn't find Roz attractive, you would have to concede she was beautiful. Her features were classically beautiful. Her eyes, her lips, the shape of her face, her neck, her outlandish hair. No wonder The Elusive Wilson had taken so many photos of her! Francine, on the other hand, had no such features! What was wrong with me? Why was I even thinking about her face?

Francine began talking. She was talking about Tony talking about us. She focused on Roz because Roz was listening to her. Me? I was more interested in looking at my old friend Topper looking at her. He looked hypnotised; in a trance; almost under a spell?

"Even academics and highly-qualified people struggle with personal relationships," I could hear Francine saying. "These high-end people make their living out of communication and diplomacy but, when it comes to a conversation with the missus about their sex life, they're as clueless as the rest of us!"

Roz nodded. She had first-hand experience of her well-bred housemates blundering through the dating game.

"What do you do?" asked Roz.

"I have my own consultancy," Francine began. "I used to work in book publishing. About 12 years. I now help writers complete their manuscripts. Take their raw material and mould it into something publishable. Work with them on structure. Work with them on that winning formula."

"Is there a winning formula?" asked Roz.

"I think so," replied Francine, putting her hand on Topper's leg and gently squeezing his knee.

I looked at Tops, who was still gazing adoringly at Francine.

"Topper!" I shouted at him. "Where are you, son?"

Tops was still struggling for words. Stuttering, gurgling and making every kind of sound but speech! Finally, after what seemed like an epic tussle between his brain and his mouth, he blurted out the words, "Isn't she beautiful?"

Now, the answer to this question was, "No!" but I wasn't going to say that. Obviously. I paused, probably too long but at least I was nodding.

"That she is!" said Roz, sparing my blushes.

"That she is!" I repeated, grateful that Roz had given me some words because – Lord knows! – I had none of my own.

Now, I'm no beauty. Not by any stretch of the imagination. I have many good qualities but I'm no pin-up boy. No runway model. Why Roz was dating me, only she could answer that question. Clearly, Roz had done her share of pretty boys. They'd dated her and discarded her, as pretty boys do. Roz didn't want to be discarded again. She wanted someone she could rely on and, even though I was no Idris Elba or Tom Hardy, she knew she could rely on me. I was as reliable as the moron at the traffic lights who will bib you when the lights turn green and you stand still for two seconds. I was as reliable as the supermarket customer that gets to check out and suddenly realises they've forgotten something 800 yards away in the home baking aisle. I was as reliable as that big piece of lime scale in the bottom of your cup of tea, even though you de-scale your kettle regularly.

For some strange, mystical, translucent, meandering, ridiculous reason, the crazy girl with the wild hair wanted to date me and, if I wanted to keep her, I had to keep it fun and, judging by the incredulous look on her face, she was having great fun. Francine was still talking about Roz and I.

"It's interesting that Tony uses the word interaction," I could hear Francine saying. "A lot of people use the word chemistry but it's over-used! Chemistry is lust! What you and Wes have is much more than lust! Tony says the interaction between you two is striking, almost as if you're Batman and Robin, fighting crime together; each with their own distinct role. There is a silent understanding. You work as a team because you gel together! That's rare! What couple wouldn't want that?"

Now Roz was in a trance! I had two mates in a trance! Clowns to the left of me, jokers to the right. Francine was ruthless in her pursuit of prey. Once she had your attention, she would reel you in with her opinions. She had her own theories on everything; cobbled together from different books on the subject.

A waitress finally approached and took our orders. We all seemed to be ravenously hungry and there were lots of side orders being added: two bowls of chips, one bowl of onion rings and an order of macaroni cheese. Two sleepy couples coming up!

Topper was still silent; unnaturally docile; either gazing at Francine or gazing into space. I did not recognise my mate. "Topper, talk to me!" I cried.

"He's tired!" Francine said. "We haven't slept!"

"Haven't slept at all?" exclaimed Roz.

"Not yet."

Topper nodded, wearily.

Without even thinking, I blurted out, "What have you been doing?"

Roz looked amused at my stupidity.

"Talking," said Francine, calmly. "Just talking."

Topper nodded again, clearly incapable of doing anything else and desperate for sleep.

Their drinks arrived and Tops glugged thirstily on his beer. It seemed to wake him up. "What a conversation!" he said. "What a conversation!" He slugged on his beer again and virtually finished it. "What a conversation!" he repeated.

Now, I was happy that Topper was talking, but I needed more than three words!

"What have you been talking about?" said Roz, impatiently, though she was absolutely loving the absurd drama of this 24-hour love affair.

"Life, love, this and that!" said Francine, a wholly unsatisfactory answer that left Roz gasping for answers.

"Tony, how about you?" prodded Roz. "Care to elaborate?"

Topper looked at us blankly for what seemed like an eternity. "What's important to you?" he asked, meekly. "Do you know? What's really important to you?"

Roz and I looked at each other. This was clearly a question for the file "To be talked about later."

"Good question, son!" I said. "What's really important?"

Thankfully, the food arrived and we didn't have to use our brains anymore. We could talk about the food, last night's party, the weather and simple subjects that didn't tax us unduly.

Despite having no sleep, Francine was still talking nine to the dozen. Maybe she was one of those clockwork toys that kept going and going and then ... stopped? Or maybe she was just excited about Topper? He was a lovely geezer! Once he'd had some sleep, she would see how nice he was! Right now, he was about to fall face first into his plate of food.

What did it matter that Francine was plain? It didn't. Why was I even fixating on it? It was almost as if Roz had given me a new arrogance? Did I actually imagine I had graduated to a higher, more aesthetically-pleasing place? Was I actually looking down my nose at someone ordinary? It was pathetic! Topper liked her and, if Topper liked her, she was alright with me! Nothing else mattered.

Topper's question had been reverberating around Roz's head. She was the kind of person that had to know, had to understand, had to make sense. She couldn't let the question lie.

"What's important to me?" she began. "A few years ago, I would've said my family. But they're okay! They're self-sufficient! They don't need me and I don't need them! These days, what's important to me is ... me! I want to grow. I want to learn. I want to evolve. And, if I do, I can be a better daughter, a better sister, a better friend."

I looked at my vivacious, erudite, articulate girlfriend and the same refrain came back at me: why would she want to date a numpty like me? She turned her head and winked at me. "A better girlfriend!" she concluded.

"Good answer!" said Francine. "I think that's what Tony and I both arrived at!"

We turned to look at Topper and he was asleep. His chin was on his chest. He still had his knife and fork in his hand.

"You've worn him out!" I said to Francine.

She smiled. "I like your friend," she said. "He's got a good heart."

"He has!" I said and, in that moment, I suddenly saw a little of what Topper saw. She appreciated my friend, truly appreciated him and, in my books, that made her an exceptional person.

With the lunch over, Roz and I got into my car and began making our way back to my place, until we got an urgent call from The Haunted House that Jill was having some kind of breakdown, so we re-routed.

"My God!" began Roz. "That Francine! She will wear us all out!"

"At least Topper is happy?"

"Topper is asleep!" replied Roz, giggling to herself. "How will he be when he wakes up?"

My phone rang. It was Marie.

"Wes, I have a crisis!"

"Not Percy again!"

"Not Percy!"

Thank God, I thought to myself. Never had I more wanted a man to have sex with my sister. I wanted them to fuck every night. I'd never known my sister to be so content. Whatever Percy was doing, he was doing a great job!

"What crisis?" I asked.

"A friend's daughter goes to the local primary school. They're having their annual Parents Pop Quiz tomorrow night and her team members have flaked-out! Me and Percy are going to help out but I don't know anything!"

"And you want me to join the team?"

I could feel Roz nodding enthusiastically beside me.

"You're in luck, babe! Roz and I are free!"

"Thank you, Wes! I owe you."

"Don't be soft!"

When we got to The Haunted House, Jill had packed all her belongings into two suitcases and seemed to be moving out.

Everybody else had tried to talk her out of it and failed, so they were all pleased to see Roz. Not necessarily the voice of reason but somebody that might get angry and shock her out of her decision.

The house was in such a chaotic and emotional state, they didn't even notice me and, if they did, they didn't care enough to acknowledge me. This time, they weren't in the warm, forgiving kitchen; they were all sprawled out in the living room. Jill and her suitcases were in the middle of the floor and, all around, stood her housemates, blocking her way. It was a clumsy impasse.

Roz entered the living room and I shuffled in behind her, not wanting to be noticed. While everyone gave Roz the quick SP on the conversation so far, I loitered quietly near the door, looking like a nervous turkey at Christmas. Roz looked around at her exhausted and exasperated friends. They'd all given Jill their own distinctive brand of logic but nothing was working!

Roz paced about menacingly and glared at Jill. Roz was about to become both good cop and bad cop; it would be a masterful performance. Jill's cheeks were still flushed with embarrassment. Above everything else, she felt ashamed. She'd set the standard, she'd made the rules and she'd broken her own rules.

"I was on my way back to my boyfriend's house to enjoy a relaxing Sunday evening!"

She emphasised the word 'boyfriend', so as to annoy Benjamin and to let the housemates know she had a life beyond them and they'd disturbed it!

"Sorry!" said Raymond, feeling foolish. "You were needed!"

"Yes, we're sorry," repeated Heston. "Maybe you can make her see reason?"

"Reason?" snapped Jill, angrily. "There is no bloody reason! I'm falling on my sword. Can't you let me have that?"

Roz continued to prowl. She noticed an unfinished glass of white wine on a table near Wendy and downed it in one. She waved the glass at me. I dived into the kitchen and brought back a bottle of white wine from the kitchen table. Roz took it from me and refilled the glass. I went back to my invisible spot near the door.

"This changes nothing!" Roz began. "No sex in the house is a good rule. It makes sense. It keeps things clean. It keeps the boundaries clear. Jill, you broke the rule but ... there are reasons for that. You were confused, you were depressed, you were vulnerable. It's nothing! It's a blip! A momentary aberration.

"Without wishing to sound melodramatic, our world will collapse without you, so you can't leave. Wendy will hate me for saying this but I think the rule should remain in place and let's just erase this incident. Christ, we've erased enough incidents down the years!"

Jill slumped down on a sofa. Heston knew this was a positive sign and rushed into the kitchen to get her a drink. Her favourite tipple: G&T. Jill sat silently, gathering her thoughts and her dignity. Heston brought her a tumbler of tipple. She drank it down.

"I've really fucked things up," said Jill. "Marrying Alistair was a stupid thing to do. What did it achieve? He lives with the mother of his children. He's never going to leave her."

"We've all fucked-up," said Raymond, edging in closer, adopting a supportive pose. "Catastrophic, life-altering mistakes."

Even the typically morose Benjamin seemed alarmed. Jill was the mother hen that made the house run smoothly; the HR lady with resources to calm even the most unstable and chaotic human. Benji needed her meticulous mind. How could be possibly be an anarchist by day if he couldn't come home to Jill's Lancashire Hotpot and conservative values?

But Roz wasn't finished yet. This time she glared at Jill and the three men. They all shuffled nervously.

"What have I done?" asked Benjamin. "I haven't done anything!"

Roz span round and pointed at me. Everyone looked. I could feel a huge beam of white light shining on me! "That one there ..."

She paused for maximum effect, choosing her words carefully, so as to offend everyone. "That one there ," she repeated, "he's my boyfriend and I like him very much. He's absolute filth in bed and we get on like a house on fire!"

I could feel my jaw dropping in shock but I really didn't want to stand there with my mouth agape.

"He's here to stay!" she said. "Be nice to him! Understood?"

"Yes, Roz," they all mumbled in virtual unison.

"We're going back to his now. Behave yourselves!"

If she'd had a cape, she'd have swished it with a flourish. Instead, she brushed past me, leaving me standing there. I offered a feeble wave and quickly followed her out.

Roz stood by my car, tapping her fingers on my roof, irritably.

"I've known them since they were teenagers. We started uni on the same day. They were gawky. Awkward. No social skills. And look at them! We're all close to 40. Jill's even a few years older! Nothing's changed! Will they ever grow up?"

As we drove home, Roz was silent, thinking. I think she was almost ashamed of her mates. When we'd first met, she'd painted them as noble, great thinkers, sensitive souls but now they were exposed! They were as flawed and irrational as me and my mates. I left her with her thoughts.

I wanted to gush and tell her how impressive she'd been but I resisted that temptation. Yes, Jill was Mother Hen, making sure the house ran smoothly, but I could now see that it was Roz who was judge and jury and, if me and the boys were to get a big house, it would be down to me to arbitrate.

The tables had turned! 12 months prior, I'd been the runt of the litter. The small, deformed one. The butt of all the jokes. Now, I was the group elder; the leader of the clan. How had that happened? The Roz Effect. Other people can make you a better person. That's what you need in your life. That's what I now had. The Roz Effect was a powerful force!

Monday

Roz and I woke together and clicked into action; moving quietly and effortlessly from bathroom to bedroom to kitchen. Yes, we were in synch. There were smiles and kisses and squeezes. Was this what a functional, loving relationship felt like? What a revelation? I quite liked it! It did actually feel like we were a team.

"Don't forget about the pop quiz tonight!"

"Send me all the details," she said. "And, when you hear from Topper, let me know what he's saying the morning after!"

I dropped Roz to a tube station and headed towards the shop.

We had lots of gear coming back, after the weekend, so the day was a constant flow of people. On Monday, more than any other day, I needed Max's stacking skills. We had to make sure, when the gear came back, it got put in the right place, and 'the right place' was, ideally, where we could find it again! Every accessory, every cable, every component had to be in the right place. By the end of the day, our backs ached!

Topper didn't call me, so I put in a call to him. I needed to hear his words in the cold light of day.

Amazingly, he acted as if nothing was different. He acted as if it was just another day. This was the man who claimed to have found 'The One' on Sunday morning.

"So, is it a thing?" I asked.

"It is," he replied, calmly. "When Tom Cruise says, 'You complete me' in 'Jerry Maguire', I get it now! I get it. With a woman like Francine, I am complete."

Topper sounded like a motivational speaker. Not necessarily logical (or even moral) but confident and assured.

"She wants nothing from me," he continued. "She just wants to be my friend. She's endured a life of being the ugly duckling. Do you know what that feels like?"

I suddenly felt really bad for fixating on her face.

"The ugly duckling never gets asked for a dance," he continued. "I danced with her on Saturday night and I made her day. Made her week!"

I really felt like shit for even having those thoughts. What did it matter what she looked like? "You are a good man, Tony! And she will enjoy every moment with you."

"We're going away this weekend. Her folks live in Great Yarmouth. We're booking a hotel and she's going to show me where she grew up."

"So soon?"

"It feels right," he said.

When it feels right, it feels right. You almost need derision and disaster. You almost need pain and perspective. When it tastes right, when it smells right, when it feels right, it's a revelation and a relief. Was I fooling myself with Roz? God, I was spending too much time asking that question! Was I fooling myself? Nah! It felt right!

"I hear you," I said to Tony. "When it feels right, you just know."

"We're going to meet her folks, drive around, share some meals. Grown-up stuff. Time to grow-up!"

"Perfect!" I said.

I couldn't get over how matter-of-fact he sounded. There was a zombie-like tone to his calm. He'd clearly had some kind of epiphany? Or maybe some kind of vision? As if he'd finally found that rare flower: the platonic relationship with a woman!

He had said, 'She wants nothing from me.' Did that mean she didn't want a physical relationship? Impossible! They'd booked a hotel room. A hotel room would involve sex. That's what hotel rooms are for! In that space, she would learn a lot about him and he would learn a lot about her! For the first time, she would discover how structured and orderly he was. Literally, a neat freak! If she was an untidy person, any sexual encounter would be dead in the water!

In truth, Topper was probably more sensitive than Francine. He had a terrible habit of falling for his conquests. Many of these girls just wanted a good time but Tops would want their number, and they'd be like, "Why do you want my number?"

My immediate thought was not that he'd get his end away. Having been with Roz and feeling that perfect fit, I wondered how it would be for them. Would it be good? Or would it be an embarrassing mess? Would she be shy? Would he be cautious? Would she be demanding? Would he be impatient? So much could go wrong! I was nervous for him.

What was I turning into? An over-thinker. Down the years, I'd ridiculed Trish for being an over-thinker; thrashing through the same information over and over again. And, here I was: second-guessing Topper's sex life. He was old enough and ugly enough to blunder through this alone. If there was a problem, he'd deal with it. Or he'd come to us!

I was really looking forward to the pop quiz and, once I'd picked up Roz from that same tube station, I began to think about trivia: dates, places, lyrics.

Even Roz was excited! "I love a good pop quiz!" she said, as she climbed into my car and gave me a soft kiss on my lips. It sent a tremor through my body. And she smelt good too!

"What is that fragrance?" I asked.

"Some new Chanel," she replied. "I was close to Selfridges today."

I began thinking about previous pop quizzes I'd been at. Questions I'd fluffed, mistakes I'd made. Grim memories began resurfacing because this was the only thing I was competitive about! I'd never played any kind of sport to any level. I was too slight to be an athlete.

When we arrived at the school, they'd decorated the assembly hall beautifully and you almost forgot you were in a primary school, until you sat on the seats and your knees were up in your armpits. There were stylish table cloths on the tables and arty lamps on every surface to create mood lighting. With a few deft touches of interior design, it felt like we were in an after-hours drinking spot!

On stage, a guitarist and a singer were playing popular songs. He was a good guitarist, she was a good singer and it perfectly set the mood for the evening. I'd never been to a pop quiz where there'd been live music and I'd been to some high profile events. Of course, live music at a pop quiz! Who'd have thunk it? Fortunately, two of the parents were really talented!

Marie and Percy bounded in, accompanied by Marie's friend, Ashley, who was immensely grateful for our involvement. She kept thanking us over and over again.

"Our pleasure!" I reassured her. "We love pop quizzes!"

"Ashley has just turned 50 and is newly-divorced, so be very nice to her!" Marie whispered in my ear.

"I'm nice to everybody!" I replied.

Percy, as ever, smelt of some expensive fragrance! I saw women's heads turn as he passed them. With time to spare, Roz and I bought a round of drinks at the makeshift bar. As they were raising money for the school, we bought loads of nibbles too!

The mums and dads were in excitable good spirits. I looked around me. Several of the men looked like record industry or media types; there was definitely a nerd or two. This would be no pushover. I could feel my excitement levels rising. This was my 10,000 metres final. This was my Ryder Cup. I wanted to win.

When we got back with the drinks, Marie and Ashley were in deep conversation. Divorce post mortem. She was putting on a brave face and knocked back her plastic glass of red wine in one!

"I've got another gig for you," I said to Percy. "A 50th birthday party. Should be a doddle! I'll send you the details."

"Thank you," replied Percy, gulping beer from a bottle and stealing a quick glance at Marie. "You've given me the confidence to offer my services. My local pub have offered me a Friday night!"

"Well done!" I said. I was genuinely pleased for him. He was a late developer but full of enthusiasm. There's nothing worse than listening to a bored DJ.

Marie and Ashley went back to the bar. Ashley had finished one drink and needed another. Roz and I winked at one another. Even in a primary school assembly hall, sitting on a ridiculously small chair, she looked sublime. Effortlessly cool. She took low maintenance to whole new depths. She was quite happy, absorbing the music, sipping on her drink, listening to the affectionate chatter of old friends.

Marie and Ashley returned. This time Ashley had two plastic glasses of red wine. This was her coping mechanism. Who was I to judge? Marie gave Percy an affectionate squeeze. He smiled with a look of pure pleasure. He had found his queen and he couldn't be happier. He was probably fantasising about her naked body and her profiteroles in equal measure.

The talented couple on stage finished their final song and the quiz mistress made a grand entrance on to the stage. She was clearly another parent but someone with a penchant for giving orders. She had a big voice and a big personality, and knew everyone in the hall, so she was able to quieten the crowd with witty, personal barbs. The school mistress outfit was probably driving certain men wild! If she wasn't already, she had a big future as a dominatrix!

The first sheet we were given was anagrams. I looked at it blankly and passed it to Roz. She gazed at it for a few seconds. "Amy Winehouse," she said. I looked at the sheet. "That's one!" I said and gave her back the sheet. Clearly good at anagrams!

The next sheet we were given just had numbers and lines. The couple on stage were going to sing a famous song and leave out a word or phrase! Contestants had to guess the word or phrase. I looked around me. Marie and Ashley were still in conversation, Roz was studying the anagrams but Percy looked keen. I gave him the sheet.

"Justin Timberlake!" said Roz. I took the sheet back from her and wrote in the name. "That's two!"

The couple on stage ran through ten songs. Everything from Blondie to Katy Perry. Roz knew a few, Percy knew a few, I knew one. I was proving to be the least effective member of the team. I gave the sheet of anagrams back to Roz.

The next round was about London concert venues. We were given a map of London with musical notes on it and we had to fill in the pubs, halls and bars. Marie and Ashley were still talking, Roz was still looking at the anagrams but Percy looked keen, so I gave him the sheet.

I couldn't remember the last time I'd been to a gig. We all went to the Royal Albert Hall to see Van Morrison but that was years ago! Before that, we all went to this tripped-out reggae festival in Germany. Thousands of white Germans dressed in red, gold and green, smoking the biggest spliffs you've ever seen, and swaying gently in a field. We were so full of irie feelings, it took us two days to come down!

Luckily, I knew my map of London, so I was able to identify the areas and that helped to identify some of the venues. Not a good round for us.

Marie now had her arm around Ashley, who was sinking lower and lower. I think she was hoping the pop quiz would prove a distraction but there was a big gap where her husband used to be.

"Bruce Springsteen!" exclaimed Roz. I took the sheet of anagrams back. "That's three!" "Let me help!" said Percy, relieving Roz of her anagram duties.

Then came a round of actual questions with a few local references thrown in. I had a quick flashback of one bad round at a pop quiz many years ago. They gave us lists of first names and we had to identify the band. They didn't even bother with John, Paul, George and Ringo. This was up a level. I saw the name Romeo and I figured it must be Showaddywaddy, as the average age of the participants was about 55? How many Romeos are there? Turns out it was So Solid Crew! My team members were NOT impressed!

One question really upset me. "Which pop music icon was born on the Benwell Road in January, 1956?" At the primary school, we were close to the Benwell Road and, having been a North Londoner all my life, I felt I should know it. 1956. I worked out his age.

"It must be Suggs?" said Roz.

"He's not that old!" said Percy. "'Baggy Trousers' was filmed in Kentish Town, so people think Madness are North London but I'm not sure they are."

We all scratched our heads and I felt deeply ashamed that I didn't know the answer. Not sure we did well on that round either! Ashley had chosen some no-hopers to help her out but I guess we were better than nothing?

When the answer was revealed to be John Lydon, I was crushed! This was meant to be my sport. I couldn't play football like Low. This was my event! Pathetic. Not that Ashley was too bothered about winning. She just needed wine, company and more wine. In that order.

Marie and Percy dropped Ashley home. I'd invited them over to see my fridge, so they came on to mine afterwards. As I opened the fridge door, they both took a step back with amazement.

"Who's it for?" asked Marie.

"I just want to be able to say, 'What would you like to drink?' Just like Mum did! Hospitality is so important! Bring them into your space. Feed them. It turns acquaintances into friends, and friends into family!"

"And look at this!" said Roz, opening the doors of a cupboard. It was filled top to bottom with goodies.

"You need a party!" said Percy.

"A social gathering is in the pipeline," I replied, grinning with carefree, childish glee. "So, what would you like to drink?"

We sat on the sofas in my small, functional front room with a selection of drinks and snacks.

"And look at this!" I said, bringing an IEA flatpack box into the room.

"What's that?" Roz asked.

"A new piece of furniture for my bedroom!"

"Looks like a little chest of drawers?" said Percy.

"For me?" asked Roz and, for my troubles, I got another nut-tingling kiss.

Marie nodded sagely. Her brother was growing up and not before time! It was a school night, so they couldn't stay late, but we enjoyed an hour of each other's company. Roz was loving Marie's embarrassing stories of our childhood. I would get the chance to meet Roz's parents soon, so I could watch her cringe.

"Thanks for helping out tonight," Marie began. "The change in Ashley has been shocking. Those eyes were once bright and smiling. She used to make us all laugh. She had great stories and an infectious laugh, but that's a distant memory. Obviously, she's sad but she's really angry too. Really angry. Angry at the time she invested in the marriage. Angry at herself for falling so deeply in love but ..."

Marie looked at Percy and he at her.

"But ...." she continued, "What can you do? If you fall, you fall! Ashley's drinking far too much now! The red wine is killing her and, fairly soon, it will affect her work! But what can you do? What are the options? Stay single forever?"

We kissed Marie and Percy good night and Roz looked down affectionately at the piece of furniture I'd bought just for her.

"Can't assemble that tonight," I said. "I'm in a good mood. Let me go to bed happy!"

Roz threw her arms around and we embraced for a few seconds. Her warm, sleepy body felt good next to mine. "You've bought me a piece of furniture!" she said.

"If this world were mine," I began, "I'd place at your feet all that I own."

She knew it was Marvin Gaye. Cheesy as hell but it made her smile.

Tuesday

I'd explained to Roz that I was going to hook up with the boys on Tuesday evening and she was more than happy to return to The Haunted House, to survey the damage. Thus, Tuesday was a series of text messages getting everybody in one place at one time. We all needed a catch-up. Significant things were occurring that would affect our routine and the social life we'd spent years perfecting!

Out of the blue, Amiable Alvin popped into the shop. I spoke to him on the phone a lot but I rarely saw him. Alvin was often my go-to guy. He was professional, punctual, flexible, polite; the model employee.

Not sure why his parents had named him Alvin but the name had given him this charming, eccentric character. He was literally on the axis between Alvin Lee, Alvin Stardust and Alvin And The Chipmunks; part rocker, part moody pop star, part wacky rodent. He had a cheerful disposition, a leather jacket and Freddie Mercury teeth! Everybody loved him! There was no customer that could phase him. Even if he didn't have their totally unsuitable request – why the hell would you ask for grime at your auntie's retirement party? – he would always have a pleasing alternative.

Max and Alvin exchanged a hearty handshake, but me and my old friend had a good old hug. I was pleased to see him.

"How are you, mate?" I asked. "What brings you round these parts?"

"Wanted to see you in person."

That sounded serious and he did not look his normal chirpy self.

"What's up?"

"No other way to tell you ..." He paused. "I've been diagnosed with prostate cancer!"

I'd been on such a high since meeting Roz. Unrealistically happy. I should've known it wouldn't last. This news totally killed my Roz-buzz! I stared at him, blankly. Not very helpful.

I had immediate flashbacks to my first meeting with him, some 10 years ago. I was still learning the ropes, getting used to inheriting my dad's disco equipment hire shop. It seemed like such a huge undertaking but having Alvin around really helped. I could rely on him. Being able to offer Alvin to clients made my job that much easier. I knew he'd always deliver; whatever music they wanted to hear!

We met at a non-descript pub in Stroud Green. I was providing the locals with a traditional Saturday night disco and we'd struck up a conversation. I immediately knew we'd be friends. He had funny faces, funny voices, terrible puns, the occasional joke and an encyclopedic knowledge of pop music. We got on well. He was easy and funny to talk to.

Back then, his hair changed colour every time I saw him. He was dating a hairdresser, who would experiment on his poor, abused barnet. There was a world of chemicals, bleaches and hair products living in his scalp. Ten years later, he shaved it all off. Now he looked like a member of Right Said Fred!

"I'm so sorry," I said. "I don't know what to say."

I hugged him again and, this time, he held on tight, just to let me know he was going to be okay.

"I've been diagnosed, I'm going to have treatment, I'll be okay."

"Really?"

I must have looked paler than usual. He pulled one of his trademark goofy faces and actually reached out to grab my hand in a sideways clench. He squeezed my hand.

"Wes, I'm strong. People get diagnosed every day, they deal with it and they get over it. Look at Nile Rodgers! He fought it twice and went back out on stage in front of thousands! The only reason I'm here is just to let you know that there may be some days when I can't work."

I laughed. "Fuck work! I want you to live!"

"I will live, Wes! Just wanted you to know what's going on with me."

I felt very humbled in the presence of this man. He was staring death in the face and taking the time to comfort me.

"Alvin, you're top drawer! You're a prince amongst men!"

"No more compliments, you soppy bastard!"

We laughed. I grabbed him again. I needed to hug him again, to let him know how much I valued him as a friend.

"I will still call," I began. "If you can't give it your all, I will find someone else. I've got this mad new bloke called Percy. He can fill in for a while?"

"If I can't give it my all, I will let you know. Now, where's my cup of tea?"

We both looked at Max.

"Maxi, what are you like? Cup of tea for my mate?"

"Coming right up!" said Max, and he disappeared into our tiny, primitive kitchen.

Alvin looked at me. He could see I was struggling with his news. What did I know about prostate cancer? Pitifully little! "I'm going to be alright, Wes."

I nodded, as if his words were a comfort, but they weren't. My happy-go-lucky bubble had burst and shit had just got very real!

While work stuff whirled around us, Alvin spent a few entertaining hours in the shop, telling us horror stories about gigs and clients and, naturally, telling us about a doctor with her finger up his bum. Somehow I knew that, if I told her this story, Roz would berate me for something. I wasn't sure what but I knew I was in for a good berating! Fortunately, I was seeing the boys tonight, so I wouldn't get berated until tomorrow.

Of course, being with Alvin made me think about my health. We only really think about health when we're in pain or a loved one is in pain. This beautiful complex machine called our body is a mystery to most people. When most people get a cold, they don't know what to do. So they buy drugs. When most people get a headache, they buy drugs. When most people are constipated, they buy drugs. Stunning levels of ignorance. Duh, I keep getting cramp, what do I do? Car owners need to take a driving test. What do humans do? Go to the pharmacist.

By the time Alvin left me, I was an itching, twitching bag of nerves. Wondering which of my aches and pains were serious, and vowing to get 'checked out'. I wasn't sure what needed 'checking' but my testicles were talking to me. It was time to step boldly into the next phase of adulthood: pro-active healthcare. After berating me, Roz would have some good ideas.

Me and the boys agreed on 7.00pm and we all agreed on one of our favourite Chinese restaurants, The Rising Sun. Not only did we love the food but we loved the owner – Geoff – a Chinese guy with a broader scouse accent than Jamie Carragher and Cilla Black combined! He'd say something in his heavy accent, we'd look at each other to see if anyone had understood, he'd laugh his head off and then wonder why we hadn't got the joke! No matter what time of the day or night, Geoff always had a pristine, starched white shirt and black tie. Yes, he was in Finsbury Park, but he was going to look Mayfair at all times!

When I arrived at the restaurant, Melvin was already there, sitting at our table and actually showing Geoff what he had in his bags. Geoff was admiring this one particular lime green shirt with multi-coloured patterns on the cuffs and collar. The kind of shirt that only Melvin could pull off but Geoff fancied himself in it.

"Christ, I could pull birds in this shirt!" Geoff said.

"And what would your wife say?" I asked.

"She'd say, 'Geoffrey, what a lovely shirt!'"

We were pleased to understand him and laughed.

He continued to dig around in Melvin's bags. "What else you got in there?" He pulled out a stylish pair of brown brogues with tartan stitched into them. "Baggers, you've got some lovely gear, son!"

"The garbs must be on point!"

"I could dance in these shoes!" Geoff said.

"Get away!" I scoffed.

"The wife loves to dance!" Geoff said. "I could wear these shoes and take her dancing!"

Low came through the door of the restaurant and could immediately see what was going on. "Geoff, you would look pukka in those shoes!"

"See?" said Geoff, to the assembled. "I've still got it!"

"Course you have!" said Low. "If you weren't married, you'd be a chick magnet!"

Unfortunately for Geoff, he was the most married man on the planet, and he didn't make a single move without his wife's say-so. When she came out to greet the customers, May was sweet as pie but, if you strayed too close to the kitchen, you could hear her giving Geoff a right earful!

We sat down with bottles of Tiger Beer and waited for the rest of them.

"Did we find out what happened to Topper?" asked Low.

"He went off with that girl, the plain one, her name is Francine."

Low laughed. A guttural, dirty laugh. "They were getting on very well! She was totally into him! I could see it."

"And then what?" asked Melvin

"I saw them necking on a sofa!"

Melvin nodded. "I saw that too. Looked like it was getting a bit handsy!"

"And then they disappeared! Not sure where they went but they talked all night. No sleep. No sex either!"

Low and Baggers stared at each other and then looked at me. Talked all night and no sex? It did not compute.

"And, this weekend," I continued, "they're going to Great Yarmouth to meet her folks! He says she's 'The One'."

"He's said that before!" said Baggers.

I couldn't remember him using those words to describe a woman. We'd talked about it. He hoped he'd find it but, as far as I knew, he hadn't.

"Don't you remember?" Baggers began. "Sheena The Window Cleaner?"

Down the decades, there'd been a lot of woman.

"Not to be confused with Vanessa The Window Dresser!" added Low, not very helpfully. "Topper liked the fact that she worked in Liberty but, after a few dates, they went back to her place and it was a total junkyard; clothes on the floor, plates in the sink. You know Tops likes to keep it tidy!"

"I don't remember Sheena The Window Cleaner!"

"She would always make sure every part of every car window was clean. She liked 100% visibility. You must remember her!"

It was slowly coming back to me. There were 52 Fridays and 52 Saturdays in every year, and we'd been mates since we were teens. I'd always been with Trish but the boys had made full use of their single years. I'd seen the boys date a lot of women. A lot!

"Tall, Scottish and a bit like Geena Davis in 'Thelma And Louise'?"

"That's her!" said Baggers. "He said that she was The One! She had a good job working at The Inland Revenue. A job for life! Her flat was spotless and she even made her own oatcakes!"

I remembered her. She was a striking girl and they made a good couple. On paper, it should have worked but it fizzled out. From memory, Tops had said there was "no spark" and that is a non-starter!

Having been with Roz a few months, I now had a finer appreciation of 'spark'. There was nothing Roz loved more than to cause mayhem in public. Her mischievous nature had no boundaries. I would watch her put her hand down the front of her knickers and she would, very discreetly, play with herself. We could be anywhere! The pub, the supermarket, my shop! And then, without warning, she would push her fingers into my mouth! 'Spark' was not an issue. I was permanently sparked! And, following each outrageous antic, she would look at me with a complete poker face, as if we'd just exchanged our views on the weather.

Try as I might, I could not stop comparing her to Trish. Trish's idea of an outrageous antic was to switch channels in the middle of my favourite programme! Whatever Tops had had with Sheena, it wasn't enough. He didn't know much but he knew he wouldn't be driving off any cliffs with her!

"So, what's special about this one?" asked Low, sceptically.

"Tops says it 'feels right'."

Low and Baggers looked at me blankly.

"He says she 'completes' him," I added.

"It's only been a few days," said Low. "Let's see what happens?"

Low loved Topper to bits and wanted him to be happy, but he didn't love relationships. Low loved women but he didn't like the role they played in relationships. In his words, he didn't like how they 'castrated' men. As far as he was concerned, most women didn't actually want a relationship, a partnership on equal footing, a meeting of minds. As far as Low was concerned, women wanted a live-in lover that could kill spiders and someone they could have on their arm in public! Low didn't need relationships! He didn't need friendship or company or advice from a woman because he had us; his crew. And he didn't need to worry about sex because there was always someone wet and willing close at hand! Low would be happy to listen to Topper's good news but knew to keep his views to himself; we all knew how Low felt about relationships!

With me, Low accepted my preference or, in his words, weakness. Long ago, I'd explained to him that I was more comfortable being part of a couple. In his own loving yet condescending way, he was happy for me, but he'd always pitied me for dating someone as homely and prosaic as Trish.

Melvin was fiddling around in his bags.

"Baggers, what ya lost?" asked Low.

"Too many bags!" he moaned.

"No kidding!"

"Found it!" said Melvin and he proudly held up a very swish-looking, silver pen. He handed it to Low, who balanced it very expertly in his palm.

"Weighty!" said Low. "Expensive!"

"My boss bought it for me! Ten years of loyal service!"

"Ten years already?" I asked.

Baggers beamed and rolled his gift between his fingers. Then he reached into another bag and pulled out a hardback notepad (for important ideas and detailed plans!)

"Right," he began, "it's my birthday soon and I want a big party! It's no special date but I want a party that is opulent, ostentatious, outrageous ... and other words that begin with O!"

"Ostrich?" I offered.

"Orgasmic?" offered Low.

"A party for us!" said Melvin. "To celebrate us!"

Mids barrelled through the door of the restaurant looking bullish and quite pleased with himself. He greeted Geoff with a smile and a handshake, and presented him with a bottle of wine.

"What's this?" asked Geoff.

"The perfect wine for your delicious food!"

"Expensive wine!" he wailed.

"Geoff!" assured Mids, resting his arm on Geoff's shoulder. "Your customers will love this wine! More customers! Better customers! You and May share this bottle and then we can agree a fair price?"

Geoff didn't look convinced but thanked Mids and took the bottle to his wife.

"Did you order?" asked Mids.

"Still waiting for Tops!" I said.

"Nah, we can order!" he said. "I'm famished! Tops will eat anything!"

So, we ordered and began having ideas for Melvin's birthday party. Melvin had an iPad and a laptop but I think he rather liked his flash pen and wanted to use it! As we gabbled furiously, he struggled to note all our ideas.

"I was thinking," Melvin began, "maybe we could use Roz's house?"

It was an iconic building with a spacious front room, almost built for parties, but I couldn't see The Addams Family going for the idea. I hesitated.

"Will you at least speak to Roz?" he asked.

"I will."

"How many people are you inviting?" asked Low.

Melvin did some quick maths in his head. "Only about a hundred."

Low looked puzzled. "I don't even know a hundred people!"

"We're going to bring everyone together! All the people we like! I want you lot to invite people too!"

"To your birthday party?" asked Mids, looking around anxiously to see where the food was.

"That's how you network! That's how you make new friends!" said Melvin, smiling like a self-help guru.

"I don't want any new friends!" said Low, grumpily.

It was weird for someone in the service industry to be so anti-social. Maybe dealing with people all day long had lessened his love for the human race? Low had these grumpy and frankly laughable turns, where he would fantasise about locking all the diners in the restaurant, leaving them in there to eat each other!

"Alright, Tony," said Melvin, well used to Low's cynicism, "don't invite anyone and don't make any friends. Do what you want!"

The food arrived and, and soon after, so did Topper. Looking more calm and assured then I'd ever seen him look. The transformation was shocking! He didn't say anything, just took off his coat and began tucking in!

He could feel us looking at him. "Hello, boys!" he said, with a mouthful of food. "Everything alright?"

"You look different!" said Low.

"I feel different!" he replied. "Pass me the duck!"

Melvin passed him the plate of shredded duck, Topper shovelled some on to his plate and continued to tuck in voraciously, but he could feel our eyes on him.

"What do you want to know?" he asked, almost impatiently.

"We want to know everything!" Melvin said.

Tops was clearly hungry and wanted to stuff his face but he could feel the gaze of a curious audience. He finished his mouthful and deliberately put down his knife and fork. He looked around the table. This was not the Topper we knew and loved. He'd always been confident and knew how to tell a story but this was a different look. He looked like Moses on the mount. He looked like a wise old man with all the answers. He cleared his throat and stiffened his back, as if he were about to share the secrets of the universe with us.

"Her name is Francine. Both parents still alive. She grew up in Croydon. Now lives in Mitcham. Never been married. Never had a steady boyfriend. Never been in love. She's very well read. Seems like her life has just been about books? She's quiet and bookish. Not much of a raver. Doesn't go out that often but she's great to talk to!

"I feel very comfortable with her. After a few dates, a woman will move into that girlfriend zone. She will act and behave like your girlfriend, you will go out and behave like boyfriend and girlfriend, she will refer to herself as your girlfriend with the hope that it will graduate to sex life to sleepovers to relationship and living together. Francine's not like that. I get none of that vibe from her. She's been the ugly duckling her whole life, so she has no expectations. She doesn't talk about relationships. She doesn't talk about a future. She doesn't talk about 'us'."

We all sat and listened. It was literally like having a new friend. This was not the personable, happy-go-lucky, chirpy-chappy we had grown up with. This was another human being altogether; a very calm and focused and together version of Topper. There was silence, as we waited for more.

"She asked me what was important to me. Have you ever thought about that? We know what we like and we do what we like, but have you thought about what's really important to you? What are your priorities? What's important to you?"

The question had stumped Roz and I, and the boys looked just as clueless. They looked at each other, hoping that someone had an answer!

"I know what's important to me," added Topper.

We all paused, mid-mouthful, not daring to speak or move. We waited.

Topper opened his arms, as if to embrace us all. "You!" he said, triumphantly. "You! You are what's important to me! My friends."

"Not her?" asked Mids.

"No, not her!" said Topper. "I barely know the woman! You, I know. You, I love. You are what's important to me!"

We were all quite stunned. Tops picked up his knife and fork and continued eating. "Pass them noodles!" he said to Melvin. Melvin obliged.

"You are my family of choice," said Topper. "I choose you!" And, as he happily continued eating, we all looked at each blankly.

There was discontent within the ranks. We weren't getting enough detail. Little of this made sense. Yes, she seemed a nice woman. Yes, she had provoked thought. Yes, Tops had made a new friend, but he looked different and was behaving in a very un-Tops-like way.

"What about her?" pleaded Low. "We want to hear about her!"

"I barely know the woman!"

"Do you like her?" asked Melvin.

"I do."

"Do you fancy her?" asked Low.

"I do."

Topper paused. Again, he put down his knife and fork, and took a sip of his beer. I watched him carefully. I could see him gathering his thoughts and recalling a memory.

"When we were at that footballer's house," Tops began, "I excused myself to go to the toilet. As I came out of the toilet, there she was waiting for me. She pushed me back into the toilet, locked the door, sat on the toilet seat and beckoned me towards her. The next thing I know, she's unbuttoning my trousers."

Low leaned back and smiled. He was content. "Ah, now it's making sense!"

"I can tell a lot by a blow job," said Topper.

"Oh, me too, mate!" said Low, swigging from his bottle of beer.

"What did you learn?" asked Mids.

Topper smiled to himself and, for the first time, actually looked a tad smitten. The hard exterior had softened and he was now smiling with pleasure.

"What did I learn from that blow job? Many things! She's a very sexual woman and a very intuitive woman. She knew what I'd like. She knew how I would respond. What else did I learn from that blow job? She loves men's bodies. Some women don't; she does! She's generous and loves to give pleasure. She's a student and loves to learn. She had read-up on her subject. She knew what she was doing! She was an expert in her field! What else did I learn? I learnt that she genuinely likes me. Me! Steady, reliable, boring me! And that felt nice."

We were all quiet. The other tables were clattering with meal-time chatter but we were all silent. We didn't know where it would go. We didn't know if Tops would ever fall in love. We didn't know if they'd ever be boyfriend and girlfriend, but he seemed happy enough, and that was enough for us.

Geoff the owner ambled back to the table. "You've hardly touched the food!" he complained. It was true. We'd all been listening intently to Topper's words and silences, so we all launched back into action, hungrily consuming May's delicious food.

"May gave you extra prawns!" said Geoff. "She says you're her favourite customers! I said, 'Nah, May, they're wankers!'"

"Will you thank May for us?" said Mids. "Tell her the grub is cracking, as usual."

It was a good evening with the boys. It felt like old times. It felt like just us, locked away in our mad little, Boysworld cocoon. When Trish had disappeared, it was shocking, then scary, then sad and finally depressing but, throughout it all, the boys were there, cracking jokes, motivating, encouraging me to go on dates with unstable women.

Our evening enjoying May's food reminded me that we'd been a tight group of Musketeers for more than 20 years; been though a lot with each other. Topper's revelations were just another step in our evolution. There was still a lot of growing-up to do but we were getting there. Whether the unsociable Low liked it or not, we were all on a learning curve and we would all soon be making new friends!

Listening to Topper was fascinating. I'd certainly never met anyone like Francine. The ugly duckling thing was doing my head in! It's so messed-up! The pretty people get everything: all the drinks, all the attention, all the proposals, while the ordinary-looking people get so little, they don't even have expectations! They expect nothing and, invariably, go home alone.

At the end of the evening, I looked at my phone to see if Roz had messaged me. I'd resisted the temptation all night. The message read, "Still pretty intense here. Exhausted. Sleep well."

As we sat back in our chairs, almost comatose, paying the bill and rubbing our bellies, Melvin asked, "Are we all out this weekend?"

"All except Topper!" said Low. "He'll be living it up in Great Yarmouth!"

"All except me," he confirmed.

"So everyone else is up for whatever I find?"

Me, Mids and Low nodded.

"What have you got planned?" I asked.

"So many options!" said Melvin.

Low fixed me with a grin. "And will there be any of the fairer sex joining us this weekend?"

It was ironic that Low should use such an expression. He didn't really view women as 'the fairer sex' in a reverential way. He didn't believe that women were nobler than he or lived life on a higher moral plain. To him, they were hustlers, just like men.

"I hope so!" I said. I knew Roz and Wendy would be up for it and I was half expecting Roz to invite someone else at some point. What would her other housemates make of our weekend jaunts? At some point, we would have to integrate them.

Wednesday

Another week had gone by and it was time for another Wesday Wednesday. Max's favourite day of the week; the day we could make lots of noise in the shop. The day when people popped-in for a mid-week boogie; the day Max's friends swung by for some education; the day curious passers-by stuck their head into the shop.

Max arrived with a record box; brand new, black and shiny. He plonked it on the counter proudly. I looked at it and then looked at him.

"Are there any records in there?"

Max pulled up his trousers, as if he meant business, and opened the record box. There were indeed records inside! Not many! About 20. He stood back and grinned. He wanted me to look at his records. I stepped forward and had a flick through. Many of the things we'd played in the shop over the past few weeks, plus a few new things I didn't even recognise!

"Have you got a turntable?" I asked.

"Saving up for one!" he proudly announced.

"Great work, Maxi! You're on your way!"

That's what I always said. What else was there to say? Max was moving forward. It was great to see him grow. One day he'd be too busy for me?

We usually started Wesday Wednesday after lunch so, once all our work was done for the day, we set ourselves up and started cranking out the tunes. I thought I'd give them hip hop breaks today and I didn't have many of those old 70s and 80s tunes on vinyl, so we were working from CD.

Max's mates had been wandering in all through lunch and, by the time 2.00 rolled around, we had an excitable group of about 12, laughing and texting loudly.

The first tune had to be James Brown's 'Funky Drummer', arguably the most sampled tune ever. The effect was instantaneous! Max's crew were frantically trying to do about three things at once: talk to the next dude, find it on Shazam, film it for posterity, play it to their mate down the phone. Bedlam!

They were all grooving in a cool and easy fashion. One step to the right, shimmy, one step to the left. They were immediately style leaders and cooler than cool. Discovering James Brown can do that to you.

But I was about to burst their bubble, destroy their illusions and pop their cherries, all with one tune. Not soul, not funk, not blues; 'When The Levee Breaks' by Led Zeppelin. I could hear their minds being blown. There was whooping and hollering, whistling and cheering and, under the din, I stopped the tune and started it again. Just so we could hear the full majesty of John Bonham's drums.

At one point, two young guys wandered in and came over to shake my hand; these were the customers that had called earlier in the week. Asif was the older of the two, his mate was called Virgil. They were both early twenties, skinny, tall, and both had record bags over their shoulders but, as they were carrying the bags with ease, I knew there weren't many records in there!

Again, these were kids born in the wrong decade. They were dressed in new, high street clothes but there were also little splashes acquired in pricey retro shops. Wide-eyed, they listened, enjoyed and nodded their heads to this earthy seventies and eighties music; the joyous smiles on their faces said it all. They didn't know what they were listening to but they loved it! They knew they had much to learn.

Max and his mates offered them a Red Bull each, which they gratefully accepted, and they instantly bonded with Max's cultured cohorts. I wasn't spinning vinyl but I was playing the kind of tunes they needed; songs that made people dance and tracks that would make them look like experts.

I wasn't sure what to say to Asif and Virgil. They had 40 years of dance music history to learn in a few days. They even tried to move to the tunes but they didn't know how. This wasn't simplistic dance music, this was rocking, sometimes funking and sometimes just floating!

What they actually needed was my two trusty boxes of floor fillers but I wasn't loaning them to anyone! All I could do was get them to make a list of the things I had in my boxes and point them in the direction of a second-hand record store so, as they listened to the tunes of Wesday Wednesday, they sat on the floor making lists.

Max had a pocket full of business cards for the shop and, as locals wandered in, lured and virtually hypnotised by the music, Max was handing out cards to (hopefully) drum-up business. The locals could see the fun we were having fun! I watched the thought process in their eyes. Hopefully, they'd be back soon to host their own parties?

With hip hop samples, it was a going to be a varied afternoon. We played 'Apache' by the Incredible Bongo Band, 'Take Me To The Mardi Gras' by Bob James and the live version of 'Long Red' by Mountain, tunes these kids had never heard. By the end of the afternoon, they understood that real hip hop was a beautiful patchwork quilt.

By the end of the day, Asif and Virgil had several sheets with scrawl over them and they were ready to go shopping! I hoped their parents were wealthy: this lot would cost them a pretty penny!

Once we'd shut up shop, I could meet up with Roz. I'd been looking forward to it all day! We'd agreed to grab something cheap and cheerful at the local kebab shop. A huge plate of shish, salad and chips! Just what was needed after a hard day's hip hop breaks.

She wrapped her arms around me and held me tight. It was a strange kind of embrace, filled with both affection and sadness.

"I have some news for you!" she began, sipping on her bottle of Keo.

"I have some news for you too!"

She looked at me with a slightly pained expression. "Not bad news!"

"Very bad news!" I said.

She was silent. "About us?" she asked.

"No!" I exclaimed. "Why would it be about us? Nothing to do with us! Well, not directly!"

"Spill!" she demanded, impatiently.

"Amiable Alvin has got prostate cancer!"

She looked as if she'd just received the prognosis herself. She gripped my hand tightly, looked into my eyes and then took a long swig of her beer. A meaningful swig, as if she wanted to get drunk and forget the words I'd just uttered.

I talked her through my conversation with Alvin, and how his treatment and recovery would affect the business. Roz said very little and absorbed the tragedy of the situation. She'd only met Alvin once but she'd loved him instantly, everyone did, and she knew how important he was to the business.

"It means I'll probably have to do a few extra gigs? Less time for us! You know, just you and me, and not a room full of punters as well!"

She acknowledged and absorbed that piece of information, and looked as if she was mentally psyching herself for her piece of news.

The food arrived. We both tucked in. It tasted authentic and hearty. We were surrounded by Cypriots. I felt at ease.

"So, here's my news: I have to go away for a month. I've been hired to work on a TV show about stand-up comedians in the north of England. I'll be based in Manchester. The production company don't want to do a month of hotels, so we're going to hire a house."

This was good news for Roz. A good job, good experience, good money but the Trish incident was still fresh in my memory, so major alarm bells began clanging in my head. The trauma was deafening. Another girlfriend was heading for the exit!

"Great news!" I said, hoping my disappointment wouldn't tarnish my sincerity. "Sounds like a great show!"

"It really does!" she said, her mouth full, chomping furiously.

True, Trish has 'disappeared' for six months and, true, I didn't know where she was but, while she was away, I had not done well. In fact, I had sunk into a depressive, almost vegetative state. No wonder the boys were happy to allow me a girlfriend!

I needed a girlfriend. I wasn't afraid to admit that. I functioned better as part of a pair. I wasn't good at the single life: the chase, the seduction, the lies, the excuses, the get-out clauses. I don't have it in me. Low could do it in his sleep but I didn't have the necessary coldness to be a single man. I liked couple stuff and couple life. It suited me.

So, it was only a month and I knew where she was. She was a phone call or a text message away. Nothing to stress about and yet I was hating her job. How often would this happen? Once a year? I was already struggling with this bit of news but I couldn't have her see that, so I changed the subject!

"The thing with Alvin has made me think about my health."

"Not surprised!" she replied, making short work of her dinner and trying to stifle a chuckle. "When it comes to health, men are hopeless! Absolutely bloody hopeless!"

The berating was on its way. I could feel it.

"Have you ever been checked for prostate or testicular cancer?"

I shook my head. I could feel the embarrassment wash across my face.

There was no berating, just a tired shake of her head. "Absolutely bloody hopeless! Good thing I live with a nurse!"

"Wendy?" I squealed, in a rather nervous voice.

Roz looked me square in the eyes. "It's your choice, genius. Either go to Wendy or go to some big, hairy male nurses with huge, hairy fingers. It's up to you."

There was no hiding the terror in my eyes.

"Hopeless!" Roz repeated. "Have you any idea what women have to go through?"

I didn't. Again, I shook my head.

"We don't have to talk about this again, do we? I can leave this in your very capable hands? You've got this sorted, right?"

I nodded furiously. She was not impressed. I was losing brownie points by the second.

"I will miss you," she said, not looking at me.

No eye contact? This was strange. Maybe this was all new to her?

"Will you?" I asked. Why the hell did I say that? What possessed me to say that?

She looked up at me. Now there was eye contact! Quite intense eye contact!

"Yes, I will miss you. Will you miss me?"

Christ, this was seriously uncharted territory! I was about to express an emotion. In truth, I was in awe of this woman. She was literally the best thing that had ever happened to me. I knew it, the boys knew it, Trish knew it, I think even Jeremy Kyle knew it! There was so much I wanted to say but this was not the time or place. Just answer the question, Wes! And say it with feeling!

I looked into the beautiful eyes of this wondrous woman and smiled. "Yes, I will miss you," I began. "I've just got used to this new and blissful existence so, yes, I will miss you."

She smiled. "It's just a month. I'll be home soon. We can make up for lost time? I'll sit on your face for a whole day?"

It was impossible not to love the crazy girl with the wild hair.

She was leaving in the morning, so I dropped her back to The Haunted House, so she could get packed. On the journey home, I tried to make inane conversation but my heart wasn't in it. I'd only just received her news and already I was sinking.

To make matters worse, I suddenly wondered if the Elusive Wilson was part of the production team. Part of me wanted to ask but part of me felt hopelessly immature. This was truly a test of the new Wes. I was enjoying my newly-acquired status within my crew and I'd even received a glowing reference from her in front of her friends; the new Wes was calm and confident, secure in his new role and new relationship.

"We'll have to do that trip to your parents when you get home?" I said, skirting aimlessly around the question I really wanted to ask.

"Definitely!" she said. "My sister, in particular, is looking forward to meeting you. I've never taken anyone home, so she knows this is a bit different."

Never before had I been so thrilled to be described as "a bit different". Different to the rest was good. I was something serious. Something worth bringing home. This filled me with confidence and a bit too much Dutch courage.

"Is the Elusive Wilson on this shoot?" I blurted out, instantly regretting my words.

She turned to look at me and smiled. "I wondered when you would ask that question!"

"I had to ask!"

"I haven't been on a shoot with him for about 18 months! Haven't even spoken to him! But somebody dropped out of his team at the last moment and, out of the blue, he called me up!"

"He knows he can rely on you."

"Yes," she said, nodding. "He knows he can rely on me. You need to know the team is good. No weak links. We've got a month to make this show. No more. He can rely on me."

Having a good team was important to me too; my delivery and set-up boys, my roster of DJs. I needed people I could rely on. I understood ... and yet she was going away for a month and living in a house with, arguably, her most significant ex. I was sliding into a depression riddled with self-doubt and envy, a very unsavoury cocktail.

When we got to her place, she turned to me. "You're not bothered about him, are you?"

"No, no!" I said very quickly. Too quickly.

"This is a man who didn't think I was good enough. I do not have feelings for men who don't think I'm good enough. As I say, I wasted a lot of time on that relationship and, after two years, he indicated very clearly that I wasn't good enough.

This is NOT someone I like. This is someone paying me shit loads of money. End of story."

"I'm cool," I said, my feet paddling frantically, desperately trying to stay afloat. "Really, I am."

"We'll speak every day."

"I'm cool," I repeated, hoping to appear strong and resolute.

She kissed me. Softly. Slowly. Deliberately. I was going to miss those kisses.

I didn't want to go home. I just couldn't face that empty bed. Not right now. I needed company but nothing too heavy.

I sent Marie a text. "If I popped by, would I be disturbing anything?"

I didn't want to discover Percy, in his undies, dancing in the front room. Idle celebrity gossip, a cuppa and some cake was what I needed.

"No. Percy's already asleep! I'm baking!" came the reply.

Perfect. I needed a friendly, non-judgemental face; someone who would totally be in my corner and see my point of view, even if I was being childish and unreasonable.

When I got to Marie's, there was not one laughing woman covered in flour and icing, there was two! Trish. I shouldn't have been surprised. She was one of Marie's oldest friends. There would be no serious pow-wow with my sister. I would NOT be sharing my pain with these two. They were giggling like naughty children. Both of them had cake mix in their hair, Trish even had a splodge of pink icing on her cheek, the sink was overflowing with bowls and utensils, but the kitchen smelt heavenly!

"By the time you make the tea, the cakes will almost be ready!"

"What have you made?"

"Something different! I can't keep making Carrot Cake or Rum Cake or Banana and Walnut Loaf! Percy will get bored!"

"We've been a bit creative," said Trish, bursting into another fit of giggles. In truth, I hadn't seen Trish look this happy in years. "When we were at school together, we had this Domestic Science teacher called Mrs. Warburton, like the bread, and she was such a miserable cow! Everything had to be done the right way: HER way! We've broken all the rules tonight! Mrs. Warburton would not have approved!"

"Wonder if she's still alive?" asked Marie.

"Probably not," said Trish, "but we will raise our cups of tea in honour of Mrs. Warburton."

I served up the brews while Marie and Trish pulled these very strange-looking cakes out of the oven. The two of them stood over the cakes, looking at them, trying to remember what they'd done.

"Did we put brandy in that one?"

"No," said Trish, we put brandy in this one and peanut butter in that one!"

"Where did we put the apricots?"

The two of them started laughing. It was obviously a private joke. It was a proper belly laugh; there was hair and flour everywhere. It took me back to their school days, when they were always plotting and giggling. Back then, I was a spotty nobody and besotted by my older sister's friends. They had boobs and disposable income; I was entranced!

I was lucky to have such a cool and tolerant older sister, and I tried my best not be the irritating sibling under her feet. I didn't want to get on her nerves. I wanted her to take me places, buy me that extra ticket and invite me to her friend's parties. I was spending my last penny of pocket money on records, so I was quite useful to her circle, making them cassettes and then CDs of hit songs.

During my time with Trish, for some bizarre reason, she and my sister had grown apart. Trish was busy with her company and being a girlfriend, while Marie was busy being depressed and wondering if she'd ever find a man, and Trish probably stayed away from her because there's only so much gloom you can take!

Anyway, here they were in Marie's kitchen again, and it was my civic duty to try both cakes. In truth, I was so nervous about my emotional well-being, I was ready to eat every cake under the sun! After three months without Trish, it was literally like having Alzheimer's! I was forgetting bookings and my body clock was upside down. I'd catch the boys giving me pitiful looks. They knew I needed that other person in my life. That rock. That pillow. That perspective.

Roz was only away for a month and away on business but, nevertheless, I could feel my soul descending into a dark and ugly place. Over the next month, I would have to keep myself very busy and very distracted. A Roz-less life would a long, cruel winter. I was grateful to Marie and my ex for providing much-needed respite.

They cut a slice of each for me and plonked them on a plate. They certainly smelt good! I bit into the brandy and apricot cake. It was eye-wateringly potent and tasty. I can only assume they'd been on the brandy too? They were eating it, savouring it, squeezing it and enjoying a different kind of sensual experience with the cake.

"That is good!" said Marie, sounding as if Percy had just kissed her pudendum!

"Yes!" moaned Trish, like a seasoned porn star, "so moist!"

A surreal way to end my day; my sister and my ex having a culinary climax! They quickly sampled the other cake and seemed equally satisfied.

"Percy will love this!" said Marie. "He loves anything to do with peanuts!"

I sipped at my tea and bit into the other cake. Equally delicious! I was very happy to be in my mum's old kitchen in our family home, taking tea with two women who had known me before I'd discovered the difference between giving blood and giving head!

"You haven't just finished work, have you?" asked Trish.

"No."

Trish could be feel me being very sparing with the details and knew exactly why! Why wouldn't she? She'd been my girlfriend for more than a decade!

"How's Roz?" she asked.

Shit! I really didn't want to get into this with Trish but, ultimately, what did it matter? I wanted her to know how I felt about Roz.

"She's fine!" I said. "She's away for a month now. She's got a great job on location." I shrugged my shoulders. "That's what she does! I'll have to get used to it!"

"What does she do precisely?" asked Marie. I was fairly certain I'd told her before. She'd been in a post-Percy haze for months!

"Film production. She'll have many jobs on location but her main role is accountant; making sure every penny is accounted for. She's the one with the petty cash tin and she's the one with the complex spreadsheet on her laptop. And when that figure at the bottom right goes to zero, they've spent the budget!"

"Good job!" said Marie.

"Good job! Good money!" I replied

"While she's gone, you'll be fine! At least you now know where the supermarket is?" Trish was smiling at me, smugly, and I let her ridicule me, the same way I allowed everyone else to ridicule me. Maybe it made them feel good about themselves? It made me wonder why I'd been so passive. Why had I allowed Trish to make all the decisions? Was she assertive? Was I a wimp? Or did it all seem unimportant to me?

Trish and Marie were talking and laughing, sampling cake and supping tea, but their conversation held no interest. And it had been like that for much of my relationship with Trish. I just wasn't interested in what she was saying. We were similar in so many ways but interesting things never came out of her mouth. Same kind of family, same school, same circle of friends, we were almost destined to go out but, when it boiled down to it, our conversations were dull as ditch water! Though even ditch water serves a purpose!

I sat in the kitchen, in a bit of a daze, staring in their general direction but my mind was elsewhere. I was wondering what The Elusive Wilson looked like. He was bound to be taller than me? Everyone was. I was doing the normal jealous boyfriend shit. What a waste of time! If I wanted my life to be better, I had to be better too. Rise above such borish behaviour. Roz required better. Roz deserved better.

"What you thinking about Wes?" Marie asked.

"He's probably thinking about his new bird!" said Trish, trying to mock me, trying to reduce Roz to a fly-by-night fad. As far as she was concerned, Roz could do better than me and would quickly move on! It was my job to prove I was The One.

"I love this old kitchen," I began. "So many memories. I can still feel Mum and Dad."

Marie stopped to listen and was suddenly caught in her own memories. "I guess that's why I like Percy," she began. "He knows how to live in a house. When we're together in this kitchen, I find us behaving like Mum and Dad. All the jokes, all the laughing, all the teasing."

I wanted that in my kitchen.

"So what were you arguing about the other night?"

Marie took a sip of her tea and tried to remember. She couldn't.

"It can't have been that important; I can't even remember!"

She pulled at a slice of cake and idly put it into her mouth. "Oh, yeah, I remember! He keeps talking about being a DJ. He wants to do more! What have you done, Wes?"

"What have I done? I introduced him to you!"

"Yeah, yeah," Marie replied, dismissively, "but, if he plays at more functions, he won't have any time for me!"

Trish and I looked at each other, and then we looked at Marie. If this was Marie's attitude, they were headed for hard times!

"Are you about to kill his dreams, love?"

Marie glared at Trish. "Oi, whose side are you on?"

Trish and I looked at each other again. Marie was not interested in our views on this matter. If she was about to battle with Percy, let battle commence!

Thursday

The next morning I sent Wendy a quick message. She was very happy to hear from me but very matter-of-fact and told me to swing by her hospital after work. I needed this over and done with because I knew that Roz would be checking up on me!

What with Amiable Alvin out of commission for possibly months, I needed to ensure my short scrawny frame was in tip top condition, and I needed to let Max and Percy know that I would be calling them to action more often! Max needed a crash course on popular music. He was a world authority on obscure genres but, in general, hipsters weren't hiring my DJs. I needed another Alvin; someone with the common touch; someone with a general appreciation of the great unwashed.

As I drove to work and pondered a thousand things, all the cars were diverted into some kind of off-road, alternative route. Burst water main or something like that! Because of one-way streets, I was virtually travelling twice my distance to work. My car was moving very slowly, snarled-up in the all-day traffic jam. To my right, there were solo drivers, talking on their phone, singing along to the radio or picking their nose (and looking at it!) I glanced to my right every now and then but, by and large, I was in my own little, Roz-less world.

Suddenly, I glanced to my right and saw two very familiar faces laughing and engrossed in conversation. Luckily, Mids and Jill didn't see me. I ducked down slightly to ensure they wouldn't. Well, this was an interesting development!

The owner of a lonely heart had finally come down off her unrealistic perch! Jill had finally come to terms with the fact that the love of her life belonged to someone else; a painful fact to face but who better to help her through the pain than my mate Mids? Tony was good company; he could show a girl a good time!

Yes, this was a very interesting development! I wondered who knew? And, if they were in a car together, she must have stayed at his? It put a smile on my face. Mids needed someone like Jill, and Jill definitely needed to re-focus.

My mates were all coupling-up? What was going on? Were we growing up? Having said that, there was no guarantee that anything would last! Three months on and we might all be on Single Street again?

Our day at the shop was quite normal: phone calls, e-mails, queries and questions. I spoke to Max about doing more gigs and possibly playing music at mainstream, commercial functions. He looked absolutely horrified!

"Christ, Wes! I don't know about that stuff!"

"Would you like to learn?"

Max paused. "I suppose so," he said, unconvincingly.

Maybe it was a bad idea? Max was a young man. Image was all important. He didn't want to be caught playing '99 Red Balloons' or 'Ice Ice Baby'. I would have to juggle the work accordingly. It looked like Percy and I would be taking the strain?

I returned to my original idea of turning Max into a music act.

"How is that big gig idea coming along?"

Max smiled. He was back on familiar territory. "It's definitely going ahead!" he began. "Bank Holiday Sunday. No work Monday. It will be an all-nighter, starting at 10 and finishing at 10! And they want me to play for an hour! To a thousand people, Wes!"

I'd never played for a thousand people. I'd played at some pretty big weddings but never for a thousand.

"I think I'm finally getting the hang of that talking thing!" By that I understood he meant 'radio'. "Getting the hang of that, my gigs are going well, I've got my own page on the radio station website, I've got good photos of myself, nice clothes ..."

Max smiled. It was a goofy, gummy smile but a smile of real satisfaction. My gawky, geeky employee was growing-up and growing into himself.

"The next thing is for you to make your own music!"

Max looked sceptical. "Not sure!" he said.

"Do you know what makes people dance?"

The penny finally dropped. "I do!" said Max. "I do know what makes people dance!"

"You know what tunes will work and what tunes won't work?"

"I do!" he exclaimed. "I really do!"

"Just a thought," I said. "Don't want to blow your mind!"

"Nah, nah, other people have mentioned it!"

"Do you know any musicians?"

"I know people that make beats!"

That probably wouldn't be enough. I had it on my agenda to talk to Roz about a musician in their circle.

At around 12.00, Belinda The Rescinder arrived with her tasty sandwiches. I bought three. One for me and Max and one just in case anyone wandered in.

"My mate who was here the other day?"

"I remember him!" said Belinda. "He bought two sandwiches and started scoffing them immediately!"

"That's him! He's got a wine company and has little parties at his warehouse. Could you provide him with sandwiches?"

Belinda looked at me quizzically. "These are chunky, lunchtime sandwiches!"

"They are! And perfect for lunchtime! You would probably need to make daintier, wine-tasting sandwiches?"

Belinda thought for a second. She was dressed in fairly dowdy sandwich-transporting jeans and hoodie, but it was clear to see she was a striking girl. Like Roz, I wasn't sure where her parents were born, or their parents, I wasn't sure if she was mixed race, or middle-eastern? Initially, I'd thought Spanish or Brazilian but I really wasn't sure now! It didn't matter. She seemed a really nice girl and I was certain she'd be a real plus at any of Mids' parties.

"Yeah, I can do that!" she announced.

"And your sandwiches really do taste good!"

"Thank you!" she blushed. "I learnt it all from my parents. They both love to cook. Mum's from Ecuador, so she brings all that South American flavour, and Dad's from Germany, so there's a bit of his seasoning in there too! Mad mixture!"

"It works. I'll let Mids know you're up for it and get him to call you. You'll get paid with money and great bottles of wine!"

She smiled and waved and disappeared off to her other customers.

I had no idea which of my crazy friends would enter my shop, unannounced; I knew someone would swing by but I was genuinely surprised when Benjamin walked through the door.

We both looked at each other.

"I was passing."

I didn't believe him.

"It's lunchtime!" he added, as if he felt he needed further justification for dropping in.

"Are you hungry?" I asked, knowing this would irritate him.

"What you got?" he asked.

"Tuna and sweetcorn." I held it up. Belinda The Rescinder's sandwiches always looked plump and delicious.

"Don't mind if I do!" Benji took the sandwich and immediately opened it.

"We'll make you some tea!" I said, winking at Max. "How do you take it?"

"Milk one" replied Benji, his mouth already full of sandwich. "This sandwich is bloody good!"

"We get them delivered every day!"

I decided to join Benji for lunch and opened my ham salad extravaganza; lettuce, tomato, cucumber and some kind of very tasty salad dressing. That Belinda was certainly gifted! Can't beat a good sandwich!

"Just passing, Benji?"

"Just passing," he assured me, his mouth stuffed with food. "The kids I teach don't care, the teachers I work with don't care, the school board: God, what a bunch of empire-builders! They just love being on a school board! It gets them into their local golf club. I hate being there. I'm certainly not going to eat my lunch in there!"

That made sense. Maybe he was just 'passing'? But why stop here? He could have gone to any coffee shop? No, that whiny toad definitely had a hidden agenda! What did he need from me? Was he still hoping I would fall on my sword? Was he still hoping I would see the error of my ways and return to my tribe?

Or maybe he just wanted to be in the presence of another miserable bastard, so we could both suffer together? Yeah, that was it! Misery loves company. That shrunken, dishevelled troll had come to help me wallow in my sadness.

I did not need his company! He was hoping for a glimmer of hope. He was hoping for a chink in my armour. He wanted to hear me say, "If she's going to bugger off for a month, I'm dumping her!" That's what he was hoping for but that wasn't going to happen!

Max came out of the kitchen with our cups of tea, while Benji and I sat either side of my counter, eating our lunch and eying each other warily! The conversation was ultra-polite and hopelessly off-topic. All either of us really wanted to talk about was the crazy girl with the wild hair.

I had to break the monotony, so I dived right in. "What do you know about this Wilson guy?"

Benji's face was truly a picture! The look of disgust that swept over his face was as if you'd just reached into your pocket and discovered a giant cart horse had taken a dump in there! It was as if you'd just kissed someone passionately in the dark and discovered it was your grandmother! The words wouldn't form in his mouth; his lips were too busy curling with utter contempt!

"What a fucking total waste of space!" Spat with force and venom. There was no love lost between he and this Wilson. "Why are smart women so stupid?"

I had nothing to contribute. This was not a question a stupid person could answer. Roz's friend Joanna had described her as "not perfect." Maybe this was what she meant?

Benji was having horrible Wilson flashbacks; his face was contorting like an exorcist was up in his grill. "Why did she like him? Why did she date him? And for so long?"

Benji had known Roz all his adult life. Only he could answer that.

Benji sipped on his tea and the warm liquid seemed to calm him. "He was a classic smoothie! An absolute bloody cliché! Smooth looking, smooth talking, smooth dresser. Why couldn't she see through him?"

Did he know she was now spending a month with him in a house in Manchester? Benji's rant was so bilious, I was nervous he would bring up his tasty sandwich!

And this Wilson character definitely explained Benji's behaviour. He sees off one contender and, almost immediately, another one slides in from the wings! Having gotten rid of Wilson, he must have really thought he was in with a shot! Benji obviously had no real understanding of how Roz viewed him. Yes, she loved him with all her heart, but like a brother, like a friend, like an accomplice. Anything but a lover!

Was he now actually hoping I would step aside? I didn't have it in my heart to tell him he was a non-starter. Not a contender in the slightest! If he'd come here to put the scares on me, I was an amused observer. I may have been intimidated a few months ago but now I knew him, now I knew what a wet rag he was; now I knew what a peripheral figure he was, I was happy to let him stomp around and express his displeasure.

With lunch over, it was time for Benjamin to return home to the "undeserving brats". What would they learn from him? At least, while Benjamin was here, I had company and conversation. I was desperate for anything to take my mind off Roz, even Benji!

As another work day came to a close, we turned off lights, pulled down shutters and went our separate ways. Doubtless Max was headed off to a harem of admirers, while I was about to endure an indignity or two. Let's call it preventative medicine?

Wendy was absolutely certain to give Roz a detailed report of my demeanour. I would need to remain calm and business-like throughout. This was nothing. This was routine. This was what adults did. I was an adult. I could do this.

Nurse Wendy embraced me at Reception and escorted me quickly and quietly to an examination room.

"Sorry to be rushing you, Wes, but I'm actually on my dinner break. I know you don't even want to be here but Roz made me promise I would see you."

I nodded. I was already turning red with embarrassment.

"It will be over in a flash. No fuss and no pain," she said, snapping on some white surgical gloves. I stood there, staring at the ground, not really wanting to make eye contact. "Let's just get this over with! Shoes, socks, trousers and pants off. Put your clothes on that chair there and lie on that table facing away from me."

I followed instructions and lay there obediently. I definitely heard the sound of lubricant being squeezed on to finger and that finger was headed my way!

"You ready?" she asked.

"I am," I said, timidly.

And then, without any fuss, her finger was between my buttocks and inside my anal passage. It felt very strange but far less painful than root canal! She was feeling for something but found nothing.

"All done!" she said. "Turn on to your back."

I obeyed. My eyes were closed. I dare not look.

I could feel her rolling my testicles between her fingers, again looking for abnormalities or some kind of lump but not finding anything.

"Okay, we're done!" She pulled-off the gloves and threw them in a bin. "Clean bill of health. Roz will be very happy!"

I lay there in stunned silence.

"You can lay there if you want but I'm going off to have my dinner!"

I sat up. "Thanks," I said and hurriedly got dressed.

Wendy turned her back to me and started looking at her phone. "What have you boys got planned for the weekend?"

"Melvin is finalising the details as we speak."

"Can I tag along?"

"Of course!" I said. Without Roz, Wendy was as lonely as me, and with Jill's head all over the place, Wendy's best option was me and my crew!

This Saturday would be interesting! There would be no Roz, no Topper (as he would be in Great Yarmouth with Francine) and, if Mids and Jill were going to play hide the sausage, we might not see him either? So, it would just be me, Wendy, Baggers and Low; two that wanted to be single and two that didn't; two that were happy being alone and two that hated it.

"How's Jill?" I asked.

"Still very down," Wendy began. "Quiet, forgetful, distracted. Not her normal tyrannical self! She went to visit her sister yesterday and stayed over! She hasn't done that in years! She doesn't even like her sister!"

Once dressed, I embraced Wendy again and thanked her for her time. "I'll text you details about Saturday," I said, as I gingerly waddled out of the surgery, still feeling Wendy's finger up my rectum. I looked like John Wayne!

Clean bill of health. I felt relieved. That had been the scariest and most uncomfortable 15 minutes of my life. A near-death experience but, thankfully, death was back at a comfortable distance. You stay right there, Death, I've got things to do!

Now, home to face my empty house and my (gulp) empty bed! I didn't really want to go home but I couldn't eat any more cake! I could have called anyone but I didn't want to! All I wanted to do was nothing ... with Roz! Christ, I was crap at this single life thing!

Trish used to say, "You men never get emotional, do you? Only when you're watching football or some You Tube clip where someone has fallen off a roof!" But, here I was, filled with emotion: love, lust, longing, yearning, pining, craving. Is that enough emotion for you, Trish? Maybe men only get emotional about women they really care about?

The house was still and quiet. I opened my fridge and it was still full to the brim with erratic bottles of exotic beer. I pulled something cold out of the fridge, grabbed the cheesy snack at the front of my goodie cupboard and headed for the front room. Surely, there would be something interesting on TV?

I looked down at my phone. A text from Alvin. "First round of treatment tomorrow. Wish me luck."

I wished him every success. I needed him to be healthy. The following night, I was spinning tunes at a swank, corporate affair. Under normal circumstances, that would be an Alvin event, but I was deputising. It would be easy money but stiff and white like your Monday morning shirt!

I flipped through TV channels. I need something to make me laugh. Something silly. Charlie Sheen in 'Hot Shots!' Perfect. I drank and munched mindlessly. Why not? Everyone else does.

Out of the corner of my eye, I noticed a lime green Post-It note stuck to a vase. I'd never noticed that before. How long had it been there? I got up and pulled it off the vase. It had just one word in the middle: strong. Definitely the work of my fabulous girlfriend! It put a huge smile on my face. I felt loved.

She'd put one Post-It note there, but where were the others? I knew there must be others! I jumped to my feet and looked around me. On a dreary Thursday night, Roz had me on an Easter Egg hunt! My living room wasn't big; so it wouldn't be hard to find more of these Post-It notes. Would it? I scoured every surface very carefully. Tucked between two books was a bright pink note with one word on it: reliable.

Was I so dozy and unobservant? How long had these notes been in my house? When did she find time alone in my house? What were these words all about? Was it a game? She knew how passionate I was about a pop quiz. Were these song titles? Or the lyrics to a song?

I concentrated hard and tried to focus my eyes on brightly-coloured bits of paper. Tucked behind a picture frame I could see a bright yellow Post-It, I pulled it down, it had just one word on it: sensitive.

And how should I play this situation? Should I talk to her about it? Or should I just keep it as our secret? Our secret, unspoken monologue? I opted for the latter. I would play it cool. If it was a test, I would keep my hand (or Post-It notes) very close to my chest. Solving this case was important but how important? Was this the deal-breaker? Christ, too much pressure! What if I failed to see the link between the words? Would I lose my remaining brownie points?

I look around me again and finally got on my knees. Were they near the skirting boards? Hidden behind my furniture? The crazy girl with the wild hair had me crawling across the floor without raising a finger. There was a large plant pot in the corner of the room and – blow me – wasn't there another sticky note round the back! I pulled it off and looked at it. One word: entertaining.

I now had four words: strong, reliable, sensitive and entertaining. How were these song lyrics? I didn't know any songs with all these words in? Undaunted, I decided to collect the words and worry about the quiz at a later date. Play it cool, Wes. Keep it fun.

Happy that I'd found all the words in my living room, I came out into the hallway. Where were the stickers? They could be anywhere! I must have looked like some kind of robot, turning my head slowly from right to left, scanning every inch of every wall. And what was that just behind my hallway mirror? Another sticker! I quickly snatched at it. One word: inspiring.

This was truly doing my head in. I needed to get into bed. It was late. I would find them all eventually. This treasure hunt would have to get completed another day. I wandered wearily up my stairs, my robot eyes scanning the walls. I needed to powder my nose. Were there any of these stickers in the bathroom? They'd be damp by now!

I don't know why I picked up the soap dish but underneath it: another sticker! I was encouraged; now I was thinking like her! The Post-It had one word on it: brave. I now had six words. A mad thought crossed my mind. Maybe these words were how she felt about me? Maybe she felt I was all of these things? Nah! Me? How was I brave?

Maybe these words described her ideal man? Maybe this is how she wanted me to be? Unrealistic expectations of a weedy numpty like me but I appreciated the love. Roz was thinking about me. I liked that.

I tossed and turned in bed. I was tired but I couldn't sleep. My mind was a rambling, epic tale of love and loss. Having Roz in my life was a beautiful thing but being without her was death by a thousand cuts. There was no way I could return to my post-Trish trauma. There was no way I could go back to that amateurish forgetfulness.

It was now finally time to create something more sophisticated than an A4 diary and a PC at work. I needed my appointments, engagements and my To-Do List all in one mobile place. It was time to get a slightly better phone with a slightly bigger screen and, most important of all, it was time to get very organised. I almost needed a sub-section of my To-Do List? A Thought-To-Task List; random ideas that could become tasks?

I needed to get some of this stuff out of my head and into some kind of note form. There was a wacky, cross-continent car race speeding around my brain; comedy, tragedy, flat tyres and over-heated engines. I couldn't go back to nodding off in shop doorways. I had to get a grip! When Roz returned home, it needed to be situations normal. She was going to say, "Was everything okay, Wes?" And I was going to say, "Yes, no problem at all!"

Friday

With the weekend approaching, there was frantic activity in the shop! Customers arrived to pick-up their gear and it was fun for me and Max to imagine what they would be doing with it! How old were they? How were they dressed? What music would they be playing? Snap judgements made on their appearance. Childish, I know!

We gave them record decks but we did not provide them with a stylus! Naturally, if they wanted a stylus, we could add that into the package (complete with deposit!) Those magical needles carried the sound! They needed to be in pristine condition!

Our first customer of the day was this stocky, bearded man, about 40, dressed in black leather from head to foot, and he had paid for two record decks complete with stylus!

He wasn't a bike messenger and he hadn't just come from a very kinky sex club. The only thing not leather was a tight black T-shirt. It was warm. He must have been sweltering but he looked very happy to be loading gear into the back of a hired white van. He was taking gear for two nights and delivering back on Monday morning because he was way out in the burbs; my delivery boys didn't go that far!

"A two-day party?" I asked him.

He smiled broadly. He had two quite prominent teeth missing but the remaining ones were straight and white.

"Me and my partner have got three things to celebrate! It's his birthday, it's our anniversary and two of our friends are having a naming ceremony for their new son! Might as well make it a two-day party? We've got an outdoor toilet, an outdoor swimming pool and space for tents. Our guests can wake up on Saturday morning, have some breakfast and start all over again!"

Max and I both looked suitably impressed!

"Sounds wicked!" said Max, not known for expressing any kind of opinion.

"Vinyl only?" I asked.

"Vinyl only!" he said, firmly and defiantly. "I don't even own a CD. Can't stand them! Don't own a CD player and we don't have one solitary CD in our house. They don't sound good. No beef in the bass! I need beef in the bass!"

Max and I nodded. We knew. We understood what he meant.

"I only have vinyl! Tons of it! It is going to be a two-day disco explosion. Two days of drinking and dancing and very decadent designs, I suspect! The theme is 'How Bare Do You Dare'! You can imagine!"

We could.

Black leather man drove off and Melvin's text arrived soon after. Sometimes he'd make a personal visit but, more often than not, Melvin's Saturday Plans text message would arrive on Friday around 11.00.

The message read: 8.00 p.m. Film Premiere, 10.00 p.m. Breakfast, 12.00 Private Party (Wandsworth). I didn't really know what this meant but I didn't need the details. If Baggers said it was worth doing, it was worth doing! We trusted our concierge!

Just after 11.00, Asif and Virgil popped back into the shop carrying a scuffed, black record box. The box looked used and abused but it was full of twelve-inch vinyl. Virgil was struggling with the weight, banging it on his thigh and wincing.

"These boxes are heavy!" he said.

"Been there!" I said.

Asif couldn't wait to show me what they'd found. He opened the box proudly. Literally stuffed with vinyl! Too many records!

I looked at him, "You might need another box, mate!"

The records were stuffed in too tightly. I couldn't even flick properly. Flicking and selecting go hand-in-hand. If you can't flick, you can't select! I pulled about 20 out and had a look at the rest.

"We worked from your list. The bloke in the shop was very helpful. He was doing that whole Amazon thing, "If you like that, you'll like this!""

My eyes were immediately drawn to something bright and yellow. Not another of Roz's Post-It notes but actual yellow vinyl; a very famous tune that had bridged the boogie and the electro era.

Asif and Virgil knew what it was but I knew Max had never heard it. I put the yellow piece of vinyl on a turntable. The bleeping and simplistic melodies of a computer game came blasting out. Max looked very confused. He stared at the vinyl and stared at the speaker, wondering if it was some kind of prank. This went on for a while. Max looked mightily confused.

Finally, the insane bleeping reached a crescendo and the groove kicked in! Asif and Virgil started dancing, or some approximation of dancing, Max started quivering like he'd seen the holy spirit and I just stood there grinning like a Cheshire Cat.

Unwise to underestimate the awesome power of 'Firecracker' by Yellow Magic Orchestra. Blasting through some huge cabinets, it sure sounded good! Weird but wonderful! When the record had finished, Max was a gibbering wreck! "What the fuck?" he said. "What a mental mash-up!"

"Anything is possible, Max! You can make that music!"

The penny dropped. "Yeah, Wes! I can do it! Anything is possible."

I left Max with his thoughts and returned to the record box. I flicked and smiled and flicked and reminisced. I didn't want to think what it had cost them but they actually had most of the tunes in my two trusty floor filler boxes!

"You boys are good to go!" I said.

"Really?" asked Asif.

"Sure!" I said. "You have a box stuffed with quality tunes. If you play good music, you can't fail!"

The two boys nodded. This was all the endorsement they need.

"We'll be back tomorrow morning for our gear," said Virgil, staggering out the door with his bulging box.

I suddenly thought to myself, I wonder where else Roz has put stickers? In the shop? In my car? In my clothes? I reached inside my jacket and there, down the inside pocket, a folded, green Post-It note, with just one word on it: respectful. I now had seven words.

Finding another word just made me miss her more. What did I miss most? I missed her soft skin, the way she smelt, the taste of her skin. I missed all of her mad hair getting in my mouth when she hugged me. I missed her sternness. She could take care of herself. I liked that.

I began looking around the shop. Could she really have put Post-It notes in here too? Max looked at me. I was looking up and around the walls like I'd seen a wasp!

"You lost something, Wes?"

I wasn't sure I should try to explain. Sometimes, couples do lovey-dovey things that are meaningless to outsiders. "Roz has been leaving me little love notes everywhere!" That seemed the simplest way to describe it.

"That's nice!" said Max. "I like her!"

People usually did like Roz but I bet she rubbed people up the wrong way. If you've got a strong opinion, you're going to run into the occasional fracas. I remembered her straightening-out everybody at The Haunted House, how quiet they'd been, how they'd listened to her, and how angry she was afterwards. Yes, she was cute and funny but, when she was laying down the law, she was formidable.

I spent the afternoon looking for Post Its but I didn't find any. I was certain there were more back at the house.

That evening, the job was to play music at the beautiful offices of a finance company close to Tower Bridge. Up some lifts to the top floor of this tall, glass tower and, once out on the terrace, the panoramic views of London were spectacular.

By all accounts, Amiable Alvin had said this was a very enjoyable and very easy gig! For the most part, it could just be background music, while people drank and networked, but they often liked a little shimmy later on?

Max and I were dropping the gear there and setting it up, while one of my other boys was coming back later to pick me up! It would be straightforward. Not the ideal way to spend my Friday evening but work was work; having said that, as venues go, this was a pleasure to play at: nice view, a free bar, waitresses walking around with delicious titbits, and well-heeled girls in dry-cleaned clothes.

Background music is a skill. It has to be low volume and chilled, but just groovy enough to arouse their curiosity. You want to plant the seed in their mind. 'Ah, this guy has some good tunes in his armoury! I may require him later?' Easy but boring. While working, I couldn't spend hours on my phone, as it would look as if I was disinterested. Some company would be nice but I really didn't want to subject anyone to this very low-key affair. So, I had to stand there and softly play music to largely disinterested parties.

I was almost set-up and ready to go when my phone pinged. Naturally, I was hoping it was a photo of Roz in her undies, but it was merely a text from Low saying, "Where are you?" I returned his text, telling him where I was and what I was doing. His reply immediately fired back, "I'll see you in 30 minutes!"

I grabbed the lovely organiser lady (very tall in very high heels), my nose was roughly in line with her navel, and told her that a colleague would be joining me. She radio'd down to Security.

Within the allotted 30 minutes, Tony G was by my side, looking suave, enjoying the view, chatting with the waitresses and guzzling beer.

"It's all falling apart, Wes!"

"What you going on about?"

"I can just about handle you and Roz, but now Topper's found a bird, it's all falling apart!"

I daren't tell him about Mids and Jill. I didn't even know if Mids and Jill was a 'thing' but I wasn't going to speculate. Low would certainly be unhappy if Mids bailed-out of Saturday night for no good reason!

"It's not falling apart!" I replied. "Don't be soft! We don't even know if Tops and Francine are going to last five minutes!"

"She's given him a blow job and he's already hearing wedding bells! Do you know how good that blow job must have been? Can you imagine?"

Low was messing with my brain. I did not want to think about Francine's mind-melding blow jobs.

"Can you imagine?" he repeated, forcing me to imagine!

"Leave it out, Low! I don't want to imagine!"

"You can tell so much about a woman by her blow job!"

"Can you?" I asked. "Can you really?"

Low looked affronted that I could be questioning his oral sex expertise.

"She might be good at blow jobs," I continued, "but it might just be a trap to lure you in? Who says they'll continue at that level and with that frequency?"

"Which is why I like to keep it casual!" he replied. "No blow job is putting any shackles on me!"

I was grateful to Low. He was bored and at a loose end, I needed company and, even though he kept bleating on about the group breaking up, it was nice to see him. I rarely saw people alone. We were always in our group. So it was amusing to spend quality time with Low, watching the quintessential single man go through his repertoire of chat-up lines. By the end of the evening, all of the waitresses were virtually circling around him waiting to be chosen.

"If Tops and Francine turns into something," I began, "he'll devote x nights to her and x nights to us. And, if she wants to come out with the group, it'll be fine! She seems okay?"

"What does he want a girlfriend for? You: we can forgive. You're different! You're a soppy tart! There's nothing we can do about you! But Topper? He's a proper bloke. He doesn't need someone to tie his shoelaces for him!"

Low hadn't abused me for a while. I'd almost missed it? Made me realise I sometimes missed him. Of course I hated the fact that he was tall, slim, muscular and good-looking but, despite being a nerdy little twerp, it was Wezza that had the girl. The jewel in the crown! It was Wezza who had the crazy girl with the wild hair.

"Why does Topper want a girlfriend?" I asked, rhetorically. "Oh, I don't know! Maybe because he wants to be deliriously happy like me?"

"Topper jealous of you?" he scoffed.

"He would probably like what I have?"

"And what have you got that's so special?"

Low was being so ridiculous, all I could do was smirk. What did I have? The only woman I had ever met who could play good cop/bad cop in the same smackdown. The only woman who had ever made me look stylish. The only woman who had ever got me to dance low and slow. The only woman that had ever made men envious of me.

"Have you met my girlfriend?" I asked.

"Yeah, yeah, mouthy chick! Loads of hair!"

"That's the one," I said. "Maybe Topper would like a bit of magic, a bit of passion, a bit of romance in his life?"

"Oh, I get enough passion!" he said, licking his lips and winking at a waitress.

Sure enough, after a few drinks, the assembled guests began to gravitate towards the music. The girls wanted to dance and, if the boys wanted to stay close to them, they'd have to dance too! Smart Move No. 1: girls like dancing so play music that girls like. Boys will follow soon after.

Low wasted no time in getting on the makeshift dance floor. This was a beautiful office, not a night club, so they were dancing on very expensive carpet. Astonishingly, these bright young minds were actually dancing and holding their drinks. Any second, a glass of red wine was going to stain that lovely carpet.

Low had immediately clicked with two girls who, shall we say, were on the plump side of curvy, but they could sure shake their money-makers! Low had the moves and the facial expressions, so both girls were laughing, smiling and flirting outrageously.

God knows how a woman can dance in a dress and heels! How do they do that? Tony's two companions certainly knew to move! I was transfixed by their hips and, bold as ever, Tony's hands were lightly resting wherever he could rest them! These were sexy and confident women, the tactile advances of a young man were as common and routine to them as adding milk to a cup of tea.

At the end of the evening, Courtney, one of my crew, arrived to help me dismantle and load the gear back into a van. Thankfully, Courtney didn't need much sleep, so he was cool to take the gear back to the shop. Which left me, Low and the two curvy girls. Naturally, Low offered them a lift home and, as I needed a lift home too, I jumped in Low's car. I was a bit nervous being in the middle of Low's sordid single life, but I needed a ride.

One was called Sharon and one was called Lola. They both lived together in a flat in Wood Green, so we wouldn't have to travel too far. Once inside the close confines of the car, I could smell that delicious blend of sweat, deodorant and perfume.

"How long have you worked there?" Low asked.

"Oh, we don't work there!" said Lola.

"But we've got a friend that does!" added Sharon.

"Her boss likes us there! He says we bring some colour to the place!"

That they did! Both girls were dressed in colourful dresses, complete with colourful head bands and jewellery. Colour was what they brought and a fair amount of flesh too! Lovers of cleavage would have been in raptures! It was definitely one of those trying-hard-not-to-look scenarios!

"So, what do you do?" asked Low.

"We both work in a similar company nearby," began Sharon. "A smaller company. We met our mate one evening at a local pub. Friday night: they all pour out of their offices and you meet people!"

"It's a nice, little community!" said Lola. "She comes to our parties and we go to her parties."

Low was being polite. There was no seduction strategy at play. He was making new friends. It might lead to something? It probably would! For the time being, Low was doing the ground work; keeping it very light and conversational. Both girls were still smiling, so it was working for them.

I snatched a quick look. Both girls were early-thirties, could have been mid-thirties? Happy, bubbly, pretty girls. The kind every club or party needs. The kind that make the world go round. They'd met men like Low before. He was nothing new or original. He was a maybe? He was a ... you never know? He was a ... why not? Pretty girls like that were spoilt for choice. Like Roz, they could have anyone they wanted.

"And what do you do?" Sharon asked Low.

"I work as a maitre d' at one of the best restaurants in one of the best hotels in London. It sounds like an amazing job and it is but it's not easy. It's not as hot and stressful as being in the kitchen, and it's not as dangerous as mending the lift, or washing the windows, but it's not easy. Most of the patrons are very polite but, some of them, if they've got a complaint – these are lawyers, judges or hard-nosed business negotiators – it can be tricky!"

Lola laughed! "I did Customer Relations at Harrods! That was enough for me! I like my job! Numbers don't talk back!"

We finally reached Wood Green and Low escorted the ladies to their front door, making sure he got a hug from both and a phone number. He got back into his car and he was smiling. A job well done! "Weren't they lovely?" he said.

"Yes, they were!"

"You didn't say a word?"

"I'm missing Roz."

"Ah, mate, not this again! You're not going to mope for a whole month, are ya?"

Low was right. It was ridiculous. Mope for a month? That would be absolutely, tragically pathetic! Who would want a man like that? Certainly not Roz! She wouldn't want a man that was reliant on her.

"You're right!" I said.

"Course I'm right," he replied. "You and me are going to invite Lola and Sharon to come out with us on Saturday night. If Tops is going to bugger off with his new piece, we have space in Mids' car for two more!"

I was now waiting to find out what Mids was doing on Saturday. If he was bringing Jill, there would not be space for two more.

And then Low began to babble! It was a detailed and dirty monologue, in which he described what kind of girls Lola and Sharon were and what we could expect from them! I'd heard this kind of analysis before. From their words, gestures and attire, Low could ascertain who would and who wouldn't put out. From their comments and references, Low could ascertain whether they were lovers or stalkers, whether they were kinksters or prudes. The last thing Low wanted was disappointment! He hated taking a gorgeous woman to bed and discovering she was a puritan in bed!

I wanted no part of it. Low could have them both; I didn't care! What I wanted was dinner and dancing with my girlfriend. What I wanted was Sunday lunch with her family. I was even looking forward to being part of the debate at The Haunted House! The single life did not appeal in the slightest. I was than happy to allow Lola and Sharon into my circle but I didn't want to be responsible for their hearts. They were strong, sexy and confident but they still shed tears!

Saturday

Saturday was our normal Saturday: lots of customers, lots of gear going out, and everything would have remained very normal until Jill wandered into my shop! I was so shocked to see her, I stood and stared for a second, double-checking. Yes, it actually was Jill in my shop, in all her matronly majesty. Dressed in casual HR clothing, she looked like she was about to approve my bank loan whereas, in fact, she wanted me to analyse her new sex partner!

I embraced her and she held on to me. How was I to interpret this hug? It was a hug of friendship, a hug of gratitude but also a hug of fear. Jill's poor heart was once again being wrenched from its moorings. She was now moving from the hopeless arms of a married man to the sensitive stirrings of my mate Mids. Mids had been burnt before and was skittish at the best of times. Jill's mood swings were interesting but alarming. This coupling had the makings of a very bad car crash.

I was very busy but I knew I had to make some time for Jill. We'd never talked before, not really talked about anything meaningful, and she looked like she needed to talk. Why did everyone imagine I had the answers? I carefully made her some tea and even opened a pack of chocolate digestives for her. I kind of knew what she had to say, so I was fairly relaxed.

She looked around for somewhere to sit and realised that all we had were uncomfortable stools adjacent to my high counter, so she carefully plonked herself on one of them. Her arse was not used to such wretched furnishing!

"I don't really know what I'm doing here," Jill began, innocently.

I did.

"It's lovely to see you," I lied, "but to what do I owe this pleasure?"

Jill sipped at her tea. It was a bit too hot. I could see her making a mental note to re-approach it in a few minutes. "Well, partly, I do know why I'm here; Roz asked me to look in on you!"

I laughed. "She thinks I'm a child!"

"She worries about you."

"She does?"

Jill nodded. "She appreciates you!"

I smiled to myself. Had Trish ever really appreciated me? No. Trish had a boyfriend because girls like having boyfriends. It could be anyone! It could be the boy next door? It could be a friend of the family? It could be a guy she met on holiday? Anything is better than loneliness! I was Trish's alternative to loneliness. She would never be lonely with me trailing around behind her, carrying her bags and promising her that her bum didn't look big in that! Trish had no real appreciation of what I was. I'm not Rafael Nadal and Barrack Obama combined but, like your beloved pet, I'm affectionate, devoted and reliable. Has that no currency? Doesn't that count for anything anymore? Trish couldn't see that.

Familiarity had definitely bred contempt. I was merely Trish's ride, merely her companion, merely her warmth in bed, merely her tea maker. Our relationship didn't make her whoop and holler with joy, it didn't even make her scream in frustration; I was just there, right there, like a forgotten ornament on a shelf. For some reason, the crazy girl with the wild hair liked me. I was a punctual person, I had to be in my line of work but, on this occasion, my timing was impeccable. I had arrived at just the right time in Roz's life.

"What I mean to say is: I don't know why I'm here making a confession!"

"A confession?" I asked. I knew what was coming. How come she was telling me? How come I was hearing the news from her? Where was an excitable Mids with some hot gossip?

"Well, maybe I do know why I'm here?"

This was a mood-swing monologue. Despite being highly-organised and highly-principled, there was a war of contradictions going on in her head. Should I? Shouldn't I? Is it wrong? Is it right? How do I really feel? Et cetera.

Thankfully, having experienced so much scene-stealing with Roz and her band of outlaws, I was ready for any new twist in the tail, though I was one step ahead of Jill; this was not going to be a shock. "Confess away!" I said, blithely.

"My confession is that, despite all my protestation, I actually do like your friend Mids. I don't do lies. I can't abide them. My father always said, 'I don't care what the truth is but don't lie to me.' So I am here to confess and apologise for lying to you. I've made my peace with everyone in the house but I had to speak with you as well."

Christ! This was quite a significant moment. It meant that Jill actually viewed me as part of their family. I had finally infiltrated their ranks! It was a surreal moment. I thought back to some of our frosty exchanges and yet, here she was: asking my forgiveness.

"You don't have to apologise to me."

"I don't do lies," she repeated, shifting uneasily on her high chair. "Dishonesty plagues me! That's why I felt such a deep sense of shame when I broke my own rules!"

It pained her to even utter those words and she shuddered again at the embarrassment. "What an ugly business!" she continued. "Shameful behaviour!"

I didn't need her apology. It was touching but not necessary. Had she really come all the way to my shop just to make a lightweight confession and a personal apology? Surely, there was more? Or was she laying the groundwork for another revelation? God, I was getting good at this!

"And ..." she continued, "I have a request."

Oh, this was getting far too surreal! A confession, an apology and a request? What next? A sonnet? Some tender words of love about my rotund, wine-guzzling friend?

"I wondered if I could tag along tonight?"

"Of course you can!" I was relieved it wasn't something more serious. "We'll probably get into Mids' people-carrier at about 7.00."

"Thank you!" Jill looked pleased and relieved. "It's usually me doing the organising but, of late, I haven't really felt like doing anything."

It felt like Jill was about to spill her guts. I really didn't want to hear the Alistair story again. Roz had recounted it to me in terrifying detail. Jill gets married to a man in the hope he'll leave the mother of his two children. It was as bewildering as it was illogical. As Benjamin had said, 'Why are smart women so stupid?'

"I know Wendy's coming out with you tonight but your friend Tony was saying I could just turn up and get in his car! It's your Saturday night out with your best friends. It's your routine; a private and sacred ceremony! I can't just turn up uninvited! I like to do things properly!"

"No problem at all," I said. "You are more than welcome! I make no promises, though; it's a boys night out!"

Jill laughed. "When you've sunk as low as me ..."

Jill paused and, suddenly, the enormity of her mistakes hit her! She was deep in thought. I could see her reliving pointless, passionate moments with her married man.

"When you've sunk as low as me," she continued, "a car full of men belching and telling dirty jokes feels like the moral high ground! It would be my pleasure to have a boys night out with you!"

The phone was ringing off the hook and Max was manfully dealing with two customers at once.

"Got to get back to work," I said.

"Of course!" said Jill. "Thanks for the tea ... and thanks for understanding."

I hadn't done anything but I smiled and hugged her.

The next customer through the door was a husband picking up some gear for his wedding anniversary party. He looked at the stuff he was taking away: two CD players, amp/mixer, two speakers and their stands.

"Looks pretty straightforward," he said, with an accent straddling London and Dublin. "I can't remember the last time I danced!"

"It's good exercise!" I said.

"I bloody need it" he said, pushing out his protruding belly.

"Big party?"

He opened his wallet and began counting out notes. "Bloody big party!" he said. "Down at my local. The landlord's an old mate. Laying on a bit of a spread for us. He'll do a roaring trade tonight! Got my relatives flying in for the party and they like a drink!"

"And what music does the missus like?"

He smiled and thought fondly of his wife. "She likes anything with a good tune! She loves Phil Collins and Billy Joel, and she's been to see Take That 13 times! 13 times! When she comes through the door, I always say to her, 'Are you back for good?' And she always smiles and says, 'Sure!' I've known her since I was 19. We've been married 40 years!"

"What's your secret?" I asked. "I've met this lovely girl and I don't want to mess it up!"

"My secret?" he said, chuckling to himself. Maybe he'd never even thought about it? "What bloody secret?" he continued. He thought for a minute.

"I don't ask too many questions," he said, stroking his grey beard. "She has her own friends, her own life, her own money. She goes out without me. If you ask a woman too many questions, she'll wonder why? She'll wonder if you trust her. She'll wonder if you want to control her. If you ask a woman too many questions, you'll make her nervous!"

"I get ya."

Roz would not appreciate a load of questions. She loved to tell you stories about her day or her evening. If she was running the show, Roz would tell you every detail you wanted to know and a few you didn't want to know! But a load of questions would not go down well! His advice was sound.

I counted the wad of notes and nodded that he'd handed me the right amount. "Let me help you load it into your car," I said.

"You've packed me a microphone, right?"

"As requested."

"My cousin Larry will want to sing. He's got a good voice, as it goes, and he'll definitely want to sing a song or two from the old country."

"Should be a good evening!"

"As long as my Roisin is happy, I'll be happy!" he said, slamming his car door and driving away.

I didn't really need his sound advice. I knew it for myself. A woman like Roz would run a mile from a possessive man. Roz didn't want to be single anymore but she definitely didn't want her every move scrutinised. As yet, I hadn't called her in

Manchester; quite a few text messages but no major phone call. I didn't want her to hear my voice, for fear she'd hear the panic setting in!

Max and I finished for the day, and I whizzed home for a quick shower and to put on this nice shirt that Roz had bought me. Purple is not a colour I would have chosen but Roz had convinced me that not only did it suit me but it was a "bold and confident" colour. Who was I to argue? Previously, the only purple in my house had been my damson jam!

I picked up one of my favourite after shaves and – lo and behold – another of Roz's Post-It notes. She knew I'd be reaching for that bottle at some stage! The words on this note were: hard working. Well, if I was nothing else, I was hard working but, tonight was Saturday and we were going to do Saturday night things: drink, laugh, chill, relax. Well, that's how it's meant to go!

By the time I got to Mids' house, everyone was in the van, raring to go.

"Film begins at 8.00!" said Melvin, tapping his watch. "We need popcorn!"

I looked inside the car and – well, well, well – there was Jill in the front seat! Normally, Melvin sat in the front, so he could navigate the best route and play his specially-compiled CDs but, on this occasion, he got bumped for Mids' new squeeze! Only I knew about them re-kindling but the seating arrangement would have aroused a lot of suspicion! Out of the corner of my eye, I could actually see Low looking for body language between Jill and Mids. He knew something was up and he needed to know!

Baggers had made a superb CD for our journey, with place names as its theme: R.Dean Taylor's 'Indiana Wants Me', The Beatles' 'Back In The USSR', Simon & Garfunkel's 'America', Toto's 'Africa', Ike & Tina Turner's 'Nutbush City Limits' etc.

The very healthy rapport between the newly re-acquainted Jill and Mids was very clear to see; lots of jokes, lots of laughter, hands on arms, hands on thighs. Low was frantically trying to make lots of eye contact with me, so he could find out what the hell was going on! The last time he'd seen the two of them together was that tense night at The Haunted House! Who could forget it?

After some afternoon delight, Jill had kicked Mids to the curb, and Mids had turned up at the house angrily looking for answers! The last time Low had seen these two together, they were glaring and spitting at each other! The tense stand-off in that kitchen would never leave me but – now? – well, it looked like things were all patched-up very nicely!

I don't even think Wendy knew! She sidled-up beside me in the back seat and whispered in my ear, "It's okay that Jill tags along, right?"

"She came to the shop and asked my permission!" I replied.

Wendy smiled. "That how she is: she likes to do things in the proper manner!"

If only she knew!

"So glad she and Mids have patched things up! Who knows?" she added, mischievously.

I smiled weakly and got a quick flashback of Wendy's greasy index finger digging around in my anal cavity!

From the shenanigans in the front seats, it was clear that Jill and Mids had done more than patch things up. She was laughing out loud, touching her hair and giving directions in an exaggerated and comical fashion. I knew that Mids hated a backseat driver, so this meant they were actually getting on famously.

Baggers was more concerned about us getting there on time and finding a parking space. The film was being shown at a small screening room in Soho, so we didn't have far to go, but parking in Central London would not be easy. We drove round and round in ever decreasing and ever frustrating circles. Finally, somebody pulled out of the last remaining parking space in Soho and we were able to nip in!

The film was a private showing of something made by one of Baggers' friends and this was the press launch. It wasn't a major studio screening room, so I knew it would be a low budget, independent film. I also knew there was a very good chance it would be about something weird. This wasn't going to be 'Forrest Gump' or 'E.T.', this was liable to be about some dysfunctional people, some unnatural sexual practices and some questionable morals. A normal family, really!

We entered through a small door and down some steps to a little reception area just behind the screening room. It was absolutely heaving with friends, relatives and members of the media. Whoever this guy was, he had a lot of supporters! We were following Melvin. We didn't really know anyone there. Finally, Melvin reached a short, twenty-ish, sun-tanned man almost being swallowed by the excitable throng around him. Everybody wanted a kiss or a selfie and he was gamely smiling, posing and receiving adulation.

Melvin ploughed straight into the middle of the crowd and hugged the young man tightly. We waited in the background and we could see Melvin saying to him, "I've brought my friends to see the film!" Melvin pointed to us and the director waved at us. Like kids on a fairground ride, we all waved back!

The tiny screening room bar was doing a roaring trade and the one over-worked barman had sweat dripping from his pencil moustache. We all headed towards him and waited patiently for our drinks and popcorn. All around us, there was excitable chatter, loud laughter, and flash bulbs going off every second. There might not have been a red carpet with recognisable slebs, but these nervous and ambitious faces were about to be plastered all over a corner of social media.

"What's it about?" Wendy asked me.

"I genuinely haven't got a clue!" I replied. "Melvin organises Saturday night and we follow him. That's why we do two and three things on a Saturday night, in case one of them isn't so great? If something's crap, we laugh about it! Whatever happens, we always have fun!"

"That's what I love about you guys; it's always an adventure!"

"Baggers is our Jill! He makes it happen! We trust him."

Just behind Wendy's head, I could see Jill and Mids tucked away in a corner, jammed pretty close together, whispering in each other's ear and finding everything funny! At some point, Wendy would work it out, or maybe she didn't care, as long as she didn't have to listen to Jill bleat on about Alistair.

Wendy turned round to see what I was looking at and we both watched Jill and Mids virtually dry-humping each other.

"Well, well!" said Wendy. "Looks like Jill has found herself a new playmate?" There was a slight look of disbelief and displeasure on her face. "Christ, when I think what she's put us through! First, she established this very strict 'no sex in the house' rule, which we all understood and bought into, then she has an emotional breakdown by falling in love with a married man, and we have to listen to her day and night dissecting another woman's relationship, then she breaks her own strict rule by having sex with your mate in our house, then she loses her confidence and authority and the running of the house goes to pot, then she threatens to leave! What next?"

And suddenly I began to fear for my friend, who was now looking like The Rebound Man! Jill was clearly a very passionate woman; passionate about rules, about systems, about manners, about protocol, and also very passionate about the men in her life. When Jill fell in love, it was clear, she fell deeply. Was Mids love or just laughter? Was he Jill's forever or just her right now? My friend hadn't had the best of luck in love, so I wasn't sure he was ready for Jill's indecision.

"Did you speak to Roz?" Wendy asked me.

I had made a conscious decision I was going to play it cool. I was not going to bury Roz beneath a mountain of lovey-dovey texts. It was a month. It was work. She'd be back soon. Roz did not need some lovelorn teenager missing her like crazy. I was going to be a man, be mature and keep it fun. Millions of men had done it before. I was evolved. I could do it.

"She seems okay?" I said. "We've been texting. I don't want to bother her."

Wendy nodded. She definitely didn't want to get in the middle of another couple. She was Nurse Wendy Patch-Up. Cool, clinical, objective. Not dishing out relationship advice. She liked that role.

In another corner of the lounge, I could see Melvin and Low doing what they did best: being chatty, being flirty and being sociable. They looked at ease and at home.

Melvin knew the director and some of his friends, while Low was making small-talk with some very young and very stylish girls. They were far too young for him but he was keeping them amused with his raffish anecdotes.

"How are the boys?" I asked Wendy. I wasn't even sure why I asked that and I wasn't even sure I liked them or cared how they were but, now that I was Roz's boyfriend, these three moody men were part of my social circle and if – big if – I married Roz, they would almost be like family!

"They're okay!" she smiled. "I shouldn't be telling you this but I think they're actually a little jealous of you and your crew. My boys can be so intense at times! Heston and Raymond are wrapped-up their work, Benjamin hates his job and the world in general. When they were younger, we all used to party together but, these days, they want to sit around the kitchen table and complain. It gets a bit much sometimes. So, to see Roz disappear every Saturday and come home beaming, it bites them! They used to be her go-to guys for fun! Not anymore!"

A truly insane thought crossed my mind. Maybe the boys could join us one evening? Yes, Benjamin was liable to be a huge millstone round my neck but – in the spirit of brotherhood – maybe this would foster good relations? It was a mad idea; having to look at Benjamin's sour puss all night filled me with dread but it would score major brownie points with Roz!

I could hear her saying, in her best Mary Poppins voice, "It's so nice to see you boys getting along!"

Over the other side of the room, I could see Melvin signalling that it was time to go in. He'd even reserved us a row of six seats! We sat back with our drinks and popcorn and waited for the lights to go down.

"What's this about?" I whispered in Melvin's ear.

"Dunno!" said Melvin.

Not even he knew! Yes, we certainly were adventurers! No doubting that! Would the boys from The Haunted House love our spontaneity? As artists, Heston and Raymond might appreciate it, but Benjamin would struggle with the random nature of our Saturday nights. What was I about to watch? I buckled-in and got ready for the ride.

100 minutes later, we were all glued to our seats, paralysed, mesmerised, jaws wide open, struggling to comprehend what we'd just seen. It had been a funny, sexy, violent, thought-provoking movie. I felt like I'd just gone ten rounds with Tyson. My head hurt! My emotions were all over the place!

The heroine was a multi-dimensional character; very attractive, very lovable but also a total fucking psychopath. You were rooting for her but also terrified by her. The mark of a good character, I guess? I turned to look at Wendy, who was still staring at the screen in disbelief.

"Wow!" she said.

"Wow, indeed!" I said. "That was amazing!"

"It sure was!" she replied.

"Hell hath no fury like a woman scorned!"

"You should know that already!" said Wendy.

I did. I had no intention of doing any scorning. I don't need fury in my life. Christ, fury was the last thing I needed!

We all stumbled out of the screening room and clambered back into the car. Melvin set the co-ordinates into Mids' SatNav and we all set sail for our next stop. A restaurant serving breakfast all day and all night! Yes, you could have the traditional fry-up; you could even have a bowl or two of cereal, but this restaurant aimed to give everyone whatever kind of breakfast they desired, all day and all night.

We all sat down at a large table and we were immediately brought a large jug of orange juice and a big pot of coffee. The menu was big, plastic, colourful and comprehensive. You could have your eggs any way you wanted, there were three different kinds of bacon, three different kinds of sausage, three different kinds of toast. The list went on and on. I was liking the look of hash browns, mushrooms and fried tomatoes, and I kind of wanted toast and chips!

There were collective oohs and aahs around the table. The photographs on the menu were having the desired effect. We were all about to eat too much.

Low, the alpha male, ever the clown, was getting very excited about the menu and threatening to try it all. Finally, he spotted the ultimate blow-out item at the very bottom of the back page and his mind was made up.

"Look at this beauty!" he announced. "The Big Bertha Breakfast! That'll do me!"

I looked at it and winced. "That's too much for me!"

"You're on your own!" said Mids.

"Oh, this looks lovely!" said Jill, pointing at a smoked salmon, avocado and scrambled egg combination. "It comes with sweet brioche buns as well!"

"Make that two!" said Wendy!

"Good call!" said Low. "Loving this place, Baggers!"

Melvin smiled with satisfaction. He loved the sound of happy friends.

Low could no longer contain himself. "So, Mids," he began, motioning towards Jill, "would you like to tell us your intentions regarding this young lady?"

Mids and Jill looked at each other, like two guilty teenagers.

"It's a friendship!" Mids wearily replied. He was well used to the group's invasive questions.

"With benefits?"

"That's none of your business, you cheeky boy!" said Jill, in her best Joyce Grenfell voice.

We all laughed because it was an audacious, Low-style question and the response was hopelessly inappropriate. If she wanted to hang with us, Jill would have to understand that every aspect of her sex life was going to be scrutinised. Just looking out for our friend, of course!

"He can't ask that kind of question, can he?"

Mids looked at Jill and shook his head. "Sister, that was nothing! Low has been known to make hookers blush!"

"Our interests are many and varied!" Low assured her. "We plan to talk about your sex life, we'll have a few words from Wezza about his non-existent sex life (now that his girlfriend is out of town), we'll speculate about Topper and what he's getting up to in Great Yarmouth and, if you ask Melvin nicely, he'll tell you a little about his preferences!"

"You've got a one-track mind, you have!" Jill said to him.

It was funny to see a woman wag her finger at Low.

"He'll get bored eventually," said Mids. "Once Low's had a little feel around, he gets bored and moves on to his next victim!"

"There will be no little feel around!"

We all laughed. Jill was fabulously ridiculous.

And then Low turned towards Wendy. "Maybe we'll get a few words from Wendy? Those doctors are pretty dishy!"

Wendy casually picked up her mobile phone, flicked through her photos and turned the phone round for all to see. What we were looking at was large, pink and erect!

"He's healthy!" said Melvin.

"Very healthy!" said Wendy.

Jill quickly realised she would now be the butt of many jokes, but she looked quite cosy sidled-up next to Mids, so she didn't seem to mind.

"So, Mids?" said Low, wanting an answer.

"Leave me alone, ya nosey bastard! Jill and I have talked, we've made our peace, we're moving on. You can see we get on well! What more do you want to know? We've already made sweet love once, so it's not really big news if we do it again! And again!"

Low smiled. He was satisfied.

Jill wasn't really that offended. After all, she lived in a house with three moody men; she knew what blokes were like!

A waiter approached us and took our order. He seemed very upbeat and talked about the food on the menu with great gusto. I began to get a good feeling about the food. What did I have? Scrambled eggs, Cumberland sausages, Maple Cured bacon, hash browns, fried mushrooms, fried tomatoes and chips! With two slices of whole wheat toast! Gimme a break: I was hungry!

The film had taken me to hell and back! The story of a really cool, kind and decent woman, the kind of woman you'd be happy to hang with, holiday with, break bread with. She falls in love with an equally cool guy, and their relationship is going well, until he decides he doesn't want a relationship any more.

She's an intelligent woman, a mature woman, and she's not shocked or surprised by his behaviour but, obviously, sad and disappointed. She's got great friends that rally around her and, just when you think she's okay, just when you think she's been dignified and mature ... she flips! Big time! Goes wild! Blood everywhere! Just when you think the film is about to dissolve into tears, snotty tissues, dark clouds and torrential rainfall, the mild-mannered heroine turns into The Terminator, Freddy Krueger and Carrie combined! Naturally, she chops up her ex but I think she even kills members of her own family, a local shopkeeper and some innocent animals! I couldn't tell; I was hiding behind my hands!

Roz and I didn't come to mind. This film was not she and I. I wanted a relationship, she wanted a relationship. We were both on the same page. Low, on the other hand, was in danger of running into such a woman!

"It's great to have you here!" said Melvin to Jill. "I can pick your brain, if that's okay?"

Jill looked a bit confused. "What can I help you with?"

"I'm organising a birthday party."

"Organising is what I do! Ask me anything! I know you've got the music sorted!" She turned to me and smiled. "How about catering?"

"Got that!" said Melvin. "And obviously Mids can help us with drinks."

"Event decorators?"

"Got that too!"

Jill looked even more puzzled now. "So, what do you need?"

"I don't know," said Melvin. "A magic ingredient! Something that will make the party unique and memorable!"

We all looked at Jill, who was processing information at an alarming rate. We could see her huge pedantic brain churning over years of events. "Hmm ..." she mused. "Let me think! Ideas I can do but magic is something different. Magic usually arrives in a blinding flash, doesn't it?"

Melvin seemed satisfied. The food began arriving and the conversation died down as we tucked into this heavenly, wholly indulgent and quite barmy meal.

"How do you know the director?" I asked Melvin.

"Friend of a friend ... of a friend."

"We should introduce him to Raymond?" said Jill.

"We should!" agreed Melvin.

The network was expanding.

"We should make a film of the party!" said Jill.

Everybody stopped in mid-mouthful. This idea was so brilliant; no one could chew or swallow.

"Raymond can shoot it, edit it and then we can send every guest a copy?"

"My God!" said Melvin. "That is inspired!"

And, in that moment, Jill became part of us. She'd displayed a quality we'd never seen before; a spark of genius. I looked at Wendy and she nodded at me. Yes, Wendy and Jill had had their problems down the years (notably Jill luring Heston into bed, despite her knowing that Wendy was sweet on him) and, yes, Jill was irrational, unpredictable and a massive pain in the arse, but she was also a maker of things; a planner, an organiser, a creative person; she was well used to working magic!

"No script!" said Mids.

"God, no!" said Jill. "Not a story with a script, just the story of the party. If you throw a little money at Raymond, he can even start a day early: the planning and the build-up to the party!"

Baggers was smiling. He loved this idea a lot and so would all his image-conscious friends; they would be thrilled to bits to see themselves on the silver screen! "No script but we should definitely get some talking heads!"

"But not 'I'm having a smashing time at Melvin's party!'" said Low, with a mouthful of breakfast.

"No, no!" said Melvin. "Much more random; stories and scandal and silliness!"

"Yes," agreed Jill, "but you must trust Raymond's editing skills. He's a very clever boy! If he turns a three-minute anecdote into a 10-second sound bite, there's a good reason!"

Baggers agreed and chowed-down on his huge and delicious-looking fruit salad (designed by him, of course), topped with yogurt and granola. No fry-ups for him! Melvin liked being slim and toned; it attracted the kind of playmates he liked!

"We won't embarrass anyone, will we? After all," continued Baggers, "all my mates will want to look as glamorous and articulate as possible."

"That's my point!" said Jill. "That's what we say to Raymond and he will ensure everyone looks and sounds amazing!"

"Thank you!" said Melvin, and you could see he really meant it! It wasn't often anyone did anything for him. Suddenly, Melvin and Jill were looking like a formidable events management team!

Low was really struggling with his Big Bertha Breakfast. On top of all the traditional ingredients, he had black pudding, kidneys and fried bread! Too much for me! He was eating at a much slower rate and had stopped contributing to the conversation.

"Don't finish it!" I said to him. "It's too much!"

Low was a very old-fashioned man. Failure was for wimps and wimping-out was not something a healthy heterosexual did! No sofa was too wide to get up the stairs, no pepper was too hot, no spirit was too potent, no breakfast was too big!

"Low!" said Nurse Wendy, very sternly. "It's too much! It's just a gimmick meal!"

When Nurse Wendy spoke about dietary matters, you listened, and this breakfast was about to put Low to sleep and send him to the toilet, hopefully not at the same time!

Low nodded, put down his knife and fork and took a swig of his beer.

"Nap in the car!" said Wendy. "At a party in Wandsworth, there's a dance floor with our names on it!"

Low smiled weakly and sat back in his seat, struggling to breathe and belching gently to himself. There was something quite significant about both Wendy's tone and Low's response. He wasn't really a huge fan of women. Oh, he loved boobs and bums and juicy orifices but, without being a misogynist, he was deeply suspicious of women. Low was quite happy to talk to (a.k.a. seduce) women but no female was ever going to influence his decision, let alone make a decision for him, and yet he had listened and obeyed Wendy. Maybe Wendy was different? She wasn't someone he could seduce (as she was in control) and she wasn't someone who desired him (well, not in an uncontrollable stalker-ish kind of way.) Wendy was different. She was like older sister or older cousin. And Wendy's simple instruction had been a caring gesture, as if she knew she was the only one he'd listen to. She was a nurse, so it was deeply ingrained into her DNA and, even on her Saturday night, she was quite happy to make sure everyone stayed injury-free and match-fit.

I thought for a second about Low and Wendy. Instant attraction, instant friendship. They'd got on well at Mids' wine warehouse event, they'd danced all night at Benjamin's birthday party and, from what I could see, the banter between them was fruity and flirty but restrained and polite, a little harsh and coarse at times but, like Jill, Wendy was well used to male frame of reference. Could they ever be a couple? Well, maybe, but Low didn't want or need a relationship. The polar opposite to me! He was more than happy to remove your clothes and shag you but talk of a relationship was a waste of everyone's time!

We'd all eaten far too much. So much so, we actually needed a few minutes to sit and digest. The party could wait. The breakfasts had been yummy but the portions were U.S. size, so the buttons on our clothes were at breaking point!

"So, where next?" said Jill to Baggers.

"I have a friend of a friend who's a milliner and she makes these huge, colourful hats. She's a bit of an extrovert and you'd need to be out-there to wear one of these hats, but this is a party to showcase her newest pieces. For my money, they're a bit Marmite; either you love 'em or you hate 'em?"

Jill was grinning from ear to ear and struggled to find right words to convey her excitement. "I am so glad I came out with you boys tonight!"

I looked at Mids. There was almost pride in his eyes; Jill was the right choice of woman and bringing Jill out with us had been the right decision. My only abiding fear was that he was The Rebound Guy. We wouldn't know until she rebounded again! I didn't want to think about that moment. Right now, they were happy and we were happy. Sure, I was missing Roz, but it was a pleasure to be entertaining her house mates and besties.

I wondered where she was? Probably, filming some radical and/or blue stand-up comedians at some smoky dive in Liverpool or Sheffield? I quickly whipped out my own phone and took a chaotic and wonky selfie of us around the table. I knew Roz would appreciate it. I sent it to her and waited for her response. Nothing. She was probably working? Or had no reception?

The females in the group had exercised some restraint but, as we stumbled back to the car, we all knew we were not in peak condition. Given the option of a bed, Low would have taken it! He napped in the car, as suggested. Melvin's playlist was superb as ever, more songs containing actual places in their title: 'Do You Know The Way To San Jose?' by Dionne Warwick, 'Baltimore' by Nina Simone, 'Vienna' by Ultravox, 'Carolina In My Mind' by James Taylor etc.

The playful ribbing between Jill and Mids continued in the front seat, Low was asleep, Melvin's eyes were everywhere, checking the route and the parking, while Wendy sat quietly next to me, staring out the window. She looked a bit sad and reflective though, being a nurse, she was probably just exhausted?

"You okay?" I asked her.

She nodded. "I'm thinking about my married doctor. I could end-up as damaged as Jill?" That was a scary thought to her! "The nights we've had trying to put her back together!"

"What can you do?"

Wendy smiled at me. It was the $64m question. What can you do? The heart wants what the heart wants. We've all fallen in love with the most unsuitable people!

"He's a lovely man," she said, "but he's married! These are the facts. I get a little of his time and that's all I'm ever going to get. Fact. I have choices. I can end it, if I want? I choose not to. These are the facts. This is my reality."

"Are you happy?"

Wendy thought about her married doctor. She thought about working with him, sharing jokes with him, having passionate sex in hotel rooms, and she thought about getting into bed alone and waking up alone.

"Sometimes," she replied. "At times, I'm really happy. Others: not so much."

"Sounds like marriage?"

She smiled again. "Yeah, it's a head fuck, whichever way you do it!"

We finally reached our party in Wandsworth. I looked up at what must have been an old council building. It had that Ealing Comedy forties look about it. It must have witnessed a million, boring meetings that ended-up in pointless bureaucracy; more road works, more traffic lights and another library closed.

There were two clipboard Nazis at the front door and a long queue of hopefuls trying to get in. Thankfully, we were with Melvin and we waltzed past them all and into the venue! If looks could kill!

We all walked in and did exactly the same; the hall was beautifully decorated from floor to ceiling, so we all looked up and collectively went, "Wow!" There was a huge net of balloons attached to the ceiling that, at some point, would be coming down. The hats were clearly full of feathers, as there was a rainforest/aviary theme, with lots of very green and exotic plants and trees, and huge and colourful but mythical, stuffed birds attached to the trees.

Predictably, there was a huge runway down the middle of the room and, with an old council building like this, the ceiling was high, so the music was just drifting up and up, not that anyone cared. The pumping commercial dance music was loud but absolutely no one was dancing. Why would they? This was a network and gossip crowd; they were all catching up on the relevant moments of the last 24 hours. Whatever trend was in that hour, me and my crew were hopelessly behind the curve, and probably stood out like sore thumbs. This was the ultra-fashionable crowd, only Melvin came close!

The bar was sponsored by some new vodka brand, so the free drinks were all vodka cocktails: with cranberry, with grapefruit, with lemonade etc. The glasses were tall and full of ice. We all thirstily gulped a cocktail and reached for another. Within minutes, the room was a blur! I looked at Wendy and she looked similarly sozzled.

"Christ, that vodka is strong!"

"We'd better slow down," she warned.

Melvin was greeting old friends and getting on famously with everyone, while Low had immediately latched on to a couple of girls that were propping up the bar; they were loving his jokes and rough-around-the-edges charm.

Wendy and I looked at each other and ordered another cocktail!

All around us, there were impossibly tall and thin girls who, for my money, were all in desperate need of a square meal. They didn't really look like women, more like flamingos wearing lipstick. I was worried they would fall off their stick-thin legs.

Jill was very excited to see the hats, so she and Mids were glued to the runaway, drinking, tickling each other and laughing. I hadn't seen Mids look that carefree since the early days of his failed marriage. I could see Jill deliberately ogling the elegant, chiselled beefcakes that wandered by, just to tease Mids! He was unaffected by her teasing and seemingly very enamoured with this striking, dynamic but quite fragile woman.

"Do you think Jill is over Alistair?" I asked Wendy.

"No!" said Wendy, quite forcefully. "She's in love with him. Present tense. Right now, Mids is a mere distraction; easing the pain. Tony seems like he's quite into her but she's still in love with Alistair and will be for some time. That kind of love doesn't evaporate; it clings on to your heart like a crab holding on to the edge of a boiling hot pan of water."

This was a little detail I would not be sharing with Mids. It wasn't my job to burst people's bubbles. I like to be honest with my family and friends but, in this instance, I couldn't. I just couldn't! Nobody wants to deal in the hypothetical. When you're at the fledgling stage of a relationship, you don't want to hear about hurdles and hiccups. You just want people to be happy for you.

You can hint at your concerns and worries and they'll say things like, "We'll cross that bridge when we get to it" or "It may never happen?" And they'd be right! For the time being: two people were making the miracle happen; they were making each other happy. Some married couples can't even do that!

What with the loud music and the excitable chatter, laughter (and squealing), the noise was almost deafening. Wendy and I did not want to shout in each other's ear all night, so we wandered. Strolled and wandered and observed and smiled. In all four corners of the room, there were gorgeous people, pushing the boundaries of fashion, some of them dressed in – for my money – dangerously impractical clothing; these were merely garments to wear at functions like this; tight pants, sheer tops, transparent shirts, and jeans with endless, tastefully-placed rips, as if they'd been dragged through a hedge forwards and backwards again for good measure!

Everywhere, there were photographers snapping everyone and everything and, as many of these people were models, they segued professionally from pose to pose. Everyone knew how to smile! Not a skill I've mastered yet! Wendy and I stood and watched these people at work. With every swivel, they found a new and provocative pose.

"How do they do that?" I asked Wendy.

"They do it all day! It takes them two hours to get ready in the morning and they don't leave the house unless they feel like a million dollars! Me? I brush my teeth and, if you ask nicely, I may even shower! The last time I did my hair was for my Sweet 16th! I own one solitary lipstick which Roz bought me for Christmas and I don't even know where it is!"

Wendy looked fucking amazing and she knew it! No effort necessary! She looked healthy and happy. It was the one major advantage she had over everyone in the room, most of whom cried themselves to sleep and hadn't seen food since their last school dinner!

Finally, the lights dimmed and there was a huge fanfare, as the models began to emerge from the end of the runway. So that clothing would not distract you from the hats, the girls were all dressed in plain-coloured swimsuits. The response from the anaemic throng was rapturous! They were loving these tall or wide creations, some of which could been hats but many of which would make excellent tree houses! Wendy and I looked at each other. Surely no one in their right mind would actually wear one of these?

Suddenly, Wendy began pointing frantically. "I want that one!" she shouted.

It was a glorious fusion of a sombrero, a scale model of Mount Vesuvius and your auntie's favourite chandelier.

"Really?" I asked.

"Yeah!" she said. "I really like it! There's something about it!"

"It must cost a fortune!"

Wendy wasn't bothered.

"I'll find out."

The show ended and I began to fight my way backstage. Like some stage-door Johnny, I loitered around the entrance to backstage and waited for the designer to emerge. Security looked at me quizzically. I wasn't a model. I wasn't a journalist. I was just some pleb holding a tall glass full of ice! Nevertheless, if I wanted to speak to the designer, I would have to fight off all the others loitering at the backstage entrance.

When she finally emerged, about 20 people rushed towards her and there was a loud flurry of kissing, screaming and camera-clicking. There was no way I was getting to her! Luckily, I saw a small, smart, efficient-looking woman standing a few paces to the right, surveying the melee. This I surmised was her assistant. I approached her carefully.

"Do you work with her?" I asked.

"I'm her PA, Eleanor. How can I help?"

"There was one hat my friend absolutely loved. How can I find out how much it costs?"

Quick as a flash, the PA reached into a pocket, pulled out a company business card and handed it to me.

"There are no prices quoted on the website. Find your hat, make an enquiry and we'll tell you how much it costs."

"Roughly?"

"It can go up to £750?"

I must have looked shocked. She looked at me, blankly. "You knew that, right?"

I nodded dumbly. This was another world. Another price bracket. Another lifestyle.

"Thank you," I said, calculating furiously how much everybody would have to contribute. I couldn't buy that hat on my own. Wendy would know that. I looked the business card. "I will definitely be in touch." The PA didn't look fussed one way or another. She was surrounded by good intentions and gossamer-thin promises.

I thanked her and wandered back to where I'd left Wendy but she'd now been joined by Mids and Jill, who looked as if they were trading insults again. The body language was aggressive and profoundly depressing. I could see Wendy in the middle, bravely keeping them apart, not that they would have come to blows.

As I got closer, I began to hear the cause of the problem.

"I said I'm sorry!" Jill was saying.

"It was bound to happen!" said Wendy to Mids.

Mids looked particularly red and exasperated. He didn't look like he wanted to talk. He looked like he wanted to scream or shout or roar; words would not express the anger and frustration he felt.

"I said I'm sorry!" Jill repeated. It wasn't helping.

"Tony, seriously," began Wendy, "it's not the last time it will happen! This man has been the complete focus of her life for the last nine years. It's all she's ever talked about. It's all we've ever heard about. It's a name that's stuck in my brain, so I'm sure it will be stuck in her brain for a while. If she calls you Ali, it means nothing! It's force of habit! That's all it is."

It all made sense but I could still see Tony seething. Wendy was so right; Jill would occasionally be calling Tony by another man's name for some time. Jill's psyche was still in the grip of the love of her life. I looked at my friend. I loved him to bits. God, we'd had some good times together! I felt powerless. I wanted to take away his pain. I put my arm around him and steered him towards the bar, leaving Wendy to pick up the pieces again.

On the way to the bar, we passed Low, who had a tall and very shapely woman attached to his arm. She was literally draped around his neck like a scarf. His ability to seduce women was a wonder to behold. He gave me a cheeky wink and continued telling her what she needed to hear.

Mids and I reached the bar and ordered two more of those potent cocktails. He knocked his back pretty quickly and ordered another. It was clear he wanted to drink his pain away. He was still shaking his head with dismay, unable to formulate the words that could express his complete disgust.

"You're the new bloke!" I said.

"I know," he said.

"You'll be the new bloke for a while!"

"I know."

Mids looked like he didn't want to talk. He was deep in thought. The long straw was carrying that long drink very quickly. I watched him survey the scene, looking at all the pretty people but, inside, wondering if he'd made the right move. After all, she'd dumped him once and he'd come back for more!

"Do you like her?" I asked.

Mids sipped through his straw and finished another of the tall drinks. He pondered the question. "You know what? I do. She's my type!"

"I know," I said. This I knew. Jill was his type. The right age, the right shape, she had the brains and the know-how; she was virtually a mirror image of Mids, except with child-bearing hips.

"I like her!" he said, triumphantly, as if he'd only just realised how much he liked her. "Fuck knows why she likes me but she does! Look at me, Wes! I'm no picture, am I? But that fiery woman thinks I'm sexy. She says I'm sexy, Wes! No woman's ever said that to me!"

No woman had ever said that to me! He was on to a winner! Worth fighting for, worth keeping, worth forgiving. None of Roz's Post-It notes had said, 'Sexy'. She loved a lot of things about me but that word had not come to mind. I was solid, reliable and faithful but, when it boiled down to it, I wasn't lighting any fires.

"That's quite something!" I said to him, almost glowing green with envy. He was starting to look more composed and less anxious. The tension began to leave his face, as he finally realised that Jill was a little bit more than a companion; a little bit more than love in the afternoon.

"I do like her!" Mids repeated. "Roz is what you need, and Jill is what I need!"

"Can't argue with that!" I said and, at that moment, Jill's arms were around his neck and she was kissing his face. They fell into a passionate embrace, leaving Wendy and I to look on at our handiwork.

Wendy pulled me away to give them some privacy, although they were in the middle of a noisy party! "So, what did they say about my hat?" she asked.

"I've got a card. We can go on their website, find the hat and find the price. It's going to be pricey, though."

"I know," said Wendy, looking disappointed.

"Maybe we can all club together for your birthday?"

Wendy's face was a picture! It looked like she was about to cry! She put her hand to her mouth to stifle the emotion. "You'd do that for me?"

"Why not?"

Wendy nodded her headed solemnly. "Roz is right. You are different!"

I squeezed her hand. "We can do this!" I said.

She looked like she was about to cry, so I said no more.

Suddenly, I felt my phone vibrate. I picked it up and looked at it. A text message from Alvin.

"Hey Wes!" it read. "This chemo has wiped me out. Got a party to do on Saturday. Definitely won't be able to do it. Sorry. Ax"

"No worries," I replied. "I'll get it covered."

Alvin was booked to play at an annual event. He'd been doing it for the last five years. They loved him and would be sorry not to see him but they would understand. The party organiser, one Waldo K. Peach, had a group of friends, all professors like him, and this group had grown down the years. It now totalled 120 people. All crammed in to his spacious house in Willesden. Pen friends flew in from around the world to attend Waldo's Peach Of A Party! It was like an academic convention without the lectures and seminars, plus a lot of alcohol and dancing. Waldo had been a white soul boy in the eighties and he just loved early Duran, early Spandau, Haircut 100 and all that vibe. Pressed on the subject, he once confessed his favourite band had been Rip, Rig & Panic (with the obligatory crush on Andrea Oliver.)

"Was that Roz?" asked Wendy.

"Nah! DJ emergency!" I replied.

We hadn't seen Melvin for a while but he eventually found us! He looked very drunk but very happy. "Weren't the hats amazing?"

"One of them in particular!" said Wendy.

"Oh?"

"We're going to buy it for Wendy."

"We are?" asked Melvin. "Did you look at the prices?"

"We'll all club together. For her birthday."

"Okay," said Melvin. "I'll speak to her PA and see if we can get a little discount?"

"Discount?" Wendy's eyes lit up.

"It won't be much but it will help."

"Good work, Baggers!" I said.

"So," he began, "I have an invitation to another party!"

I looked at Wendy. "Wanna go?"

"Do you?" I could see she didn't. Three events was more than enough.

"No."

"I think we'll pass."

Melvin nodded, hugged us both and disappeared into the distance.

We could see Low wandering towards us. He did not look best pleased.

"Let's go!" he said.

"You done for the night?" asked Wendy.

"After speaking to this girl for the best part of two hours, she finally tells me she has a boyfriend and they've always wanted a threesome!"

Low did not look happy. Wendy struggled to stifle a smile.

"We just need to find Mids and Jill and we can go," I said.

"You stay here!" said Low. "I'll find them!" Low was in a hurry to leave. Occupational hazard for The Lothario, I guess? Wasted time. That's why I was so happy not to be single. I don't have time to waste chatting-up endless women. It's exhausting!

Within minutes, we were back in Mids' car slowly winding our way back to North London. This time, wisely, with Jill at the wheel. Mids had consumed one too many of those tall drinks. He was cracking bad jokes in the front and keeping Jill entertained. Wendy dozed silently against the window, while Low stewed in the back seat. I could hear him frantically sending texts, looking for a last minute booty call, but even that didn't deliver! Occupational hazard for The Lothario, I guess? There's no such thing as sex on tap!

When we got back to Mids' house, Jill went inside, Low jumped into his car, and I took Wendy home.

"Nice of you to drop me," said Wendy.

"No problem."

"You don't really have to get me that hat!" she said.

"If you want it, we will find a way."

She looked genuinely touched. It was the least I could do for Roz's bezzie!

We'd had another memorable Saturday night: the shocking film, the breakfast restaurant and the fashion show/party. It was after 3.00 and my eyes were closing.

As I finally got into my bed, I looked at Roz's Post-It notes stuck to my bedroom wall. I wondered where she was and what she was doing but I wasn't going to worry. Occupational hazard for the person in love, I guess? Missing someone was not fun!

Sunday

When I woke up on Sunday morning, my first thought was Roz. I was trying hard not to feel pangs of jealousy but – damn it! – in the immortal words of Phil Oakey, I'm only human! I wanted to speak to Roz, hear that voice, hear those torturously long stories, hear her black and barbed jokes, and how badly did I want to suck her nipples! I wanted the full-on Roz experience but there was no way I was calling her! There was no way I was going to come off looking needy and, by the looks of things, she was doing the same! No phone calls, just a few texts. She definitely didn't want to reveal the extent of her affection for me.

Yes, I'd found the Post-It notes from her but I still didn't know what they meant, or even if they referred to me! I badly want to call her but it wasn't going to be me! I was going to be calm, mature and assured; I was going to let her work. She was a professional, she was on the job. She didn't need some drippy dork like me wheezing down the phone!

I looked up at the Post-It notes again: strong, reliable, sensitive, entertaining, inspiring, brave, respectful and hard working. Was she describing me or what she hoped I'd become? Surely I was all of those things? Surely she was describing me? Good thing she hadn't written 'self-esteem'!

I pulled on my dressing gown and wandered down to the kitchen. As I approached my kitchen, I could smell toast. I stopped on the stairs. There was somebody in my kitchen making toast! A burglar would NOT pause to put some bread into my toaster, would he? Did Marie have a key to my house? Did Trish still have a key?

I slowly pushed open the kitchen door and there stood Roz, looking sensational in the plainest jeans and the plainest T-shirt. She wasn't even wearing her customary bright colours but her aura filled the whole room.

"I wanted to make us breakfast?" she said, timidly, unable to give the words her normal bite and energy. I was so used to the hyper-animated Roz, this hushed, almost nervous version of Roz was hard to comprehend.

She stood there looking at me. I couldn't believe it was her, so I stood there dumbly for a few seconds, wondering what to say, wondering what to do.

"It's my day-off," she began. "I thought I'd surprise you?"

I slowly began to walk towards her. I wanted to hold her but she wasn't moving towards me. She was definitely holding back. She didn't want me to see and hear her emotions. I wrapped my arms around her and I could feel her holding me tight; very tight, as if she wouldn't be letting go. In fact, I could feel her put her whole body into the embrace, as if she wanted to be inside me! As if she wanted to hide inside my body and feel protected.

"God, I've missed you!" I could hear her say.

The embrace seemed to last forever. She was holding on tight. I relaxed to give her the chance to break away but she seemed quite happy holding on to me. I could feel her smiling and humming, as if she was quite content to just hold me. We stood, toe to toe, breast bone to breast bone, locked in this co-dependent, blood transfusion of an embrace, until she finally broke away and glared at me.

"Why didn't you call me, you bastard?"

I was ready for this power exchange.

"Why didn't you call me?" I replied.

Stalemate. She continued to glare at me.

"I've missed you!" she spat. Ah, this was more like the Roz I knew and loved! "You don't give a fuck about me!"

This statement was not even worthy of a response. She knew she was being a moody, unreasonable cow! As soon as the words left her lips, she could feel her power draining away.

I looked at her. She was not happy. Not necessarily unhappy with me, more unhappy with herself for missing me. I didn't say a word. And that upset her even more!

"You should have called! Any normal person would have called!"

Normal? Are we going to use the word 'normal' here? I thought.

"You're playing some weird, little game, and I don't like it!" she said, waving a finger at me. "If you wanted to call, you should have just called!"

Just to be looking at her, just to be hearing her voice, even if it was accusing me of nonsense, I was beyond happiness; I was teetering on the verge of ecstasy but holding it together manfully. How I'd missed her crazy hair and her soft lips!

"Say something, you cruel and heartless bastard!"

I laughed. Big mistake.

"You want to laugh at me?" she shrieked. "Really? You give me all your quaint, North London, white boy loving and then you throw me in the freezer like some unwanted carcass!"

I laughed again. Why did I do that? Big mistake. She continued glaring at me.

I wanted to tell her how much I'd missed her but I felt committed to my position. I didn't want to use those same old words. I didn't want to be the normal boyfriend. Talk is cheap. I wanted to be constant. I wanted to be strong and reliable. I wanted to lead by example.

Words just seemed soppy. I was fed up of looking soppy. The boys already thought I was a pussy-whipped wimp. I didn't want to be that guy anymore. It hadn't got me anywhere! Being the doting boyfriend, according to Trish, had relegated me from suitable to unsuitable father. I needed to exude some masculinity.

With Roz still glaring at me, I held out my hand. I must have looked quite serious because she suddenly looked quite worried! As if I was about to dump her! As if! She took my hand and we looked into each other's eyes.

"I love you," I began, "but can you please stop talking?"

She smiled and let go of my hand. "I was making you breakfast. The toast is cold!"

She pulled the toast out of the toaster, threw it in the bin and put four more slices of bread in the toaster. I sat down at my kitchen table and watched her cook. I think I was almost too happy to talk. Too relieved to talk! I was more than happy watching her cook breakfast, occasionally bending over to check on the sausages and bacon.

Here she was: in my kitchen. I had a million questions to ask her, none of which I wanted to ask. I had a clutch of soppy emotions to express, none of which would be leaving my lips. And I would not be asking her about the Post-It notes. The sticky pieces of paper were our secret, our private joke, our lovey-dovey game. All would be revealed soon.

She finally put two huge plates of food in front of us and we sat down to eat. We both knew that neither of us would be finishing our plates. It was a ridiculous, excessive amount of food. I loved her hopeless sense of proportion. A cup was either half full or over-flowing. It's a delightful trait in brilliant people, like great writers that can't spell!

The sun was streaming through my kitchen windows and I got up to adjust the blinds. It looked like it was going to be a hot day. Roz was manfully working her way through the food but it was far too much for her. She was sipping frantically at her coffee, trying to wash it down. It reminded me of our very first date. That epic breakfast we shared together; me trying to explain why I'd fallen asleep in an office doorway and her trying to calculate whether I was a habitual liar or not.

Thankfully, there had been something in my performance that she'd found believable and trustworthy. Thankfully, there was something about me she liked and here we were, months later, both standing at the precipice. It's one thing to say, "I love you," but it's another thing altogether to fully appreciate what it means. You're basically saying, "I need you" or "I want you in my life" and, ultimately, "I can't live without you." Well, I probably could live without Roz, but I'd be an ugly, snotty mess, honking my nose into endless tissues and wailing very loudly!

We both kind of knew we were standing at the edge of a cliff. Maybe that's why the conversation was stunted and stilted? We were both coming to terms with our feelings. It's clear we had both missed each other but we were both trying to play it cool. We chit-chatted about the documentary, about the region, about the comedians, about her crew, about the accommodation and, finally, about The Elusive Wilson. As she spoke about him, that familiar, endearing venom came hurtling out of her mouth! God, she hated him! Not because he wasn't a good man but because he'd rejected her. Despite all they'd shared, in the shakedown, he'd scored her poorly. He'd put all the information into the matrix and the results were not good and, for Roz, this was very hard to take. In her estimation, she scored highly in every discipline! Having The Elusive Wilson judge her to be an 'also ran' was absolute fuel to the fire; her hatred of him was behind words, but he was paying her bills, so she would be professional to the last.

In my sad, insecure brain, it was an absolute joy to hear her describe him in such unflattering terms. As far as I could see, she would not be falling back into his loving arms. I felt stupid for having such thoughts. The Elusive Wilson was The Excluded Wilson; he would no longer play a part in her life (unless he was her employer!)

And then I suddenly remembered we'd first met at a cafe near Chiswick. Why was she coming from Chiswick?

"Where does he live?" I asked.

"Chiswick," she replied.

"So you were coming from his place to meet me?"

"I was at that crap bar on that Saturday night because he was off with one of his harem. When you disappeared, I hung around for a while but I'm standing there thinking, 'Wilson's buggered-off with some floozie and now this new one's buggered-off God knows where!' At that point, I thought, 'Sod this!' and I decided to return his front door key to him. I'd had enough! So, I drove all the way back to Chiswick! God knows how I got there! I'd drunk a lot and, when I reached his place, I decided to crash out on his couch. He didn't even come home! On Sunday morning, I had a shower, left his key on his kitchen table and let myself out."

"From the frying pan into the fire?" I suggested.

"No, Wes! You are totally, totally different!" She paused. She didn't want to get too mushy! She didn't want me to know her every thought. "You are a proper boyfriend. You actually want to date me!"

"I do," I said, trying not to sound too enthusiastic.

She looked at me and smiled. How I'd missed that face, that smile, that impertinence and that sweet but gravelly voice.

"I know it's only been a few days but I've missed you," she said. "I've missed our adventures, I've missed your crew, I've missed knowing where you are and knowing you're always there, always there for me."

We were now wading into some serious expressions of emotion. I could sense she was about to get very animated and, given I didn't need much encouragement, if she'd started, fairly soon I'd be trotting behind her with some heavyweight declarations of love! This woman had seriously got under my skin and it was scary but it was where I wanted to be.

She put her knife and fork down and leaned back in her chair. "I'm too full to have sex!"

"We've got the whole day, right?"

"My train leaves Euston at 8.00."

"We've got time."

My phone dinged and I looked at it. A text from Topper to all of us. "Great Yarmouth is a lovely town. We're having a good time. Her family are nice people. Francine's a bit intense but she's very loving. Early days. Back tonight. What are we doing this week?"

I gave my phone to Roz, so she could read the text.

"They're not going to make it!" she said.

"Probably not!" I agreed.

"There's no passion in that text."

"He's quite reserved."

"We'll see."

I couldn't really worry about Topper and his new girlfriend. I was in the middle of a moment with mine! The day was going to contain sex, now I just had to make sure I didn't screw things up by saying the wrong thing! On my day off, I was treading carefully through a minefield. One insensitive remark and the whole day could blow up in my face!

I didn't want to talk about the Amiable Alvin; that would make her sad. I didn't want to talk about Mids and Jill; that would just make her anxious. And I didn't want to talk about life without Roz; that was depressing beyond words. So I decided to talk about Max and my plans for him! Roz listened with interest.

"I'm going to turn him into the next Derek B or the next Paul Oakenfold. He knows how to make people dance, so he should be making his own dance music."

Roz nodded with approval. "I'm liking this! You could operate a number of businesses out of the shop? Day-to-day business plus artist management company and, eventually, record company?"

I was just shooting the breeze but she was way out ahead of me. She was designing a future for me! And then I suddenly realised what was expected of me! I couldn't just stand still, I had to make plans, I had to expand, I had to move up in the world. She wanted a go-getter! She wanted Mr. Reliable for a season but then she needed me to become The CEO.

This wasn't in my immediate plans but hesitancy was not sexy! I needed to exude confidence. "Good idea," I said, chirpily.

"You can do this, Wes!" She had more faith in me than me!

I thought about Max. He didn't have to try. He was young, handsome, cool and he was right at the very cutting edge of new music. If I couldn't turn him into a pop star, I was an imposter and a wastrel!

"I know I can," I said. "I can't keep hiring out that grimy, old gear! I have to move with the times. Equipment is changing, music is changing."

"Everything revolves around you," she began. "You know that, right? You are virtually managing this group of people. All of your crew look to you for guidance and approval, and now Wendy and Jill can't stop singing your praises!"

I looked at her blankly. Me? I didn't say that out loud but I looked pretty confused. "Really?" I asked.

"Definitely!" said Roz. "Jill is a hard nut to crack but she is a big fan of yours. She loves a good manager and she says you do it with such ease!"

I wasn't used to receiving personal compliments. Every so often, a customer would compliment us on our customer service, but actual personal compliments were few and far between! This one was resting uneasily with me. A good manager? I'd never even thought of myself as a manager!

"You are a facilitator and an enabler!"

Now I was really confused.

"You let people be themselves. They are comfortable being themselves. You make it happen."

Trish had never complimented me on anything! Not even my rock-solid reliability! No, she had never complimented me on anything! I thought about it. What did she even like about me? I was a boyfriend and girls like having a boyfriend. That was it.

"I guess so?" I agreed, dumbly, not fully understanding what I was doing. "I don't over-think it."

"No, you don't but you always manage to do the right thing! Did you know that?"

This was one compliment too many. I would have to put a swift end to this. I changed the subject. "Did you get all the details from Saturday night?"

"Some," said Roz. "Not all."

"Baggers needed a great idea for his party and Jill came up with it."

"Not surprised! It's what she does!"

"We're going to get Raymond to make a film of the party and then send a copy to everyone that attends."

Roz looked stunned for a moment. "That's a great idea! And Raymond will do a good job!"

"We just need a venue?"

"Do it at ours!" said Roz.

"Really?"

I'd been too terrified to ask.

"Yeah, why not? Melvin's friends are going to be what? Models, designers, journalists, bloggers?"

"Probably. Heston won't mind?"

"Miserable git! He'll be happy to see some pretty, young things!"

Problem solved. What a relief! Melvin was going to be overjoyed.

Roz yawned. "That breakfast has knocked me out! I'm going to lie on the sofa."

She got up gingerly and moved into my front room. I watched her take off her shoes and curl up on my sofa. The TV was purring quietly with some news channel.

"I've been up since five!"

And those were the last words she said. She was out like a light. I put a light blanket over her and pulled the curtains.

Suddenly, my phone began to vibrate. I picked up the call. It was my No. 1 delivery and set-up guy, Courtney.

"Wes, I'm being held hostage!"

This was a new word in my line of business. There were spillages and breakages, there were late payers and non-payers, there were arrogant customers and clueless customers, but none of my staff had ever been taken hostage!

"I'll be there as soon as soon as I can!"

Courtney sent me the address, I threw on some clothes and jumped in my car. A short drive to Bounds Green.

Sure enough, sitting in the front room: one employee, arms folded, looking very frustrated, and one very tall, very perplexed fifty-ish woman, holding her invoice and waving it at me aggressively.

"The music last night was terrible! Wholly unsuitable! I hardly knew any of the songs!"

From memory, I didn't recall her requesting one of our DJs.

"Madame, can I just look at your invoice?"

She handed it to me. Sure enough: equipment hire, delivery, set-up and collection the next day.

"Madame, we didn't supply you with a DJ!"

She looked even more confused. "I distinctly remember looking at that page on your website! It was a page of faces and what musics they specialised in."

"Yes, madame, you may have looked at that page, but you didn't select a DJ, and we certainly haven't charged you for one!"

"Well, who was he?"

Courtney and I looked at each other. Damned if we knew!

"Roughly how old was he?"

The woman thought. "About 21, maybe 22?"

"Do you have a daughter?"

"Yes."

"How old is she?"

"She'll be 22 in August."

"I would suggest it was one of your daughter's friends?"

Having got to the bottom of the mystery, Courtney stood up.

"You just wait a second!" she said, glaring at him with menopausal menace.

Courtney sat back down again.

"My party was ruined!" she said.

"Madame, that is not our fault!"

"You should have recommended a DJ!"

"With all due respect, I don't do hard sell. I find it patronising. If you wanted one, you should have asked!"

A 21-year-old daughter wandered into the front room, wearing pyjamas and much of last night's make-up. Her green hair was pointing in several different directions.

"Who are they?" she asked her mother.

"They've come to pick up the equipment. Maude, darling, do you know who the DJ was last night?"

"My mate, Jason. You know Jason!"

"Do I?"

"Course you do, Mum! He was brilliant! Got everyone up dancing!"

"Darling, I didn't know any of the songs!"

"That's 'cause you're old!"

The daughter stumbled into the kitchen and began rifling through the contents of their fridge.

We definitely didn't want to get in the middle of this rather spiky mother and daughter moment. The woman looked crestfallen, not just because she'd kept Courtney hostage under false pretences, but because time was passing quickly and she was no longer abreast of party favourites. With those cutting words from her daughter, I could see her feeling fragile and vulnerable.

I didn't owe her an apology and I didn't owe her a penny but I wanted to put a smile on her face. She'd probably been looking forward to this party and probably not enjoyed a moment!

"I tell you what," I began, "let me invite you to a party! I am DJ-ing at a party next Saturday. Really lovely people. Regular customers. Why don't you and a friend come to this party, and I guarantee you'll know all the songs!"

The woman looked up at me. She almost looked tearful. "That is a very sweet gesture, young man. I'm touched."

"A genuine offer!"

She nodded. "I know. I appreciate it."

The daughter came back into the front room. "Mum, what are we having for lunch?"

"So, will I see you next Saturday?" I asked her.

"We'll see," she said, but I got the impression that I'd never see her again.

Courtney got up warily, looked at the woman and, once he'd established the conflict was over, he began to dismantle the sound system. I helped him get loaded and we were out of there sharpish.

Courtney looked at me, shook his head and smiled. What could you say? All in a day's work.

"Sorry about that, mate!" I said.

Courtney was a quiet guy, a shy guy. A private man. More at home in his bedroom building a PC or an amplifier than being out at parties like us! He didn't say much and, when he said it, it was virtually a whisper.

"No problem," he mumbled, softly.

"Are you ready to do gigs for me, Courtney?"

Courtney looked at me and laughed. "You know I can't do that, Wes! Never done it in my life!"

"But, Courtney," I began, "you know about gear and you know about music! You're a short hop from doing parties!"

Courtney gave me his shy, little laugh and almost blushed. "Nah, Wes! That's not me!"

"Okay, mate! You tell me when you're ready."

Courtney gave me a quick smile and was gone with the gear.

When I got home, Roz was no longer on my sofa, or in my kitchen so, with my pulse racing, I climbed the stairs and there, in my bed: the crazy girl with the wild hair, smiling at me.

"Get your arse in here!" she said, persuasively.

I looked at the wall behind my bed. All of the Post-It notes were gone. I didn't have time to worry about that. She pulled back the duvet and shook her boobs at me suggestively. I didn't need an invitation!

When we finally woke up, it was after six. Her train would be leaving soon. She quickly jumped in the shower, while I went downstairs and packed her some snacks for the journey. Within the hour, she was dressed and downstairs with wet hair, looking happy and relaxed.

There wasn't much to say. We'd said it all in my bed. Her actions were expressions of love and I felt loved. Surely she must have felt how much I'd missed her, how much I desired her, how much I wanted to please her? I don't want to gush and spill my guts; she'd heard all those promises before. I didn't want to say more than I had to. I wanted my actions and gestures to carry my message.

"Will you call me?" she asked.

"I assume you're busy?"

"Call me anyway."

"Can I call you Sugarlips?"

She rolled her eyes.

Once I'd dropped her at the station and we'd kissed goodbye, I put quick call in to Melvin. I needed to know what I was doing. Our concierge had the answers.

"Let's do dinner on Tuesday. Just us boys!"

"Yes!" I affirmed. "Just us boys!"

"And then we'll have a big Saturday night with the girls?"

We agreed to return to one of our favourite venues on Tuesday, The Sanderson Hotel; classic decor, a long bar full of happy tourists, gloriously English and great grub! It never failed.

I was anxious to hear about Topper's time away with Francine. I wasn't holding out much hope. She was a strange one but, if he was happy, I was happy.

When I got home, I thought about my Post-It notes. Where had they gone? I went to my fridge, still full to the brim, pulled out a can of Coke, threw that into a glass, closely followed by a slug of Jack Daniels.

When I got back into my front room, the TV was still on that same news channel. I watched it carelessly, not really taking in every detail but my eye was suddenly taken by a lime green Post-It note stuck to my bookcase. I got up and pulled it off, it said, 'Skilful'. I smiled to myself.

My phone vibrated again.

"We've got an invitation to dinner!" said Low, sounding highly excited.

"You and me?"

"Yes, just you and me!"

"With who?"

"With Lola and Sharon, those two lovely girls we dropped back to Wood Green the other night!"

The prospect of this filled me with dread. Reading between the lines, Low wanted to sleep with one of them (the one who'd shown the most interest in him, whoever that was) and I was there to keep the other one occupied!

This was our equivalent of 'taking one for the team'. I tried to hide my displeasure. "That sounds splendid!" I said.

I tried to think, had Low ever done the same for me? Nah! My life had been very simple. Trish. Full stop. Although Low's muscle and foolish bravery had got us out of more than a few tight scrapes.

I remember one particularly crap disco just off Bond Street, full of flash, Middle Eastern guys. They took offence to us having so much fun. What were we supposed to do? Pay big money at the door and stand around like wall flowers? No, we were drinking and laughing and dancing, and their female friends were having fun with us on the dance floor!

These dullards got upset. Frankly, I'd have got upset with their stylist! They were all wearing these garish shirts that even I knew were naff as old boots! Probably paid a fortune for them! Anyway, these Neanderthals strode on to the dance floor, looking to mark their turf, with their ten ton medallions hanging from their necks! In situations like that, you need Low. He's tall, charming, fearless and a modern-day, urban diplomat. Perfect for a Middle East crisis!

He explained to the morons, in no uncertain terms, that we merely wanted to have a good time and we would be occupying that section of the dance floor, while they could have this corner. And, if they didn't like their girls fraternising with us, it was down to them to provide some entertainment, which would involve a few drinks, a few dance moves and not a clanking bit of metal!

Yes, in those kind of situations, Low was the perfect man to have at your side. It almost felt like we were The Avengers, each with own unique super-power. Christ, what was mine? According to Roz, I was The Enabler. Didn't sound much like a Marvel character!

So, I knew exactly how the evening with Lola and Sharon was going to pan out, now I just had to play my part; smile sweetly, make conversation but, if Low thought I was going to service the other girl; that would not be happening! Not be happening!

How would she feel? Rejected? Unloved? Hung out to dry? In truth, one girl was going to be making whoopee, while the other would have to put up with me! Not fair but Low did not care. In his world, nothing was more important than him getting his end away.

I reluctantly agreed and we arranged to go to the girls' house for 7.30. They would be cooking dinner and we were to bring bottles and dessert. In a way, I really felt guilty being party to this plan. Maybe I could privately contact the other girl to let her know how the evening was going to go down? Or was I being presumptuous? Maybe she had no interest in me at all?

After an afternoon of lovemaking with Roz, I was drowsy and ready for bed. I couldn't really over-think Low's double date; I had better memories to swim in. My afternoon had been a dream; one of those situations where you pinch yourself and think, "Wow! Am I really here?"

Kissing the smooth skin of this beautiful woman was like being in high-end, studio porn! Was it really me? Yes, it was! This cool and velvety woman desired me! Little old me! I just wanted to ensure I kissed every damn part of her mouth-watering body and I did! And with those pleasing images still racing through my mind, I was soon asleep.

Monday

Monday was a standard day; customers returning gear to the shop; packing, stacking and break-backing. A very physical day. Thankfully, I was still on Cloud 9 following my afternoon with Roz. Our session had released a lot of happy chemicals in me, so not even an arduous Monday could dampen my spirits.

I was dating the most beautiful girl on the planet and I wanted to tell the world, only I needed to keep it quiet; I didn't want Roz knowing how I felt!

Max was walking tall, maybe even an inch taller! He was on top of the world. Well, his world! In the places he went, he was the rising star; he was loving the adulation!

I talked to Max about Alvin and asked him again if he thought he could step into his shoes. Max did not look convinced. In fact, he looked terrified!

"I can't play all that stuff he plays!" he wailed. "Alvin's got music from before I was born! Percy's your man! Percy to the rescue, bruv! Percy loves doing gigs!"

Max was right. Percy loved doing gigs but he was an acquired taste. Plus, he was very opinionated. The winning thing about Alvin was that he kept his trap shut. The customer was always right. I wasn't convinced Percy had mastered that skill yet but, whatever his negotiating skills, I needed him this Saturday. I'd sent him a text, I was just waiting for his reply.

I needed Percy for Waldo K. Peach's 'Peach Of A Party'. He definitely had the music. I just needed there to be some chemistry between he and Waldo. Waldo was used to Alvin and trusted him. Even if Waldo got a sudden craving for A Certain Ratio or Gang Of Four, or something contemporary like Talking Heads, Alvin could seamlessly blend it in!

I hadn't booked Percy to do anything for me but he was now a soul trader, booking his own gigs and forming his own bonds. Maybe he already had a gig on Saturday?

As we worked, Max's phone was pinging away! He was certainly a man in demand. I was dreading the day he would get too big for my shop. My only way of keeping him was to do as Roz had suggested, establish new companies within the shop, manage Max the artist and put out his music. It was a conversation for me and the boys tomorrow night! That was Tuesday, I still had Monday to get through!

I was not looking forward to my evening with Lola and Sharon. Not that they were boring or tiresome or anything! They were lovely girls; genuinely warm people. I definitely got that from them. But Low's ploy was treating them like cattle. They deserved better.

As the day progressed, I got more and more angry with Low. What had he roped me into? Why did he need me to get himself laid? He didn't! He was perfectly capable of picking up girls anywhere! Literally, anywhere! He even got laid at a funeral!

Would it be Lola or Sharon? Which girl would I be disappointing? I hated myself for being so obliging and hated Low for using one girl to bed another. It was all very sordid. I almost needed Roz The Enforcer to sort him out? Or maybe Nurse Wendy would be more effective? For some reason, when Wendy spoke, Low listened.

I needed to drive because I knew I wouldn't be staying over, so I met Low at Wood Green tube and we drove to the girls' flat, stopping at a supermarket to buy bubbly and some Ben & Jerry's.

Once we got inside, the flat proved to be spacious. The walls were covered with framed, black & white photos; beautiful shots of countryside, beaches, architecture and faces.

"Who's the photographer?" I asked.

"That's my brother, Sam," replied Sharon. "Always had this bloody fixation with cameras, always pointing a camera in my face! Me and my friends used to run!"

"Very classy!" I replied and made a mental note to ask Sharon for Sam's number.

They had a huge kitchen-diner that extended into a front room and, as we sat on a sofa, the smells from the kitchen were making me hungry. I had to ask Sharon, "What are you cooking? It smells amazing!"

"We can both cook!" she replied, handing me a flute of Prosecco, "but Lola drew the short straw, so she's making one of her signature dishes."

"What is it?" I asked, impatiently.

"You wait and see!"

I'd only had a sandwich (from Belinda The Rescinder), so I was ravenous! The bubbly was going straight to my head. Much more of this and I would be powerless to hold off a girl's advances! Sharon kept topping up our glasses, so she'd definitely decided getting us drunk was the way to go. It was almost like role reversal? My defences were being attacked. I needed some of that food to absorb the alcohol.

The conversation was light and fluffy, lots of anecdotes about men, lots of suggestive remarks, lots of laughter and, from what I could see, lots of very unnecessary posing! Both girls were – shall we say? – blessed and both girls were wearing low-cut tops. Their breasts were virtually falling out! It was unsubtle seduction and I was virtually powerless to stop it.

Having said that, after my second glass, my vision was blurred, so I couldn't really focus on what was falling out! When Lola announced, "Dinner is served!" I couldn't get the table quick enough and, as she dished it out, I still couldn't work out what it was but, as I began to gobble it down, I really didn't care! It was so tasty! Really tasty! And so more-ish! It was some kind of meat and vegetable stew but God knows what! As the others gabbled away, I was stuffing food into my mouth like I was in a hurry. I looked down and my plate was empty!

"My God!" said Lola, "did it even touch the sides?"

"Would you like some more?" asked Sharon.

I nodded. I wasn't sure answering was a wise move. My head was spinning, my belly was full and warm, and my taste buds were virtually singing songs of praise. Whatever this concoction was, I needed more. Now. Please.

It tasted like corned beef. Could it really be corned beef? All I knew was: it was addictive comfort food. I watched as Low and the girls enjoyed their flirtatious banter. Every so often, Sharon would look over to see if I was alive. I was very quiet and still consuming but, by now, I had slowed to a civilised pace.

"He's a bit quiet, your mate!" said Lola.

"He's a thinker," said Low, covering furiously. "He sits and listens and takes it all in."

"And what does he do with it?" A not unreasonable question from Sharon.

Low was stumped but kept busking. "He can make sense of any situation."

The girls looked confused. Not even I was sure where he was going, but I was squiffy!

Low was thinking on his feet. "What I mean is: Wes is a keen observer of people. He can read between the lines. Someone might be saying one thing but mean another!"

"Like a hidden agenda?" said Lola.

"Yes!" Low agreed.

"So, what's my hidden agenda?" asked Sharon, moving her eyebrows up and down suggestively.

My defences were down. There was no holding my mouth anymore. "You want to get me drunk, so you can seduce me."

Sharon smiled. "You're not wrong!"

And, with those words, we were all now on a carnal collision course! It was merely a matter of getting through the meal before the inevitable happened. Lola looked at Low and he winked back at her. That was the only communication they required. It was on! Dessert was a mere formality. Once that had been consumed, Lord knows what would happen? Was I really going to have to fight this woman off?

The ice cream we'd bought was a godsend. It was light and cooling and didn't take up too much room in my bulging belly. Lola had now left the kitchen area and was sat on one sofa next to Low, while Sharon was edging ever closer to me on the other sofa.

"My glass is almost empty!" Lola shrieked.

Sharon leapt up, pulled another bottle of bubbly out of the fridge and expertly opened it. Her hand yanked that cork out with little problem. These were strong hands! She would not be easy to wrestle, should it come to that! Surely it wasn't going to come down to a physical tussle?

Sharon re-filled Low and Lola's glasses and they both toasted.

"To new friends!" said Low.

"To new adventures!" said Lola.

I looked over at them. They were starting to get very close. Sharon sat down next to me and tried to give me some more.

"No more for me," I said.

"Really?" she said, filling her glass. "We drink so much Prosecco every week; it feels like Cream Soda to me these days!" She raised her glass. "Health and happiness!"

Low and Lola raised their glasses and repeated, "Health and happiness!"

With all the drinking, toasting and laughing, I felt like I was in some kind of bawdy, medieval romp. At any moment, the court jester would be appearing and make us all laugh with saucy, topical songs. I definitely did not feel present, like I was tripping and, as I'd already written the story and knew what was about to happen, it felt like a dream I couldn't wake up from!

Out of the corner of my eye, I saw Lola and Low disappear into her bedroom, and now I was alone with Sharon! Within seconds, her shapely thighs were draped over my lap and she was that much closer to me.

"You're worrying me, Wes. You do find me attractive, don't you?"

Having drunk so much, lying was pointless.

"I do," I confessed. "I find you very attractive."

And, quick as a flash, she was up and sitting on my lap facing me. Our lips were almost touching. Her scent was a sweet, fragrant mix of cocoa and citrus fruits, and that cleavage was headed in my direction.

"I'm not single!" I finally said. "I'm attached!"

Her shapely breasts were now resting on my chest.

"I like 'attached'," she said. "That means you won't get attached to me!"

And, before I knew it, her lips were on mine.

Mustering all my strength, I grabbed on to her shoulders and pushed her away.

"I can't," I said.

Sharon looked into my eyes to see if I was serious and, once she could see that I was, she slowly got up from my lap. This stunning woman had no need to beg. With that face and that body, she would be any man's dream. Tomorrow would be another day and she would have more suitors sniffing around her.

"I hear you," she said. "You're a good man, Wes. She's a lucky girl!"

"I'm sorry," I said.

"Don't apologise for being a good man! One day I'll need a good man like you."

"You must have so many admirers?"

"Yes but they just want to sleep with me! No one wants to love me."

I could hear echoes of Roz's words. She'd virtually said the same; lots of hungry, temporary wolves but no noble beast amongst them.

Sharon sat back down on the sofa and slung her legs over my lap. She looked deflated. "Well, this is shit!" she said.

"I'm sorry!" I said. I couldn't think of anything else to say. If only I'd been able to get to her 24 hours prior, we could have avoided this embarrassing scene!

"You don't have to keep saying sorry!" she said. "I've been rejected before!"

I had never rejected a woman before. This was all new. Instinctively, I began massaging Sharon's feet. Something Trish had taught me.

Sharon looked shocked. "Oooh, what are you doing?"

"One of my exes taught me. Does it feel good?"

"Hell, yes!" said Sharon, as she began to sink deeper into her sofa. With all her moaning and groaning, Lola and Low must have heard her, and probably thought I was giving her the ride of her life but all that was happening was she was slowing falling asleep and, sure enough, within seconds, Sharon was out. Like a light! I stopped massaging her feet and sat very still. I didn't want to wake her.

The ridiculousness of it! In the distance, I could hear bed springs pinging and the feint moans of Lola while here, in the front room, nothing was going on! Nothing! I was pinned to the sofa under Sharon's powerful thighs, unable to move and she, softly snoring, was dead to the world. I sat there, pondering the ridiculous situations I allowed myself to get into. I was trapped. For how long? Low owed me!

I thought about Roz. Where was she? What would she say if she could see me now? She'd probably laugh. Having lived with five people for so long, she must have found herself in this situation before. We were the givers and the foot-massagers. We were the listeners. The reasonable ones. We were the ones that covered the stranger sleeping on the couch.

I was still inebriated and I could feel my eyes closing. Fairly soon, I was asleep too and I would've gone the whole night if Sharon hadn't suddenly woken up with a jolt!

"What happened?" she asked.

"I was massaging your feet and you nodded off!"

Sharon looked at me. "You're a good man, Wes! If it doesn't work out with you and your girl ..."

I smiled. This was all new to me. Now, I had a smart, beautiful and voluptuous woman asking to be put on the sub's bench. My life had certainly changed!

"I need to get home but I can't drive!"

"I'll drive you home!" she said. "Prosecco's nothing to me anymore! It has no effect!"

"And how will you get home?"

"You'll call me a cab!"

So, we got into my car and headed back to mine, and we would've got there if my phone hadn't rung! It was a frantic Marie wanting me to come over immediately. Christ, what now?

"We need to take a detour!"

Sharon laughed. "Road trip!" she squealed. "I love a road trip!"

"We need to go to my sister's house. She's got this new-ish boyfriend. They are nuts about each other. Nuts! But it's stormy! Always bloody arguments!"

"Been there!" said Sharon. "I dated a bloke like that. God, I loved that man! God, I loved him! It couldn't last, though."

"Don't say that!"

"The arguments were exhausting! They squeezed all the love out of the relationship."

This was good. Sharon had given me a line. I didn't want to be mediator but I was going to have to get in the middle of these two numbskulls! The arguments will kill the love. That was my line. It was a good line.

When we got to Marie's, there was no love in the air. It was cold, dark and sickly. Percy and Marie sat either side of the kitchen table, glaring at one another. Sharon and I came in and looked at them: motionless, glum stalemate. Neither had noticed it wasn't Roz.

Suddenly, Marie looked up. "Oh, hello, love! Who are you?"

"Sharon. Friend of Wes."

"Would you like a cuppa and a bit of cake?"

Sharon was suddenly wide awake. "Cake?"

"Yes, darling: fruit cake, carrot cake, coffee & walnut, banana bread and my new creation, orange pound cake!"

"Some of that last one!" said Sharon.

Marie turned on the kettle and began slicing. "Percy likes cake!" she said.

"Yes," said Percy, through gritted teeth, "Percy likes cake!"

Marie's stock phrase was starting to grate. I doubt if he was tired of all the cake but once Marie had a decent cliché, she could rinse it to death!

"But," she continued, in a much more menacing tone, "if Percy keeps buggering off to do gigs, Marie won't be able to feed him cake!"

And here was the nub of the problem: Marie was not happy about Percy working so hard. Most women love a man with a good work ethic but not Marie! She wanted Percy at home, so they could sample culinary and carnal delights. Baking and bonking. What more could a man want?

How the hell could I get in the middle of this? I had turned Percy into a DJ and was about to make him even busier! This argument was basically my fault! I needed Percy this Saturday and, with The Amiable Alvin out of action, I would need him a lot more. I had a vested interest and, as far as Marie was concerned, I was the problem, not the solution! So why had she called me?

"First of all," I began. "You must stop arguing! Arguments will kill the love!"

Percy finally looked up. "Wes is right! More discussion. Less emotion!"

"Yeah, yeah!" said Marie. This was her standard, I've-got-it-under-control response.

"Here you are, love!" she said to Sharon, presenting her with a hot beverage and a generous slice of orange pound cake.

Sharon thought she'd died and gone to Heaven. "True love, foot massages and cake? I like your family, Wes!"

Yep, that was us: givers and nurturers. Just like my mum and dad. The way it should be.

"More discussion. Less emotion!" I repeated.

"Yeah, yeah," said Marie.

"Arguments will kill the love, Marie! You don't want that!"

Percy and Marie looked into each other's eyes and he held out an apologetic hand. She reached out and squeezed it.

"But what about all these bloody gigs, Wes! He keeps going out to work!"

Sharon snorted with laughter.

Marie slowly turned towards Sharon and looked very upset that Sharon's only contribution to the debate was a snort! "Do you have something to say?" she asked, in quite a threatening manner.

"I used to go out with this geezer. Tall, handsome, good in the sack but, Christ, he was lazy! He used to sit on my sofa all day and play computer games! He'd even invite friends over to play computer games and then they'd empty my bloody fridge! And, when I got home from work, he'd say, 'What's for dinner?' Cheeky bastard! I got shot of him! He was fun at night but he was too bloody lazy! Now, you, you've got a man, a man that clearly loves you, and he's running from job to job! Sounds like a good relationship to me!"

"It's not a relationship anymore!" spat Marie.

Sharon seemed unphased.

I was already out of ideas so, if anything was moving this evening, it was down to this woman I barely knew! Maybe she'd had some training or experience in this field?

Sharon's plate was empty and she waited patiently for an offer of another piece. Marie's generosity had deserted her. Sharon knew she had to get her back onside. I watched her concoct a new strategy.

"This would work well with peaches," said Sharon.

Marie digested this suggestion and approved of it. They shared a quick baking moment.

"Another piece?" offered Marie.

"Yes, please," replied Sharon. "I don't have a lot of home baked cakes in my life. When I was growing up, my whole house smelt of cinnamon and nutmeg! My mum was always baking cakes for her church, for their coffee mornings, for the prayer group, for the church fete."

Marie handed Sharon another generous slice and, having heard tales of her cake-less life, she suddenly felt guilty for being so snappy.

"Is Mum still around?" she asked.

"We lost her four years ago," said Sharon. "I can bake a half-decent rum cake but they never taste like my mum's."

Sharon was winning. I watched the balance of power shift. If you truly appreciated the raw beauty of home-baked cake, Marie could talk to you. Talk to you on a higher level!

"So what's with the cake?" asked Sharon. "It seems to be a big part of things around here."

This was Marie's cue. I knew what she was going to say and Percy readied himself for further repetition of Marie's stock phrase. Marie did not disappoint.

"Percy loves cake," she chirped, and I could see Percy cringing in his seat. He needed to alter the language of his relationship, alter the dynamic, alter the expectations.

"That's love!" said Sharon. These were words Marie wanted to hear. "You make him cake to please him and he works two jobs to please you!"

"It doesn't please me!" Marie said, in frustration.

Sharon looked at her. It was a proper, 'Come on, bitch! You're being unreasonable!' look. Marie seemed to understand.

"Your man wants to please you. He wants you to be proud of him."

"I am! I am!" exclaimed Marie.

"Let your man please you!" said Sharon. "It's very important to a man."

Again, these were words Marie needed to hear. She wanted she and Percy to be strong and resilient. She needed to know how to behave and I was still fumbling in the dark with my relationship, so I was no help.

"Keep it fun!" I offered. It wasn't much but it was my creed at the moment. These were the words guiding me and, without wishing to blow my own trumpet, they were working.

Sharon seemed to like them. She sipped at her tea and wiped her mouth on a napkin. "Keep it fun!" she repeated. "Arguments will kill the love!"

Percy hadn't said anything but he looked exhausted! He slowly raised his head, trying to gauge if the gunfire had ceased. "Well?" he asked.

"You want to please me!" declared Marie, as if she'd just solved a fairly significant mystery of the universe.

"I do!" said Percy. "Of course I do!"

There was something decidedly sexual about Percy's response and I got the distinct feeling he was about to jump on my sister.

"I think our work is done here!"

Marie quickly rose to her feet and wrapped another piece of cake in some tin foil. She and Sharon exchanged a grateful hug and didn't my girl look happy with her piece of cake? That was surely for teatime tomorrow?

We said our goodbyes and made our exit. Messy fireworks were about to occur. I needed to get the hell out. I was now sober, so I got behind the wheel.

"I'll take you home," I said.

"You sure?"

"It's the least I can do! You saved my arse in there!"

I heard a loud ding and my 'Please Refuel' light was on.

"Sorry!" I said. "I need to put petrol in or I'll forget about it!"

"No problem!" said Sharon, blissed-out with cake and enjoying her first Wes adventure.

We stopped and I put £40 in. Having paid at the cash window, I turned round to find someone talking to Sharon through her car window. Trish had an uncanny habit of turning-up in the wrong places.

"Hello, Wes!" said Trish, looking very smug. "What a charming, young lady!"

"What are you doing here?"

"You're asking me what I'm doing at a petrol station? The same as you!"

"Why here? Why now? Are you following me?"

Trish laughed. Really laughed. I hadn't heard her laugh like that in ages. Was it genuine or the nervous jitter of a stalker. I couldn't tell.

"Oh, Wes, you are funny!" she said, sarcastically.

Trish waved at Sharon in the car, Sharon waved back, then Trish turned on her heels and got into her car, speeding into the distance.

I got back into my car and tried to make sense of what had just happened.

"An ex?" asked Sharon.

"Yes."

"I think she still likes you! She immediately came to talk to me, to find out who I was. If it was just a friendship, she would have come and talked to you!"

"You've done this before, right?"

"Social worker. It's what I was trained to do," replied Sharon, suddenly getting a million flashbacks of her past.

"But you ended-up in The City?"

"Couldn't take the stress!" she replied. "So much anger! So much sadness! So many broken marriages, broken families, broken people."

"And now?"

"My job is simple. I do it, get paid, go home. No stress."

Social Services' loss was my gain. This clever cookie could be an asset! But how was I going to bring a rejected woman into my social circle? I dropped Sharon back to their flat and she turned to look at me. I was literally petrified she was going to kiss me again. I was still recovering from the last kiss!

"Thanks for a lovely evening!" she said.

"Very funny!"

"No, serious!" she replied. "99.9% of the time, my dates finish and I'm either glad it's over, or I know I'll never see him again. With you, I'm not glad it's over and I know I'll see you again!"

"You will?"

"What?" she exclaimed, indignantly. "You don't want to be my friend?"

"Oh, I do!" I quickly replied.

"I know," she said, confidently. "I'm a smooth operator. You like that!"

I did. I really did. She was slick.

"Please don't kiss me again!" I pleaded.

She smiled. "You liked that, huh?"

There was no denying it. She winked at me and got out the car. Before closing the door, she stuck her head back in. "Shall we exchange numbers?"

It seemed harmless enough, so we did.

"I'm gonna need those healing hands of yours again!" she said.

I was too embarrassed and flustered to reply. She disappeared into her front door. Was I tempted? In truth, no! Cheating wasn't my thing. All I wanted was Roz. The crazy girl with the wild hair was more than enough for me.

Tuesday

Melvin had originally wanted us to go back to The Sanderson but had changed plans on Tuesday morning. Something new and very interesting had arrived in his inbox and he wanted us all to try it; a special night at a French restaurant way out west, close to Richmond. We knew nothing about the restaurant or the evening ahead. As usual, we were all totally in the dark but it didn't matter, we trusted Melvin implicitly.

Having said that, Baggers was always right! He'd found us a Romanian restaurant once, way up in NW10. The restaurant didn't look like much but the food had completely floored us! Low was so blown away, he wanted to talk to the chefs, and this was a man who worked in a high-class restaurant! What could these Romanian chefs tell him? Low had actually knocked on the kitchen door to ask a few questions.

"They make it with love!" said Low, scowling with disappointment. "That's not very bloody helpful!"

So, if Melvin told us it was worth visiting, it probably was!

When I arrived at the restaurant, Topper was already there, smiling, drinking a beer. He got up to hug me!

"Feels like I haven't seen you in ages!" he said.

I laughed. "Daft bugger! It's only been a few days! It's probably 'cause you've been away!"

I ordered myself a Kronenbourg and sat at our table.

"Well?" I asked, gulping beer too quickly. "How's it going?"

Tony The Jeweller had always been very precise and succinct. In his line of work, it was all about fine detail. Tiny parts, tiny jewels, tiny links. He always had a magnifying glass attached to his head. Modest home, modest workshop, modest lifestyle. Short sentences, simple thoughts, small gestures.

But he was changing! He wanted to scale up! He wanted to super-size his life! It was he who had mentioned all of us boys living together in a big house, with big walls and big paintings, and he was definitely ready to be more expansive. Spread his wings, in every way. It was his idea! I hadn't discussed it with the boys yet.

As he began to talk, I could immediately see; this was a different Topper. The body language was completely different! This was an animated, gesticulating man, waving his arms and flexing his fingers, like he was telling me some epic, biblical tale, though he was merely recounting his weekend in Great Yarmouth.

A very pretty waitress approached us. 'What a great face!' I thought to myself. She was bleached-blonde, tall, slender and graceful, literally gliding through life with such poise and elegance, I wondered what the hell she was doing in there! She looked like a high-powered diplomat, able to negotiate our future with a firm, assured hand.

"Our other friends will be with us shortly," I said.

She acknowledged, smiled and went to wait at another table. I liked her smile and she seemed to like mine. Something very strange was going on. I was becoming attractive to the opposite sex. Roz had me, Trish wanted me back, Sharon wanted to sample me, and now I had a waitress clearly making eye contact with me. What in me had changed? Are attached men attractive? And did I look and smell like an attached man?

"Her family are lovely people!" Topper began. "Real salt of the earth people! Her mum cooked us Sunday lunch! You should have seen my plate! It was like a sharing platter for five! Big slices of lamb and beef, the biggest potatoes I've seen in ages, huge Yorkshire puddings and she must have put her whole back garden on my plate!"

It sounded good! I was hungry.

"Her family didn't ask about Francine and me," he continued. "They wanted to hear about London, about my work, about my friends, about our adventures! Francine sat there, looking pleased as punch. She says I impressed them."

"And were you impressed?" I asked.

"I was!" he replied. "Lovely people! You can tell a lot about a person by their family, can't you? Those sexy women we date are probably going to grow up to become their mother!"

This was true. I was a clone of my dad. I thought about Roz's mum. What was she like? I would find out soon.

Mids strolled through the door, also looking very pleased with himself! This was a man with a new girlfriend, getting lots of sex and probably living life even larger than usual. He hugged us both.

"Just catching up with Tops," I said.

"You're looking well!" said Mids to Topper.

"I feel great!"

"Nah, mate!" said Mids, "You look really bloody well! Almost like a fully-developed adult!"

"Having a girlfriend is the best, isn't it?" said Topper.

"It certainly is!"

Mids waved my bottle in the air and the pretty waitress seemed to understand.

What was happening to my group of awowed singletons? They used to ridicule me mercilessly. None of them could understand why I needed a girlfriend. Why would I willingly ditch my freedom? And yet, here they were, both getting cosy with a woman, and talking about them in glowing terms! Were these two lovable rogues really going to get married before me?

Talk of marriage was premature. In truth, they barely knew these women, but they both looked in a state of rapture, both rambling and talking over one another, comparing notes on their new squeezes.

With me, it was accepted: I would always have a girlfriend. I had Roz. But if these two bumpkins became very attached, with all the additional complications that brought, the group would surely fall apart! If we were all off doing couple things; we (as a gang) would be no more; no dinners, no adventures, no holidays together. Surely not?

It made me sad; could that really happen? No, it couldn't! What was wrong with me? Such thoughts were pathetic beyond words! I stopped and took stock. It was a non-sensical fear. Friends make time for one another. Full stop. We had Melvin. Melvin set dates and times. Girlfriends would have to live with those arrangements!

"She makes me feel very powerful!" Topper continued. "As if I'm sitting on untapped potential. We talked about my skills and assets, talked about my hopes and dreams, and she made me realise I have good, attainable ideas. She's made me realise that I can actually push my plans forward. I don't have to tread water anymore!"

Mids and I stared at him. Tops had changed beyond all recognition, in just a matter of days! He was using words he never used! "She's very loquacious!" he said.

Mids and I turned to look at one another. He was in the grip of a literate woman. Not necessarily a bad thing.

While Topper and Mids carried on talking about their new girlfriends, I looked around the restaurant. Every table was full and there was an exceptionally noisy buzz of expectancy.

Low strolled through the door, looking triumphant. He hugged and greeted us all, but I could barely hear him above the hubbub. What had we walked into? Was it a party? Was it a showcase? I couldn't see any instruments or a mixing desk. Was it a performance? I couldn't see a stage.

It was almost 8.00. Melvin had told us to get there for 7.30. He was late! At 7.55, the one with the bags staggered the door, apologising profusely. I smiled at my lovely waitress again. "Can we get some more beers?" She nodded and smiled back at me. This was so strange. She really seemed into me.

At 8.00, a tall, handsome, grey-haired chef came through the kitchen doors and there was a loud and long round of applause! He waved down the adulation and spoke to us.

"We have prepared something very special for you all. Some fantastic dishes! Take time to savour them all. We hope you enjoy them? Dinner is served! Bon appétit!" More applause and the chef disappeared back into his kitchen.

"What is this?" I asked Melvin.

"Sit back and savour!" he replied, with a gleam in his eye

This was all part of the Melvin mystique. He loved plots and plans and surprises, and he loved the theatre of us not knowing what we'd let ourselves in for!

So, I sat back and enjoyed and, one by one, these dishes just came and came and came, each one more delicious than the last! Pate, sea food dishes, fish dishes, meat dishes, risotto, Sushi; a constant stream of delicious delicacies.

The excitable chatter continued at the other tables and, though we had much to discuss, conversation just couldn't take place. It was too noisy, there was too much food and, to be honest, with some of these dishes, you wanted to hold them on your tongue and moan softly.

Mids had called for the wine list and we were all now drinking very dry, very fruity and, no doubt, very expensive champagne. It was the necessary accompaniment for this remarkable food.

I turned to Melvin. "What is this?"

"A tasting menu!"

"Fuck me!" Not the cleverest thing I'd ever said but I was virtually at a loss for words. "It's too much, mate! Too much flavour, too many spices, my senses are being overloaded!"

Melvin laughed. "Shut up and enjoy it! He's one of best chefs in the UK. He's only here once a month!"

"We need to talk!"

Melvin nodded in agreement. "We'll find some quiet bar afterwards."

Mids and Topper finally stopped talking about their women and began to fully appreciate what they were eating!

"So tender!" said Topper, putting some steak in his mouth.

"Top drawer, Baggers!" said Low, who gave him an enthusiastic double thumbs-up, as he consumed a delicious piece of Dim Sum.

And when the plates finally stopped arriving, and we were all holding our fat bellies contentedly, the chef came back out to more rapturous applause.

"I hope you enjoyed that!"

"Bravo!" shouted someone from the back. Everyone laughed.

"We plan to come back here next month! Make sure you book early!"

The chef waved and, as the room burst into applause again, he blew kisses and went back into his kitchen.

It's not that I was stuffed full; my tastebuds were alight with excitement. I felt as though I had taken a trip around the world and sampled every cuisine. I looked again at Melvin. He was beaming! He loved getting it right and exposing his friends to new experiences. I was still licking my lips and contemplating licking my fingers too! In the different corners of my tongue, I could still taste a few of the dishes. Why have one dish when you can have 20? It made the standard menu look dull.

"Wow!" was all I could say. After that experience, I was feeling very good about life but, out of the corner of my eye, I could see a little conflict occurring. I tuned in my ears to see what was being said. Low was sat between Topper and Mids and, from what I could glean; Low was ridiculing their new relationships so they, in turn, had both turned on him. Low was leaning back in his chair as both Mids and Topper leaned in! Not that Low was scared of either.

"You do your thing, mate!" said Mids.

"I will! I'm just saying: don't imagine a woman is the key to your happiness. A woman can only give you so much. In the long run, it's down to you! Don't get too reliant on her! They can give you their love but, just as quickly, take it away!"

Christ, I really didn't want to get in the middle of this fundamentalist discussion. Single Man v. Married Man was an argument no one was winning. I didn't want to get into it. I wanted to talk about Lola and Sharon, I wanted to talk about The Amiable Alvin's prostate cancer and launching new businesses out of my shop and, of course, Melvin wanted to talk about his birthday party! We needed a nice quiet bar. It would take a while to digest all this rich food.

"Can't you just be happy for me?" asked Topper.

"I love you, mate! I'm trying to protect you!"

Christ, the 'trying to protect you' manoeuvre! A killer play!

If someone disagrees with you and you give them that 'trying to protect you' move; you'll be stuck in stalemate for a while!

I got up to see if I could attract our waitress's attention. I could see she was busy settling bills. Suddenly, the owner of the restaurant shouted the name, "Yvette!" in her direction and she turned round. She was with customers, so she motioned she'd be with him in a moment. Yvette. The perfect name for her.

My phone vibrated. A text from Sharon. "Where are you?"

"In a restaurant!" I replied. Why was she texting me? She would have to get out of that habit! I could not have women like that sending me random texts!

"Are you in the middle of one of your adventures?" Sharon asked.

To my right, I could hear raised voices. Low, Topper and Mids were all now standing up and the body language was not healthy! Topper and Mids were leaning in towards Low in a very aggressive manner, while Low was just standing back, smiling, being as provocative as possible, winding-up his mates because winding-up his mates was his idea of fun!

"You can be a fucking pain when you want!" said Topper to Low. "I finally meet somebody decent and you want to destroy it! Why? Why don't you want me to be happy?"

"I do!" said Low. "I do want you to be happy! That's the point!"

"Then stay the fuck away from me!" replied Topper.

This had got very heated very quickly! There would be no 'staying the fuck away'! We were family! We would work through our problems.

"Come on, guys," began Melvin. "There's a nice pub nearby with a garden terrace. Let's just chill."

"As long as we don't have to listen to relationship advice from this idiot?" said Mids, angrily pointing at Low who, for some very perverse reason, almost seemed to be enjoying the conflict. Sure, we'd had conflict before. Terrible arguments! But, come the end of the evening, we'd always been able to resolve it.

"Yes!" I replied to Sharon's text. "Another tense stand-off!"

"Send me the address!" she pleaded. It was insanity bringing a strange woman into my social circle but, in this instance, I actually needed Sharon's calm, objective viewpoint. I could put out the occasional fire but I was no fireman! She was a pro.

Yvette finally came to give us our bill and we all contributed. She and I didn't really say much but it was very polite and pleasant, and there was a lot of wholly organic smiling. I was making her smile and she was making me smile. I was not used to this.

For some bizarre reason, she seemed to be into me. She even made a point of putting a restaurant business card in my hard. "Book early for next month!" she said.

"We will!" I assured her.

And then we all ambled and stumbled down to this nice, quiet pub and plonked ourselves out in the garden. We were all very full and content after a big meal but there was also this simmering tension between Low and the two newly-coupled ones. A tension I had to break somehow! Topper and Mids couldn't even look at Low while he, cocky as ever, smiled as if no problem existed.

"Forgot to tell you!" said Mids to Baggers, "Jill says you can borrow the house for your birthday party. Heston is completely cool with it. He knows your friends will be fine."

Melvin almost looked overwhelmed with joy and gratitude. "Well, that's one item off the agenda! I wanted to talk about that and get your feedback?"

"Cross it off your agenda, son!" said Mids. "Jill is now a big fan of our group! Turn up for the books, eh? Remember how hostile she was?"

How could I forget? At one point, Jill had actually suggested I wasn't "good enough" for her Roz. How times had changed! And that made me think about Roz. Where was the crazy girl with the wild hair? I thought back to my Sunday afternoon with her. Her lips kissing my chest and down across my stomach. What a visual image I was getting!

"And, Tops," Melvin began, "the key bit of information we need to tell you: Jill also had a great idea for the party! She's going to get Raymond to make a short film about the party and we'll then mail it to all the guests!"

Topper looked struck by this. "That is a great idea! As long as he's not going to try and tell some story?"

"No story! No angle! No opinion!" said Melvin. "Just a record of the event; a little memento for my guests."

"Nice touch!" Topper added.

Everyone was talking in very clipped tones and there was still tension in the air. Mids and Topper were still seething, and Low knew it, but didn't really care!

"So, I've got the venue, I've got the booze, I've got the music, so what about the food?"

"Thai!" said Low.

"Mexican!" said Mids.

"BBQ!" said Topper.

I looked at them. Had they all deliberately said something different? Just to be difficult? More silence. No playful banter at all, just a painful silence.

"Come on guys," said Low, condescendingly, "Food is my thing!"

Christ, did he really just say that? We were all tip-toeing through a minefield. It was about to blow.

"You work in a restaurant but front of house, not in the kitchen!" spat Topper, in a very confrontational way. "You're not a chef! We all know as much about food as you!"

I was startled at the ferocity. Francine had given him a new confidence but also a gritty edge as well. He'd suffered a lot of shit from Low down the years but that was stopping right now! Low was shocked too. These words had rattled his chain. He glared at Tops, as if he wanted to say something cruel but was biting his tongue. How the hell had this escalated so quickly?

"You know as much about food as me?" said Low, getting very close to Topper's face.

"What the hell is going on here?" I shouted. The other drinkers in the garden turned round to see what was happening. This was out of character for me. I never raised my voice. "This is not us! A bit of banter is fine but this is getting personal! We're not a bunch of strangers, we've known each other most of our lives. This is us!"

"Yeah, this is us!" said Low, "But if these two go off and play happy families, what will happen to us?"

"Is that all you're worried about?" asked Mids.

"I had that same thought, Low. Trust me: I did! Even if there are three couples in this group, we can make it work. Friends make time for friendships!"

"Well, this is a lovely gathering!" said Sharon, striding through the garden door. Low looked very confused and turned to me. "Wezza, what is going on?"

"Sharon was at a loose end this evening ..."

"A loose end?" he said.

Shaped as she was, Sharon could do very little to hide her magnificent curves. The jeans hugged her every contour and the low-cut top was struggling with her bosom. She looked dynamite and she knew it. She wanted to make a good impression on the group. I'd talked about them enough the night before!

"Are you going to introduce us, Wes?" asked Mids.

"So, people, this is Sharon!"

Sharon smiled and curtsied.

"Me and Low met Sharon and her flatmate Lola last week at an event. And your mate Low decides he wants to get his end away with Sharon's friend Lola. So he books me into a double date at their flat!"

While Baggers and Mids shook their head in disbelief, Topper looked disgusted!

"And you went along with this plan, Wezza?"

"I did."

"Why do you humour him?" asked Mids.

"He's my mate and I love him."

I looked at Sharon. She was thrilled to be in the middle of another of my adventures. She and Lola probably got into a whole heap of trouble on a regular basis but this was different.

And then Low started getting upset with me! "Why is she here? This is one of our evenings. Just the boys! Why is she here?"

"The evening is not going well, Low." I began. "Our evenings together are always very pleasant."

"What's that got to do with me?" asked Low, getting ever more tetchy and glaring daggers at everyone.

Mids swigged from his bottle and took a deep breath. "What's it got to do with you? You poisoned the evening, son."

"Poisoned the evening? Bit dramatic, mate!"

"Tell me more about this double date!" said Melvin, anxious to hear some juicy details about Low's scandalous private life.

Sharon took up the story. "So, we cook dinner for these two! Well, Lola did. Her signature dish: corned beef and cabbage. And, once we'd had dessert and a little more bubbly, Low and my mate Lola disappear into her bedroom."

"And?" said Melvin, loving every moment of Low's discomfort.

"And," continued Sharon, gesturing towards me, "I thought I'd be able to lure your mate here into my bedroom!"

"And?" asked Melvin again.

"He turned me down!" She ran her fingers slowly down the sides of her body. "He turned down all of this!" She then she turned round and gave her arse a little wiggle, before turning full circle. "All of this!" she repeated.

Melvin looked at me and laughed. "Wezza! What the fuck were you even doing there?"

"Good question!" I said. "Thankfully, the evening introduced me to Sharon and, she won't mind me for saying, she is a diamond!"

Sharon smiled and blushed. "Aww, shucks!"

"We've double dated before!" began Low. "I've double-dated with all of you! At the end of the evening, you make your fun!"

"Oh, I get it!" said Sharon. "There's always one in every group. Low is the one with the questionable morals?"

"What the fuck have morals got to do with anything?" Now he was getting angry with Sharon, who looked non-plussed. "I'm a single man. End of story. If you wanna do it, we can do it! If you don't, that's cool too! What have morals got to do with it?"

"It's not even the morality!" said Topper. "It's his single man soapbox that gets me! If you want to be single, that's fine but, if I find a girl, don't tell me there's no point because she's going to break my heart!"

"Interesting!" said Sharon. "As you say, he's not amoral, it's more a mistrust of women and a general cynicism about relationships!"

"Hey!" shouted Low. "Who the fuck are you and why are you in the middle of our discussion?"

I could see the other patrons turning round to see if this was about to turn ugly. I managed to smile and wave my hands, as if to suggest this was a very minor dispute.

Just to antagonise Low, Sharon sat down and made herself comfortable. She smiled and looked around her. It was amusing to watch someone do a 'Low' on Low. Sharon suddenly noticed Melvin who, being non-confrontational, had been sitting in the corner trying to be invisible and hoping all the nastiness would die down.

"You're a lovely thing!" said Sharon. "You must be Melvin! I've heard all about you. In fact, I couldn't get your friend to stop talking about you! He loves you very much, did you know that?"

Melvin smiled and blushed slightly. "Yes, I know. We're very lucky to have each other."

"Yes, you are!" said Sharon. "I've known a lot of men in my time and, yes, I've become acquainted with a fair few, so I know what I'm talking about. Men don't express emotion at the best of times. So, when a straight man tells me he loves another man, that's big!"

"Why is she here?" asked Low, pointing a derisory digit in Sharon's general direction.

"She was at a loose end," I repeated.

"I don't get it!" said Low. "What purpose does she serve here?"

Sharon tutted loudly. Which aggravated Low. "What purpose do I serve? So, if we were fucking, I'd serve a purpose but, as we're not, I don't serve a purpose!"

"Why is she here?" Low repeated, looking at me with increasingly menace. I don't think I'd ever seen Low look so angry. We were all threatening the safety and security of his social circle. His gang was going up in smoke and it scared the shit out of him!

"She's trained for this kind of family conflict."

Low looked at me quizzically.

"I had a major problem with Marie and Percy last night, and this young lady was very helpful!"

Sharon sat back in her chair and offered a huge, toothy grin. "Ain't no one going to offer me a drink?"

"Christ!" said Mids. "Where are my manners?" And he disappeared into the bar to get in a round of drinks.

Melvin was still loving the sheer awfulness of last night and turned to Sharon.

"Sorry to keep asking questions but ... were you led to believe that Wes would be – how shall I put this? – a willing participant in this arrangement?"

At this point, Low knew he was about to be humiliated. He had dragged me into a difficult situation – God knows why! – and he had simultaneously inconvenienced three people ... just to get his end away! There was no point in him getting angry with anyone (about anything) when he had acted like such a prawn!

Topper relaxed. The conflict was over. Low was quiet. There was nothing more he could say. Low could no longer torment he and Mids, he could no longer berate me, and he could no longer question Sharon's involvement. Low knew why I'd invited Sharon: to quieten his arse down!

"I was led to believe," began Sharon, loving her moment in the spotlight, "that Wes was a very charming man, and that he is! I was led to believe that Wes and Low were on the same page. A double date. A double deed. But, oh no!" She pushed out her fabulous chest to illustrate the point. "Wes was not interested in these at all! He told me he was 'attached' which, of course, I totally respect. The funny thing is: I had a really good evening! I got to meet two of you, then I got to meet Wes's sister and her boyfriend, and here I am this evening! I feel like I've crossed into a parallel dimension; a group of handsome men who all love each other! This is wonderful! You will be great role models for future generations!"

Mids re-entered with a tray of drinks and immediately noticed a calm. He handed out the bottles and a lone glass of bubbly for Sharon. "Are we all good now?" he asked.

"I think we are," I said. "Sharon to the rescue again! I told you she was good!"

"And what about Roz?" said Low, still looking to cause trouble.

"What about her?" I said.

"Roz is a lucky woman, isn't she?" began Sharon. "I put it on a plate and he turned it down! Put it on a plate!" She adjusted her low cut top, just so her breasts would bounce a little. "Men don't turn this down!"

I could see Mids, Low and Topper trying not to leer at Sharon and failing miserably. It seemed ridiculous and inconceivable. What kind of man would turn it down? Lovelorn me! That's who.

Melvin was still on the edge of his seat, anxious to prise even more details from Sharon about Monday's lurid liaison. "So, what actually happened? Did you try to seduce Wes?"

"I did!" said Sharon, almost proudly. "I sat on his lap and my chest was against his. I could feel his heart beating. He told me he was 'attached' and I said I didn't mind if he was 'attached' but, when I looked into his eyes, I knew what he meant by 'attached'! It meant that Sharon should get off his lap!"

"You are my fucking hero!" said Mids.

I held out my arms, like a not-so-innocent footballer who's just raked his studs down an opponent's calf, "I am attached. End of story. It's me and Roz. We're a couple."

"Long may it last, I say!" said Low, sitting back down in his chair and straightening the collar on his shirt. He was now calm and composed, and could go back to provoking people.

"You don't mean that!" said Topper. "You don't want a relationship, you don't believe in relationships ..."

"They're not real!" said Low.

Everybody stopped and processed and absorbed these words.

"Relationships are not real?" asked Sharon.

"They're just friendships with a bit of sex thrown in. And, when the sex ends, the friendship dies, and the relationship gets shown up for what it was: a lie!"

We were all struck by this and paused again to think about his words.

Was he right? Maybe in some cases? In some cases, maybe some people were fooling themselves; deluding themselves into thinking they were tight? In some cases but not in my love affair! Oh, no! Not in mine!

"Luckily," I began, "my friendship with Roz is going very well. It's good. It's rich. It's strong. We're good friends. We keep it fun."

"Got to keep it fun!" said Sharon, with purpose. "That's why I plan to hang with Wes. I love his adventures!"

"Really?" said Low, cynically. "Are we stuck with you now?"

Sharon smiled and shook her head. A less confident woman would have responded quickly with something short and abusive.

"You know what, Tony? You will grow to love me. Because, one day, I will solve one of your problems!"

Low did not look convinced but suspected she was right. She was like a male version of him. Like him, she confronted danger and disarmed a situation. Like him, she was not afraid to roll up her sleeves. And, like him, she did as she pleased. The opinions of others did not affect her. I could see him appreciating her strength. They were both like two battle-hardened warriors.

"Alright," said Low, "you're in!"

Sharon smiled with satisfaction.

"What now?" said Low.

"What now? We still need to agree on cuisine for Baggers' party!" I turned to Melvin. "What do you fancy, mate?"

"Thai sounds nice!" He turned to Low. "Do you know someone?"

"Of course I do! Chefs pass through my restaurant, start their own catering companies."

"Are we all happy now?" said Mids, standing up and stretching. "After that bloody meal, I need my bed."

Melvin looked happy and relieved. "Thai it is!"

"What's the occasion?" Sharon asked Melvin.

"No special birthday!" he began. "I just love a party!"

"Who do I have to sleep with to get an invitation?" she asked.

"No one!" I assured her.

She looked disappointed.

Sharon had come straight from work, so she needed a lift home. I volunteered to drive her home. I barely knew this women but I liked the way she thought. She was incisive. She got right to the nub of a matter very quickly.

"What's happening on Saturday?" Topper asked Melvin. "What's the plan?"

"You'll get your itinerary on Friday, as usual!" he said, winking mischievously. He loved surprising us and we loved his surprises.

"I might have to duck out!" I said. "Percy is covering one of Alvin's gigs. An important annual gig! I might have to go along for moral support?"

"What's wrong with Alvin?" asked Low.

"I've been waiting for an opportunity to tell you: prostate cancer. He's started chemo and, naturally, he's feeling weak. He'll be out of action for a while!"

Everybody looked at me blankly. No one could speak. Always quick with a retort, Low had nothing. He looked deflated. "Christ!" he finally said. "Poor bugger!"

"It's Alvin!" I said. "He will beat it!"

"Course he will!" said Topper, with conviction. "Many beat it! Alvin will!"

Everyone was silent. I could feel Sharon looking at all of us. She was witnessing quite a poignant moment. We all liked The Amiable Alvin. Everyone did.

"I've been waiting for the right moment to tell you all," I said. "This evening has been a bit ... fractious?"

"Will you give him our best?" said Mids, trying to sound upbeat.

The Alvin news was quite shocking. I'd killed the vibe with a few words.

"Look! Go and get yourself checked! Roz made me promise I would and I did!"

"Checked?" asked Low, wincing.

"Yes, tough guy, checked!" I replied.

We all hugged and went our separate ways.

Sharon and I got into my car and I made sure the Bluetooth in my phone was on. I always expected calls. We'd only got a few miles down the road, when the phone rang. I could see the name 'Roz'. I put my finger to my lips, so Sharon understood I needed her to stay very quiet.

"Unexpected surprise!" I said.

"I needed to hear your voice!" said Roz, who sounded croaky and a bit choked-up.

"Are you okay?"

"I am so glad to be here!" she began. "I'm so glad I get to spend every day and night with The Elusive Wilson."

Sharon and I exchanged confused glances.

"I'm so glad to be spending this time with him because he was a poor excuse for a boyfriend and you're such a good boyfriend! He's an arrogant, self-centred shit! What did I ever see in him? He was never interested in me! If he has a heart, he keeps it to himself. Now that I've had connection with you, I realise I had no connection with him. He keeps it all to himself! He actually gives you nothing! You might think you're getting love but you're not! You're just getting enough affection to keep you locked down. There was no love. He keeps it all to himself. What's he saving it for?"

Sharon and I exchanged glances again. She put her hand under her chin, as if to suggest I should keep my chin up and encourage Roz to do the same!

"It's lovely to hear your voice!" I said, changing the subject and trying to sound upbeat. "I miss you!"

"God, I miss you!" she wailed. "I can't wait to open your ridiculous fridge, pull out some mad beer and just chill on your sofa. I'll be finished soon. I can't wait to get home, soak in a bath, sleep in my own bed, or your bed! Either would be nice?"

"You and me both!" I said. "Your little side table looks very sad and lonely. It misses your clutter!"

"I love my little side table!" she said, sounding even sadder. I wasn't really helping. I looked across at Sharon who still had her hand under her chin! Sharon's sign language for keep it light, keep it fluffy and keep it affectionate.

"When you get home," I began, "I promise, we can do lots of fun stuff, just you and me. We can go to the National Portrait Gallery! And eat in their lovely restaurant!"

"Aww, I love you, Wezza! I'm not gonna say it often because I don't want your big head to get any bigger, but I do! You are my secret getaway! When I'm with you, all of the madness disappears and all of the narcissists crawl back into their holes!"

I looked at Sharon. She had her hand on her heart, her signal I should express some emotion.

"I love you too, my little fruit bat! I cannot wait to pick your damp towel off my bed and mop up the flood in my bathroom!"

"Very funny, you swine! Look, I'm knackered. I'm going to bed. And no wanking!"

I looked at Sharon, she held her hands up, as if to say, 'You're on your own with this one, matey!'

"Really?" I asked.

"I'll be home soon. Love you!"

"Love ya too!"

Click. Gone.

Sharon and I exchanged another glance. She was puffing out her cheeks, as if in a state of disbelief. "Wow, she's really into you!"

"You think so?"

"Oh, yes!" said Sharon, assuredly. "Not only does she like you but you give her that safety and security women crave. When she's with you, she can relax and be herself. When she's with you, she feels safe. That's what women want."

I listened and absorbed and processed. It was good to hear that I was doing it right. You can't attend 'How To Be A Decent Boyfriend 1.01' at night school. We have to work it for ourselves, often using our father as a role model. Thankfully, my father was a kind man. He loved my mum and she loved being loved by him. My dad wasn't a mad, impetuous person. My mum would never have asked him to keep it fun and, if she had, he might not have known what to do, but he was always very kind, and kind to everyone, and my mother always looked very content; I'd catch them smiling at one another and that left a big impression on me. If they were still smiling, he was keeping it fun.

Sharon sat contentedly in the passenger seat, mulling over her thoughts; she was like my own personal Yoda. I liked having her around. How would I explain her to Roz? Personal trainers were acceptable but a personal Yoda? I couldn't see that flying!

"And what about tonight?" I asked.

"What about it?" she asked.

"Do we have a problem?"

"Nah!" she replied, dismissively. "It's a group of friends. You're not all going to be the same! Where's the fun in that?"

"Low winds people up! He loves winding people up! He can be really irritating!"

"So what?" she began. "Ignore him! Why do you let him bother you? I've only known your mate a few weeks! You've known him a lifetime! Why would anyone take relationship advice from a dog? He's a dog! No point him having a girlfriend; he'd only cheat on her! He's got a big dick and everything but Lola says it was like fucking a robot. She got nothing from him! No soul, no emotion, no conviction, no connection, no appreciation. She didn't feel like she'd been touched. It was just sex!"

It was shocking having Low's sexual performance dissected by a third party but, if you have sex with a woman, another woman's going to hear about it! You can be guaranteed! Who did Roz talk to? Who knew about my dimensions? What did it matter? She liked me and she couldn't wait to get back into my bed!

"The last decent man in London!" began Sharon. "To be riding in his car! How privileged am I?"

"Don't be daft!" I replied.

"I'm nearly 40! Time's running out!"

Despite being so clever, Sharon still had her own irrational insecurities. Even the wisest people have an inferiority complex. I dropped her to her front door and she kissed me softly on my cheek. She wasn't going to be putting any more moves on me. I was relieved. I went home to my small, empty house. There on the doormat were the normal utility bills and junk mail, plus a bawdy seaside postcard with an old married man and a young, blonde girl in a revealing bikini. On the back, it just had one word: resilient. My tenth word: resilient. Those ten qualities: was I really all those things? Roz was clearly lost in some teenage crush mist. Suddenly, from being a depressed reject, I was all ten of those outstanding characteristics. Yeah, I knew Roz liked me but this was over the top. I was a good boyfriend and, according to Sharon, the last decent man in London but all of those things? Really?

Wednesday

Our Hump Day was Wesday Wednesday and Max just couldn't wait! He'd invited his mates, as usual, a few girls he wanted to impress, plus a few club promoters. Not sure why he'd invited club promoters? He didn't play the mad music I played. Maybe he just wanted to impress them with the company he kept?

It gave us a chance to show that our gear actually sounded good and, even though we were playing it pretty damn loud, our neighbours left us alone because we were almost bringing people to the area.

The morning was really frantic! Lots of enquiries, lots of quotes. Hopefully, at a later date, concrete bookings? Not that we weren't busy! Customers were picking up gear and dropping off gear, getting all excited at the prospect of being DJ for the night at their local church hall, village fete or school disco.

One young man came in with his dad and this was clearly going to be his debut appearance at his school. He had all his music on two memory sticks, now all he needed was some gear.

"You can't really make a living out of being a DJ, can you?" asked his father.

"I am surrounded by people that do!" I replied.

The father didn't look convinced. "I'd still like him to go to university!"

"Universities always need good DJs!"

Now, the father looked very alarmed. "I won't be sending him there just to play music!"

"Better he does that than drinks away his student grant! If he's the DJ, drinks are free!"

The father liked the logic of this a lot. He put his arm round his son. "There you go, Adam!" he said. "You can do it all: your degree, DJ in the evening and your drinks will be free!"

The son looked very relieved that his father was coming to terms with his passion. He couldn't wait to carry the CDJs into his father's car! In his eyes, these grimy, black boxes were the key to his future! If only he knew? With practice, he could be as much of a failure as me!

I looked in the diary, The Amiable Alvin's next gig was the following Saturday. I couldn't see him being ready for that either. I quickly sent a text to Percy. I needed The Lanky One to put it in his diary. He quickly fired back a text saying he would. I looked at the gig details. It was a large and very grand 60th at a posh hotel with a special requirement for "extra Motown". This was something Percy could do with ease.

I definitely did not want to be gigging every Saturday night, so I needed Alvin to get well soon and I needed Percy to step-up! Marie was unlikely to be happy about this but, if she missed him that much, she did have the option to go with him! When did she last go out, anyway? The night she met Percy! Months ago!

My music knowledge was for emergencies and special occasions only. I needed my weekends. I had a girlfriend. Girlfriends need dates and good times, so I couldn't have a diary full of grubby gigs. I really needed an extra body; an enthusiastic amateur, like Percy.

I looked around the shop. It looked grimy and dishevelled as ever. If we were going to continue with these day-time raves every Wednesday, I needed to find some time to clean (or find a cleaner!) Maybe a big bunch of flowers wouldn't go amiss? Rather we smelt of lilies than stale beer!

Belinda The Rescinder turned up at 12.45 and I was happy to see her! Her tuna and sweet corn baps were doing my head in! I dreamt about them!

"I'll take two!" I said.

"Hungry?" she asked.

"Starving!" I said. "And I'll take two of your breakfast baps for Max! He posts pictures of them on his Snapchat account!"

Belinda smiled. Thankfully, she didn't find me attractive!

"Did Mids ever call you?"

"He did!" she replied. "I'm taking some stuff to him on Friday evening! Some of his regular customers are coming over for a tasting. I'm making him traditional, thinner triangles. Delicate little nibbles, not these door-stoppers!"

"I love your door-stoppers! I might even sneak in there and pretend I'm a client!"

Belinda looked amused by my madness. "You could buy an extra one for later?"

"Now, why didn't I think of that? I'll take three!"

"Three, Wes? You'll get sick of them!"

"I'll cross that bridge when I get to it!" I needed fortifying for Wesday Wednesday.

I'd been deliberating a theme and I'd decided it might be fun to hit them with some classic house? What was Max's birth date? Something ridiculous like 1999! The first house tunes were made before he was born! This would be fun! I had a little section at the back of a record box devoted to classic house. 'Someday' by Ce Ce Rogers and 'The Promised Land' by Joe Smooth were about to cause mayhem!

Just after 1.00, Max's crew started drifting in. Just to warm up the speakers, I put on 'Voodoo Ray' by A Guy Called Gerald. Oh my god! How good did it sound? I could see by the puzzled looks, absolutely no one knew the tune but they were loving it! Max and his crew started jerking involuntarily which, to them, was probably dancing! As ever, curious passers-by began sticking their head in, wondering what the hell was going on and, fairly soon, there were people actually dancing in the shop. Two tall guys with thick, chaotic locks put their thumbs up in appreciation and got into the groove!

The object of the exercise was to encourage trade, so Max was moving to the music, chatting with his mates, filming on his phone and posting it (immediately), and giving out business cards to anyone that stuck their head in. Two young mothers wheeled their pushchairs straight through the door and just stood there, drinking Frappuccino and nodding their heads. They looked old enough to remember these tunes but, with the bass drum pounding, their poor toddlers were probably wondering if they'd stepped inside a volcano?

After three hours of Chicago, Detroit and New Jersey nu-wave disco, I gave the decks to Max, so I could get on with some work, although phone calls would not be an option. I replied to my e-mails and scanned through the random texts that people had sent me.

Low had sent me some dirty jokes, Mids had sent me a photo of a bottle of wine, Topper had sent me holiday snaps of he and Francine in Great Yarmouth, while Baggers had sent me a photo of a shirt, asking me if I liked it. It was grey with bold, black, vertical stripes. I was no expert but it looked smart and eye-catching. In the absence of Roz, I was happy to let Melvin buy my clothes. I sent him a text saying I liked it and he said, "Good. I've bought it already, it was on sale. Dirt cheap!" In Melvin's world, 'dirt cheap' could mean £60 but, if he was happy buying me shirts, I was happy.

Wendy had taken to sharing medical jokes, sent to her by the doctors and nurses in her world. I'm sure I was missing a few of the nuances but I was happy to be in her circle. And now Sharon was sending me all manner of madness; eye-popping memes that would make a sailor blush but she was not the kind of girl to be shocked by anything. She was certainly a character! I thought about the lovely photos on the walls of her flat, taken by her brother, and I wondered if she had any other creative brothers?

"Bit of a random text," I began typing, "but do you know anyone that makes music?"

"Yes," she replied. "My brother Solomon has a nice little set-up in his house. Why?"

Well, well, Sharon was turning into quite a find, and if I could hook-up Max and her brother, the odd text from Sharon would not look too suspect.

"I've got this bright kid working in my shop, who is turning into quite a DJ star (on his scene.) His next move is to make music. Do you think Solomon would be interested?"

"I will ask him," replied Sharon.

We were shutting the shop at 6.00, so Max played his last tune and, after a million elaborate handshakes, the shop emptied. Still buzzing from the day, Max went off to the pub with his mates and, just as I was about to turn off the lights and shut up shop, I could feel Trish in the doorway.

"Hello!" she said, innocently, trying not to seem as if she was about to interrogate me and find out my every move over the last week. "How are things?"

"Good!" I said, vaguely, knowing it would irritate and frustrate the hell out of her.

"Who was that Sharon girl?"

"Not that it's any of your business!" I said, sternly.

Trish knew full well that it was none of her business but she badly needed to know about this new player in the game.

I locked the shop, pulled down the shutters and began walking to my car. Trish followed me.

"What? Am I spending the evening with you?" I asked.

"How you got any plans?"

She knew I had no plans. With Roz out of town, I was about to go home and mope, and Trish knew it!

"I'll buy you dinner?" she offered, hoping this would butter me up and act like some kind of truth serum.

"I want pizza!" I said, sounding like a spoilt child.

She needed my co-operation, so she wasn't about to argue.

We ordered the food and sat in the restaurant waiting for it.

"Low and I met two girls at a corporate event. Your friend Low took a shine to one of them and, instead of just calling her and making a date, he decides to create this double date situation for the four of us!"

Trish looked amused but also disgusted with me.

"A double date with Low? That's only headed in one direction! So, did you shag her?"

"Not that it's any of your business!" I repeated.

Trish knew she was being a nosey cow and, having left me in the lurch, she knew she had absolutely no right to ask me anything, but she was going to anyway.

"You don't know me very well, do you?"

Trish sniggered. "I've known you long enough, haven't I?"

"Well, that's pretty sad, love, because you clearly weren't paying attention!"

"You're a man!" she said, blithely.

It was all coming back to me. Despite the fact that she was older and wore the trousers, I'd always found Trish naive, as if she were living in a black and white movie, while we'd all graduated to the brave new world of colour.

In her world, she was her mother and I was a pale imitation of her father. In her world, men were predictable, slaves to their genitals, not noticing that her own boyfriend was quite happy being faithful. It made me quite angry to hear her nonsense again. It brought back bad memories.

"Ah, the bad old days," I began. "You think I'm still that person, don't you? I'm not. I'm not just Marie's little brother. I'm not just your shadow. I'm not just your tag-a-long accomplice. And I'm not that clichéd man. That's not me. If you knew me, you wouldn't ask that question."

"Don't give me that, Wes! You're a man! Who could resist those huge boobs?"

Anybody looking at us must have thought we were a couple. Roughly the same age. Dressed similarly (jeans and T-shirt.) From our body language, anybody could have seen we weren't strangers. We were interacting like old friends, bickering like lovers, and yet this was the woman who had walked out on me! Left me twisting in the wind for six months and then returned home, with her tail between her legs, acting like nothing had happened.

This was the woman who had decided I wasn't ready to be a father and, for that reason, had gone AWOL for six months to decide if I was the right man for her! Me, like an idiot, I'd actually waited a while. And then I'd met Roz, who'd showed Trish up for what she was: naive.

"Is this how it's going to be from now on, Trish?"

"What?" she replied, feigning innocence.

"Are you now going to be documenting my sexual encounters and rifling through my rubbish bins?"

"I don't care who you shag, stupid boy! I'm just trying to protect you!"

Well, well! The 'trying to protect you' manoeuvre! These are the words of someone who thinks they know better than you. The words of someone who wants to control you. And, in Trish's case, the words of someone who wants to put you back in your little box, where you belong.

I didn't plan on being Trish's lapdog again. I was done with dysfunctional relationships. Roz and I were going try something new: happiness. It was ambitious but it was worth a go.

The pizza arrived and we took it to my car.

"Where are we going Trish?"

"Your place?"

I sighed as silently as possible. "Okay, we'll eat this pizza and then I'll drive you home."

"Why?" asked Trish. "Have you got a hot date with those huge tits?"

What had I seen in Trish? What had I honestly seen in this woman? Maybe, when I was young, I was grateful to have a girlfriend but, with hindsight, it got me thinking: what the hell was the attraction?

She was pretty enough, shapely enough, smart enough but why had I fallen so deeply in love? Why had her disappearance caused me such pain? With hindsight, was she really all that? Driving in my car, listening to her irrational nonsense, I understood why Low stayed single! Amazing! We'd dated for so many years and she still didn't know me.

"There's nothing between me and Sharon. I can't do what single men do. I'm not made like that. I don't have the confidence. I don't have the blarney. And you should know that!"

"You're a man, Wes! End of story. She's a beautiful woman with big breasts: end of story!"

In most cases, Trish was right. In most cases, most men looked temptation square in the eye and went, "Ah, fuck it!" Sharon was not used to men turning her down. But how right was Trish? Did 'most cases' mean 70%? 80% of cases? Maybe more? But, not me! Poor, sad, insecure me! I had turned it down! Why? Because I'd struck gold: the crazy girl with the wild hair, and I wasn't going to jeopardise it!

There was only way to straighten this out!

I called Sharon. "What you doing?"

"Nothing," she replied.

"I need you for a couple of hours."

"Another Wes adventure?"

"Something like that."

I gave Sharon my address and looked across at Trish, who was in a state of shock. "What did you do that for?"

"To shut you up!"

"This won't prove anything!" she said.

"When you meet Sharon, you will see; that will be all the proof you need! This is a woman who takes what she needs! This is a woman who is not used to being turned down but I did!"

"So, why do you get on so well?"

I thought about it. Why did we get on so well? Subconsciously, we assemble a cast of characters, all with different strengths. We create a circle of friends who each bring something different into our lives. I had Low, Mids, Topper and Baggers, I had Max, Alvin, Courtney and all my crew at work, I had Percy and Marie, and now I had Roz! And, through Roz, I had Wendy and Jill and, at some stage, Heston, Raymond and Benjamin would become part of my circle. What a motley crew! And now I had Sharon! My own personal Yoda!

"We get on well because she's a real person. A wonderful whirlwind of a woman! And I want people like that in my life!"

Trish looked at me as if I was talking another language. The taming of this shrew seemed aeons ago! She did not remember this Wes! Within myself, I still felt insecure and insignificant but, compared to how I used to be, I was a titan of industry! Compared to how I used to be, I was now a major dick-swinging playa!

"You didn't have to bring her into it!"

"Oh, I did! Besides, she loves my world! For her, we're a soap opera! She got to see Percy and Marie go at it on Monday, she got to see Low being a pompous idiot last night, and tonight she will meet you!"

"I'm not a performing seal!" Trish replied, indignantly.

I wanted her to feel like a freak show because that's what she'd become: a pantomime villain; a ridiculous figure of fun, stalking me on petrol station forecourts to see what I was up to. I wanted her to experience the full force of Sharon, in all her tactless, busty glory.

We arrived at my house and sat down to enjoy pizza. Even though I'd had two of Belinda's baps, I was still hungry. (I'd have the third one for breakfast!) I tore into slice after slice but Trish picked at her one slice, almost too nervous to talk, as if she could feel the storm approaching.

My mouth was full, so I didn't want to talk, but Trish wasn't making any conversation, so I chattered away. I talked about every subject that might make Trish feel jealous and/or uncomfortable: Roz, my new record label, Saturday's adventure, our forthcoming holiday plans. Am I spiteful? Maybe I am? I don't have many bad qualities but this girl was really irritating me! I hated the way she thought she knew me! She didn't know me! And now her image of me was contradictory! Back in the day, she viewed me as a pliable wimp and, now all of a sudden, I was a heartless Casanova! Really, love?

She looked around my kitchen to see what had changed. What in my life had turned me into this impudent, thoughtless monster? She bit into her slice of pizza and chewed it absent-mindedly. I got up to get us drinks. Inside my fridge, I now had potent, European beer and (courtesy of Mids) the odd impressive bottle of wine. I poured her a glass of Chablis and she gulped at it thirstily.

"No need to drag her into this," she mumbled.

Too late. The plan was in motion. My box of tricks was on her way. I really got a good feeling from this girl. Sharon was like the final page of the book. She saved you reading it by getting straight to the conclusion, the point and the moral simultaneously. Whatever scrape you'd got yourself into, Sharon would rescue you with her no-nonsense approach to problems. If your brain was confused, Sharon would literally reach inside your head and untangle you. I got the feeling Sharon was going to play a part. I didn't need her for sex but I knew I'd need her.

There was a knock at the door. Sharon had got to mine in double-quick time. She just couldn't wait for the next instalment of her soap opera. She hugged me warmly and strode into the kitchen, holding out her hand. Trish shook it. Sharon was grinning from ear-to-ear. She could barely contain her excitement. What was this new plot twist?

"The jealous ex!" she said, triumphantly.

Trish turned and glared at me. "What have you been saying?" She did not look happy.

"Wes hasn't told me anything! I've got two eyes. I've got a brain. I can see what's happening here!"

"Me? Jealous?" protested Trish.

"Save it, darling! I've been in your shoes. I had a good man once. He wasn't much to look at but he loved me! He loved me! I thought I could do better, so I dumped him. I told my friends that he wasn't 'ambitious', I told my friends that I'd 'outgrown' him. A few months later, I started to miss him! Too late! He'd found himself a new girl. And she wasn't much to look at either but she loved him ... and he loved her."

Sharon took her coat off and slung it over a chair. Still standing and smiling, she looked around the kitchen. Not much to look at, so she sat down and made herself at home, wiggling her arse into a comfortable position. Trish could not hide her disdain. Not only was this gorgeous woman in my life, she was comfortable in my kitchen and felt quite at home in my personal life!

"Here!" said Trish, gesturing towards me. "You've found yourself another good man!"

"He turned me down!"

"Really?" said Trish, still unable to believe that I had.

"Put it on a plate for him!"

"So, why are you here?"

Sharon laughed loudly. She was beginning to see how damaged Trish was. "Why am I here?" she asked. "To meet you! I plan to meet everyone in Wes's world. All of my mates have got married, or moved away, or just turned into cat ladies! My family are a bunch of spongers! My flatmate Lola's the only fun person I know. So I am very happy to know Wes. He's quality, isn't he? Why did you let him go?"

Trish slumped into one of my kitchen chairs and picked up her cold slice of pizza. It didn't seem very appetising, so she put it back down. Trish had no answer, or no answer she wanted to confess to a total stranger. She looked up at Sharon, who still perched on the edge of her seat. "Why did I walk out? I'll tell you one day."

"The thing is," began Sharon, "whatever you've got to say, I bet I've been there before! Look at me! Been with so many men and I'm still single! It would knock most people's confidence but not mine! I know my prince is out there! He's probably stuck in traffic on the North Circular Road!"

"Can I offer you something to drink?" I asked.

"You sure can!"

I opened my fridge, which was still full to the brim with a million exotic bottles.

"Fuck me, Wes! Expecting company?"

"My parents always had a full fridge."

"Got any bubbly?" asked Sharon.

"That's a good idea!" I said. "Let's celebrate!"

"Celebrate what?" said Trish, looking thoroughly fed-up.

"New friendships!" said Sharon.

I popped a bottle of Prosecco and poured some into a flute.

Sharon picked up a slice of pizza and bit into it. "And not just him!" she continued. "His friends are quality too! You walked out on a man with his own business and a good circle of male friends? Sounds like a keeper to me!"

Trish had had more than enough of my friends. They tolerated her because she was my girlfriend but, when she walked out on me, they were quick to turn. Melvin, in particular, had always felt she emasculated me which, of course, she had! Ironically, despite being gay, he was our expert on masculinity! These days, she couldn't count on a cordial relationship with my mates; they were frosty, at best. She was the ex that had walked out on me. Their loyalty was strong and touching.

"Oh, yeah!" said Trish, sipping from her glasses, and then downing it in one. "They're a delightful bunch!"

"Ah, yes! Your relationship will be strained for a while."

Trish looked at her in disbelief. "Who are you and how do you know so much about us?"

"As I say," said Sharon, finishing one slice and tucking into another, "I've got two eyes and I've got a brain. And, anyway, this is not an uncommon scene. As we speak, this is happening all round the world: the man, his friends, the new girlfriend, the ex-girlfriend. It's an old story!"

There was something disconcerting but compelling about Sharon's outlook on life. She felt like she had the answer to every question. I was so glad she was my own personal Yoda! I could see Trish twitching, as if she wanted to ask her a question. She was sorely tempted to see if Sharon had any perspective on her situation.

"So, in my situation, what do I do?"

Sharon bit into her second slice and thought. I sat there enthralled. It was fascinating to watch these two women communicate. Trish didn't even want to be in the same room as this woman but, here she was, asking Sharon to look into her crystal ball.

"In your situation," she began, "I'd busy myself with work; unless you want more uncomfortable evenings like this? The thing is: things change. That's the only thing in life you can count on! Change! People change! Relationships change! Feelings change! Circumstances change! Who knows who I'll be dating in six months? It might be one of Wes's mates? Who knows? Wes doesn't know where he'll be!"

And, at that moment, Sharon's sagacity began to lose its charm! No, I didn't know where my relationship was headed, but I didn't need reminding. All my fears and doubts began flooding back. I'd finally struck gold but now I was jittery.

Sharon wasn't finished. "In your situation," she continued, "I'd just hang in there! You never know what's going to happen?"

And that seemed to pacify Trish. These were some cryptic yet calming crumbs of comfort. I didn't like the thought that she was now encouraged and, with Sharon's words echoing in her ears, should I mess up my relationship, Trish would be there to pounce! The thought of going out with Trish again terrified me! It appalled me and actually repulsed me! Who the hell wants to drive in the middle lane? I want sixth gear and the open highway!

Sharon sat and looked around my kitchen. "Bit threadbare!"

"Typical single man's kitchen," I said.

"But you weren't single for many years!" Sharon looked at Trish and gestured towards her. "And this was your woman. Was your relationship a bit threadbare too?"

Trish stood up. "You can't say stuff like that!" she shouted at Sharon. "You don't know us. You don't know any of us!"

The kitchen door swung open and there stood Roz, wearing my dressing gown. "What's all the noise?" she said, bleary-eyed. "Some of us are trying to sleep!"

Suddenly, she caught sight of the pizza and walked towards it. We all watched her. She tore off a slice and bit into it. She gobbled hungrily. "Shouldn't really be eating this late!"

I think I felt a bit embarrassed. There were two women in my house. I had some explaining to do. I was rooted to the spot, watching Roz finish slice one and bite into slice two. She put a greasy hand on my head and ruffled my hair. "Hey, baby!"

We watched her walk over to the fridge. She opened it. "Too much choice!" she said. She tugged at a cold bottle of beer, closed the fridge, opened the bottle and swigged from it. There was one place left to sit at my kitchen table, so Roz plonked herself down. "Well, this is a cosy party!" We dare not speak.

She pointed at Trish. "You: I know." Then she pointed at Sharon. "You: I don't know."

"Long story!" said Sharon.

"Is it a good story?" asked Roz.

"It involves Low being a total knob!"

Roz laughed. "What's new?"

I'd managed to compose myself. "You're here!"

"I am," said Roz. She stopped eating and looked quite sad and then quite angry.

"Last night, he knocked on my door. Last night, he actually thought he could just knock on my door and I would let him in. After everything. Despite the fact I've got a boyfriend." She tossed her pizza slice down with disgust, as if she was now – finally – dissolving her friendship with The Elusive Wilson.

Roz suddenly realised that Trish and Sharon were not up to speed. She addressed both of them. "I've been on location with this guy I used to date. Well, not date, we went out for two years."

The two women nodded and waited for the rest of the story.

"I won't work with him again," she continued. "He actually thought he could knock on my door and treat me like some piece of skirt." She looked at me. "Do you know how disrespectful that is?" She looked at the two women. "Do you know how that made me feel?" Rhetorical questions. We sat and listened.

"I packed my stuff and got on the first train. I can do the rest of my work over the phone or online. I won't work with him again." She swigged from her bottle of beer. We could see a look of absolute disgust on her face. "Yeah, we dated! Yeah, we were close ... but he made it very clear ..." she paused for emphasis, "... he made it very clear that he didn't want a future with me. 'I don't do that lovey-dovey stuff!' he would say. So, we went our separate ways. We wanted different things. And yet, after everything, he still felt he could knock on my door! How arrogant and self-centred is he?"

It was getting late. Roz looked weary.

"So," she continued, "enough about me! What were you all talking about?"

We all looked at each other, wondering who would lie first.

"Shall I go first?" asked Sharon.

Trish and I must have both looked relieved.

"I met Wes at a corporate function a few weeks ago. Met Low there too! And Wes was saying that he had a talented DJ working in his shop who needs to start making music, and my brother Solomon has a nice little studio set-up in his flat."

Roz smiled at me. "My clever boyfriend!" Then, she turned to Trish and looked at her quizzically. "And why are you here?"

Trish was not good at lying, she never had been, and she wasn't about to start lying. She looked at Roz, hoping for some sympathy. Roz just needed an answer.

"I'm trying to work out what I'm supposed to do."

Roz nodded. She understood. Trish wasn't getting any sympathy but Roz was happy with that response. It was a bit icky and possibly too honest but at least it wasn't flannel and bullshit. She nodded. "I hear ya. When The Elusive Wilson told me I didn't have a part to play in his future, I was like, 'Shit, what do I do now?' I just got on with my life, you know?"

"That's what I told her!" said Sharon. "I've been there! Invested a lot of time!"

"Take it from us," said Roz, in an almost sisterly fashion.

God, it was surreal! My current giving my ex relationship advice, with a naughty third party sat close by! Did Roz ever have to know the Sharon story? In a way, it was best if I told her early doors. Didn't want it waiting in the wings, ready to leap out at any stage! After all, I had behaved nobly, but it might put Sharon in a bad light! Intuitively, I knew this woman was going to be useful in a number of ways.

Roz thought for a second. "But why are you all here eating pizza?"

At this point, I thought I should interject, to convey the image that I had designed the evening. "Sharon was at the shop," I began. "We were talking music. Trish arrived at the shop but I definitely didn't want to trawl through old details with Trish all night, so I dragged Sharon back here to keep the conversation light."

"And if a man offers to buy me dinner, I'm saying, 'Yes!' Sharon smiled and still looked very pleased to be in the middle of my adventures.

Roz was too tired to smile and nodded. "Okay!" she said. "I'm going back to bed."

"I quickly need to drop the girls home."

Roz nodded. She would have to get used to her man being busier. With The Amiable Alvin out of action and Max's music career in my hands, I was going to have to become something I'd never been: dynamic!

"Good night all!" she said, waving feebly and wandering back upstairs.

We all looked at each other. We'd all lied to Roz. We all looked quite sick with guilt. With a choice selection of grimaces, I think we all now had an understanding; we were never going to get into this situation again. No more lying, especially to Roz!

Thursday

In the middle of Thursday afternoon, Percy bowled into the shop looking as pleased as a crate digger who's found a tune that's been eluding him for years! He stood in the middle of the shop, arms folded, grinning like a teenager with a dirty secret.

"Hello, mate!" I said. "To what do we owe this pleasure?"

Max looked at him with amusement. Max found Percy very funny. Who wouldn't? Not only did he smell like a department store after shave department, but he was wearing a bright yellow handkerchief in his breast pocket, and was now sporting a stylish manbag over shoulder, big enough to carry headphones, CDs, memory sticks and essentials.

"What you looking so happy about?" I asked.

"This time, last year, I was a bored, single, lonely, bus driver. Today, look at me!"

We did. It was a faintly ridiculous sight but we were happy for him. His quiff was positively bouncing with glee.

"You ready for Saturday?" I asked.

"I am!" said Percy confidently. "That's my era! I've got it all. I used to have a mate at Virgin Records near Tottenham Court Road. He kept me abreast of everything. I've got all these cool 12-inch singles that came and went very quickly. Picture discs, colour discs, shaped discs; it was an exuberant time!"

"Waldo can be quite challenging!"

"Don't worry, Wes. I've got it all."

Well, this was a turn-up for the books! A few days ago, I was sorting out his relationship (well, Sharon was) and here he was – 48 hours later – telling me not to worry. But I wasn't out of the woods yet. I had a few gigs that needed a DJ and I was short on personnel. I might need a new employee?

"How about next Saturday? You okay for that?"

"No problem, Wes!" said Percy, opening his manbag and producing a KitKat, which he proceeded to offer out. We both declined. Max and I were both still stuffed from Belinda's baps and her new line in Danish pastries.

"I suppose that's why I'm feeling so good," he said. "For the first time in my life, I've got it all: job, career and girlfriend! I've got it all!"

He smiled again and chomped down his KitKat, standing tall and proud in the middle of our shop floor.

"Max will make you a cuppa!" I said.

Max dived into the kitchen, and this allowed me to talk about adult stuff that Max didn't want to hear.

"Is everything good with Marie?" I asked.

Percy smiled which, naturally, worried the hell out of me! Marie is my sister, after all!

"Things are good and, I suppose, that's another reason I'm so happy! Think I've finally got the hang of this boyfriend thing! I've had girlfriends in the past. We all have. When I was younger, I didn't know what I was doing. I do now! I know how to treat a woman."

I was half-tempted to ask him for his theory but I wondered if it would change our employer/employee dynamic. I'm meant to know more than him, damn it! But curiosity got the better of me.

"So, what do you think, Percy? How do you treat a woman?"

Percy pointed up at the sign on my wall. Our shop motto. Whatever makes them dance. "You created that sign, Wes! You know the secret! Do whatever is necessary to make it work. If you want it to work ... it can work!"

"Of course!" I said, calmly, completing forgetting that I'd written and created that sign. "Whatever makes them dance."

"Marie and I are good. When you left the other night, I turned to your sister and I said, 'We can't keep dragging Wes into our nonsense!' We shouldn't need help. Not from anyone! If it goes awry, that's normal. If it goes sour, that's normal."

Roz had made me a better man and Marie had definitely turned Percy into a decent, upstanding citizen. He finished his KitKat, licked his fingers and tossed the wrapper into a bin. Max came back with his cuppa, which he gratefully accepted.

"And it feels good to be part of this family. This little DJ fraternity we've got. You boys understand me. You know what it takes to make people feel good and want to dance."

We did. I'd never thought about us as a family but we were: me, Max, Percy, Alvin, Courtney and the crew; a merry band of travellers, making people smile, sing, dance, fall over, get up again and carry on dancing. We had a role to play.

I looked to my right. There was an imposing man standing in the doorway. He had one of those Cruise/Clooney Hollywood handsome faces, and he was wearing designer jeans, tan suede loafers and a navy cashmere crew neck. He almost didn't want to come in.

Percy broke the silence. "Come in, my friend. How can we help you?"

The man sauntered in and looked around him. He finally focused on me and seemed to recognise me.

"Where is she?" he asked.

This was Wilson. Not so elusive. Here he was: in the flesh.

Max and Percy had no idea what was going on.

"Where is she?" he repeated. I looked at him. He really was as self-centred as she had described. No 'Hello, my name's Wilson.' No handshake. No formalities. No grace. No manners. And no communication skills either! I stared at him, which made him angry. It was truly a pleasure to watch this narcissist suffer. He definitely wasn't the centre of my universe!

"I need to talk to her."

"Call her!" I said, confidently.

"She won't pick up. I went to the house; she's not there."

"Do you know who I am?" I asked.

"Yes," he said. "You're Wes. She's told me about you. Showed me photos."

"I'm not just Wes," I said. "I'm her boyfriend and, as her boyfriend, it's my job to protect her from people like you!"

"People like me?" smirked Wilson.

"The ex-boyfriends," I said. "The ex-boyfriends who still think they matter."

Wilson fixed me with a confrontational look. This dickhead was actually going to stake his claim.

"We've been talking," he began. "About old times."

"Really?" I said, with as much sarcasm as I could muster.

"I've had a change of heart."

"That's nice for you, mate!"

I'd never met anyone so arrogant. He made Benjamin seem modest and self-effacing! Max and Percy could barely believe what they were seeing, while I was having enormous fun aggravating this enormous tool.

I pointed to myself. "I am boyfriend." I pointed to him. "You are ex-boyfriend. You had your chance. You blew it!"

"We've been talking!" he repeated, this time more forcefully. "She has good memories of me."

This idiot was beyond help. He couldn't quite grasp that he had missed the boat and, by knocking on her door last night, he'd done something inappropriate. In his tiny mind, all women were in orbit around him.

Wilson stiffened his back, as if he was about to say something important. "We were in love."

"I think you'll find," I began, "that she may have been in love with you and, had you reciprocated, you'd still be an item."

"That's not true!" he shouted.

At this point, my security team took one step forward. To his right, Wilson could suddenly feel both Max and Percy breathing down his collar. He looked up at Percy, who looked more strange than menacing.

"That's not true!" he repeated, much more softly. "We were in love."

I held the aces and I didn't even need Sharon!

I'd dealt with the trite and mawkish Benjamin, and now I was going to deal with The Elusive Wilson. The man who had finally shown his face! Too little, too late.

"Whatever you think you had ..."

Wilson knew where this sentence was headed and began to turn, but I was going to have my day in court. He was going to hear me out.

"Whatever you think you had ... it's over!"

"We'll see about that!" he said and strode out of the door.

Max and Percy looked at me. I smiled. "Roz's ex," I explained. "Back then, he wasn't interested! They dated for two years but he couldn't commit, so Roz left him! And now he's had a change of heart?"

For the first time, I really felt like Roz's boyfriend; strong enough to bat away suitors and intruders; confident enough to keep her past in the past. She was in my bed. In fact, she liked being in my bed.

Where was she?

I sent her a quick text. "You okay?"

She quickly replied. "I'm sitting at your kitchen table working. I'm not wearing any knickers. When are you coming home?"

These were the kind of texts I liked to receive.

"Be home just after 6.00," I replied.

Max and Percy looked concerned. I'd handled a potentially explosive situation like I was ordering my dinner.

"That could have gone badly wrong!" said Percy. "He doesn't look that stable."

To me, The Elusive Wilson hadn't posed a threat. He was never going to throw a punch. Any kind of conflict might have ruined his hair! Having said that, he definitely wasn't stable! He had de-stabilised himself. In his own tiny, little world, he was used to getting his own way. Narcissists imagine that everything revolves around them so, when a troublesome third party like me gets involved, it was always going to throw the poor boy into a tailspin! He hadn't anticipated that Roz would find someone new. People waited for Wilson. Waited to be summoned to his chambers!

In a way, Wilson was even more pathetic than Low. Low was a hit and run. Pure and simple. Wilson would give you some sugar, bugger off and expect you to be waiting for his return. Low never returned!

Max and Percy still looked concerned.

"As you probably know," I began, "Roz is way out of my league! She's gorgeous, she's glamorous, she's smarter than me, she's more ambitious than me; she's going places! If you date a woman like that, there will be competition. Even if you get married, there will still be men lying in wait, like quiet and calculating cheetahs, waiting to pounce."

"Christ!" said Percy, though I couldn't see him fighting off too many men. I loved my sister but she was no Roz.

"Max will tell you, we had a scene in here with Benjamin, one of the blokes she lives with! He's clearly head over heels and probably always has been. He came in here wanting to know my intentions!"

Percy looked at Max. Max nodded, to verify my story.

"I sent him packing!" I said, feeling very cocksure. "And there will probably be others who fancy their chances?"

At this point, any reasonable man would have asked, "So, what does Roz see in you?" but, thankfully, these two weren't that curious. What did Roz see in me? I'd heard her explain the attraction in front of her friends at The Haunted House, but it was still difficult for me to accept. I guess I have my own self-esteem issues?

At that point, Wilson came back through the door of the shop. The audacity of the man! What did he want now? We all looked at him. He was smartly dressed but standing awkwardly. He wasn't sure what to say. We hadn't been that impressed with him last time he'd opened his mouth! He knew he needed a new tack. He knew he needed something he wasn't used to using: diplomacy.

He began with an apology. "Look, I'm sorry for the way I behaved, but I need to talk to Roz."

"Call her!" I said, firmly.

"She's not picking up!"

"I wonder why?" I replied, twisting the jagged blade already imbedded in his chest.

"Look I don't know what you've heard ..."

"It doesn't matter, mate!" At last, the ugly side of North London was coming out of me. Not genteel Highgate or Hampstead. This was the grimy backstreets of Finsbury Park! This was the unbridled aggression of a fracas on Tottenham High Road.

The Elusive Wilson was now The Perplexed Wilson. In his world, everything went for him. People agreed with him. But now, for the first time, he couldn't get his own way.

Finally, he came clean! The pitiful words cascaded out of his mouth like the desperate cries of a hungry baby. "I've made a mistake!"

And there it was! He'd fucked up and now, publically, he was having to admit it. I now had two people in my life that had made a major mistake. Their regret hung in the air like a truly foul stench. Trish was a mess, and now I had The (Not Very) Elusive Wilson crying into his milkshake, like a humiliated bully.

I didn't have it within me to be the bigger man. See? I told you. I'm not perfect! I could've been sympathetic but I really disliked this man. He'd treated Roz like a flimsy piece of skirt and she was much more than one of his acolytes! She deserved better! In fact, she deserved better than me, but I would do for the time being!

I had nothing to say to him, which aggravated the hell out of him and even caused him to hop with frustration.

"Say something!" he cried.

I looked at him blankly. There were a number of things I could have said to him, all of which would have sounded like gloating. Guys like me don't gloat. Guys like me count their blessings.

"When you finally get hold of her," I began, staring him straight in his eyes, "make sure you listen to what she says. I think you only hear what you want hear. She's a friendly, conversational girl but she's definitely not interested in taking a step backwards with you!"

"You don't know her!" he spat, and maybe I didn't? "We were in love," he repeated, and this was clearly a mantra he was going to repeat, hopefully to bring it to life?

I definitely had no more words for him. I was shocked to find myself dragged into a cat fight. This was not how I behaved. I wanted better for us. I wanted art galleries and tasting menus.

The only way I could get rid of him was by being cooperative. "I'll let her know you're looking for her," I said.

"Thank you," he replied and vacated the shop.

Max and Percy looked at me. Max put two thumbs up. "You handled that well!" said Percy.

"All in a day's work," I replied, calmly, though my heart was racing. I didn't like these suitors and potential hazards.

With the drama over, Percy went back to work and the day began coming to a close, when suddenly we were joined by another stranger in the shop, a much friendlier stranger, a smiling man bearing gifts.

"I was just in the area," he began. "Thought I'd pop in? I'm Sharon's brother, Solomon."

I took his hand and shook it warmly.

"Really pleased to meet you!"

I got close to him, so I could whisper in his ear. "I'll introduce you to Max in a moment. Can we play some music first and see if he responds?"

"No problem!" he replied, winking, and handed me a CD.

I quickly popped the CD in a player and cranked it to a nice volume.

Out of the speakers came four to the floor dance music but it was so much more than that! There were influences from everywhere! A bit of afrobeat, a bit of bhangra, some dancehall, some salsa, and even some Vivaldi-esque strings!

Max looked in a trance. The groove was causing him to tremble and quiver, though it may have been a new dance move? I could see he liked it. He was nodding and smiling and pointing excitedly at the speakers!

It mesmerised us both for about five minutes and then faded away.

"Sick!" said Max

"Max, I'd like to introduce you to my new friend Solomon."

The two boys shook hands. Solomon was about five years older than Max but probably still moving in similar circles.

"Do you like it?" I asked.

"Sick!" was all Max could say. "Can I hear it again?"

"Remember I was talking about you making music?"

Max nodded.

"Solomon is a friend of a friend and, if you hit it off, maybe you can work together?"

There was terror in Max's eyes. Stage fright. "Me?" he asked Solomon. "Work with you?"

"Do you have any ideas?" asked Solomon.

Max thought for a second. "When I'm playing in a club, I know what should come next, but I sometimes don't have that kind tune. I'd like to fill the gaps, so I always have the right tune to play."

Solomon understood him and nodded. "Would you like to hear something else?"

Max nodded enthusiastically and Solomon pressed 'Play'. There were no vocals and it seemed quite repetitive to me, but it was clear that this guy had music coming out of his pores. Everything we heard was like kitchen-sink stew, full of nutritious ingredients. This was a boy that loved all kinds of musics, so he was alright in my books. If he and Max could find some common ground, they would make beautiful noises.

I sent Sharon a quick text. "Here with Solomon. He's a nice bloke and a talented musician. Thank you."

"My pleasure," she replied. "Here's something that will blow your mind: Low is back in Lola's bedroom!"

It took me a while to digest that. I was almost too stunned to answer. Low never went back for seconds. Lola hadn't been overawed with Low's performance either, so why were they back in bed again? My brain was trying to process this but failing. Luckily, Max and Solomon were already deep in conversation and sharing some jokes, so I was no longer needed.

I wandered outside to get some air and think more clearly. Low never went back for seconds. Lola hadn't been impressed but there was clearly something about her that he liked and wanted more of!

The sun had gone in but it was still warm. The kids were all home, so most of the people getting off buses were weary and dishevelled commuters. I could see the frantic look in their eyes. They were desperate to get through that front door, so they could unclip that bra, kick off those shoes and/or consume that cold tin of beer they knew was waiting in their fridge.

I looked around me. I owned a dirty shop on a busy, dusty road. Things would have to change. I didn't just have to keep it fun, I had to show growth and progression.

I had to show Roz that I had plans and that I planned ahead. Probably, the first thing to do was ... erm ... plan ahead!

If Solomon and Max liked each other, they would make music. If the music was good, we could press some vinyl and create an imprint. But, if I was running a record label out of my shop, shouldn't it be clean and shiny? Shouldn't it have glass offices and coffee machines? Or was that only the sanitised and very corporate labels? Maybe dirty bass lines deserved a grimy office? Well, our shop was certainly grimy, but it still needed a cleaner! Maybe Sharon could hook me up with a cleaner too?

I went back into the shop. The music was blaring but, somehow, Solomon and Max were deep in conversation. A text went ding in my phone. It said that me and Roz were 'cordially' invited by Topper and Francine to a 'formal' dinner at Francine's house the following Tuesday. This, I assumed meant we'd have to dress smartly. Enjoyable for Roz but not for me.

We normally dined out on a Tuesday but there would be no need this week. Topper and Francine were taking giant steps into coupledom. I felt embarrassed. In all my years, I'd never held a dinner party at my house. Maybe because Trish had no need to spend her private time with my friends! Maybe, after everything, despite the elaborate yarn Trish had spun, maybe the major problem with me was my friends? She didn't like them – or was jealous of them – and, in truth, they weren't that fond of her! Although they'd never verbalised it, I don't think they thought she was right for me and, when she buggered off, I think they were quite relieved. She didn't think I was 'father material' and my mates didn't view her as 'girlfriend material'!

I looked at the text. I was happy for Topper. God, he'd tried so many women! So many different types, but they'd never been quite right! The dinner party was to be held at his house but she was designing the menu and doing the cooking! Topper would've told her that Low was a *maître d'* at a posh restaurant and that Mids was a wine connoisseur but, undaunted, she wanted to cook for us all. You had to be impressed! I was happy for Tops. Even though he wasn't a huge Trish fan, he'd always wanted a partner, and now that I had snared the crazy girl with the wild hair, he wanted it badly.

I was excited to tell Roz about the dinner party. There was a beautiful girl in my house and she wasn't wearing any undies. I couldn't wait to get home. I called her mobile. No reply. I called my house phone. No reply. Where was she? And, suddenly, I had that sinking feeling! Maybe The Elusive Wilson had finally got hold of her? What did that slimeball want? What did he really want?

And then my mind began playing tricks on me! I should know better! Am I not the new and improved Wes? Am I not a mature, evolved and confident man? Was I not, in Jill's words, the "pivot" in my group? So what if she was meeting-up with The Elusive

Wilson? It would only be to put him straight. I tried to keep my brain from going to dark places.

Finally, the music ceased and Max and Solomon looked at me. They were both grinning. "We're going to make music!" said Max, triumphantly.

The plan was coming together. Keeping it fun is just a small part of it. Dates and dinners and dancing are just a start. Giving her pleasure with your body is just one minor aspect. A woman wants to see your brain working. It's the most powerful organ you've got and she wants to see it flex and pump: inspired and spontaneous ideas, a bold and audacious imagination plus, as her warrior, she wants to see you impose your superiority over your peers! Within your circle, she wants to be the other half of the power couple!

Having said that, I couldn't brag about how clever I was because now I couldn't find Roz! Maybe The Elusive Wilson had tracked her down and taken her back to his evil lair? What were they saying and doing now? What were these former lovers discussing? My brain was absolutely tormenting me! I kept visualising Roz and Wilson locked in fond embrace. Come on, you idiot, snap out of it!

I needed to occupy my brain. I needed to stop worrying about me, about her and about us. I needed to do something selfless. I suddenly remembered Wendy's hat. I'd promised to collect money and buy it for her birthday. I didn't have the patience for that right now. I needed to be pro-active. I pulled my wallet out of my jacket and found the business card I'd been given by her PA. I called the number.

"Eleanor? I don't know if you remember me? I approached you at the Wandsworth show?"

I could hear the cogs in her brain whirring. In her job, she met a lot of wannabes and outsiders, each with their own uniquely ridiculous question.

"I'm a friend of Melvin's?"

"Ah, yes, I remember!"

"I'm still interested in that hat!"

"Good!" she said.

"It's a lot of money!" I said.

"Yes it is."

I was just another wannabe or outsider trying to hustle her.

"I know this might sound strange ..." I began.

These were almost certainly six words she heard on a regular basis.

"... but I'm fairly certain," I continued, "I could provide you with a service. I'm sure I've got something you need!"

There was silence down the other end of the phone. I could hear her thinking, "Who is this nutter?"

I began busking. Not really knowing where I was going.

"I run a disco equipment hire shop and we provide DJs as well. Music is massively important at fashion shows. You need music that compliments the clothes or hats or swimwear or whatever! The music has to reflect the character of the show. Your boss makes hats that are full of life, full of pizzazz, laced with traditional British humour. Faceless, tuneless, anonymous dance music just isn't right? You need music with personality."

Eleanor was still silent, absorbing my words.

"You know what?" she began. "You have a point."

"Can we talk about it?"

"Sure," she said.

"Now?"

"Now? Bit late, isn't it?"

"I feel energised!" I said.

Eleanor thought for a second. "Ah, what the hell! She'll probably have me working here until midnight again!"

I got the studio address, got into my car and headed down there. No phone call and no text from Roz. I was imagining the worst. I had to keep my mind occupied. The studio was in a quiet industrial estate in Willesden. By the time I got there, all the businesses were dark except for this one manic milliner. I rang the door bell and the exhausted Eleanor answered the door. She looked less than impressed.

"Are you okay?" I asked.

"I started work at 10.00, it's now 7.00, and I haven't even had lunch!"

"Can I go and get you something?"

Eleanor looked at me in disbelief. She had not been afforded an act of kindness all day. "I don't even know your name!"

"My name's Wes. What can I get you?"

Eleanor shook her head and almost seemed on the verge of tears.

"Some Chinese?" I suggested. "And a can of Coke?"

Eleanor looked deeply touched but was still wondering if I was some kind of practical joker.

"I'll be back as soon as I can," I said.

She was speechless and nodded, numbly.

I quickly found a local Chinese take away and was back at the studio within 20 minutes. I don't think she thought she'd ever see me again but, here I was, bearing gifts. She let me in and sat me down in a chair in a small, junk-filled office.

She knew I wanted to talk but I knew she wanted to eat. "I'll sit here, quietly," I said. "Eat it while it's hot."

She didn't argue, gratefully began to tuck in and consumed it all within minutes. She looked up at me. The colour had returned to her cheeks. "Thank you," she said, softly, almost too grateful to speak. "I needed that."

I didn't need to say anymore. She knew what I wanted, she knew what I could offer. All that remained was for me to make small talk and make a new friend. Mercenary, I know, but I wanted Wendy to have that hat.

"Long hours?" I asked.

"I can't complain," said Eleanor, "I'm in my dream job!"

"Ellie!!" screamed a voice down the corridor but, before she could get up, her boss was in the office, bearing down on her. "I need some fags! I'm going to be up all night! And I need a cuppa!"

Her boss was short and very slight with insane, multi-coloured dreadlocks full of jewellery. She was wearing a functional, denim jump suit, that made her look like a pixie, and had orange Dr. Martens on her feet.

She suddenly noticed me. "Hello! Who are you?"

"Friend of Ellie's," I said.

"And what do you do?"

"I own a disco equipment hire shop and we provide DJs too! I was saying to Ellie, I was at the Wandsworth show and I didn't think the music was right."

"Oh?" asked the milliner.

"Bland dance music is not you! Your hats are anything but bland. You need a proper selection of songs with wit, with character, with personality; you need some slightly eccentric songs to suit your hats!"

The milliner laughed. "Are my hats only slightly eccentric? I must try harder!"

"Didn't mean to offend."

"No offence taken. So what do you plan? Can you provide us with this glorious soundtrack?"

"That's what I do!"

"We're out of almond milk," said Eleanor.

"Me and Ellie'll pop out and get you some. Back in a jiff!" I said. God knows why I said 'jiff'! I never said 'jiff'. It just seemed right at that moment.

The milliner smiled and wandered back out to her workshop.

Eleanor looked at me. "She likes you. I haven't seen her smile in years!"

Mission accomplished. I'd made my trade. We would play at her next show and I would get that hat at a greatly reduced rate.

We arrived back at the studio, made the maestro some tea and stood to observe. Her workshop was a carnival of different coloured fabrics and there were huge feathers everywhere. She seemed oblivious to our presence but then she stopped and turned.

"Do you wear hats, Wes?"

"I don't even own a hat! Of any kind!"

The milliner shook her head with disappointment. "You don't know what you're missing!"

"Where would I wear a hat?" I asked.

"Wherever you want! In truth, if you had a hat you loved, you would wear it everywhere!"

No disputing this logic. "I guess so?"

"Ellie, give this young man the date of our next show. It's a smaller, more intimate event but, as you say, we will need the right music."

Ellie and I exchanged details and said our goodbyes. She almost seemed sad to see me go. "I'll come back and see you soon." She smiled in appreciation. She'd appreciated the company.

By the time I got home, Roz was still in my kitchen, staring at her laptop. As I came through the door, she jumped up to greet me. "I've missed you," she said, as she sank into my arms. It felt good to hold her close.

"I called here and there was no reply," I said.

"I went back to the house to get some clothes."

"And I called your mobile."

"Sorry! I left that here!"

I dared not tell her what I'd been thinking. My mind had gone to dark and unnecessary places. I'd tormented myself. I deserved nothing less than pain, shame and embarrassment.

We said nothing for a few seconds, we just hugged. She seemed relieved that her nightmare was over, I was happy to have her in my house. She'd been home to get clothes, so she was staying a few nights.

"So much to tell you!" I said.

"Save it for the morning," she said.

Friday

Friday ended-up being really bloody strange.

Waking up next to Roz was pleasurable and having breakfast with her was as lively and entertaining (as ever) but it quickly went downhill from there. Business in the shop was brisk but all the stuff around it was perplexing. I felt like I was in the middle of a multi-car pile-up. Twisted metal and bloody bodies everywhere!

Roz needed work and it didn't matter where she looked for work, so she made herself comfy at my kitchen table, opened her laptop and began foraging. She had her coffee, she had her croissants and, from what I could see, she still had no underwear on but, in this office, not necessary.

"I'll see you later," she said, cheerily, not knowing that I was about to walk into a shit storm! In truth, I wish I could've stayed at home and played with her juicy bits but … you know … duty calls.

Max did not arrive alone. On this day, he was accompanied by a young man called Dexter. Dexter was his age, tall, athletic-looking, with a smiley, confident face. He looked charming and spoke with a likable ease.

"Wes, this is my mate, Dexter!" We shook hands. "Dexter is going to be my business manager."

I stifled a chuckle and took another quick look at Max to make sure it wasn't a wind-up.

"Seriously?" I asked. Which might have been a bit insensitive?

"Things are going good!" said Max. "Lots of gigs and now I'm going to be making music with Solomon ..."

"So pleased you two get on!"

"Nah, he's safe!"

Max was buzzing! Radio show, new clothes, new gigs, new friends and he was about to do something he'd only ever dreamt of: making music. And he figured, with somebody like Dexter at his side, he was about to do something very grown-up: make proper money!

I turned to Dexter, who was looking very pleased at his new role in Max's life. At this point, try as I might, I couldn't bring myself to like the guy. He was one of two things: either a complete fool or someone who had come to leech off Max. Max was my boy, I was very protective of him and no one – repeat no one – was going to abuse his good nature!

"So, tell me about you, mate! Have you ever managed anyone before?"

"No."

"So, what have you been doing up 'til now? What's your experience?"

Dexter looked nervously at Max and, with a look, Max conveyed that Dexter should probably answer my questions, as I was vastly experienced in these matters. Well, I wasn't, but Max thought I was The Oracle and I kinda liked that rep.

"I do a show on the station. Thursday from 9.00 – 11.00. Playing all kinds of house. I do clubs, like Max. I know everyone on the scene and," he added, proudly, "everyone knows Dexter!"

Then, he paused. Not sure what else to add. Not sure what else would be relevant.

"I used to have a Saturday job in Lidl!"

He was not pulling up any trees but then he was just a kid. Not skilled, not experienced and definitely NOT business manager material!

"Okay," I said.

Dexter flashed a winning smile, as if he'd passed the audition. He had a mobile in his hand, expecting an important call at any moment, and was expertly twirling it, as if it were his nervous twitch.

How had I got myself into this situation? I was Max's boss, I was his friend and, I guess, I was his mentor, but I was not his mum. It was not my job to protect him from predators. It wasn't my job to polish his antennae and keep this judgement sharp and yet, if I was going to be a record label boss, I was suddenly an A&R man! So, Trish, I'm not 'father material' but I'm father enough to guide an artist's career?

"Max knows he has my support," I said. "I trust his judgement."

Max and Dexter looked very pleased to have my endorsement. They shook hands in a deal-clinching way, as if they'd sealed a pact with the devil and they were now free to go off and cause mayhem.

"So," began Dexter, "when will I get paid?"

I took another quick look at Max to make sure it wasn't a wind-up. Max clearly didn't think it was.

I turned to Dexter but my mild amusement had now disappeared. I suddenly had a glum vision of all these hustlers coming out of the woodwork, trying to steal a slice of Max's glory. "Do you know what a business manager does?"

"Manage someone's business?" offered Dexter.

My heart sank. I was more than friend and mentor, more than mentor and A&R man, I was a fucking witch sent to ward-off evil spirits

"True," I replied, "but it will also be your job to drum-up business; get Max work and put him into situations where he can earn money. Business managers work on commission. YOU get paid when HE gets paid!"

The tingly mood of optimism was now shot to shit. This sounded like a lot of hard work to Dexter. I could see him physically shrink in stature. He began to look quite nervous and edgy; Max hadn't seen this side of him.

"You alright, mate?" I asked him.

Dexter began to stutter and shuffle uneasily in his designer trainers. "Maybe ..."

"Maybe what?" I asked.

"Maybe ... maybe I'm not ready to be a business manager?" Dexter suggested. "What do you think?"

Dexter nodded like one of those decorative dogs you used to see in people's back windows. He seemed to be throwing in the towel already.

"Thanks, man, I didn't understand," he said to me. I tried to nod in a supportive way. I definitely didn't need to see his stupid face again. He stood there looking impotent for a few seconds and finally said, "I'd better go."

Dexter and Max exchanged a convoluted handshake and his not-so-slick mate beat a hasty retreat.

Max looked confused. "I thought he could help?"

I shrugged my shoulders. "Don't worry about it, Maxi! Even Elton John had problems with his business manager!"

"Who?" said Max.

I didn't bother explaining.

The phone was ringing, e-mails were arriving and I really should have been taking care of my business but the next one through the door was Percy, looking as if his latest epiphany was literally about to blow his mind.

"Wes, sorry to come barging in!"

"Any time, mate."

"Wes, I've been thinking. It came to be last night. In a flash! I want to do this full time. I want to give up driving a bus. I want to become a full-time entertainer!"

You had to love Percy: his energy, his enthusiasm, his endearing naivety. He was a purist and an idealist; a beautiful daisy-age hippie in a sea of mobile disco mediocrity. In Percy's world, there was just great music and smiling faces. Nothing gave him more pleasure than playing popular songs and making people happy (other than Marie's very moist meatloaf!) I didn't want to burst his condom and put out the passion of that disco inferno.

"We've got Friday and Saturday work, mate, but not enough to pay your mortgage!"

"Well, that's the thing," Percy continued, really getting up a head of steam, "if we can give people more, we can put up our prices! We can do it! We can give them more! Turn it from just a DJ playing some tunes ... turn it into a spectacle! Sound and vision! A multi-media show! Big screens showing movies, videos, images, song lyrics whatever; a bit of razzle dazzle!"

I appreciated his idea and I loved the fact that he was thinking about our business, even as he lay in bed (Christ, even I switched off once I was under the duvet) but I didn't think I had the headspace for a 'multi-media' experience. Not at that precise moment. I was just reaching a place of comfort and I quite liked it! Yeah, I said it! I was comfortable in my comfort zone.

Right now, my priorities were making sure Percy did a great job at Waldo's party, keeping Roz safe from her loony ex, overseeing the first recordings of my fledgling record label and finding a cleaner to rid my shop of several decades of dust and grime!

"I've done the sums, Wes!" He reached into the back pocket of his trousers and yanked out a folded piece of paper, which he unfolded. Holding it before him, he read it out like a proclamation. "With three gigs a week and a 25% increase in our prices, I can give up driving a bus!"

I needed to tread carefully. I didn't want to upset Percy. Right now, he was my go-to guy and I needed him all happy and smiley for not only his gigs but Alvin's too! Nevertheless, Percy's idea was coming to me on the wrong day and at the wrong time; his plans were not in synch with mine, plus Max's mate Dexter had upset me, plus I was ready for Belinda's baps, so my stomach was rumbling, plus I needed to take a was (not was) plus the phone was ringing off the hook!

Percy's excitable smile was lighting up the shop and he was virtually hopping with delight at the brilliance of his idea. I needed to arrest this development and put it on the back burner. It could happen ... but not right now. I needed to find the necessary smarm of a line manager; some management speak to soften the blow. I wasn't trained for this.

I smiled (like a stoned skateboarder) and tried to give the impression that I was seriously considering every aspect of Percy's plan. "It's a brilliant idea, Percy. Great to know you're having ideas!"

Percy began to flail his long arms like a body-popping octopus. I was glad there was no one else in the shop or he would've smacked someone in the chops! He was growing happier by the minute. It almost seemed like he was growing taller but it may have just been his quiff bouncing?

"But I'm just not ready to go multi-media. Not just yet. I've got other things I want to do. Look, I've got all of Alvin's gigs for you and, if you can hustle a few more, as you've been doing, the sums might add-up?"

Percy's arms stopped waving and he began to calm down. I could see him doing the sums in his head. "Hmmm!" he hummed to himself. "You might be right, matey?"

My join the dots management skills weren't so bad after all! I would need them to help Max avoid parasites and to keep Percy's lofty ambitions out of the clouds. Though, thinking about it, I was now also nurse maid to my circle of friends.

Percy seemed happy. "Wes, you're the best!" he said, shaking my hand very firmly. "One day, we'll be ready!"

He turned on his heels and went back to the bus garage. His time there was shortening. Our boy had big plans! I could see what he was suggesting but I wasn't ready yet. His plan would require investment and I needed somebody clever to do some sums for me.

And, as soon as Percy had left, Mids was straight through the door, carrying a bottle of wine (he never liked to arrive empty-handed) and he did not look happy. Since when had my humble disco equipment hire shop become a doctor's surgery? And how would business get done if I kept having to put out fires?

Mids plonked himself on one of the stools at my reception desk and began idly fiddling with his phone.

"Morning, Mids! Nice day!"

Mids grunted.

"So, you've got your thing tonight? Your little soiree? And Belinda's going to make you some tasty nibbles?"

"Yeah!" said Mids, looking and sounding glum.

"You'd better fix your face, son. You've got guests to entertain! If you want to sell some cases of booze, you need to find your happy place and stay there!"

I had not been employed as a cheerleader. It was not my job to shake my pom poms and make Mids smile! What was going on? I liked my new status as group leader but I didn't have the energy to lift everyone's spirits. Damn, people, why don't you take drugs like everyone else?

I looked at Mids and let him sit and stew for a few minutes. I figured, eventually, he would spill the beans. He seemed more concerned with his phone, so I just carried on working. "I'll always be the rebound guy," he finally said.

Ah, this again! The recurring Alistair problem.

"She insists on talking about him! No matter how much she slates him, she keeps talking about him. 'Ali introduced me to them', 'Ali and I went to that festival in 2012', Ali fucking Ali fucking Ali! Everything is Ali!"

I loved my mate and I hated to see him pain. This woman was dangerous. Dangerous to his self-esteem and a threat to his future! He'd already had his heart and his world torn asunder once, he didn't need a repeat performance!

"We're all rebound guys," I said.

Mids looked up at me. His eyes looked tired and watery. "Yeah?" he asked.

"If you're dating someone who's previously had a boyfriend, then you're the rebound guy! We all are! I am!"

"You are?"

"Sure," I said. "Roz doesn't just talk about The Elusive Wilson incessantly, she actually went to work for him last month!"

"Really?" asked Mids.

"I can't get rid of the twerp!" I said. "He was in my shop yesterday, saying he'd made a mistake!"

Mids' mouth was agape. "What did you say?"

"I said, 'Good luck with that conversation, son!' She doesn't want to speak to him! She wouldn't spit on him but – oh no – I have to deal with him!"

Mids took a deep breath. What else can the man in love do? Breathe deeply and stiffen your back. Buckle yourself in. The ride is liable to be bumpy!

At that moment, light relief, Belinda The Rescinder arrived! As soon as Mids saw her, he perked up! The baps in her basket looked even juicier than ever!

"We alright for tonight?" he asked.

"Absolutely," said Belinda. "My first catering job! You bet!"

"You're always so cheerful!" Mids said.

Belinda paused for a second, as if no one had ever pointed it out, as if she'd never realised it. "I suppose I am."

"How do you do it?" Mids asked.

Not the kind of question Belinda got asked on her rounds every day.

Belinda paused again and thought. If we didn't buy so many of her baps every day, she wouldn't have given us the time of day, but she humoured us. "I'm a positive person," she began. "As a self-employed person, you have to be. As a one-woman catering empire, I have to be! I'm cook, cleaner and bottle washer. I'm the public persona. I'm the face. I'm the image, the reputation, in fact, I'm the final word!"

Mids stood back, amazed, and suddenly looked quite humbled by this formidable woman. By God, her baps were heavenly but she was also a huge and colourful billboard for the single woman, the solo artist and the fiercely independent feminist. She had to make it work and, in her own delicious way, she got on with it.

Mids fell to his knees and placed his hands on her feet. "I bow before you, Belinda The Rescinder. As your humble servant, I live to please you."

Belinda looked at me and we both looked at Mids, prostrate on the pavement.

I shrugged my shoulders and smiled feebly. "He's prone to the melodramatic. He'll be alright tonight. You watch him. He's the master salesman!"

Belinda flashed us a dazzling smile (which Mids missed 'cause he was still kneeling on the pavement), took my money and got back on her bike. "I'll be there at 5.00 to set up!"

"Thank you, my queen!" said Mids, raising his palms to the sky.

"You can see why he's so successful!" I said to Belinda. She laughed and rode off.

I looked down at Mids, who was now attracting the attention of people walking by. "Shall we have some lunch?" I suggested.

Mids dragged himself to his feet. "Bloody women!" he said. "Why do they induce such passion?"

Now, that was a good question!

As Mids, Max and I tucked into our lunch, Mids opened his bottle of wine, and I thought about his question. Yes, Trish had induced heightened feelings in me, but they were merely sadness, frustration and, eventually, anger. Roz, on the other hand, was definitely inducing passion in me. New passions! Good passions! Warm, caring, loving, lustful passions! I wanted to hold that little cutie in my arms all day and lick her extremities!

I was lucky! Mids: not so lucky. His first wife had cheated on him and left him for another man, and now he had the insatiable but unstable Jill yanking his chain!

"So, how's it going with Jill?"

Mids thought for a long while before answering. In fact, I'd finished my bap before he started talking! He knew he'd have to give me a decent answer or I'd just badger him for clarification.

"I really like her!" he began. "That's my problem! I really like her!"

I looked at him and formulated my response. What had my life become? It felt like I was a million miles from cleaning sticky lager residue from my fader channels. Back then, life was simple! Now, I was a bloody agony uncle; allegedly, some kind of expert!

"What's the problem with you liking her, mate?"

"I don't want to fall in love, Wezza."

And this is the crucial bit of this conversation. This is the crossroads. This is the fine balance between sanity and insanity. This is the dilemma that separates the men from the boys. This is the bittersweet nectar that poisons a million relationships. This is the factor that causes men to take a step back from a woman.

"You don't want to fall in love?"

"I can't, Wezza! I just can't!"

Ah, poor bugger! As he sat there munching on Belinda's delicious baps, I didn't know how to break it to him. Naturally, I had to break it to him gently but I had to choose my words.

"This isn't petrol, Mids. You have no choice! You have no say in the matter. If your car needs unleaded, your choice is unleaded. Don't put diesel in there! With love, you have no choice! You can't sit there are go, 'Hmm … I'll just keep it platonic!' or 'I think I'll just be her fuck buddy!' You have no choice, mate!"

Mids looked up at me gloomily. Not even Belinda's baps could take this edge off this painful moment.

"If love grabs you by the testicles, that's it! If love digs its claws into you, you will not – will not – be able to wrestle free from its powerful grip."

Mids finished his bap, finished his plastic cup of white wine and poured himself another. I saw Max look nervously at us. The last thing he needed was two drunk men shouting at one another! He'd seen this before!

"Oh crap!" cried Mids. "Not more pain! I can't handle any more!"

"There doesn't have to be pain, Mids!"

"Oh, there will be!"

A fatalistic approach to his future. What could I say to turn him around? My untrained brain just didn't have the vocabulary.

Or maybe he was right? Maybe she would be the next woman to break his heart? Who knew? Nobody knew. I didn't know where I was headed with Roz. Topper didn't know where he was headed with Francine. We were all in amusement arcades, playing the slots. There was no way of knowing if that endless stream of coins was ever going to pay out?

"So, what do I do?" asked Mids, glugging from his cup of wine and starting to slur his words.

"You've got a soiree this evening, you mad bugger! Stop drinking!"

"Takes more than a few cups of wine to get me pissed! Don't worry!" said Mids, putting down his cup and clasping me by my shoulders. "Now, Wezza, what do I do?"

Looking me square in the eyes, I knew he was serious. Hard to know what to say? Yeah, maybe I was now some kind of point guard but Mids was my peer; we were equals. It seemed insane for him to be asking my advice.

"Since when did I become the expert?" I replied.

Mids broke free in anguish and span around like an Olympic ice skater. Having done 180 degrees, he was now face to face with Heston! Christ, what was he doing in my shop? This was turning into a traditional, English whodunnit; a constant stream of suspicious characters coming in and out of doors.

There was complete silence. Max had never met Heston before and seemed transfixed by this rugged, man mountain. Mids had met him before and looked as surprised as me. Actually, I wasn't surprised at all. Who hadn't visited the shop today? I was half expecting the Welsh water polo team and the cast of 'Hamilton'.

"Hello!" said Mids, extending a hand to Heston. "Nice to see you! How have you been?"

Heston leaned forward to shake his hand. "We've been alright," he said.

"Heston: meet my employee, Max." The two shook hands.

"We've been alright," continued Heston, "but …" He wasn't one for a position of weakness. He didn't like to admit he needed help and didn't like to ask for help.

"But?" I asked.

"The house is very quiet."

Hmm, I hadn't thought of that! Roz was with me, Jill was with Mids; we had totally upset the chemical balance at The Haunted House. Three men, three women. It had always worked. They'd known each other from uni days. First, they'd lived in a big flat (with no bedrooms) and now they lived in big house, inherited by Heston from his grandmother.

I definitely couldn't say, 'Oops, sorry!' What could I say? Roz wanted to be with me, I'd introduced Mids to Jill and now Jill wanted to be with him! What could I say? It was evolution. In Mids' case, I couldn't really say it was 'progress' but ... well ... these things happen! People meet, people get on, people share a bed.

The only problem was: Heston genuinely looked quite sad. Now, this was a tall, handsome geezer! An artist: a painter and a sculptor. This was a man surrounded by beautiful, creative women all day, every day. How could you not be happy? And yet Heston missed the three man/three woman dynamic in the house; the rhythms, the love, the camaraderie, the bickering; family life! Roz and Jill weren't just housemates, they were Heston's family.

First Dexter, then Percy, then Mids and now Heston. It was a lot to deal with. My head was starting to throb. These were not problems or emergencies, just issues for my brain to deal with. And, if I diversified, my life would become even more complex. I didn't just need a cleaner, I needed an HR person!

And then I thought about Roz. How impressed would she be if I emerged from this day unscathed? Yeah, I needed to keep it fun but I also needed to be an exceptional man; Superman: complete with shiny red underpants and cape! That's what women want, right? All of those words on those Post-It notes. They need their man to be all those things and more!

I took a deep breath and surveyed the scene. Heston looking to me for answers, Mids looking to me for answers and Max just looked confused, though he was now used to the madness in our shop. Since the arrival of Roz, our lives had become 'Dallas' and 'Dynasty' combined.

"Mids bought me a delicious Riesling!" I said, holding up the bottle for Heston to see. "Can I interest you in a plastic cup?"

Heston looked a bit taken aback but finally said, "Yeah, sure. Why not?"

He seemed a bit tense and angry at someone. Surely not me? He took the cup and sipped. He knew about wines, so he knew what he was drinking.

"Nice, eh?" said Mids.

Heston nodded in agreement. "Crisp. Nice apricot note!"

For Mids, if you appreciated wine, you went straight to the top of the evolutionary scale. "Yes!" said Mids, triumphantly. "This man knows!"

Heston, despite being so tall and broad and masculine, looked quite diminutive today, as if someone had burst his balloon. There's only so much talking you can do. I was virtually talked-out for the day. I wasn't even sure I had the words for him. If I was now Mother Theresa, the Dalai Lama and Nelson Mandela combined, I needed a nap and an energy drink!

My phone dinged and it was a text from Sharon. It was full of laughing emojis and the words, 'Low is STILL in Lola's bedroom!'. Well, this was very good news! Or was it? If Low coupled-off with Lola, Baggers would be the only single man in the group. How could the group possibly survive? The band would surely have to break-up?

If Heston had group dynamic issues, so did I? But what could I do? Low, Mids and Topper all now had bed partners!

I sent Sharon a quick text back. "If you're feeling lonely, come hang with us! I'll be at the shop until 6.00."

I got a big smiley emoji in return. Sharon didn't know what Friday night entailed but adventures with Uncle Wes were always fun.

I shrugged my shoulders and tried to give Heston some comfort or guidance. "I'm really sorry, my friend, the crazy girl with the wild hair has captured my heart and kidnapped my very soul!"

Heston nodded in acknowledgement. He'd known this woman since she was a teen. He knew how charismatic she was, he knew how irresistible she was, and he probably knew a good many more secrets about her! He'd known Roz when she barely had beer money and he'd watched her mature into a compassionate, sophisticated, articulate Velociraptor, capable of love and warmth but also capable of biting into your flesh and tearing you limb from limb!

"What could I do? I was powerless."

Heston nodded. He knew I was mere putty in her hands.

"And I guess I have to apologise too?" Mids began. "I'm partly to blame."

Heston finished his cup of wine and looked towards the bottle to see if there was any more. I quickly grabbed the bottle and poured him another cupful. Were we really at 'drowning your sorrows' already?

"The house is not the way it was. Jill always made sure everything ran smoothly. I notice little things: we ran out of bitter lemon the other day and Jill always used to make sure there were no cups and plates in the sink."

Quietly, I was not impressed. These grown men still needed a mother in their home, but it was distressing to see this virile beast in such a pitiful state.

"Having said that," continued Heston, "whenever I see Jill, she looks really happy!"

"She does?" asked Mids.

"Oh, yes!" confirmed Heston. "She's been up and down for years; deliriously jovial one minute and down in the bowels of depression the next. The Alistair affair gave her seismic mood swings. That shit was difficult to live with!"

Heston had helped me. Mids' mood had instantly lifted. He didn't want to fall in love with Jill but at least he now knew he made her happy. He smiled with contentment. Heston had helped me but how could we help him?

"What can I do, Heston? You want me to send the girls home?"

"Could you?" he asked.

The conversation had reached a fairly comical moment. These were two grown women! Not just fiercely independent but bloody fierce! I was not going to tell Roz and Jill to go home! They did as they pleased and Heston knew it!

At that precise moment, there was a vision of beauty at the door. Sharon just stood in my shop doorway posing. She's a poser. No getting away from it! She waited until all eyes were on her before moving. As ever, she was wearing a dazzling outfit that showed off curves we knew she had and a few curves we didn't know she had!

She embraced me, embraced Mids and then looked at the two men she didn't know. "This must be Max!" she said. Max didn't know who she was and, when she clasped him to her maternal bosom, his eyes almost popped out.

Then Sharon turned towards Heston and looked him up and down. Literally. Looked him up and down, and up and down again. "You're a fine specimen, aren't you?" she said, placing her hand on his chest.

Heston looked down at the hand on this chest and then looked down at Sharon, who's hand, in the meantime, had moved down from his chest to his stomach.

"I am Heston," he proclaimed, giving himself an untamed savage voice to go with his body.

Thankfully, Sharon's hand didn't go any further down! She stepped back and took hold of his hand, to inspect his fingers and nails. She was literally checking him out, inch by inch. I almost felt like a voyeur but our eyes were glued to this remarkable spectacle. Even by her own bold and brassy standards, Sharon was surpassing herself! Heston was rooted to the spot, bemused by this complete stranger scrutinising him.

Sharon stood back and walked around him. Checking him out from every angle. Max's face was a picture. He'd met girls before and, in recent months, quite forward girls, but none of them went about their business like this!

Mids looked at me. He'd experienced Sharon before. He'd witnessed her taking Low down a peg or two. In fact, she'd ridiculed Low to his face and he'd still come out liking her! Quite a feat! I had a few questions to ask her about Lola and Low, but I didn't want to disturb a craftswoman at work!

"And what do you do?" Sharon asked Heston, as she ran her hands down his arms.

"I'm a painter and a sculptor."

Sharon couldn't really be impressed because she didn't know any painters or sculptors, but I could see she was intrigued.

"Where do you work?" she asked.

"I have a small, grubby workshop in Angel, Islington."

Sharon was suddenly aroused. "I'd like to see your small, grubby workshop in Angel, Islington," she said.

I didn't know Sharon that well but I was fairly certain I knew why she wanted to go to his small, grubby workshop in Angel, Islington. Either to strip off and get painted, strip off and get sculpted, or just have grubby sex. Knowing Sharon, she was probably hoping for all three!

Sharon now had her hand back on Heston's broad chest, as if she were a doctor checking his heartbeat. Heston had not moved from the spot. Never, in all his horny, gory teens had he ever met someone as mad and meticulous as Sharon.

"Are you single?" asked Sharon.

"I am."

"Have you ever been married?"

"No."

"Do you have any kids?"

"No."

We watched as Sharon covered all the bases, asking him pertinent questions and a few impertinent ones too!

"Have you ever had an STD?"

"No."

Finally, she had finished with the questions and she took a step back. She twirled. Not for any reason. She just twirled. Ensuring that we could all see every part of her shapely frame.

"Do you find me attractive, Heston?"

"I do."

She smiled with satisfaction and turned to me. "Wes, what's on the agenda tonight?"

I had been so hypnotised by Sharon's diagnostic check, I was in a bit of a trance and took a while to answer.

"Mids has a wine-tasting event this evening. I am going along to lend my support, make some small talk with Mids' customers and sample delicious wine."

Sharon turned to Mids. "Can I come?"

"Of course!" said Mids. "All functions need glamour!"

"Can I bring Heston?" she asked.

"Of course!" said Mids. "Heston knows his wine!"

Sharon looked at Heston and he at her. He was no longer talking about his house being 'quiet'. Now, he was caught-up in a very dangerous but very fragrant web. He was as intrigued with her as she was with him! They came from very different worlds but there was something raw and animalistic about Sharon that Heston liked. Capturing her image would almost be like a wildlife study! She was brash and passionate like a huge splash of abstract colour. In my head, I could see them crashing against each other like a treacherous storm.

"Well, that's settled then," began Sharon. "Our evening is planned."

Max sat back and watched. Over the last few months, he'd seen some pretty strange things going on in the shop. Today's performances had been right up there! Tomorrow would be another busy day full of the regular stuff and, doubtless, the irregular. I did not need any more men dealing with some kind of mid-life crisis!

We closed up the shop for the evening. "It's Friday night, Maxi. What you up to?"

"I'm going to Solomon's!" he said, excitedly.

"No gig?" I asked.

"Much later," he said. "I go on at 2.00."

I smiled to myself. I was no slouch but, by 2.00am, I would be tucked-up in my bed with my honey, who I couldn't wait to see! If it wasn't for the half-naked Roz selfies on my phone, Friday would have been a complete downer!

Now, I had the delicate task of trying to explain to Roz why Sharon was at the wine tasting party and why she was attached to Heston's body. Literally, like Siamese Twins!

By the time Roz arrived at Mids' warehouse, she had been frustrated by an unproductive day and was badly in need of some wine. Mids was happy to furnish her with a glass and she embraced him warmly. The warehouse was already half full with Mids' customers, mightily glad to not only be tasting new wines but sampling Belinda's magical morsels.

"I've looked forward to this all day!" Roz said, as she fell into my arms. I'd definitely been looking forward to seeing her. She looked divine in a patterned, lilac dress. Bright colours looked so good on her!

"Shit day!" she said. "Not a lot out there."

Roz held me close and I could feel her loving and appreciating me. What a priceless feeling! I'd never felt that with Trish. Our embraces had always been utilitarian and underwhelming. Maybe we didn't fit? Thankfully, Roz's eyes were closed and she still hadn't spotted Heston, who was still in a deep Sharon trance. Out of the corner of my eye, I could see him watching and listening to Sharon. She wasn't saying much but he was listening intently. He seemed in a primed-for-seduction stupor. If Lola was going to spend the whole day in bed, Sharon was too!

"Heston!" Roz said, suddenly spotting him. "Did you invite Heston? Why did you invite Heston?"

"Problem?"

"Not at all!" Roz said, breaking free of my clutches and rushing over to greet her old friend. I followed her. There would doubtless be a few Sharon questions?

Roz put her arms around Heston's sturdy frame and kissed his cheek. "Everything okay?"

"Yes," he replied.

"You're here?"

"I went to see Wes this afternoon and he invited me!"

Roz was now caught between several questions. She wanted to know why Heston had come to my shop but the more pressing matters were why Sharon was at the wine tasting and why she virtually inside Heston's shirt!

"Sharon, right?" Roz asked.

Sharon nodded enthusiastically.

"You two know each other?"

"We met a few hours ago!"

Roz did some mental calculations. "So, you were at the shop today as well?"

"Your boyfriend thinks I'm his personal helpdesk. As it happens, I don't mind. I like connecting people. Wes asked if I knew a cleaner and I do!"

Sharon was thinking on her feet and doing a great job.

"A cleaner?" asked Roz.

"For the shop!"

Roz looked at me. "For the shop?"

"It's disgusting! If I hope to run a record label out of there, I need a cleaner!"

Roz nodded. It made sense.

"I'm finally getting my shit together!" I said, proudly.

"You know a cleaner?" Roz asked Sharon.

"I've got a mate with a cleaning company! Her people clean offices all over London! I've had a look at the shop. Wes is right! It needs about eight hours of deep cleaning! Two women, four hours each. It smells like a pub in there!"

Roz nodded and looked at me. "She's right!"

I gestured towards Sharon and Heston. "And I've introduced these two and ... well ... they seem to like each other!"

Sharon looked very comfortable being in close proximity to Heston. Doubtless, she had plans to suck the very life out of him, and he clearly didn't mind! He was old and ugly enough to take care of himself; whatever kind of deep cleaning she had in mind for him, he was up for it!

Roz looked at the happy couple. "So, I see! Heston has impeccable taste. When we were at university, he never let us drink poor quality wine. I knew we'd always be friends!"

Sharon beamed. She loved the sound of a man with impeccable taste. Maybe she'd only been with pretenders and wannabes? If she'd now been able to snare and hypnotise a man with impeccable taste, that was a job well done! I gestured to Roz that maybe we should leave Heston and Sharon alone. They both looked in the zone and anxious to learn more about one another. I took Roz over to meet Belinda The Rescinder; the woman who had come to Mids' rescue on more than one occasion.

While we were standing there making chit-chat with Belinda, one of Mids' customers came over to see what kind of nibbles were available. He was a stocky man with a thick head of orange hair and a ruddy complexion. He looked very outdoorsy.

Belinda had fried some little fish cakes and had a pot of sweet chili sauce to go with them. The man picked one up, dipped it in the sauce and popped it in his mouth. We audibly heard him moan with pleasure.

"By Christ," he began, with a broad Irish accent, "what the hell are these?"

Belinda smiled. "Fish cakes."

"Fish cakes?" he squealed. "Fish cakes? These are Heaven on earth, that's what they are!"

Belinda smiled again.

"She delivers sandwiches and baps to my shop every day!" I added.

The man turned to me. "Well, you're a lucky bugger, aren't you?"

"Sets me up for the day!"

"I bet!"

The man picked-up a business card at the front the table and popped it into the breast pocket of his shirt.

"May I?" he asked Belinda, hoping for another fish cake.

"They've all got to be eaten!"

The man ate another and moaned with genuine pleasure. "Delicious! What's in them?"

Belinda smiled shyly and trotted out her standard answer. "If I told you, I'd have to kill you!"

The Irish man laughed and held up his hands. "Fair enough!"

He then caught sight of some chicken nugget-looking things, picked up a cocktail stick and popped one into his mouth. Same response. He looked like a man who enjoyed his food. He pulled the business card out of his breast pocket. "Belinda?"

"That's me!" she replied.

She'd also made some very polite, triangular sandwiches. The Irish man could not resist. He popped one in his mouth and smiled with delight.

"Young lady!" he began, "this is exceptional catering!"

At that moment, Mids swung by with two bottles of wine. "What are you drinking, Des?"

"I'm drinking that Reisling," said the Irish man.

"What a beaut, eh?"

"Very tasty," he replied, "and where have you been hiding this young lady?"

"This is Belinda The Rescinder!" announced Mids. "She will turn your bad mood around! If you're feeling low, her food lifts you up!"

"That it does!" said Des. "This grub compliments a good wine!"

Des picked up the bottle of Reisling and looked at the label. "You can put me down for 40 cases of this! Let me go and grab the missus! She needs to taste this food!"

The Irish man walked over to his wife and we all looked at one another.

"My God!" said Mids to Belinda. "You are worth every penny!"

"Who was that geezer?" I asked.

"He owns two hotels and two restaurants! He's about the richest man I know!"

Mids disappeared, waving his bottles of wine and Belinda smiled at me. "Thank you, Wes! Thanks for the hook-up!"

"I think that Des bloke might be contacting you too!"

Belinda looked up to heavens and crossed her fingers! "Hope so!"

Roz grabbed another chicken nugget and we moved away to make space for other guests.

Roz looked up at me. "You've been busy!"

"You have no idea!"

They say that men can't multi-task! What Roz didn't know was that her boy had turned into some kind of super-strength empath; a plate-spinning circus act; a pioneering entrepreneur, marriage guidance counsellor and social worker combined! Or maybe that's what a woman is anyway?

Yes, I had been busy. The scope of my influence was now stretching out to her circle of friends! Whatever kind of marks I was scoring, I knew I was doing a good job, and modesty and humility will score you extra, so I had to stay cool. No point whipping it out, waving it about and looking for approval! Had I finally reached maturity? Being humble was some powerful shit!

"Why did Heston come to the shop?"

I wondered if I should tell her the truth? It would almost emasculate him? To be honest, I really didn't know. Roz going to her boyfriend was an occasional and understandable blip but Jill going to her boyfriend on the same night was noticeable. The house dynamic was being affected. Now poor Wendy had to deal with The Three Degrees on her own!

Actions and consequences. All this coupling was affecting everyone's lives! In truth, Heston was asking me press the Reset button. That would be nice, wouldn't it? Press the Reset button and get everything back to the way it was. Ah, the way we were! But what Reset button to press? Back to your twenties? Back to your teens? Christ, no! The teenage Wes was clueless!

"He says the house is 'quiet'."

She thought about this for a second. "Maybe you can stay over at mine?"

Consequences and actions.

Jill had instituted a strict No Sex In The House rule and, for decades, it had worked. Before they'd lived in the house, they'd all lived in a big flat with no bedrooms; if you wanted sex, you had go elsewhere. The rule had now been transferred to the house and, even though they all had their own bedrooms, the No Sex In The House rule carried over. There was a huge 'No Strangers At The Breakfast Table' sign in the kitchen.

Nevertheless, she who had created the rule had broken it! Trying to sneak Mids in and out of the house without anyone noticing had thrown everything into disarray. It was almost as if Jill no longer cared for her house rules? Understandable. After all, they'd been observing them for almost 20 years!

My suspicion was that Jill just didn't care anymore. The Alistair business had caused her to go 'Fuck it!' in large red letters. What's the point in having rules and regulations; what's the point in having morals and principles when everyone is just living freestyle, doing what the fuck they want!

"Stay over at yours?" I asked. "Not sure Benjamin will want to see my face first thing in the morning!"

"He will have to get used to it! And Mids should come over as well? If anyone complains, we'll say Heston said the house was 'quiet'. Did Heston actually say that?"

"That's the word he used."

"We'll tell them that Heston said the house was 'quiet'."

Actions and consequences. We were about to stage a revolution! Me and Mids staying over would bring not one but two strangers to the breakfast table. If Raymond and Benjamin had a problem, they could take it up with Heston. There was no magic Reset button that anyone could press. If Heston wanted Roz and Jill back in the house, they now came with bed partners! And if Heston brought Sharon back to the house? My God! It would be one action-packed breakfast!

Personally, I suspected Sharon would take Heston back to her place, lock the door and literally throw the key out the window. Fuck it, you could almost smell the animal attraction! Every time we looked over at them, they were gazing into each other's eyes!

"That's a strange couple!" Roz said. "Heston usually likes women from his world, so they can talk about art and culture."

"She's a bright girl! They'll have plenty to talk about!"

Mids' soiree seemed to be going very well! People were arriving and staying! The wine was flowing, Belinda's snacks were almost done and the hubbub of chatter was deafening. The only person missing was Jill! I could see Mids periodically looking at the door. Not that he needed her there, he just liked having her around.

Just as people began drifting away, Jill arrived looking flustered. She checked to see that Mids wasn't with a client and gave him a quick peck on his cheek. She whispered something in his ear. He nodded in acknowledgement and carried on schmoozing! Then she wandered over to where we were and fell into Roz's arms. What she needed was a comforting hug but she didn't want to fling her arms around the host.

Roz looked at her old mate. "What's wrong, Jilly?"

"Just hate my job, babe!"

Jill then hugged me. "I love your boyfriend!" she said to Roz.

"He has his moments!" Roz replied, winking at me.

"In many ways, Wes has turned my life around!"

This was proper endorsement. I couldn't help but let a cheesy grin creep around my face.

"Yes," said Roz. "I can see he's been busy!"

I wondered how Mids would respond to Jill's late arrival. He wasn't as easy-going as me. When the final guest left, an exhausted Mids came over to our corner and squeezed Jill in an affectionate but also quite a sexual way! He was loving her wobbly bits!

"So sorry I'm late!" said Jill, very apologetically.

Mids wasn't even that bothered. "That was a success!" He looked down on his phone, where he'd been keeping track of orders. I could see him totting-up numbers. "A big success!" he reiterated.

"And can we please have round of applause for Belinda The Rescinder!"

We all gave Belinda some applause and, as ever, she blushed furiously.

"I might be inclined to say that YOU made the difference!" Mids said to her.

Belinda shook her head furiously. "God, no! They're just snacks!"

"Food is a feel good thing! You made my customers smile!"

Belinda accepted the praise and continued packing up.

Heston and Sharon had gone! Gone! We knew not where! I would find out soon enough. Sharon loved to share these little nuggets with me.

Roz turned to Jill. "Heston says the house is 'quiet'."

Jill was still looking flustered and needed to sit down somewhere comfortable with a long, cool drink. She absorbed Roz's words and we all stood there waiting for her response. The revolution was either about to happen or it was going to be put in a small drawer for future use.

"Quiet?" Jill asked.

"You know Heston!" said Roz, snorting with derision. "He's an old-fashioned guy! He's not good with change. He likes going to sleep knowing we are tucked-up in our beds!"

"Heston won't be home tonight!" I said.

They all looked at me!

"Wes introduced Heston to this girl called Sharon," Roz said to Jill. "Huge tits! They were here earlier, it was disgusting, she had her hands all over him, he was loving it, of course!"

"Christ!" said Mids. "She is a handful!"

Jill gave him a disapproving look.

"Heston won't be home tonight and I'll be very surprised if he comes home tomorrow," I added.

The girls looked shocked.

"You're quite the matchmaker, aren't you, my sweet?" said Roz.

I shrugged my shoulders and tried to look as if this were not my plan and, in truth, I hadn't planned a thing! Two people had just found each other: Mids and Jill, Topper and Francine, Low and Lola, and now Heston and Sharon. Christ, if I could find the miserable Benjamin a woman, I would then require iconic status!

My phone dinged and I looked at my phone. It was from Sharon. "Low has just come out of Lola's bedroom. He looks broken." This was followed by lots of laughing emojis. I smiled to myself and shook my head. Low had met his match.

"What's up?" said Roz.

"Low pulled a sickie to spend a day in bed with Sharon's flatmate and they've just finished!"

Roz looked confused. "What is going on, Wes? When I met you, you were the only one in your group with a partner! Now, Melvin's the only single one! This bloody relationship thing is spreading like wildfire!"

She wasn't the only confused one! I knew my friends. They were not relationship people. There had always been a problem. Always. It had never worked for one trivial reason or another. Topper had tried before, Mids had tried before, even Melvin had once claimed to be in love, but it had never lasted.

Have people stopped being good at relationships? I knew there were more twists in this tale but, in the meantime, I was going to smile and be happy for everyone. Christ, who was I? Not an expert and not a married man ... yet!

Roz and I got into my car. It had been an eventful and satisfying evening. Everyone was happy! Mids, Jill, Belinda, the customers and now even Heston had a smile on his face! We began to drive home.

"You know you're going to have to tell me about Sharon, don't you?"

This: I knew. It was like going to see the headmaster for the slipper. There was no getting away from it.

"Start at the beginning," she said, ominously.

I was nervous. I didn't know why. I hadn't done anything wrong. Okay, maybe I had been sparing with the facts, but we all do that! We ALL do that! If I can admit it, so can you! Why had I been sparing with the facts? Because my relationship with Sharon wasn't normal! It had become very intimate very quickly. Obviously, not physical but, in a very short space of time, she'd become quite integral to my life. How do you explain that to your girlfriend?

"I was covering one of Alvin's regular gigs. Swish company in the city, gorgeous building, canapés, free drinks etc. And these two girls come over because they like the music. They don't work for the company but their mate does and she'd invited them over. Anyway, Low does what Low normally does; he flirts with both of them, figuring one of them will take the bait. A few days later, he informs me that he and I have been invited to dinner by these two girls."

I could hear Roz periodically go, "Hmm hmm!" It was a light-hearted noise. As if she found the story intriguing but also ridiculous. "So he drags you over there, so he can find out which one fancies him, leaving you to babysit the other one?"

"Something like that!" I replied.

Roz shook her head and giggled. "I did the same once."

"Really?"

"Long time ago."

That didn't make it any better. My mind was already racing.

"I dragged Wendy over to this guy's place and she had to babysit his mate! Actually, I don't think she minded? She ended-up going out with him for a few months. Mine turned out to be a dead loss!" I loved hearing about dead losses!

Okay, I was over one hurdle, now to continue with the story. "So, Low disappears into the bedroom with Lola, and her friend Sharon is under the impression that I'm going to be down for whatever!"

"And who gave her that impression?" She already knew the answer. "I shall be having a quiet word with your friend Low. He is NOT to drag my boyfriend into any more compromising situations like that. So, what did Sharon do? Dim the lights and put on some Teddy Pendergrass?"

"Pretty much!" I said.

"And what did you do?"

I was silent. Why was she asking me that question? Was it so hard to believe that someone could resist Sharon? Heston had been powerless. He couldn't resist and he probably didn't want to resist! Where was he now? Probably underneath those huge, pendulous breasts, wondering why Christmas had arrived so early?

"You told her you were attached?"

"Of course I did!"

"And what did she say?"

"She was disappointed and she told me you were a 'lucky woman'. When it's put on a plate, men rarely resist!"

"I've never been turned down!"

"Well, there you go!" Second hurdle completed.

"But that's not the end of the story, is it, Wes?"

Now, we were coming to the tricky bit. Who was Sharon and what was she to me?

"So, she's been plying me with drink all night and, when I decide to go, I realise I'm too pissed to drive, so she says she'll drive me home and get a cab back!"

"Alcohol has no effect on her?"

"Not Prosecco, she says. So, we're driving home, and I get an emergency call from Marie."

I could hear Roz giggling beside me. She knew what was coming. She knew it was going to involve tea and cake, and she knew it was going to involve some non-sensical, non-existent problem.

"I liked her when I first met her at that swish gig. I liked her conversation at dinner. And, having turned her down, I liked her attitude. I later discovered she had a background in social work but she left because it was too stressful. So, Sharon drives me to Marie's, we have tea and cake, but I'm not making any impression. My words are not working. I'm being calm, rational and logical and I'm having no effect at all. As usual, Marie is making it into a huge drama. So, Sharon gets involved; a few choice words and she cleans up! Sharon talked to Marie, and Marie was straight within a matter of minutes. Bosh! She's impressive!"

"I see!" said Roz.

What could she see? She certainly couldn't see how impressive Sharon was. In order to be convinced, she would have to see it for herself!

"Is there more?" Roz continued.

"Oh, yes," I said proudly, feeling confident I could complete this task without sabotaging my own relationship. "The following night, I go out with the boys and Low is being a total shit to Topper and Mids. When he wants to pick a fight – hell! – there is no one better than Low! Single-handedly, he destroyed the evening. Topper and Low arrive all loved-up and happy and, by the end of the evening, they're snapping and snarling at one another!"

"What's his problem?"

"He doesn't trust women, he doesn't believe in relationships and he thinks that, if we all find girlfriends, the group will break up!"

Roz did not look impressed. We arrived home, parked the car and went inside. Roz went straight to the kitchen and put the kettle on. "So, what happened next? Don't tell me you called Sharon to sort it out!"

"I did!" I replied.

"You couldn't sort it out yourself?"

"I was becoming blah blah blah!" I replied. "They weren't listening to me!"

"Sharon to the rescue again!" Roz replied and I could almost hear a touch of sarcasm in there, as if to say, a real man would have dealt with it himself! "And now she's found you a collaborator for Max and found you a cleaning company to clean the shop? Resourceful, ain't she?"

There was something bothering me about Roz's words. No sincerity, no conviction. Surely this mature, evolved and modern woman wasn't threatened by Sharon?

"More than anything else," I began, "I think she likes us. Her flatmate Lola is the only other person she likes and trusts. She says her family are 'spongers'. I think ..." I continued, finally finding my voice, "... I think that people are going to want to be our friend. My group, your group; together, we make a good group of people. People are going to want to join our gang. Sharon probably figured I'd be able to introduce her to decent, new people and, as you saw for yourself, the chemistry between she and Heston was electric!"

"He's a tart!" said Roz, dismissively.

"I doubt that Sharon is hoping it will result in marriage and babies!"

Roz still didn't seem sure. There was something about my friendship with Sharon that didn't seem right. I was walking on deeply unfamiliar ground. I genuinely didn't have a clue what to say, and this from a man who had done a hell of a lot of talking earlier; I'd saved Max, I'd pacified Percy, I'd comforted Mids and I'd even removed the frown from Heston's face but, in this instance, I couldn't find the words. If I'd had sex with Sharon, it might've been easier to understand, but we had a level of intimacy that was troubling Roz.

Roz made us both a cup of tea and opened a plastic box full of flapjack. We both sat and enjoyed our beverage.

"She's not my first phone call!" I finally said.

"No?"

"You're still my first phone call."

"You sure?" Roz asked. "I don't need to be your be-all and end-all. I just need to know I'm the only one."

I chuckled to myself. How did I get here? Two women? Two women was not me. Two women was not what I did. I looked at the crazy girl with the wild hair. She had a mouthful of flapjack and was savouring it on her taste buds. "You are the only one," I said.

"When I was dating The Elusive Wilson," she began, with her mouth still half full, "there was this man he always used to hire. A sound man. Andriy. I think he was Ukrainian? Lovely man. God, he could drink! We got on great! I didn't fancy him. He was a bit flirtatious but nothing heavy. He knew I was dating Wilson. If Wilson was off organising something, we'd carry on drinking and laughing into the night. One day, Wilson shut it down. Stopped employing him. So, I know about platonic friendships. I'm not an idiot!"

And, at that moment, I suppose, I realised how much I loved her. I couldn't even speak. I sat there with this stupid grin on my face, which I knew she deplored! It's the 'I've-Just-Had-Sex' grin. Smug and juvenile. "Stop grinning!" she eventually shouted.

"I'm sorry," I said. "I love you."

"Do ya?"

"I does."

"She's a texty person, right?"

I nodded.

"So, I've got to get used to lots of texts from this girl?"

I nodded again. "But it looks like Heston is her focus now?"

Roz smiled. "He's a tart!"

I'd been well and truly grilled by Roz. She'd made me squirm, which was unfair, as I'd dealt with her ex that afternoon, and not just an ex, someone who'd actually put moves on her the night before!

As I sat there thinking about Wilson, I realised I should have punched his lights out. Cheeky fuck! He's knocking on my girlfriend's door in the middle of the night and then he turns up at my shop expecting me to help him find her! That's arrogance beyond arrogance! Not only had he no respect for Roz, but he was looking to treat me like nothing, like I was minor pothole in the road, like I was small obstacle preventing him from getting to his destiny. He literally believed everyone and everything revolved around him.

Roz wasn't getting off that easy. "You know Wilson came to my shop this afternoon?"

She looked genuinely shocked. "He's in London? And when were you going to tell me this?"

"I'm telling you now."

Not my normal polite response. Roz looked surprised.

"And?" she asked.

"He was looking for you. Said he couldn't get through to you on the phone."

"And what did you say?"

"Well, I wasn't going to give him my home address, was I?"

Again, not my normal polite response. As a non-confrontational person, I kept things very simple and respectful. My customer service skills were 24/7 but I shouldn't have been so stern with her. After all, she'd been through a traumatic experience. Having said that, she did have prior knowledge of this man! She must have known what she was getting into?

I felt guilty but I really didn't want to see this guy's face. I had no option but to ram my point home. "I don't want him turning up at my shop when he can't find you!"

Roz shook her head and kind of smirked to herself. "He is something else! Totally, totally self-absorbed and self-centred; like he's The Chosen One or The Golden Child!" She paused. Her love for him had long since evaporated. Now, he was just a problem. "I'll talk to him," she said. "You have better things to do!"

"I do!" I said. If I was going to keep it fun, dealing with her exes was not a good use of my time.

"I'll talk to him," she repeated. "You won't have to deal with him again."

I didn't believe her. That reflection always looks so satisfying to the narcissist; he would be back!

Saturday

I'd heard tell of Waldo K. Peach's Peach Of A Party but I'd never actually been. Down the years, The Amiable Alvin had always taken care of it and the customer had always been very satisfied.

Alvin had said to me that it was the most perfect 'party house' he'd ever seen; a huge kitchen-diner and big patio doors leading out to a spacious garden. It was vast without being a mansion and an acre of land; huge yet intimate. In truth, a large, terraced, suburban house and, for one night of the year, the neighbours knew what they were getting: disco into the early hours!

I think Waldo invited them all: the neighbours on either side and the ones at the bottom of his garden. He behaved properly. If they didn't show, at least they'd been invited?

Alvin had also spoken (at length) about Mrs. Peach's delicious chilli con carne. Alvin described it as almost 'health food'; the normal ingredients but with generous portions of vegetables and some kind of fruit (maybe a pear?) giving it a sweetness. I was looking forward to sampling it.

At 4.00, I put in a call to Courtney to find out if everything was alright at Waldo's. Courtney confirmed that Waldo had hired the customary gazebo so, should there be rain; we would be covered.

Max and I shut up shop and I went home to pick up Roz. She had endured another fruitless day and needed alcohol, hilarity and snogging (in that order!)

"I don't know what's going on?" she complained. "I can't get on anything! I know people are making TV programmes but maybe they don't have someone like me in the budget? I may have to take a staff job? Work for a big company! A desk job!"

I could see her shudder at the thought. She loved the freedom and variety of being freelance. She'd done offices and she hated them; according to her, there were too many cheap and cheerful kids doing a poor job, too many people talking shit all day and not much working being done!

"Quite looking forward to this!" she said, putting the finishing touches to her make-up. She knew it was a left-field eighties bash, so she looked decidedly gothy. I quite liked her vamp look; there was a sexy menace to it!

"Might as well enjoy my Saturday night?" she continued. "I've just had a text from Wendy, Low has taken Lola out with the Saturday night crew! Should be interesting? If you take a girl out on a date, you're moving into a new phase of the relationship"

Roz was right and this was very uncharacteristic of Low. Low did not do dates and he did not do relationships. What was he doing? Hoping that Lola would just be happy to be part of the crew?

Not only had Low gone back for more (again something he rarely did) but he was actually bringing Lola out into the big wide world. This involved conversation and courtesy, this involved menus and manners! This was not what Low did! And hadn't he given Topper and Mids merry hell for having girlfriends? What would Mids say to him? I didn't have my ambassador on hand.

So, while Roz and I were with Percy, and Topper and Francine were at home planning their dinner party, the Saturday night crew had an unfamiliar line-up: Mids and Jill, Low and Lola, Baggers and Wendy. It didn't matter. The crew were together, the crew was growing and morphing but, essentially, the gang was still together. Melvin's plans were always intricate and imaginative, and they were sure to show the girls a good time. As long as Low and Mids could stay civil!

"I've told her to send me photos!" said Roz, putting on some angry, spiky earrings and pulling a studded leather jacket over her shoulders. She loved dressing up! "Right, I'm ready!"

I'd told Waldo we were coming and he was very happy to finally meet me; we'd only communicated via phone and beautifully-worded e-mails and, of course, he was curious to see if my recommendation could fill Alvin's shoes.

When we arrived, Courtney had set-up the gear as normal, as expected, but Percy had placed a laptop at the front and was screening this remarkable montage of images from Waldo's favourite period, the dark side of the eighties. It must have taken Percy ages to do but ... maybe not? Maybe these were some of Percy's favourite photos, collected down the years?

You couldn't help but be sucked into the montage: old photos of Duran Duran at The Rum Runner in Birmingham, Spandau Ballet at The Camden Palace, Patti Smith at Max's Kansas City, The Ramones at CBGB, an emotional journey through David Bowie's different images, UB40 walking around the streets of a Birmingham suburb, The Selector playing at a sweaty dive in Coventry, plus countless beautiful, black and white images of punks, Goths, new romantics, sound system men proudly displaying their speakers and punky rastas smoking the hugest spliffs ever!

Behind the console stood Percy, absolutely beaming with pleasure! I had to admire his initiative. It was pleasing to have these complementary images flickering away. I knew Percy's idea was good but I just couldn't commit time and resources to it.

"Cool, eh?" Percy asked.

"Very!" I said. "Must have taken a lot of work?"

"Nah!" said Percy, waving away the suggestion.

Roz greeted Percy warmly. It was a comical mis-match; he was about two feet taller. "Hello, lover boy!" she teased. "How's Marie?"

Percy rolled his eyes.

"You know she adores you!"

"I know," said Percy, with a sigh of resignation. He was now learning that being in love is not just hazardous and arduous; it can tax the finest mind with its complexities.

The house was just as Alvin had described. It was a terraced house but very, very wide, which afforded Waldo and his wife this huge, football pitch-shaped garden, which was now full of these very happy academics, no longer teaching their chosen subjects, just drinking and singing at the tops of their voices.

None of the guests had gone full-blown fancy dress, that was too fussy for these elder statesmen and women, but there were some outrageous wigs, some shocking, iridescent and garish colours, and there was also some very experimental make-up. Attired in black eyeliner with black lipstick to match, your history tutor looked very different!

Percy, as ever, was being as literal and pedantic as ever, Waldo wanted left-field eighties, and Percy was serving that up in a massive spoonfuls. Waldo didn't want 'Club Tropicana' and 'The Safety Dance', he wanted 'Slippery People' and 'Save It For Later'. If Percy had a specialist field, this was it!

Even the bar had themed cocktails! You could have a Thomas Hardy Wallbanger or a Bloody Mary Shelley or, if you were feeling adventurous, a Mai Tai Zetterling!

And when we finally reached Mrs. Peach's infamous chilli con carne, we had to pause and inhale for a few seconds; it smelled so good! It was one of those dishes you wanted to keep eating and we both could have eaten ourselves into a food coma but we had to pace it; we'd promised we'd meet the Saturday crew at their third pit stop.

We sat down at a bench to eat our plates of food. The first mouthfuls went in and we looked at each other.

"You've brought me to an ordinary, suburban house in Brent. We're sitting on wooden benches, eating off paper plates with plastic cutlery. We're surrounded by the UK's finest nerds, some of whom can dance, some of whom will need a hip replacement in the morning."

I nodded. All of these facts were true and, to an outsider, it might've seemed like she was complaining, but I knew she wasn't. This was Roz-speak; her own way of talking, her own grammar and punctuation, her own way of expressing herself. I loved that I could now understand Roz-speak and she did too.

What was she saying? It thrilled me to hear her words. She was actually saying, 'I love you'. I nodded and smiled. Yes, we were in a far from perfect environment; not, cool, not sexy but, somehow, absolutely the right place to be and she was thanking me for bringing her to this bizarre bash.

The chilli tasted so good, I didn't want to swallow it. I wanted to roll it around in my mouth like some spicy gobstopper. I ate very slowly, savouring every morsel; if I'd finished my plate, I'd have to ask for more (and more) and I didn't want to commandeer the grub!

"God, this is good!" she said.

"It really is! Alvin used to talk about it and I'd be thinking, 'It's just chilli con carne, mate! It all tastes the same!'"

"You know who'd love this? Wendy. She makes a mean chilli herself but this? This has a little something extra!"

Roz looked around her; a happy group of 5o and 60 year olds, dancing on a lawn, absolutely losing themselves in the music and the memories; a world away from the stresses and strains of insolent students and power-hungry principals. Waldo and his fellow teachers and professors were back where it all began: their misspent youth or, in the case of these people, perfect attendance and straight As.

Waldo rushed up to us, exhausted and excitable, his face shiny and red, accompanied by a short, plump friend who looked as though he couldn't stop smiling.

"This is Ambrose!" Waldo announced. "He comes all the way from Patagonia every year to attend my party."

We shook Ambrose's hand.

"He teaches economics at the National University. Tell them what you said to me, Ambrose."

"This music is a drug," began Ambrose. "I am high!"

The two of them certainly looked off their trollies but the strongest they'd probably imbibed was some real ale!

I looked at my lanky soon-to-be brother-in-law. Percy was writhing with joy to 'I Love A Man In Uniform' by Gang Of Four. "I shall make sure I tell the DJ," I replied.

Waldo and Ambrose returned to the dance floor. How long would these guys last? They were both in their fifties! Scattered around the lawn, there were deck chairs for party-goers to collapse into and huge ice buckets full of bottles of water, so guests could re-hydrate and recover.

The South Americans know a bit about drugs, so I figured Percy would take this as high praise. Maybe I shouldn't have been so worried about Percy? Maybe I should've known that an eccentric like him would be perfect for this crowd? We didn't really need to stay much longer. Percy had it under control. Waldo seemed to like him. We were good.

The only thing holding us at this party was Roz, who wanted another plate of food and another cocktail. I raised an eyebrow. "Seriously?"

"Just a little more," she said, not looking guilty in the slightest. I certainly didn't mind her stuffing her face! She was conventionally slim with curves, and those curves needed feeding! I returned to the jovial Mrs. Peach, who was more than happy to furnish Roz with another plate of food.

I returned to the bar. I quite liked the look of Sex On The Beach House, so I got one for Roz and I. We'd already both had an Attack On Pearl Harbour, so at least we were sticking to vodka. Roz was positively purring. "It's all the extra vegetables!" she began. "I bet there's sweet potato in here?"

This party was such an epic piece of theatre, we probably could've stayed and chilled for a few more hours but the texts began arriving as soon as I'd begun sipping my drink. The first text came from Melvin saying, "That Mids and Low stand-off is occurring again!" The second text came from Mids saying, "You are required. And maybe bring Sharon?"

I definitely didn't want to call Sharon. I'd had my Sharon conversation with Roz and I hadn't come out of it looking good! Calling Sharon to bail me out of two situations was not a very masculine look. Yes, I had to keep it fun but, just as important; I had to be a man. I had to fight my own battles, kill spiders, catch mice, charm her parents, mix a decent Martini, bring home the bacon and ensure I could get that dress zipped-up without too much pain. Being a man was a tall order!

Roz's phone was lighting up too. She showed me a text from Wendy, a photo of Mids and Low, toe-to-toe, arguing over a moot point, and in front of Lola too! We wanted Lola's first Saturday experience to be memorable (for the right reasons) and I didn't know if she had the thick skin of her friend.

What did Sharon care? She was probably still stroking Hestons's chest?

"Finish up and we'll go." I looked at my phone to check Melvin's detailed Saturday schedule. They were doing cocktails at one bar, dinner at a restaurant and moving on to a club night afterwards. Judging by Melvin's detailed plans, we figured we'd be in time for dessert at the restaurant?

In a weird kind of way, my priority was Lola, the newcomer. Everyone else was used to Low and Mids but Lola was probably wondering if this banter was friendly. What could they possibly be scrapping over? They both had their girls with them. Surely they were happy?

When we finally got to the restaurant, right in the heart of Hampstead, there was complete silence. Everybody was eating quietly, not saying a word, not exchanging a glance, for fear it might kick off again. We embraced everyone and the waiters quickly found us chairs. I positioned myself next to Lola and put Roz's chair the other side of Low, so we had him in a pincer movement. Intuitively, I knew Low was the culprit.

"Welcome to the Saturday Night Crew!" I smiled.

Lola looked sceptical. "It looks like I've caused a bit of a problem?"

"You haven't!" said Mids, quickly. "But your friend over there has no manners!"

"Keep your nose out of my business!" Low snarled.

I still wasn't totally sure what the conflict was about. Whatever it was, I needed to keep Lola away from it. No need for her to be exposed to pointless, tactless, breast-beating! If these two idiots wanted to duke it out, they could do it somewhere private.

"It's really not a problem," said Lola.

"Not sure what's going on, hun!" said Roz. "Can you summarise it?"

"It seems that Low gave Mids a hard time about having a girlfriend and, when I show up, Mids asks Low if he's not being a bit hypocritical. Low said it wasn't the same, as I'm not his girlfriend."

"Is that fair summary?" I asked.

"That's about it!" said Low.

"I felt it was insensitive," said Mids.

"It's none of your business!" I could see Low starting to get really angry again. It didn't happen often but, when it did, it really scared me. By nature, he wasn't an angry or aggressive person. Yes, I'd used him as my 'muscle' when I need protection but, by nature, Low was gentle as a lamb.

Melvin was his normal quiet and restrained self, just sitting and observing but, out of the corner of my eye, I could see him wanting to speak. I turned to him. "You okay, Baggers?"

"No, I'm not!" He looked on the verge of kicking off as well. "No, I'm not!" he repeated, more forcibly. "You think I'm going to bust my arse planning our Saturday nights, planning our dinners, planning our holidays. You think I'm going to make a million phone calls, send a million e-mails and suck-up to people all week long just for this? For this? I don't need these kind of Saturday nights! I can do my own thing!"

Melvin was glaring at Mids and Low, in particular. The girls were quiet and looking decidedly uncomfortable. This wasn't their idea of a night out either."

Lola turned to Mids. "I really appreciate your concern. Really, I do. I'm very touched. You're all very nice people but, if Low doesn't want to define me as his 'girlfriend', it's cool! 200% cool. Things are different these days. There are many kinds of friendship. Low is good people. I need friends like that. I'm happy."

"Thank you, Lola," I said. "Are we cool now?" I looked at Mids and Low. They both looked shamefaced. I hadn't actually diffused the time bomb single-handedly but I'd supervised it! That's good enough, isn't it?

Jill squeezed Mids hand and he pulled her hand to his lips. Low kissed Lola on the cheek and she smiled with pleasure. The smiles began to return to our table but Melvin still wasn't done. "No more arguments, please! Or you can find some other bitch to do your bidding!"

"We hear you!" I said.

Mids waved his hand at a waiter and chose us all a nice bottle of bubbly. It arrived with a tray full of flutes.

"Let's have some dessert," he began, "and raise our glasses to another Saturday night and, as always, a big thank you to Baggers for making it happen and putting up with our shit!"

We all toasted Melvin and each other.

"I promise you," I said to Lola, "our Saturday nights are not normally like this. We're normally guaranteed good vibes!"

"I know," she said. "Sharon recommended you all highly. Even Low!"

"Have you heard from Sharon?" Roz asked.

"Her phone's still off!"

Roz shook her head. "Wow! Intense!"

"She hasn't had sex for ten months!"

There was a collective gasp of shock around the table.

"Well, that explains it!" said Roz.

Like Sharon, Lola was a sweet-natured girl; accepting, tolerant, forgiving and always thinking the best of people. The best approach when dealing with Low. It was true, even though he'd gone back for more, it meant nothing. Even though he'd taken her out with his inner circle, it meant nothing. I suppose the bit that stuck in my throat was his public proclamation that she wasn't his girlfriend and, despite her brave face, I'm sure that must have hurt Lola. That was unnecessary but that was how Low liked to keep it: 100% honest. If nothing else, he was totally honest with everyone which, in a world of half-truths, is quite refreshing.

As she wasn't his girlfriend, Lola couldn't really commit herself to our group and our evening. As she'd described to Sharon, Lola could feel that Low was holding back. How could there be a connection? Low didn't want to connect. For whatever reason, he was holding back. Holding back what, none of us knew!

We then went on to this brilliant, old skool hip hop club night; who doesn't love sing-a-long rap anthems? When he dropped 'Hip Hop Hooray', it was amusing to see all these 30 and 40-year-olds swaying to the beat and, when he played 'Jump Around', everyone leapt in the air like they were 16 all over again.

Lola was smiling and singing and swaying but, like Low, she was holding back. I could see she was happy to be with us but there was no point in her making that investment; she might never see us again? For that reason, I felt really bad for her and, for the first time, really quite angry at Low's choice. Yes, maybe I was weak and soft but at least I was all-in; I committed; I made a statement. Roz knew where she stood with me. She knew I loved her and I made sure I expressed myself, in a million soppy ways.

And there was no doubting Roz loved my affection but this was all new to her. She'd had many men but none that actually loved her; none that expressed anything. She'd say to me, "Do you really?" as if I was playing some cruel practical joke on her, and I'd say, "Yes, really!"

In fact, there was so much jumping around, we all looked knackered by about 2.00!

"You do this every Saturday?" asked Lola.

"That's why we love Melvin so much!" I said. "He organises all of this for us every weekend, and that's why he got so angry; it takes up a lot of his time!"

Intuitively, I felt that Lola quite liked the idea of being part of our circle, but she had no way of knowing if she'd been accepted, or ever would be! She seemed to want to talk but I suspected she wanted to talk about Low and I had nothing to tell her! I didn't know how he felt. I didn't know what he was doing and he probably didn't either!

As we all fell into Mids van and made our way home, there was laughter and banter and, despite the bust-up, it seemed as if everyone had had a good Saturday night. Roz and I had certainly had an eclectic evening! She looked at me and smiled. It was a 'You Done Good' smile. If your girlfriend says she's proud of you, you can really walk tall.

We dropped Melvin off at an address (we didn't ask any questions), we dropped Wendy at The Haunted House and then, to my surprise, we dropped Lola and Low's at his place. This was unprecedented! Both Mids and I exchanged a look. If she wasn't Low's girlfriend, she was well on her way to becoming something significant! Lola was quite happy to go into Low's flat. Her flat was probably still a bubbling cauldron!

And then Mids dropped Roz and I home. Thankfully, we all lived quite close.

"Sorry about that!" said Mids to me.

"Don't apologise to me, mate! Felt sorry for that girl!"

"She's a lovely, young thing!" said Jill, still quite chirpy, despite a vigorous evening of Prosecco and Public Enemy. "But Low is right!"

"He is?" said Mids.

"Yes, he is. It's none of our business. If she didn't want to come out, she would've stayed at home! But she came out and had fun with us! What she and Low have is none of our business."

Mids wasn't going to argue. Roz was used to Jill's approach to life and love. We got out of the van, went through the front door and, without even a cuppa, we collapsed into bed. Roz fell straight to sleep, softly snoring. (Not that I'd ever mention it!) I lay there for a while, wondering where my Post-It Notes had gone. What had Roz done with them? Had she changed her mind? Was I no longer all of those things? This foolish train of thought soon sent me to sleep.

Sunday

When I woke up on Sunday morning, Roz was already awake, a cup of coffee at her side, rifling through her e-mails, looking for glimmers of hope. She had about nine tabs open and was methodically looking in every nook and cranny for work. I bent down and kissed her cheek.

"There's nothing out there!" she growled. "And I won't work for peanuts!"

"Sleep well?" I asked.

"I guess so?" she said. "I passed out and didn't stir. Must have been a deep sleep?"

I made myself some coffee but I wasn't quite ready for breakfast, so I opened my laptop too. There in my inbox was an e-mail from Trish. What fresh hell was this? I opened the attachment. She had designed a logo for my record company. I hadn't even given it a name but she had named it Wheels Of Steel, after the shop. It was really good! I shouldn't have been surprised; graphic design was what she did, with a small greetings card business paying her bills.

Trish's style was very girly, pink and fluffy; lots of bunny rabbits, kittens and unicorns, but this logo was bold, stylish, slightly edgy and it actually promised good quality music. It was optimistic and very un-Trish-like.

I stared at it. Yes, it was very classy but what was Trish trying to do? Win me back? No, she knew that was futile. Be my friend? Well, she would always be my friend but ... from a distance! She had blown her credibility long ago! So, what? Was she really just happy to contribute to the business and my future? Which begged the question: was she actually capable of a selfless gesture? I had to take it at face value.

I turned my laptop around, so Roz could see.

"Wow!" she said. "That is good! Who did that?"

"Trish."

"Did you ask her to do it?" she asked.

"No."

"Must be a peace offering?"

That seemed logical. I sent her back a brief e-mail thanking her. I figured I'd show it to a few more people and get their feedback? Maybe Max and Solomon? Maybe the boys as well?

I had just put my toast down when the phone dinged. It was Melvin, wondering where I was. I told him I was at home. He asked if he could pop over quickly.

"You don't mind if Melvin stops in for coffee, do you?"

"Of course not!" said Roz.

And, as Melvin never arrived empty-handed, he came through the front door with coffee shop coffees, delicious Danish pastries, one holdall, one sports bag and a man bag over his shoulder.

He sat down, made himself at home and we tucked in!

"What's on your mind, mate?"

Melvin looked nervously at Roz. He knew she'd be at my place because he'd bought her coffee but he actually needed to talk about her and, now he was here, he was a bit nervous. "I know Roz won't mind me speaking plainly."

Roz loved Baggers. "No," she began, "Roz won't mind you speaking plainly."

Melvin summoned all his courage and took another sip of his hot chocolate, fairly smothered in whipped cream! "I think I agree with Low. I think the girlfriends are affecting the group. You know I love the girlfriends! I love Roz and Jill, Lola is a gem, and I'm look forward to getting to know Francine but ..."

Baggers took another sip of his hot chocolate and had to lick whipped cream off his lips. "... but, we need to make some time for just us boys. Just us."

"I don't think the girlfriends have caused the problems!" I said.

"No, they haven't," Baggers quickly added. "Not at all. We have caused our own problems, as usual! I just think ..."

"Say whatever you want to say, honey!" prompted Roz. "You can say what you want!"

"I just think ... we need to have some evenings where it is just us."

I looked at Roz. She seemed fine.

"I agree!" said Roz.

Melvin needed to clarify further and took a deep breath. Deep down, the master concierge was relatively shy; funny, fabulous and flamboyant in so many ways but, by nature, reserved; quite happy to be an observer.

"It's not that I need to spend more time with men. I spend enough time with men! Our group: we need to be stronger; we need to sort out our own issues before we approach partners; we need to be more selective, more principled, more decisive and, frankly, more manly!"

Roz and I looked at one another. What Melvin was saying was perfectly valid but profoundly embarrassing! The gay guy was telling us to man-up but, in a way, it was completely logical; he had a 360 degree view of masculinity.

"You're right!" I said. "In the immortal words of Supertramp, you're bloody well right!"

Melvin looked relieved. Despite it being early Sunday morning, Melvin was showered and dressed and looking as smart as ever. Wherever he was last night, those bags had served their purpose. "I didn't know how you'd respond! I know nothing stays forever."

Roz and I looked at each other. I winked at her. She now spoke Wes-Speak. She knew my wink contained a myriad of loving feelings. She knew my wink was rapport and understanding and camaraderie and unwritten rules combined.

"Some things must stay forever," said Roz. "You five are where it all began. You five must stay tight and love one another."

I looked at Melvin. "Some of these girlfriends may not stick around?"

Melvin looked edgy again, as if he had something else to say. We could see him shifting nervously and clumsily picking up pastry crumbs from the coffee shop paper bag.

"What's up, Melvin?" Roz had little patience. In her world, there was no need for hesitancy and, often, no need for diplomacy and etiquette either! "Spit it out!" was one of her most-used phrases! She would rather you got to the point!

"I don't think Mids and Jill are going to make it!"

I think Roz and I were both shocked by this. We both said nothing and gawped at Melvin like goldfish. Had he really just said those words?

"What makes you say that?" asked Roz.

Melvin didn't really have an answer. It was an intuitive thing. He tried forming a sentence but it wasn't forthcoming. He kept shrugging his shoulders, shaking his head, and dipping his pinkie finger in his whipped cream. None of which was helping us reach an informed opinion.

"I don't see a spark," he finally said. "He wants it to work (for his reasons) and she wants it to work (for her reasons) but I don't see any spark between them. I see them kiss and cuddle and touch and get quite raunchy at times but ..."

"But?" I prompted.

"You know me, Wezza. I sit and watch. Sit and watch. I've seen couples in public, I've seen couples in private, and I've seen all kinds of couples. I think 'spark' is my specialist subject."

He paused and looked sad and reflective. We both watched him, waiting for him to speak. "I suppose," he began, "spark interests me because I've never felt it! I've observed it but I've never felt it! I've felt a lot of things! Naturally, I've felt a lot of lust but never that ... spark ... but I know what it looks like!"

This was disappointing news for Roz and I. We both loved Mids and Jill as a couple, and we both had a long history with one of them; we wanted them to be happy, but Mids had looked a sorry state in my shop on Friday. Not just frustrated but close to depressed. With a warehouse full of booze at his disposal, I could easily see him hitting the bottle. Part of me didn't want Mids in a relationship that was going to mess with his head. Who needs it? If the object is to keep it fun, the last thing you want is uncertainty!

"She's not over that guy!" Melvin said. "You can see that in her eyes. There are too many moments when she is living in the past. She can't live in the moment if she doesn't currently reside there!"

There was little Roz and I could say. We both hoped he was wrong. Time would tell. It was true: Melvin did sit and watch. He'd always been the silent partner; clocking everything, looking out for danger for us and looking out for partners for himself. I trusted his instincts on everything. I trusted him to organise our weekends, book restaurants, book holidays and even buy me clothes! He was always right. On this occasion, I hoped he was wrong.

I was quite enjoying my morning with Melvin. It reminded me that I wanted to stage a dinner party at my house. I'd always wanted to but never got around to it. Dinner parties involve cooking, washing up, dressing up, no belching at the table. A group of five straight guys don't do dinner parties but, now that there were girls involved, it seemed like a good idea? Outside caterers, of course!

I think Melvin was just about to make a move when my phone dinged again. Amazingly, Low was checking to see if it was okay if he popped in, on his own. I looked at Roz. "Now Low wants to pop in!"

"It's like our first date, sunshine. Breakfast into lunch."

"You don't mind, do you?" I asked Melvin.

"Why would I?"

Low hadn't done the maths. He thought I'd be alone. Why would he think that? Sometimes, Low was completely illogical; disconnecting himself from his brain like he was unplugging the Hoover! So, when Low came into my kitchen, he was shocked to see Roz.

"Ah!" he said, looking surprised!

"Good morning to you too!" said Roz, getting up to embrace him.

"And what are you doing here?" he said to Melvin, playfully.

"Probably here for the same reason as you?"

Melvin knew something else I didn't know; buggered if I knew why Low was in my kitchen!

"Well, this is cosy!" Low began, trying to keep it conversational. "Any chance of a cuppa?"

"Can we do you some toast?" asked Roz.

"That will go down a treat!"

This was a very unusual start to my Sunday. After a Saturday night out, there'd usually be a flurry of texts and the occasional phone call but, normally, after a long evening together, we'd give each other space! And yet, here they were, getting comfy underneath my kitchen table! Roz and I put away our laptops to make more space and avoid soggy keyboards.

I now had another person in my kitchen who had something to say but wasn't quite sure how to say it. Low made short work of his toast and was skirting around the issue with some stories from last night. "I didn't expect Roz to be here!" he finally blurted out.

"If I play my cards right and keep my nose clean," I began, "you will find Roz here more often than not!"

"Right, right!" said Low, realising how dim he'd been. "I was going to tell you about Lola."

"Do you want me to go?" asked Roz.

"See?" said Melvin. "This is my point! We need Guy Time!"

"We do!" agreed Low.

"Do you want me to go?" Roz asked again.

"No!" said Low, very firmly. "Not running you out of your kitchen on a Sunday morning!"

"Not embarrassed, are you, Tony?"

Bold as brass and as cocksure as he could possibly be, no one could ever suggest such a thing! Low did not want to be seen in public with the word 'embarrassment'. Low loved to conserve this reputation of being brave and fearless; unafraid to mix it with the girls, even when they were talking about the messy details. "Nah, nah! Embarrassed? Me? Nah!"

"Spare us no detail!" said Roz, grinning mischievously.

Christ, what had she unleashed? Roz was about to hear some messy details she might want to forget?

"Me and Lola talked last night," Low began. "She said she's cool and she really is! She says she can't remember the last time she actually called a man her 'boyfriend'! Look, we get on really well! Amazing chemistry! She doesn't need to be defined as my 'girlfriend'. What does it mean? A geezer will introduce you to his girlfriend and, the next time you see him, they've broken up! A name can't hold us together."

Low looked quite pleased with himself and had another sip of his tea. When it came to sex and women's bodies, nobody knew more than Low; he was our own personal reference book, but what he knew about the female brain would barely fit on a cherry pip! Roz, Melvin and I looked at one another. Low truly didn't have a clue. I left it to Roz to start the dissection.

Roz took a deep breath. Unsure if her words or her logic would actually make any difference. "Lola says she's 'cool' but she likes you, she wants to be with you and she's going to say whatever keeps you sweet. She doesn't want to put you under any pressure. Most men run from pressure. So, she's always going to say she's cool but ... there are very, very few women that are blissfully happy being a fuck buddy! Trust me! I know! So, she says she's 'cool' but I'm not so sure?"

Low looked bitterly disappointed. Crushed, actually. With Lola, he thought he'd found the ideal relationship. Ideal for him!

"Are you sure?" he asked. "She says she doesn't want a boyfriend. She says she doesn't want to live with a man again. She likes her own space!"

We all looked at each other. It was a possibility?

"Just don't get angry with me!" Low continued. "Don't get angry with me because of what I've been told. Don't shoot the messenger! I can only go on what I've been told! If she says she's cool ..."

"Low," Melvin began, very solemnly, "we know what you've been told. We know what you've been told but we all suspect the girl may actually feel differently. If she's into you, there is a little part of her heart that is hoping (and praying) that chemistry will evolve into something else. Most women do not want to be a booty call! You could stay in her bedroom for two days, three days! Most women want some kind of relationship. She may not say it because she doesn't want to freak you out but, deep down, she would love to be loved by you!"

Now, Low looked terrified. "You think so?"

We all nodded.

Low was grappling with some unfamiliar feelings and thoughts. He'd kind of been down the road before but never this far! In the past, there'd been women, there'd been chemistry, there'd been civilised discussion but, pretty quickly, both parties had backed away. A one-night stand: it is what it is. When the phone call doesn't arrive, smart women know what time it is!

"So, you think she's lying?" Low asked.

We all nodded.

Low thought about this. He clearly liked Lola and wanted to spend time with her. We could all see him coming to a conclusion in his head. "Yes, she may be lying? But maybe not? If she's happy with our arrangement, then so am I?"

He still wasn't getting it but what could we say. Lola was a grown woman; old enough to make her own decisions. We'd tried to help Low but he wasn't hearing us and it really wasn't our place to speak to Lola. From what I knew of Sharon, they seemed like very down-to-earth types. Christ, they'd both met many men like Low before! They knew what they were getting (or not getting!)

I had Roz, Baggers and Low around my kitchen table. I could barely keep the smile off my face. It felt like home. We were chit-chatting about nothing in particular but there was teasing and laughter and inappropriateness and I loved it. It felt like my parents' house. It felt like a house should be.

There was a knock on the door. Deliveries on a Sunday? Nope. I hadn't ordered anything. The electoral register? Nope. Not on a Sunday. I got up to open the door. There stood Topper, looking frazzled.

"I've been walking," he said. "I needed some fresh air."

I stood there looking at him.

"Have I called at a bad time?"

I opened my door and ushered him in. I don't think my kitchen had ever had so many people in it!

Topper came into the kitchen, and was so stunned to see everyone else, he began to laugh. I wasn't sure why. Maybe it was a nervous laugh? Or a laugh of embarrassment? Or it may have been that laugh of shock and disgust when you discover your parents having sex in the front room?

Topper was laughing but we couldn't see what the joke was, so we just stared at him until he'd calmed down. Once he'd composed himself, he began trying to work out why we were all gathered in my kitchen. We could see the cogs in his brain turning.

Topper looked at me. "Am I disturbing something?"

"No." I said, so he began embracing everyone round the table.

I actually only had four kitchen table chairs, so I went under my stairs and got Topper a deck chair. As it was slightly lower than my kitchen table chairs, he looked up at us, rather like a toddler waiting for his small plate of pre-cut lunch.

"What's going on here?" he asked.

We all looked at each other. It was quite a long story which somebody had to tell. Nobody volunteered, so I began. "Baggers is here because he thinks we should have more evenings where it's just us guys. No girlfriends!"

Topper nodded. "I agree. I hope you don't mind me saying that, Roz?"

"Why would I mind?" she asked.

"What you missed last night," I continued, "was a disagreement between Low and Mids. When introducing her, Low didn't describe Lola as his 'girlfriend', Mids viewed that as insensitive and, as usual, Low and Mids began bickering. So, Low came here this morning to state his case and, accordingly to Low, Lola is perfectly cool not being described as his 'girlfriend'."

"I see," said Topper. "So this is the 24-hour sex session one?"

Low nodded. Despite all his bravado, he was blushing slightly.

Topper continued. "You meet her, you sleep with her on the first date, you sleep with her on the second date (numerous times) and then you take her out with our

Saturday night crew? Our sacred, inner circle? So, what shall we call her? Your concubine? Your paramour?"

Low raised his eyebrow. Topper and he had frequently argued about partners. Topper yearned to find true love and Low had told him (on numerous occasions) that he was a "soppy tart". So, to find Low behaving in a very lovey-dovey and couply way irritated Topper no end.

"What are you afraid of?" Topper asked Low.

Low was terrified, no doubt about it, but doing an expert job of holding it down. In his mind, he was very anxious to hold on to this exceptional women but he wasn't going to express his emotions to anyone and he wasn't going to call her his 'girlfriend'. Everything needed to be loose and free and casual.

"I'm afraid of death," Low began, "but, as it happens, I've had a good life. Can't complain!"

"Okay, forget about the title!" Topper continued. "Forget about the introduction, but what you must do is treat her right!"

"I do!" Low protested.

"This is a beautiful girl who has given you a lot; committed herself to you in quite a significant way; laid her cards on the table! It's honest and courageous and you should feel flattered!"

"I do."

"You must take care of her and take care of her feelings!"

"I will. I will."

Low had his shield up, protecting himself from the blows raining down. Topper viewed himself as an authority on such matters, Low didn't! Hence, the locking of horns! Low did not appreciate the attack and, having defended himself, we all knew that he would fire back with something. He did not disappoint. "Out walking, Tops? Taking in some fresh air, were you?"

"So hard to believe?" replied Topper, not very convincingly.

"Last time I saw you, you were loved-up to the eyeballs! Don't you take a Sunday morning stroll with a girlfriend?"

In all the time I had known him, Topper had never dropped by unannounced. We'd known each other for years and this had never occurred. Topper was here for a reason and we all knew it, so we patiently sat and waited for him to spill the beans.

"It's so nice to take an early morning stroll with your girlfriend!" continued Low.

Topper squirmed in his deck chair, which I knew wasn't very comfortable. "Any chance of a cuppa?" he asked.

Roz had been forced into the mother role but she didn't mind. Watching men stutter and suffer and confront their emotions was ample payment. "Some toast, Tony?"

Getting some unfiltered love was much needed. "Thank you!" he said and gobbled down his breakfast gratefully.

We were all making small talk about last night; filling-in Tops with all the juicy (and all the not so juicy) details. Topper smiled and said little, happy to be in my kitchen.

"Everything okay, Tops?" asked Melvin.

"Trouble in Paradise?" suggested Low.

Topper paused and thought about his response. "It's never going to be perfect, is it?" he finally said.

Now, of all the things he could have said, this was not a great start. "It's never going to be perfect, is it?" Of all the things he could say, this did not inspire me with confidence!

We all stared at him in disbelief and waited for more beans to spill. Topper knew he'd started badly and that he quickly needed to make up ground. "She is a truly remarkable woman!" he proclaimed.

None of us could even muster a response to such a droopy statement.

Topper looked up at the ceiling and all over my walls. "Bit bare, isn't it?"

Roz laughed. "I could fill this house with stuff – paintings, shelves, plant pots – but Wes doesn't want that, do you, my love?" She could see the look of terror in my eye and laughed again. She knew what an unfussy person I was.

Commenting on my kitchen was procrastination and we knew it. Rather than talk about Francine, Topper decided to go on a little wander around my tiny kitchen. He opened the fridge and, true to my word and in the spirit of my parents, it was full to the brim with bottles of drink (with one shelf reserved for actual food.)

"Christ!" he said. "When's the party?"

"My mum and dad always had a full fridge and full food cupboards. I want to be able to offer my guests a drink."

Topper looked his watch. "It's almost midday!" he said.

"Help yourself!" I said.

Topper began digging around in my fridge, holding up bottles and screwing up his face. "What is this stuff?" he asked.

"Found it in the supermarket!" I replied. "I want to be able offer my guests variety."

"Hand it here!" said Low. "I'll try it!"

Every moment Topper was in my fridge, he was putting off the inevitable. Eventually, he would have to tell us why he'd ended-up at my front door, unannounced, on a Sunday morning. He eventually found a bottle of beer he liked, Roz handed him a bottle opener and he sat back down in his deck chair. We all waited, patiently.

He could feel us looking at him. "What do you want to know?"

Low laughed. "Topper, stop being a large, hairy fanny and tell us what's on your mind!"

"I came here to see Wes!" Topper replied, defiantly. "I figured Roz would be here too. I thought it might be nice to get some second opinions on a few things?" Topper glared at Low. "I didn't know The Prince Of Darkness would be here too!"

"Don't you worry about me, son!" Low sipped on his beer, sat back and looked very smug. "I'm in a good place!"

"Are you?" said Topper, sceptically.

"You conduct your affairs how you want and I'll do things my way. So many bloody experts everywhere! Who knew that single men could be such experts on relationships?"

Silence. We all sat and reflected. Just like me and Roz's first date, breakfast had become lunch. We'd drifted into the afternoon. Yes, the conversation was prickly and the atmosphere tense, but it felt good (and very natural) to have my kitchen full of the people I loved. It reminded me of the family home. Mum loved to feed anyone that passed by. It might just have been a Spanish Omelette or some cheese on toast but, if you've got food and good people around a kitchen table, the magic will follow.

I looked around my own kitchen. Yes, it was bare. I was rarely there! But, also, this wasn't my forte! Interior decorating? Christ, I was just getting round to cleaning my shop. And, as if by magic, my phone dinged. I looked down. A text from Sharon. "Gladys and Sophia from my friend's company will be at your shop at 11.00am tomorrow. Give them £40 cash each."

Roz looked at me. "Problem?"

"The shop finally gets cleaned tomorrow!"

"A text from Sharon?"

I nodded.

Roz chuckled to herself. "I guess they've finally come out of her bedroom?"

"Those girls!" said Low, chuckling like Sid James. "Now, that's passion! That's what it's all about! Passion! If there's no passion, what's the point?"

We all thought about this for a second. "What about love?" asked Melvin.

"Come on, Baggers!" said Low, dismissively. "Given a choice between the two, what would you choose?"

Roz looked at me. "So, Wes, if you could only have one, which would you choose?"

I definitely wasn't answering that question. It was time for some procrastination of my own. "Shall we think about lunch?" I asked.

We all looked at Baggers, our own personal restaurant guide.

"I assume you want a Sunday roast?" he asked.

"God, yes!" said Roz, sounding like a studio porn star.

"But first ..." said Low, still trying to get Topper to open up, "... Topper's going to tell us what's on his mind. Are you dragging your feet because Francine isn't what you thought she was?"

A pointed question that Topper had to respond to.

"I like her a lot," he began. "Really, I do. She makes me a taller man. She gives me confidence, she gives me courage. That's a rare gift!"

"It is," said Roz. She turned to me. "Do I do that for you, honey?"

"Look at me!" I said. "I'm growing. Moving from record-playing to record-making! You make it happen!"

Roz smiled with pleasure and satisfaction, and turned back to Topper. "That's a good quality, Tony, but I sense you have a few reservations about her?"

Topper ummed and aahed and looked decidedly uncomfortable but, having come this far, he had to talk. "It's all happening so fast!" he finally said. "We've done the trip to see her parents, we're inviting my mates over to dinner, she's been looking at holiday destinations on line, she's been looking at property on line, she's been looking at wedding venues on line!"

We all looked at each other. It was touching but also quite sad.

"She's happy!" said Roz.

"I get that," said Topper, despondently.

I'd never seen someone look so sad about happiness.

"She's too happy!" he said.

It took a while for this to sink in. It had stopped being touching and suddenly become creepy. 'Too happy' meant desperate. Even I knew that! 'Too happy' meant this poor woman had waited a long, long time to attract a decent man and, now he was here, she was going to rush him through customs without any formalities! Topper was now on a (very) fast track to the future. Slowing this woman down would be problematic. She was on a roll!

We all looked at Topper and there was a collective wave of sympathy towards him. This is a guy who wanted a girlfriend and brought a lot to the party, but Francine was no longer looking like a contender. She had a ton of good qualities but she was just ... too happy! 'Too happy' also meant that Topper was about to become the centre of her universe. She would devote herself to him.

With Roz and me, it was different. She had her own money, her own friends and she made decisions for both of us. Even her housemates deferred to her judgement! I was not the centre of her universe and I never would be! I had a job to do and woe betide me if my performance levels dropped!

"She's too happy!" began Topper, "And she's too 'us'. It's all happening too fast! Everything is 'we'! When did I become part of a 'we'?"

"Hold on," said Low, "do not tell me about treating a woman right! You can't say shit to me unless you treat this woman right! She's into you! Really into you! You're telling me to be sensitive and be gentle! That goes for you too!"

Christ! Had Low finally got it? I couldn't remember so much sense coming out of his mouth! The last time he'd made that much sense was when Melvin got delivered a medium-to-well steak that barely looked as if it had touched the pan! Being a *maitre d'*, he had the courage and the vocabulary to argue with the chef!

"You're right," said Topper. Two words he rarely said to Low.

"Yes, he's right," said Roz, "but how do you feel about Francine?"

Topper had to think hard about this. He gazed out of my small kitchen window for some inspiration. The sky was full of cloud and my back garden was badly overgrown. He wouldn't find much inspiration there.

"In terms of feelings, I'm down here, and she ..." He raised his palms as high as he could. "She ... is way up there! Way, way up there! I am miles behind her!"

"That's natural," said Roz. "Women fall in love quicker and deeper."

"But I'm way behind her!" complained Topper. "There's too much pressure on me to catch up!"

This was true. It was a wholly unbalanced relationship. Francine had got there far too quickly. It hadn't even been a month! It set off alarm bells in all of us. Their relationship would be far from 'fun'. It would be Francine tapping her fingers, waiting for Mids to catch up. It would be Francine doubting his heart, doubting his intentions and making him feel wretched. Not fun.

We were all silent, feeling Topper's pain. Friendship turns us all into empaths. It was like sitting at Topper's hospital bedside. There he was: banged-up and bandaged, and what could we do? Nothing. Bring him flowers and Lucozade. This was Topper's problem/issue/situation to sort out. All we could do is watch in the wings and be there with a towel!

Even Low was quiet. He could see that his mate was in trouble and he knew Topper didn't have the heart to just cut her free. Topper's predicament had somewhat killed the vibe.

"And what about Tuesday?" asked Melvin.

Topper suddenly remembered he had invited us all for dinner! "Oh, Christ! Have to go ahead with it! She's been talking about it all weekend!"

"Starting tomorrow," Roz began, "you'll have to start applying the brakes. Slowly." It sounded painful but Roz was right. Relationships and friendships need to get re-aligned sometimes; make sure everyone is on the same page!

I could feel the whole mood of my blissful Sunday morning turn to mush. "Come on, let's go and eat!" I suggested. I knew food would put a smile on everyone's faces, even Topper's!

"I assume you know the best local place for a Sunday roast?" I asked Baggers.

"Oh, yes!" he grinned.

Monday

I don't know why I'd waited so long to Spring clean. Many Springs had come and gone.

Max and I gave the shop a cursory spit and polish every now and then but it could hardly be described as cleaning.

Why had I put it off? Life. Life had got in the way: work, my social life, my haphazard love life, my depression, my apathy.

This then was a symbolic day. Not only a day of cleaning but the day my shop began to resemble an office; the home of a record label.

Monday would have to be a normal Monday; noisy, chaotic and messy but, with Sophia and Gladys arriving at 11.00, we would have to find a way of working around our new cleaning ladies.

And, when Max arrived, there was another symbolic moment.

"Would you like to hear what we've done?"

This was it: my first tune on my new record label.

"Course I would!" I said.

Max was trembling with excitement; his first tune and his first piece of A&R feedback. He pulled a memory stick from his trouser pocket, shoved it into a CDJ and cranked it up to typical Max volume.

Just like the stuff Solomon had played us, this track was squarely based in African music; majestic, tribal beats with many other influences and noises layered on top: Latin percussion, a folksy acoustic guitar, a sample of a classical string section, a mad jazzy saxophone line, dub effects in the production, and a sweet, female vocal melody on top.

"Who's the singer?" I asked.

"Some friend of Solomon's."

"I like it," I said. This wasn't the kind of stuff I played and I didn't really know what I was listening to but I liked it. I was cool enough to know it was cool.

"Will your punters like it?"

Max smiled. "They will love it!"

The flow of customers throughout the morning was steady. We'd seen these faces before; exhaustion and relief. We were their last stop; the ordeal was over.

"How did it go?" I asked one weary customer.

"I've got another daughter," he began, "but she's not getting married! I'll be buggered if I go through that again!"

He must have originally come from Yorkshire. There were still slight traces in his accent. "We left the wedding at 4.00am," he continued, "and then my family had to be up at 9.00am to go back to the hall and finish the clearing-up. Seems they had a children's birthday party in there in the afternoon? Someone had broken a sink in the gent's toilet! You can guess who'll be paying for that?"

My gear looked fine, so I gave him back his deposit. He looked relieved.

Just after 11.00, these two cheerful ladies arrived. Lovely, smiley faces and brightly-coloured, flower-pattern dresses. We shook their hands, they hung up their coats, put their handbags underneath my desk and put on some well-worn aprons.

They surveyed the shop and smiled.

"Big job!" said one of them (not sure which.)

"Yes!" I guiltily replied.

They both had huge, Mary Poppins-style bags, which they reached into and began pulling out buckets, mops, dusters and assorted magic potions. They did a quick walk around the shop and began talking to each other in another language. Whatever they were saying, it was making them laugh. It didn't surprise me: this monumental task was a joke!

They filled their buckets with clean water and disinfectant and, within minutes, they were back at my sink pouring out black water. Back and forth they went. Back and forth; chattering, laughing and taking a keen interest in me, Max and my customers. I couldn't understand what they were saying but I knew they were talking about us. There were looks and facial expressions and laughing but, as they seemed happy, I left them to get on.

After two hours, it was 1.00 and time for lunch. They asked Max to make them some tea and they pulled these long, elaborate sandwiches out of their handbags. We'd got our grub from Belinda The Rescinder, so we all ate together.

Max had been playing his tune all morning. Over and over again. Initially, the girls had been dancing but, with repeated plays, they began singing along.

"Who's Sophia?" I asked.

One of them put her hand up.

"And you're Gladys!" I said to the other. She smiled. Sparkling white teeth with a prominent gap between the front two.

"Who made the song?" asked Gladys.

Max shyly put his hand up.

"You?" said Sophia, incredulously.

"With some help from my friend, Solomon."

"Ah, Solomon!" said Sophia. Now it made sense. "It's good!"

Max's second good review; he was in Dreamland.

The shop now smelled of pine disinfectant; infinitely preferable to the ingrained smell of fags and booze. I went and had a look where they'd been working, and was amazed to see sunlight bouncing off floors, surfaces and gear. It was a start but the shop was still cluttered. Ultimately, we would have to create more space to make it look more office-y.

Just after lunch, Courtney arrived with a collection job, bringing more gear into the shop. Gladys and Sophia seemed very pleased to see him. They clearly felt he was someone they could tease on a higher level. Courtney was a lovely geezer; totally reliable with a commendable 'can do' attitude but very quiet and reserved. The cleaners actually refused him entry into the shop! Courtney looked totally bemused, which made me laugh.

Amazingly, the girls were able to clean, talk, harass the boys and dance to the music. I kept my head down. I had paperwork and e-mails to send. And then, as if they weren't enough madness in my shop, Percy arrived, looking triumphant.

To celebrate his success, Percy had bought himself a sunshine orange cravat. His pleased-as-Punch smile filled the room. "Did we slay or what?"

I shook his hand. "Great job, Percy! Loved the montage and Waldo was thrilled with the music. When you played 'The Sweetest Girl' by Scritti Politti, he almost wept!"

"All credit to you, Wes! Whatever makes them dance! That's the motto and it works!"

I could see that Gladys and Sophia were now totally distracted by the human Totem Pole. They had stropped cleaning and were staring at Percy in his starched bus driver's uniform and orange cravat. Percy turned to greet them.

"We've got some cleaners, Percy!"

"They are doing a beautiful job!"

Gladys and Sophia smiled and blushed. Percy was clearly wearing his flattery pants!

"You drive a bus?" asked Gladys.

"And I am a DJ!"

"A DJ too?" asked Gladys.

Percy smiled with pride and could not have felt prouder. It had been his life's ambition to be described as a DJ.

"Have a look at this!" I said to him, showing him Trish's logo.

It seemed to have a profound effect on Percy. "A record company!" he said, in total awe. "You're really doing it!"

"I am," I said, and I probably had that same stupid smile on my face! I'd always fantasised about being Richard Branson or Chris Blackwell and here I was: launching my very own 'Tubular Bells'.

I wondered if I should play him Max's debut single. I'd seen him dance before. His moves were un-co-ordinated, clumsy and comical in turns. He would definitely cause distress and then I thought, 'Ah, sod it! If he dances, that's a good sign!'

"Maxi, will you play Percy our first single."

Max loved the sound of that. Debut single. New artist. New record label. He was buzzing like an expensive vibrator!

The tune came on and Percy cocked an ear. The girls watched him closely, wondering what he would do; first the feet, then the legs, then the arms. The girls were mesmerised and, from what I could see, getting quite aroused; watching this man respond caused them to respond! To my amazement, they threw down their rubber gloves and began dancing with him. Percy's whole body was now convulsing in time and, even though the girls had never seen these moves, they had a few complementary moves of their own.

Only in my shop! I looked at Max; he was loving the response. I looked at Courtney; he looked even more bemused and was still trying to get his gear into the shop! The more I listened to Max and Solomon's track, the more I liked it. It was getting under my skin.

It wasn't even Wesday Wednesday and there was already a party in my shop! The tune finished and everyone clapped their hands. Max gratefully received the applause by bowing his head and clasping his hands, as if in prayer.

"Wow, Wes!" said Percy. "You're on your way!"

It felt good. I didn't really know what I had but it made people dance and I liked it.

Percy had already done a sterling job of distracting Sophia and Gladys but, when Heston strode the door, I couldn't see how they were going to finish their work! Percy went back to his bus garage, Max and Courtney carried on humping gear, while Heston stood there, looking perplexed.

Carrying buckets full of black water, the girls paused momentarily to look at Heston. He'd already had a traumatic experience with a woman in my shop, so he seemed unfazed.

"Good afternoon!" he said in his rich baritone.

"Good afternoon!" the girls replied, clearly impressed with his voice. In their heads, they were doing maths. Voice + height = virility. Though I wasn't sure how much juice Heston had left in him. He'd been locked in a bedroom with Sharon for almost two days!

"Sorry to drop in on you!"

"No problem!" I said to him.

"So ..." he began, "... this Sharon: how well do you know her?"

"Not very well."

Not the answer Heston wanted. He wants facts, anecdotes or, at the very least, clues. He wanted to know if this woman was constant or flaky and skittish. He wanted to know if she was genuine or fake. He wanted to know if she could be trusted. What could I tell him? My view was 100% intuitive.

"Shit!" he said. "I've never met anyone like her. I don't know what I'm going into!"

The hunk had never met anyone like her? I was surprised. Maybe he'd always taken the easy road and seduced the impressionable?

"I don't really know her at all," I began, "but, what I've seen, I really like. For my money, I think she'd make a good business partner. I could see her being very helpful. She's logical and pragmatic. I need some of that in my life. I guess we all do? And ..."

"And?"

"... and Roz actually feels a little threatened by her. Have you ever known Roz to feel threatened by another woman?"

"No!" Heston replied in shock. "Why?"

"Because she's a proper, grown-up woman; she's got it all!"

Heston listened and nodded. "Look, I've only had one relationship before." I could see his brain recounting a few images and emotions. "It didn't end well."

Sharon had not only sexed him to within an inch of his life, she had clearly awoken some dormant feelings in him. He was having good and bad flashbacks of his last major relationship.

"I've brought her into my circle. That should tell you how I view her. I'm happy to hang with her and I don't bring just anyone into my life!"

"Okay," said Heston. "I hear that."

The girls came back from the sink with fresh buckets of water and disinfectant.

"Are you married?" Sophia asked Heston

Heston looked at me.

"Yes, he is!" I said.

"Shame!" said Gladys.

The girls walked off despondently.

"I think she's powerful and potent," I said to Heston. "I think everyone in your house is going to like her. Sitting around your kitchen table, she'll be able to hold her own."

This meant something to Heston. I had not been an overnight success. The housemates had been resistant, to say the least! It had taken months for them to warm to me and the boys. Heston wanted someone who would instantly make a good impression. Sharon would certainly do that!

Tuesday

Tuesday was a day of numerous texts.

It was important to bring Mids up to speed.

Topper had expressed his concerns to us on Sunday and now we were all going to have to endure what was, to all intents and purposes, The Last Supper.

We had a group conversation going all day; some of it serious, some of it stupid, some of it dirty.

Low was bringing his non-girlfriend to the dinner and Mids expressed surprise that Low had found time to pull his dick out of Lola! Low assured him that it had come out and gone back in again! Low wanted to know about the whip marks on Mids' back. Mids assured him they were merely Jill's nails at the high of ecstasy.

Melvin wanted to know if he should bring a bottle. Mids told him to bring chocolate or flowers, as he was bringing bottles for all of us. Topper told us we didn't have to be on our best behaviour, as Francine was not a prude. Personally, I felt that was asking for trouble!

Roz and I were not the first to arrive at Topper's flat. Low and Lola were already there, sipping bubbly and sitting close together on the sofa. I think I even saw their fingers touch! Very un-Low-like!

The delicious smell of roast meat was the first thing that hit us.

Roz and I looked at each other.

"She can cook!" said Roz.

"It appears so!"

"Taste one of these!" said Low. "Stuffed mushrooms!"

Francine presented Roz and I with flutes of champagne.

I popped one of the starters into my mouth. There seemed to be warm gruyere cheese on my tongue. "Delicious!" I said.

Low raised his eyebrows. Francine had skills. No matter Topper's reservations, Francine knew what she was doing in the kitchen!

Topper's one-bedroom, single man's flat had always looked quite sparse but, within a couple of days, Francine had brought colour, style and fresh flowers to his abode. It actually looked like a home and Topper appeared very comfortable in it.

Baggers was followed by Mids and Jill, and we all stood around, over-indulging on these stuffed mushrooms!

"I've got my first track by Max and his collaborator Solomon with me!"

"Let's hear it!" said Melvin.

I didn't want to steal Topper's thunder. "I'll play it later."

"Is it good?" Melvin asked.

"It is!"

We probably should have invited Wendy but there was barely room for us! Topper had joined two small tables to make one long table and it stretched the entire length of his sitting room. As it was, we would all be elbow to elbow!

I think we all ate too many of the stuffed mushrooms because, when we sat down to eat, we were sluggish! Roz struggled to stifle a yawn and I could see Mids loosening the belt on his trousers!

The table was immaculately laid out: perfectly symmetrical cutlery, pristine white heated plates, three glasses (water, wine and champagne) and small vases of flowers to add colour to the table. Even without food on it, the table looked superb.

The first thing Francine served-up was carrot & coriander soup. Topper handed out crusty brown bread to dip in the soup. It wasn't an adventurous and experimental menu but – by God! – it tasted good! I was trying not slurp (honest, I was!) but sometimes a slurp escaped. Roz did not look impressed and then, to make matters worse, I actually dripped soup on my shirt! Francine had given us starched white serviettes. Roz picked mine up and tucked it into my shirt. "That's what it's for?" she scolded. Everyone laughed.

Melvin was mightily impressed! "This is my favourite soup!" he said to Francine. "This is exceptional! What's your secret?"

Francine laughed. "You want to share secrets with me, Melvin?"

Melvin smiled and carried on drinking his soup.

Naturally, as people always do, we dipped too much bread into our soup and, after too many stuffed mushrooms, we were already full, and Francine hadn't even brought out the roast meat!

Topper could see we were enjoying ourselves. Around the table, there was lively chit-chat, compliments about the food, good natured ribbing of Topper (because that was always fun) and a suggestion from Low that Mids eating soup sounded like a man going down on a woman!

Lola found all the sexual banter very funny. "You boys always bring it back to sex!"

"You'll get used to it!" said Roz. "I've lived with three men for more than two decades. Men don't even think of it as 'sexual'. To them, it's just conversation. It could be the weather or last night's 'Emmerdale Farm'?" To men, sexual innuendo is just humour, like a knock-knock joke."

"Men are desensitised to sex," said Jill. "It's just a bodily function, like breathing or blinking!"

"Is that true?" Lola asked Low. "Is sex meaningless to you?"

"Mids' sex life is meaningless!" said Low. "Jill needs a whole bottle of gin before she can face it!"

Jill laughed. "You can't talk about my man like that! He's sexy!"

"After a bottle of gin, anyone's sexy!" said Low. "Even Wes!"

Roz laughed. "Tony, don't start on me! You'll regret it!"

Topper cleared up the soup plates and we all put our hands on our fat bellies.

"Stuffed!" said Jill.

"Me too!" said Melvin.

Francine had made a huge leg of lamb with six different vegetables plus gravy. The crispy roast potatoes sat in a Pyrex dish of melted butter. We all cooed with pleasure but we were already full of food.

"Francine, what are you doing to us?" asked Roz.

"Darling, it's an honour to have you here! We hope to entertain you all on a regular basis. We love entertaining!"

We had all heard that 'we'. Clear as a bell. That 'we' was a statement of intent. That 'we' meant: he and I are a functioning, ongoing couple. No matter how Topper felt, Francine was part of a 'we'.

How could she say, "We love entertaining!" She didn't know what he loved. She didn't know him well enough to say stuff like that. We all quickly exchanged glances. Roz winked at me. Roz-Speak for, 'Don't worry, honey. We're built on more solid ground.'

Topper carved the leg of lamb and it fairly fell off the bone. Even the gravy was seasoned with onions and peppers! Nobody piled their plate high. I could see everybody being very cautious.

Lola, in particular, was really struggling! Francine even said, "Is that all you're taking, darling?"

"I'll come back for seconds," Lola expertly lied.

We'd all heard Topper's concerns and fears about Francine. It all made sense. It had only been a few weeks but she was already making plans; she knew what kind of photo album she was having for her wedding and what kind of ornaments they would have in their front garden. Topper was trailing way behind! He was on Page Two or Three, while she was at the penultimate chapter! On Sunday, we'd seen that look of despair on his face but it was impossible not to be impressed by Francine. This was turning into a great evening!

After the main course, we all breathed a sigh of relief, imagining we'd reached the end of the meal but – oh, no! – Francine then produced this light as a feather Strawberry cheesecake. One of my weaknesses. I had to try it! It sat in my mouth and melted down the back of my throat. This kind of dessert really reminded me of my mum. At that moment, Francine was looking really good!

Roz looked at me. "How can you?"

I put some cheesecake on a spoon and offered it to her. She accepted my spoon and, seconds later, her eyes lit up! "Fuck, that's good!"

Having heard such a forceful endorsement, everyone realised they should at least have a spoonful! Jill moaned very loudly and Lola's moans followed soon after. Anyone passing Topper's flat must've wondered if we were shooting an adult movie! We all agreed it was the perfect end to a very special meal. Francine sat back in her chair and looked immensely pleased with herself.

"Thank you!" I finally said. I could barely talk.

"My pleasure!" said Francine. "The first of many!"

Melvin had eaten himself to a standstill. He was struggling to breathe let alone talk! "Thank you!" was all he could muster. "It was all so delicious!"

"My mum put on a good spread," Francine began, "and her mum before her!"

I looked at Topper. Maybe he was bricking it inside but he looked happy enough? He knew Francine had done a number on us but he also knew he had to apply the brakes. It was vital they stayed on the same page. No point Francine making plans! Not yet.

I looked around the table: smiling, exhausted faces; Lola and Low tickling each other, affectionately; Mids filling up Jill's glass; Melvin checking his phone. I looked at Roz. She winked at me. Roz-Speak for, 'I think I might be ready for bed?'

"Okay," said Francine. "Time for some parlour games!"

We all looked up in horror.

"Does it involve moving?" asked Mids.

"No," said Francine, smiling.

This is interesting, I thought. What is she going to pull out of her bag now? Parlour games? Five male friends do not play 'parlour games'.

"What do you want to play?" asked Baggers, the only one of us who had probably played 'parlour games'.

"We can play Adam & Eve?" Francine began. "You get the chance to play God. Design the perfect man or woman! Wes?"

Roz glared at me. "Don't you dare describe me!"

"What kind of woman do you want me to describe?" I asked.

Only Roz could look this upset about being paid a compliment! "If you were God, would you make a woman that looked like me?"

I looked at her blankly. It was a silly question. "I wouldn't change a thing!" I said.

"You're no good at this game!" Roz said. "Jill, you are God in The Garden Of Eden. Design man!"

Jill looked flustered. "Don't put me on the spot!" She thought for a second. "He would be taller than me, strong, kind, skilled, expressive eyes, sensitive ..."

Jill's list went on and on.

"... witty, sexual, tactful, resourceful ..."

On and on. Much like Roz's list of 10 words! Where were those bloody Post-It notes? They'd dried up. Maybe Roz no longer felt that way about me. Maybe, after all, I was just a normal bloke? Just another boyfriend.

Wednesday

On Wednesday morning, I woke up and Roz was already crouched over her laptop.

"Did you sleep?" I asked, kissing her cheek.

"A bit," she said. "I'm restless."

Poor baby! She hated not having work. It wasn't the money so much, it was more the boredom. An active brain needs activity. She loved being in the thick of things: the travel, the drama, solving problems, meeting deadlines, the finished product, the ratings, the awards.

I made myself some coffee. "Maybe we can do something nice after work, to cheer you up?"

"Well," she began, hesitantly, "there is one piece of work I've been offered. Two weeks in Crete. Good money."

"That's great!" I said. "Why don't you sound excited?" And, without an answer, I knew who was offering her the work!

"Well, well!" I began. "He's not so elusive anymore! Wilson's found the perfect way to spend time with you: offer you a job in a foreign country!"

Roz looked at me. "It's work."

I was trying hard to be the better man. Really, I was! "And what happens when you get that knock on your bedroom door at 3.00 in the morning?"

Roz looked disgusted. "It's like you don't listen to me, Wes."

I immediately felt like an insecure, jealous teenager. What's the point in getting older if you don't grow up?

She stood up and stretched. "You don't listen to me, Wes."

"I do, I do!" I protested, but I'd already shown myself to be weak and irrational.

She moved over to the kettle and switched it back on. "You know how I feel about Wilson. I've told you our story in great detail."

And now I wanted the ground to open up and swallow me. "You have."

She made herself another cup of coffee and sat back down. "If I tell you I'm working with Wilson, I don't want this response. I've straightened things out with him. It's just work. There will be no knocking at my bedroom door in the middle of the night. He's got other girls he can call. I know two of them personally and there are many more!"

Suitably chastised, I sat down at the kitchen table and attempted to beg for forgiveness. "I'm sorry," I said. "I'm not blessed with brains."

"Do you think I want to work for him? Do you really think I want to look at his face every day for two weeks?"

I shook my head. I was too depressed to talk.

"It's work," she repeated. "Nothing more. We fly out early tomorrow morning."

I nodded. I would have to get used to this. Christ, I had enough on my plate! What was I fretting about? "I'll miss you," I said.

"And I'll miss you too! Get ready for a lot of FaceTime conversations at weird hours of the morning!"

I smiled, weakly. It was difficult to keep it fun at moments like this. This was not fun at all. I loved having her at my side. I loved the way she stole my toast. I loved the way she sat on my lap and pressed her chest to my nose. I loved the way she winked at me.

When I got home from work, Roz was gone. She'd gone back to The Haunted House to pack two weeks' worth of clothes. The house felt cold and lifeless, devoid of her noise, her perfume and her aura.

There was no one sitting at my kitchen table and definitely no one in my bed. I would have to focus on work, the label and turning myself into a man worthy of a woman like Roz. Based on my performance that morning, I was a feeble wretch. For some insane reason, she liked me!

I wandered it to my front room with a bowl of cereal and a mug of tea and there, sitting on my sofa: a package with my name on the front. It was gift-wrapped with a glittery, red bow.

I stared at it for a second. We were nowhere near my birthday, or Christmas, or our anniversary. I opened it carefully. Inside, I found a T-shirt; navy blue with bold, white print. I opened it out to read it. "My boyfriend is: strong, reliable, sensitive, entertaining, inspiring, brave, respectful, hard-working, skilful and resilient ..."

I turned it over, "... and he belongs to me!"

The 10 Post-It notes. This made me well-up a bit but, when I thought of her chastising me that morning, I quickly sobered-up. I had to learn to trust her. Trust her instincts. Trust her judgement.

I put on my new T-shirt and looked at myself in the hallway mirror. She wasn't there but I could feel her arms around me, embracing me, protecting me.

I sat back down in my front room with my cereal and thought about the fortnight ahead. When she returned, Roz would want to see progress, and progress is what she would get!

November 9, 2018

Printed in Great Britain
by Amazon

38351748R00135